The Bodacious Descendant
2010 © by Darrell Swanson

Publisher's note: This book is a work of fiction. Names, characters, places and incidents are the product of the author's imagination or are used fictitiously, and any resemblance to actual persons living or dead, events or locales is entirely coincidental.

ISBN: 978-193651-7213 - *Perfect*

Published by: Off The Book Shelf

Editing: www.aribert-editinghouse.com
Cover design: Roxane Christ – roxanec@telus.net
Cover photo of the Ice Man – courtesy of:
Landespolizeikommando für Tirol

Dedication

This book is dedicated to my loving wife, Joy, who sacrificed a lot in order for me to complete this work. She has been a wonderful support, inspiration and a never-ending source of encouragement.

Thanks to those who contributed toward my scientific research and also to those who pointed me in the right direction along the path of publishing a book. I am deeply indebted to you all for your time and sharing of your knowledge as well as believing in the story.

Thanks to my friends and family who have supported and encouraged me to complete this work.

Thanks to all the reviewers; without your comments, I would have never known whether or not it was a credible story.

And, thanks to you who are reading this; I truly hope you enjoy the book.

Prologue

Jared jumped behind her and froze. He stared into the ice and got down on his hands and knees. Sally continued on her way.

"Sally! Hey! Come here," Jared yelled. "Look at this!" He was waving at her furiously.

The young woman scrambled back to where Jared was, digging away at something.

"Look at this. As I was jumping over the crevasse, I saw something. It looked like a doll. But look, it's a body!" Jared stood up and continued staring at his find.

The lower region of the body was frozen about three inches under the clear ice. They could see one arm outstretched over its head; the ice was about eighteen to twenty inches thick around the torso. What looked like a quiver was lying beside it, close to the surface. There were bits of debris frozen around it, too.

All they could say was "wow", over and over again.

"Wonder how long it's been here? Nobody from the village told us about anyone gone missing recently. Maybe it's one of those funky mystical mountain people we heard about?"

Kneeling down, they used rocks to chip away at the icy grave.

All of a sudden Jared stopped. "Wait a minute. What if…, what if this is really, really old? What if this is our woolly mammoth we've been wanting to get our hands on?"

They stared into each other's eyes with thrilling intensity.

"Sal, this could be it, everything we've been waiting for. Think about it. What if we have stumbled on to one of the greatest finds ever? Look at this body, perfectly preserved in ideal conditions."

"No way. What if this person went missing a couple of years ago and they gave up the search? You're being a big dreamer, Jared. I can't see it. Besides, we need to report it to the authorities as soon as possible."

"True, but I'd like to believe we have something here. C'mon Sal, this is really important to me."

He turned back to his find, broke through the ice and managed to get the quiver free with some remains of arrows still in it. He was very careful not to mishandle them.

5

"This is really old, look at these arrows – this is not a recent death."

"Wow!" Sally looked at the artifacts, visibly amazed. "They are perfectly preserved."

She began to see the possibilities and got down on her knees again, closer to the mummified body. They very carefully chipped at the ice around the lower part of the remains. Crude footwear made from decayed grass covered the feet, and the remnants of some kind of animal skin enveloped the corpse.

Without disturbing the surroundings, Jared carefully peeled back the animal skin cover, revealing perfectly preserved ankles and lower calves. The brownish, frozen skin was taut but not deteriorated.

The ice had entirely entombed its victim and as the two worked to free parts of the body, they accidentally broke off a piece of it. Jared cursed as he pulled the chunk of ice away and examined it closely. "Well, we know it's a man." He showed the chunk of ice to Sally. They could see the outline of the genitals through the glassy encasement.

"Wait a minute; this is all we need, Sal. This is all we need," Jared shouted jumping to his feet. "We can take this and do our experiments. You never know, there could be frozen sperm. There could be cells. This is all we need. Wow, jackpot!"

They looked at each other with incredulity. They could not believe for one moment they had actually found such a treasure, which would be the departure point into one of their most fantastic life's adventures.

"This is too good to be true." Jared hugged Sally with what seemed endless enthusiasm.

"What are we going to do with the body?" Sally asked as she took picture after picture of the mummy lying at their feet.

"Are you kidding? We've got to leave it here. We have no way of getting it out anyway. Besides, we don't have a jackhammer to get that upper part out. That ice is a couple of feet thick and really old, look at how hard it was to get where we did and it was only a few inches thick." Jared paused, still staring down at the frozen remains. "I think we need to get back to the village as soon as we can and have our find preserved. I think we should be very careful who we mention this to."

"Why is that?" Sally was not convinced that they should keep their find quiet.

"Well, what if we go and tell the authorities and they come and find part of it dug up and its genitals missing? We'd be toast, charged with messing with archeological findings."

"Are we just going to keep quiet about it?'

Jared looked at his girlfriend for a second. "I think we should get somebody else to find it." Sally was staring at her companion now. "I know, we'll tell other hikers about the caves and give them detailed instructions how to stumble across the body in the process."

Sally hesitated for a bit before she said, "Good idea, but what happens if no one finds it even then?"

"Somebody will find it. We'll leave markers for the trail. But, we'll be long gone and forgotten by the time anyone connects us with the missing family jewels. We'll make sure we don't give out our address and phone number. C'mon, we gotta get out of here. Let's see what we can put these body parts in."

They replaced the broken ice over the body and packed snow all around it to make sure it was not exposed to the elements and decaying agents. They quickly rummaged through their backpacks and found some plastic bags.

They had started down the hill when Sally stopped and yelled, "Wait a minute, the markers, for the trail?"

Jared cursed and turned around.

They piled rocks in neat formations leading to the caves, the glacier and across the crevasse, and kept making them behind themselves all the way down to the village of Maso Corto.

Darrell Swanson

Chapter 1

The sun had dipped below the smaller mountain between them and the village. The wind was up and howling around them, clouds were forming in the west.

"We should try to get to our first camp site up there, so we can get this on ice again. Hope it isn't as hot again tomorrow."

It was pitch black by the time they reached the campsite and it was just as cold as the first night. Jared buried the bag under some ice and kicked snow over the top of it.

They were both exhausted and famished. Sally cooked up the last of the dried stew mix, which they ate avidly around a small fire. They turned in quickly in the hastily made tent.

The wind blew with gale force all night and they woke up to the sound of rain pounding on their tent. They had slept like the proverbial babies from the pure over exertion of the previous day.

"I guess I got my wish for a weather change," mumbled a stiff Jared as he stretched and yawned.

They quickly broke down camp, dug out their treasure and started back up over the summit of the first mountain. The wind whipped the dense fog around them and the driving rain stung their faces all the way down the often-steep hillside.

They were used to inclement weather, being from the Pacific Northwest, so they were prepared with proper rain gear. Their only problem was remembering the way home.

Jared hauled out his compass and took a reading. Being experienced in reading landscape and compasses and even hiking in white-out conditions, they found their way back down through the rugged topography with little difficulty. Their only handicap was Jared who had stiffened considerably from the slide incident. That was an experience Sally would never forget. It had been the preamble of their unexpected discovery.

As they descended through the clouds, they were able to see more and more of the mountain until they got below the cloud cover and could see the village of Maso Corto spread out over to their far left in the valley below.

The rest of the journey down the mountain was wet, but uneventful.

They arrived back at the hostel in time for a late dinner. Jared got his treasure into the kitchen freezer as quickly as possible. It hadn't thawed in the slightest, much to their relief. He made sure it was well marked with his name on it and packaged tightly to keep curious eyes from prying into the contents. He had to get the jewels into liquid nitrogen or dry ice to ensure they would stay good and frozen for the journey home.

Jared's nose was quite red and swollen which gave him the idea to see a doctor so he could find out about a local supplier of dry ice.

The village doctor wasn't much help. His English was so poor that Jared had a hard time explaining what he wanted to be examined for, let alone asking about dry ice. After several attempts, Jared finally got the information he needed. They had to go back to Bolzano, about two hours away by bus. He graciously thanked and paid the doctor who prescribed aspirin for the swelling and pain.

"Damn," he muttered under his breath as he left the doctor's office.

As soon as Jared reached the hostel and explained the change of plans to Sally, they got on the phone and re-scheduled their flights.

In the morning they called home and arrange pick up from their excited families at Seatac Airport, checked out of the hostel and made their way back to Bolzano and then on to Rome as quickly as possible. Before leaving, they were so excited about the find as well as getting out of there that they almost forgot to tell fellow hikers about directions to the caves. Sally scribbled out a map and posted it on the bulletin board, making sure nobody saw her pinning it up.

"Let's not act too hastily about leaving – somebody might get suspicious." Sally calmly tried to damper Jared's enthusiasm.

In Bolzano, they managed to find some dry-ice to pack their treasure before they caught the train to Rome.

On the train, they never stopped talking about the possibilities; Jared, his mind racing a mile a minute, emphasized his view on the genetic make up of his ancient friend while Sally babbled about a stronger immune system. Ultimately, Jared always wanted to clone a human.

10

"Let's call him Jarsal," Sally piped up.

"Ummm, how about Salrad? No-no, I mean *Salad*, especially the way he's packed." That remark sparked a roar of nervous laughter out of the two young biologists turned amateur archeologists.

"Seriously, let's think of a cool name. It would be our code word as well, so we can refer to him instead of "it" or "the thing"."

They bantered back and forth with corny names and finally decided on Giuseppe just to authenticate it a bit more – given "it" came from Italy.

Chapter 2

Sally and Jared had met during their freshman year at the University of Washington and became first good friends, and eventually lovers. Both biology majors, they were fascinated by the possibilities of the fledgling world of DNA mapping. Jared was a young man with a brilliant mind. He was top of his class all the way through high school and his hunger for anthropological sciences was unquenchable. Now, celebrating their graduation, they hoped to continue ground-breaking methods of mapping the human DNA beyond university. With a few prospects for a job in the wings, taking this break was the last hurrah for quite awhile.

Jared was like a Christopher Columbus of the new science of the human body. He wanted to map the human DNA and secretly clone a human. His sinewy six-foot frame matched the questioning blue eyes and shoulder-length, curly red hair that fell around his face and down the nape of his neck. The angle of his nose and high cheekbones gave him a rugged outdoorsman look. Along with Sally, they loved hiking in the Cascade Mountains near their home town of Seattle.

Sally's interest lay in disease research and the effects on the genetic make up of humans. She, too, was a true scientist. She excelled in biology and associated sciences throughout school, and her parents encouraged her to pursue her dreams. Sally was a willowy, five-foot-nine, dirty blonde that bleached white in the sun. Her compelling hazel eyes inset in a strikingly, pretty face were magnets for the average college male. Her statuesque figure and natural beauty was model material. However, she was far more interested in her scientific passion than in the fashion runways.

Jared and Sally had had hours and hours of discussions on their theories of the origins of species and diseases and their impact on civilization. They had a unique way of agreeing and disagreeing. They seldom argued but would reason with each other in tenuous debates. It was as if they were bringing forth something deep from their own heart while they encouraged each other to be more vulnerable.

They had discussed the possibilities of a superior pre-historic human. They both believed that our human forefathers along with prehistoric animals had a better genetic make up, better resistance to disease; maybe even more use of gray matter and possibly, other characteristics now extinct in modern man. Ultimately, they would have liked to get a hold of some cells off frozen Siberian woolly mammoth or other pre-historic animals that had been discovered over the years – anything to prove their theories. Along with animal cloning, they eventually hoped to discover why dinosaurs became extinct. More importantly, they believed there may be a link to a better understanding to the genetic origins of disease.

Sally and Jared, the rebels of their class, wanted to pursue all the possibilities. Their quest for adventure was enormous.

Now, finally finished with their formal education, the discussions focused on marriage, careers and kids. While they had spent most of their college days together, they had chosen to live with their own families. Although, they had a deep love for each other, they would have probably compromised their education if they had moved in together.

Sally, being a scientist first, was always the realist. She had been voted in high school as Miss Congeniality. She liked calculated risk. Unlike Jared, she would never take life-threatening chances – she was too practical. Her parents had wanted her to be a nurse. She loved taking care of people, but she had this wild, adventurous side to her. She loved to travel and loved the outdoors, but ultimately she wanted to make a mark on society with the cure to cancer or MS or, as a matter of fact, any incurable disease.

Chapter 3
Rome, Italy – August

The 7:30AM train lurched in motion as Sally and Jared, settled into their seats facing other passengers in the crowded car. Soon, the conductor came through the car and asked for tickets and passports. The hubbub and noise of excited tourists amidst the acrid cigarette smoke was typical. Many of the faces were local travelers; others were like them, young American students getting ready for careers or getting ready to go back to school. Some were backpacking, others were staying in luxury hotels, and there would be those who opted for the B&B type of accommodations called "pensiones".

There were some looking to challenge the fabulous hiking in the Alps that bordered Italy, Austria, and Switzerland. The region had experienced an unusually warm winter and the glaciers in the high alpine were considerably smaller, allowing hikers to explore more of the beauty not seen in years.

Jared had brought a walkman with him and he popped in the latest *Police* tape and slipped on his earphones. He loved to play the guitar and was already missing it back in Seattle.

Hope Mom is taking good care of my baby, he thought about his guitar as he pulled his sunglasses down from the top of his head. He wrapped his arm around Sally's shoulders and gave her a kiss on the cheek. His mind was beginning to empty itself of school and he was thinking of the trip they had been on, his buddies back home and what it would be like to be married to Sally.

Sally was busy studying the map sitting in her lap as she marked off points of interest while the train meandered through the colorful Italian countryside, squealing and scraping its way past farms and through little red roofed villages. The stops were brief and locals got on and off waving their arms at each other as the Italian expletives filled the air. The sun was low in the sky and a slight overcast created a misty haze.

"Jared, what do you think of this for an idea?" Sally said.

Jared stopped the tape and pulled off the earphones.

"What was that?"

"Let's get off at Bolzano and take the bus to Maso Corto. I think that's what we should do, because we've got only five days to do this part of Italy and then we need to get back to Rome for the sightseeing thing for the rest of the trip and then back home." Again, Sally was the practical traveler, planning their trek almost to the minute.

"Sounds good to me, but, why up there?"

"Well, I think it would be good to be able to see three countries from the one vantage point – you see, it says right here 'see three countries' from this summit – the Schnal ... stal Glacier. I think that's how you pronounce it."

"Okay…, that's sounds like a good idea – Schnalstal it is," exclaimed Jared, putting his headphones back on and hitting the play button.

Conversation then ignited in the seats across from them as they discovered where each hiker was from, where they were going and the great hiking conditions they were hearing about from the locals. This kind of trip usually spawned new relationships and many pen pals.

Eventually, half of the compartment went to sleep, mouths opened, and snoring and heavy breathing was drowned out by the clickety-clack and screeching of the train along with the frequent whistles of road crossings.

The train pulled in to Sally and Jared's station at Bolzano. They had both been sleeping and had to hustle to get their back packs off their car quickly before the train left.

The fresh evening air soon jarred them awake as they stepped on to the platform. Some of the other Americans got off as well and they staggered toward the station exit.

They hadn't made any reservations at the local hostel so they hustled there way to a phone as quickly as possible and called ahead for reservations as well as directions. Fortunately, the hostel was only a ten minute walk from the station and they just happen to have two beds left.

The hostel was a clean, quaint, five-hundred-year-old dwelling that had been operating as a hostel since shortly after the Second World War. It had a castle look to it with huge pillars framing the entrance way and enormous wooden doors scarred with years of use.

The doors opened into a vaulted foyer that echoed scurrying footsteps from one of the two hallways that led to the men and ladies' sleeping quarters.

It was 10:45PM and the dining room was closed. "Thank goodness for vending machines," Jared muttered as he found two or three of them lining the back passage to their respective rooms.

The next morning they caught the bus to Maso Corto. Maso Corto was becoming known as a destination for a few diehard snow skiers who would stay there and ski the Schnalstal Glacier all summer.

It was gloriously sunny and the scene around them was nothing short of spectacular. As they disembarked a couple of hours later, they were in awe. A few hundred feet to their right was the tram that took passengers up the side of the Val Senales that led into the T-bars and ski runs that streaked down the mountainside. The unusually warm conditions made the glaciers look ragged and spent, even from the low vantage point.

The roar of melting snow could be heard from the streams cascading down the mountainside, which in itself sounded foreboding somehow.

Sally and Jared decided to take it easy the first day and explore the local village and find out about the mountain from the locals before they planned their hike.

Through broken English mixed with the local Italian brogue, they managed to find out about some of the trails and spots worth exploring in the region. They decided on day two they would take a shot at scaling some of the recommended trails. Sally really wanted to get to the peak where three countries could be seen, and they mapped out the most accessible trails to that point.

The mountains were so different from the Cascades. These were severely peaked and rugged with little flora. The climate was quite dry and even though the winters would produce great skiing conditions, the rocky formations didn't allow for green, lush forests except in the valleys where there were plenty of streams. Most of the trees ended around a thousand feet, a surprisingly low altitude, considering that three quarters of the mountain range was still above the tree line.

In some places, the icicle shaped, mocha-colored rock formations were formidable at the very least. Iron deposits ran like rusty tears down the barren rock faces. Trails meandered around treacherously steep drop-offs. There were plenty of glaciers and bathing-suited hikers could be seen tromping across them like colorful ants.

Their hostel was a great resource and they learned about the locals and walked about the town, gleaning and discovering information about the history of the region. Because they were so close to Austria, there was a definite influence from the culture and the locals could switch between several languages in a moment.

Sally and Jared learned about the local folklore; how the mountain had "mystical" properties. The story went that it was residence for a community of people who lived a way up the mountainside and they somehow had supernatural strength. Apparently, they would roll huge boulders down the mountain if the locals failed to have an annual "mountainfest" around harvest time. So, it had become a great excuse for everyone to get together once a year to party and honor the "mountain people's" request.

The tale went on to say that the last contact from the mountain people around the turn of the century had been a chilly warning to keep the celebrations going or else. The local authorities had decided to cancel the festival for one year due to poor weather conditions and, unfortunately, a huge boulder had rolled down and had crushed the local tavern, killing three patrons. The site had then been turned into a tourist attraction and, of course, they had reinstated the annual festival. Today, hikers were adamantly warned not to anger or harm the elusive mountain people, "it would be bad luck," the locals claimed.

Sally and Jared had a good laugh over the tall tale and commented that they would love to meet one of these mountain people. The locals pretended to be very serious because they knew it would otherwise keep the tourists from coming back.

They decided they needed to camp out, at least one, maybe two nights on the side of the mountain so they stocked up with some bread, cheese and other supplies for their trek up to the Schnalstal Glacier.

Chapter 4

The first rays of the sunrise caught Sally and Jared working their way up the well worn trails of the lower part of the south face of the mountain. Their ultimate goal was to reach their intended destination some ten thousand feet above sea level where the panoramic view of the three countries could be seen. The Schnalstal Glacier was behind a lower peak where the ski lifts were located, so hikers would have to scale one smaller peak that topped out at ninety-five hundred feet, and then descended down about four thousand feet and backup toward the glacier.

By noon, they were well up the side of the first peak and the trails were starting to disperse into narrow little foot paths, etching their way through dry, tufted grass and tiny, colorful leaves, dried up from the alpine sun. Little, powder-blue flowers were still blooming despite the late season and dry conditions. The panorama was unbelievable. Every direction unfolded a canvas of unprecedented expanse and majesty. The sun was hot but not unbearable. They had long since stripped off excess clothing and put on sun tan lotion, hoping to brown up in the last days of a tanning sun. Sweat dripped from under their arms as well as dampened their foreheads. Other hikers they met or passed by commented on the heat of the day, but nobody complained, it was truly hikers' heaven.

As they progressed on the trail, all sorts of human-like shapes began to emerge out of the icicle rock formations. They laughed as they pointed to recognizable figures and caricature faces of mutual acquaintances – teachers and friends – carved into the limestone landscape. They snapped one photo after another as they caught each other's poses.

"Hey, Sally, look at this, this is *the* Kodak moment we've been looking for!" Jared pointed to a large rock. It likened an old wizened troll, while three smaller fellows stood in a circle, all facing each other. Their bulbous noses and enormous ears reminded one of three of Snow White's dwarves.

"Grab the Coke and some chocolate bars, we're gonna have a rock party."

They took off their backpacks and dug out four cans of Coke and chocolate bars, and placed them on the rocks as if the dwarves and troll were having a party.

They howled and laughed until tears wetted their eyes as they each took pictures, hamming it up around the troll family.

The break was a nice relief and they made notes of their trek. The glaciers were seriously melting and in a lot of cases, there was very little left of once large plots of ice and snow. The sound of the cascading run-off could be heard at every turn.

"Man, the locals were right, it's been warm up here, look at how dry the lichen is and what's left of the edelweiss," Jared remarked.

"I'm sooo glad we are doing this…. Hey, we could do Mt Everest someday!" Sally said as loud as she could between breaths. The rarified oxygen made speaking more difficult at every step they took.

"Jared, what do you think? Mt Everest? Wouldn't that be a blast? I could see the WHOLE world from there!"

"OK, Sir Hilary, let's do Schnalstal first. We've got a long way to go."

They reached the first peak around dinnertime and the sun was rapidly disappearing toward the western horizon. Long shadows were cast in the valleys far below. Fellow hikers were becoming less frequent. Sally and Jared's legs were starting to feel rubbery and they were quite hungry. The thin air and cool breeze reminded them to start thinking of setting up camp. However, they decided to press on for another hour down the north face, heading toward the summit of the Glacier. Going down a mountain is harder than climbing up and being in the shadow. The north face was much colder. The glaciers were considerably larger and the air coming off them was like an air conditioning blast, cooling the two trekkers down to a shivering cold. The clothing went back on rapidly and they silently stepped up the pace.

Most hikers rarely ventured beyond the first peak, so there were no trails. Being experienced hikers, Jared and Sally knew it was important to take compass readings and leave markers in order to find their way back – distance could be very deceiving and disorienting.

Darrell Swanson

Living in the Pacific Northwest had given them unparalleled mountain knowledge and they were very aware of the dangers lurking in the unknown alpine. Many of their hiking and mountaineering friends had had close calls with perilous experience.

They put-up camp about one quarter down the chilly side of the north face. They had a sumptuous feast cooked over a portable stove and collapsed in their tent and sleeping bags within minutes.

Chapter 5

As soon as the sun poked its head over the crags, they ate breakfast, quickly packed up and left toward the sunny valley below. The terrain was much the same, except not so "bleached" due to the lack of sun, and what little vegetation there was, it appeared more lush.

Through binoculars, they could see some dark shadows that looked like caves on the western face. They decided to take one route up to the summit and come back a different way, making a figure nine. The eastern side of the mountain looked less rocky so they headed that way up. Their only concern was the rapid whitewater river that carved its way between them and their destination. Making its way through the verdant valley amidst tall stands of ash, willow, viburnum – hopefully it would be easy to cross. Beautiful couldn't describe the scene that spread out before them.

They were motivated by the present cold and the reward they would receive getting into the glorious sun that washed the dale. There wasn't a cloud in the sky and from their vantage point; they truly felt like they were taking on Mt Everest.

They finally got into the sun and started taking off clothes. The shadows on the mountain in front of them could be seen better now and through binoculars, they could definitely make out the telltale indentations made by the presence of caves.

They stopped for lunch in a meadow surrounded by leafy ash that were starting to turn color, welcoming the pending fall season. The green needles of pine contrasted in perfect harmony with the deciduous trees clustered about, and their scent permeated the air. A couple of deer cautiously walk through the trees on their way to the river.

"This is surreal," Sally cooed with undisguised enthusiasm.

"Yeah and we're all alone."

"And what do you mean by that, Mr. Houghton?"

Both silently took in the absolute beauty of the surroundings while leaning back on their arms in the grassy meadow. Jared leaned over and kissed Sally on the neck. They made out unashamedly in the presence of the beauty enveloping them and proceeded to fall asleep in each other's arms.

An ant crawling across Sally's neck tickled her awake. She suddenly came to life and jerked Jared awake. "Hey? How long have we been sleeping?"

"I dunno; a couple of hours." Jared stretched, looking at his watch.

"C'mon, seriously?"

"I never looked at my watch, can't have been too long, the sun is still in the same position. I guess we'd better get going."

In order to cross the river, they decided to go eastward a few hundred yards where the rapids were shallow and the current was fast. They took off their hiking boots and watched their feet turn blue as they jumped around, squealing in the glacial water. Fortunately, the water never got over their knees.

"Man that's co…co…cold!" Jared yelled above the rush of the stream.

The terrain was much the same on the north side of the river and they easily made their way through the meadows and stands of trees. They started on the incline around the east side as planned. The sound of the river started fading off slowly while they began their climb up the slope.

They could see more glaciers and the numerous waterfalls from the melting ice and snow.

"Soon this whole area will be covered in several feet of snow and this whole cycle will start over," Jared commented as if mesmerized by the scenery.

The heat of the sun off the rocks and the cool breeze was deceiving. Both Jared and Sally had stripped down to the minimum and were starting to feel the effects of the bearing-down sun coupled with the altitude. They constantly drank water. They slowed down the pace as they worked their way through the rocky moraine and the eerie landscape. Vegetation was becoming scarce as the view became more and more spectacular. They said little to each other as they puff their way up the increasingly sharp inclines. The climbing was relatively easy in terms of mountain climbing and they could see that rappelling would not be necessary.

They came across some faded candy wrappers discarded by previous hikers and put them in their pockets to be disposed of later. The sun was slowly arcing its way in the west when they reached the final base of the summit. They picked up the pace. Their hearts were pounding with exhilaration and exhaustion as they neared the top. The peak that looked like a needle from a distance was actually a fairly gentle slope that required some rock climbing technique to reach.

They had long put some of their clothes back on as the wind off the glacier at the top was chilly. They had to be very careful with their footing in the slippery sections of the glacier since they didn't have crampons or other ice footwear. The real danger lurked in the snow and ice bridges over crevasses. Many hikers and climbers had lost their lives falling through these dangerous traps, especially when there were lots of sharp peaks such as along this mountain range.

Jared was in the lead. Suddenly and unnoticeably at first, he began to slide backward rapidly down the steep face of the glacier. He knew he had to fall toward the mountain to slow his momentum.

Sally yelled, "Fall forward! Fall forward, Jared!"

He fell into the mountain and spread out his arms and legs; as if he was hugging the slope. As quickly as he started, he stopped, his face was burrowed into the icy snow, he didn't move.

"Are you alright?"

Slowly he lifted his head and yelled, "I'm OK! Gonna check to see if I can get out of this slide."

Just as he finished his words, he began sliding off again and began picking up speed. Sally watched horrified as Jared skidded down the steep ice pack, clawing in with all his might. Amazingly he stayed in the same position without losing his balance. If he had started rolling, it would have been all over. The end of the glacier was approaching rapidly and all that was left to slow him was a natural ski jump – probably formed over top a huge rock underneath.

"Press in harder! Press in harder," Sally shouted.

Jared dug in with his arms and knees and began to slow down. He finally stopped on the edge of the "ski jump". He cautiously raised his head and surveyed his situation. He was laying on about a ten-degree angle with snow piled up around him like a carpet that had gone askew. He saw blood dripping into the snow and felt around his numbed face for cuts. The pain was coming from his nose.

"Jared! Jared!" Sally's voice was way off in the distance.

He slowly rose himself to all fours. The blood stopped dripping from his nose as he grabbed a handful of snow and wiped the excess off his face.

"I'm alright, just a nose bleed. Must have banged it during the slide," Jared shouted back.

He looked behind him and had to admit he was very lucky he didn't go another two feet or he would have been gone. Fortunately, he had slid in a slight westerly direction and was in a better position to complete his traverse across the glacier.

Still in shock, he remained in the prone position holding on to his nose.

"Jared, speak to me!" Having surveyed a safer route through the glacier, Sally began inching her way across the slippery surface toward him.

"I'm OK, just a little shook up that's all. Be *really* careful." He pointed to what seemed an easier path from his vantage point in order for Sally to join him.

She worked her way across the icy field and about twenty minutes later she got to Jared. They were both on their knees and hugged each other; Jared was shivering violently by now.

"You're in shock, Honey, let me warm you up," Sally whispered through her tears as she lovingly stroked Jared's snowy, matted hair while holding him tightly until he stopped shaking.

"I love you, Sal. I love you," Jared spluttered through his tears. "I could have been a goner."

"I love you, too," Sally said tenderly as she held onto him.

They embrace for what seemed like forever.

"We better make that summit before it gets too late," Jared muttered, regaining a smidgen of composure and a bit of his confidence. "How do I look? Blood gone off my face?"

"You look like a circus clown," laughed Sally, breaking up the seriousness of the moment. "Your nose is all red and swollen."

They got up finally and worked their way off the glacier onto the rocky moraine leading up to the summit.

All the pains and memories quickly disappeared as they stood atop of the Schnalstal Glacier at some nine thousand feet.

The view was all encompassing. Peaks of the surrounding Alps stuck up like frosting on an angel food cake.

Sally surveyed the horizon with her binoculars and pointed out to Jared the three countries she could see. They stood there snapping pictures, laboring in their breathing from the altitude.

"Wish we had a flag," Jared suggested patriotically. "Let's build a little memorial with something to say we've been here."

They noticed they weren't the first to do that; there were several neat piles of rocks littering the top. Some had been there a long time. There were even names.

Jose and Maria and Lucia Armallo, Barcelona, Spain.
Franz and Johann Sweitzer, Vienna, Austria.

There were remnants of flags tied to sticks. Some had been there a long time. There were stones in the shape of letters and dates.

They quickly built a little shrine. Sally wrote a note and stuffed it inside the rocks.

"Let's get going, Hon, we want to spend the night in the valley." Jared waved to Sally as she lingered, taking more pictures.

"What a view. I can hardly wait to see the pictures, even though they can never reproduce the moment," Sally mumbled. "You know we should take a break before we head down," she suggested with concern lacing the tone of her voice. "You just finished sliding half way down the mountain."

They dug out some Coke and chocolate bars and celebrated for a few moments.

The westerly side of the summit was relatively easy to descend; certainly a lot easier than the east side was to ascend and certainly a lot easier than it looked from across the valley.

They worked their way through the rocky escarps and came across another glacier they had to cross about halfway down the mountain. Jared was still a little shaky from his fall and his nose and head throbbed from the blow he received during the slide. Despite the handicap, he was still adventurous, albeit a bit more cautious. He was always known as a chance maker; he liked to live his life on the edge. He was the first among his friends to try bungee-jumping, sky-diving and deep-sea diving. He had been pulled over at fourteen for drag racing with his parents' pick up. During hiking trips back home, he liked to take enormous chances. He was just like that.

His parents thought he would be great US Marine material and pressed him hard to sign up. He still remembered the words of his father. "Son, the Marines may not pay huge money, but, once you're in, you're never out, unless you do something really stupid. You can retire at fifty five with a great pension and have done all the things you've wanted to; fight for your country, see the world while you're getting paid and have a woman at every port of call." He respected his father but thought that the Marines just weren't for him, even though days filled with adventure quests appealed to him. However, he knew too many Marines living in the Seattle area that were bored to tears. He always dreamed of being a scientist and nothing was going to stop his curious mind from exploring the impossible.

The caves were around the corner out of sight from their vantage point. They would have to come back across it to descend to the valley. They crossed easily over the top part of the glacier and made their way through the rock formations and came in sight of the caves. They had to descend into a steep gully and back up toward a natural ledge where the cave openings were located.

They were quite excited about the possibilities and their pace quickened in anticipation. Upon arriving at the ledge where the caves opened out, they caught a view of the little meadow where they had made out earlier and commented on what God must have seen from His viewpoint. Marriage was definitely in their plans and this glorious view of the valley coupled with the adventure cemented their love even more.

They caught their breaths and worked their way around the natural apron leading to the first of the three cave openings. The first two openings were about twenty feet high and fifteen feet across. One was in the shape of an arch and the other was shaped like a teepee. The sun was at a low angle so the interior lit up, showing strange writing and pictures on the walls.

"Look, Jared, what the heck is this?"

They crowded around some of the designs and laughed at the crude drawings of animals made on the rock with something sharp that was signed by somebody from Rome.

The cave was an enormous bowl shape with rocks scattered all over the place. It looked as if it wanted to carry on but it was blocked with boulders and rock debris.

"Wonder if that goes anywhere?" Jared asked musingly as he surveyed the seemingly insurmountable amount of blockage.

They spent a few more minutes exploring and taking pictures. They then signed their names in the soft rock wall with a picture of a heart and arrow. *Jared and Sally, forever in love, Seattle, USA.*

The teepee shaped cave entrance was about fifteen feet tall; the largest portion of the opening being about eight feet wide at its base. It, too, opened into a large rectangular shaped room and was blocked like the first one. There were more crude modern drawings and names, but less than in the first cave.

They stayed for only a few minutes, taking some pictures, and left. The third opening was up a three foot "stair step" to their right and was only about five feet across in the shape of a lop-sided rectangle. Because of the angle, the light didn't penetrate the interior very well and it had a big chunk of ice blocking its hallway. It was cold and damp and there was nothing very interesting about it. They dug out their flashlights and quickly surveyed the shallow room.

"There's nothing here, Sal. Let's get going. We need to get down to the valley before we lose the sun."

They took a few more pictures of the inside of that last cave as well as the outside and were soon on their way down toward the valley.

The easiest way was to cross over the bottom part of the glacier, following the same path they had taken to reach the caves, in reverse. Rocks stuck out as centurions guarding the place, while a rushing stream emerged from underneath the ice sheet, forming a shallow rocky crevasse where clear ice showed frozen rocks beneath it. Sally easily jumped across the crevasse – the same crevasse that opened up to the couple finding their *Ice Man.*

Chapter 6

The train ride back to Rome seemed as if it would take forever. They were by themselves in a compartment so they could talk freely. Jared grew quiet as they rumbled along the beautiful countryside. Everything was so romantic that he, all of a sudden, felt so much love for Sally that he turned and nuzzled his mouth into her ear, and whispered, "I love you."

She looked back with loving eyes. "I love you, too."

Tears welled up in Jared's eyes, and fighting to hold back the emotion, he quietly blurted out, "Will you marry me?"

Sally, sensitive to Jared's vulnerability, gazed back, and almost as a matter-of-factly replied, "Yes," breaking down as she began to weep.

They gave each other a long hug and wept with joy as the swan song of their vacation came to a grand finale. They swayed with the rhythm of the train and kissed and held onto each other for a long time.

"I was going to ask you on top of the mountain, but, I guess we needed to find Giuseppe."

They laughed and discussed plans for the wedding and who all would be coming.

"You know, Sally, if this DNA experiment works, the first child we will be birthing will be Giuseppe's off spring."

Sally, in shocking dismay pushed herself away. "You sure know how to ruin a romantic moment!"

"I'm sorry, Hon, I thought we kind of had that understanding."

Sally folded her arms, backed in her seat, her eyes narrowed, and she lowered her head. "Yeah, but I didn't need to be reminded of it at this moment. We're talking about a lab experiment and a lifetime commitment all in the same breath here. *You* don't have to carry Giuseppe's kid for nine months."

"Hey, hey, hey, look – he's not even *my* kid. He or she will be somebody else's. He or she would be a descendant of a past civilization. Besides, we don't even know if this is going to work, we don't need to get bent out of shape over this…. I…, I don't know why I said that, I'm sorry."

They made up quickly and continued with their wedding plans.

They arrived at the Rome International airport and Sally called her parents to announce their earlier than expected arrival home after re-booking their flights. Then they began worrying about getting their treasure through customs. Should they do a carry-on? Leave it in checked baggage? What if they got caught with this very unusual find? If they do carry-on, what about the dry ice? X-rays?

"Let's ask someone, Jared," Sally suggested, finally breaking their quandary while they were about to get into the check-in queue. "We have enough time, let's look for the special baggage handling department – if they have one."

They looked up the Italian spelling for "special baggage" and came across a sign pointing in the direction of the "OGGETTI Speciale"—*Perishable Packaging*—department, which was way to the other side of the terminal.

Fortunately, the clerk spoke enough English for them to discover it was okay to take up to one pound of dry ice on board; tourists used it frequently for perishables apparently. As it is a gas in a solid form, they were told it could be dangerous when water was poured on it and it was not to be touched with bare-hands. They patiently listened to the lengthy discourse about something they already knew, politely bowed out of their class and made their way back to the check-in line.

Jared stopped. "And, what are we going to say when customs decides to inspect our bags, Baby-Doll? *Oh, these are my family jewels we're bringing back from the old country?*"

Sally turned to him, smiled and shook her head. Jared was right; they had a problem. While they walked through the duty free shop, they pondered on how they could bring it through without getting detected. Back home they could use a salmon container, but, Italy?

"Here it is," she whispered as she grabbed Jared and led him over to a counter while pointing to some fancy Italian sausage and pepperoni done up in an attractive tourist package and costing way too much. It looked like a miniature crate containing a vacuum-packed sausage. "We'll do the swap and carry the contents on board."

Jared stared at it for a few seconds, thinking carefully how it would work. He then decided to ask the clerk if it could pass through customs in the States. The salesperson fortunately spoke English. He promptly told them that vacuum packaging was the only way they could get any perishable into the US. "Other packages would be confiscated," the clerk said.

Jared and Sally looked at each other before Jared said, "Okay, we'll get the medium size one. But, are you sure the package inside won't be taken once we go through customs."

"Absolutely, Signore."

Reassured, Jared paid for the purchase and had it tagged to go through customs before leaving the store.

Sally was practically dancing in one spot when they left the shop. "How are you going to reseal the package once we've got it open?"

"Ah-ah...," Jared replied, a smug look on his face. "That's where a man's know-how comes in my dear." He took Sally by the hand then and led her to a corner of the departure's hall – out of earshot. "Listen," he began, "this little crate is high enough to contain both – our treasure and the pepperoni on top." He pulled the box out of the bag. "Look, all we have to do is put our little sealed pack of ice under the sausage and "Bingo," we've got a crate of pepperoni to check in the luggage – not the carryon."

Sally was still staring at the little crate when she said, "Okay, that might work, but how sure are you that our family jewels aren't going to leak?"

"We'll just have to get some Krazy-Glue to seal the plastic bag." Jared sounded pleased.

"Alright, Mr. Handyman, let's find some Krazy-Glue and get this crate on its way to America!"

They did the switch, being careful to reseal the little crate carefully and stuffed the package into a backpack which they checked through to Seattle. Their biggest concern was not having control over where the checked-in luggage went and how long it would sit in the sun and other warm areas. However, the greatest benefit to having it in the belly of the aircraft is that it would be nice and cold, at least while in the air.

Once on the plane, the chilling reality settled in and Jared's mind raced. How would he do this? He had wrestled with the moral side of cloning over and over... *How am I going to convince myself if Sally gets pregnant from this, that this kid is not mine? I mean, I am raising another man's child for God's sake; even if he is some super human. Would he be able to lead a normal life and have offspring...? What if he is a freak or has some crazy disease or disability? What would society do to this kid? What would happen to me and Sal, and even our families? Would the scientific community black-ball us and ban us from any further scientific work? I guess we could find other careers. I know our folks would totally be against this ... even our friends.... But I have to do this. It's never been done. This is as big as man walking on the moon. This would re-write medical history ... maybe even history, period. I know Sal wants to make a mark with her research on ancient cellular and DNA integrity. But, how am I going to do this? I need some pretty specialized equipment. I may have to create my own.*

"Sal, you know this is going to take some pretty specialized equipment to pull off. Who can you think of that makes specialized lab gear?"

"I dunno. I'm too tired to think about it. Let's get home first and then see if we can get into the lab at the university. I'm sure we will find someone."

"I just thought of someone who can help.... Dennis. He once told me the CIA has the most advanced stuff anyone can imagine."

"Dennis, your brother Dennis? Really? The CIA? What would they need a lab for?"

"I dunno." Jared shrugged. "They might do some kind of research."

Sally closed her eyes and shuffled her position on the seat to nestle her head against Jared's chest. "I don't want to talk about it anymore. I'm too wiped."

"OK, Babe." He stuck the ear-buds in and flipped on the Walkman and went off into a musical dream land with some tunes off a compilation tape he had put together before they left.

Several hours later they arrived in Seattle, tired and yet charged with excitement. They picked up their backpacks and headed toward customs.

They handed the officer the claims form. The officer was an aging African-American with a sizable stomach hanging over his belt buckle. He eyed the two of them up and down.

"Y'all open your back-packs, please."

31

Sally and Jared, trying not to appear nervous slowly unbuckled and unzipped their packs.

"Been away awhile?"

"Uh, three-and-a-half weeks," Jared answered, while the officer started pulling out the contents.

"What countries you've been to?"

"France, Italy, Germany, Switzer..., well..., almost to Switzerland," laughed Sally nervously. "We liked Italy and decided to spend more time there." She could feel her cheeks flushing and her pulse starting to race as she quickly glanced at Jared.

He clenched his teeth and said nothing, staring at his pack being emptied on the floor.

The officer came across the sealed crate and turned it over carefully. Jared and Sally were holding their breath; Sally was ready to spill her guts, Jared was almost going into shock.

"This'll make some good pizza topping, I've had it myself," the officer finally said to the two terror-stricken young travelers. "My wife says she'd go back to Italy just for their sausages, if we had the time, but with the grand-kids now...." He set the pack back down and continued to unzip all the little pouches and pockets in their packs. He looked up at Jared. "How'd you get that swollen nose?"

Jared was almost speechless. "I..., I..., I fell while mountain climbing ... in the Alps, the Italian ones..., Alps," he stammered, "is it *still* that noticeable?" trying to act surprised as he glanced over at Sally.

The officer grunted, shaking his head. "You can go on through." He chuckled.

Sally and Jared quickly shoved their belongings back into their packs and left the customs area.

Both parents and their brothers and sisters met them in the public waiting area. Hugs and kisses from the welcoming party quickly dissipated the nervous relief that almost got them caught.

"We've got some news we'd like to share with you all, seeing that everyone is here, and no, Sally and I didn't have a fight." Jared pointed to his nose. "I had a fight with a guy named Giuseppe on Mount Schnalstal." Everyone had a laugh. "First, I'd like to ask you Mr. Stephenson,"—Jared turned slowly toward him—"will you grant me the privilege of marrying your wonderful daughter? I promise I won't let her hit me like this again!"

Again, laughter and accolades of surprise met the young couple's return.

Mr. Stephenson reached out his hand and fighting back tears, he replied, "If you came home early just to ask me this, Jared Houghton...." He paused. "We've been waiting for this for a long, long time..., of course..., from her mom and me, YES!" He grabbed Jared and pulled him in and gave him a big hug. "Welcome to the Stephenson family, son." He choked up, trying to hide his emotions.

Everyone exchanged more hugs with them both before making their way to the exit.

Both Jared and Sally convinced everyone they were too tired to party and wanted to get to bed as quickly as possible. Jared could hardly wait to get the genitals into the deep freezer at home.

Chapter 7

They were in the school's lab, a few days later, after they had made special arrangements with one of their former professors.

"I've found some frozen sperms," Jared yelped, lifting his head from a microscope located in the empty laboratory while Sally kept her eyes on the hallway for any intruders coming toward them. They wanted to keep things under cover as much as possible even though other students and old college friends streamed in and out and wanted to talk about Europe or about their own work on various projects.

"We've got to keep this under wraps," Jared whispered. "I think we have something much bigger than we know."

They finished up their initial investigations, packed up and left. Jared had convinced someone to give him a locking liquid nitrogen container. They could keep the contents under wraps and take miniscule amounts off for sampling and keep them in a common refrigerator.

They walked quickly out of the laboratory and exited the building.

"I think we have one of the most important ancient human finds – ever – as a matter of fact. I think we can prove some or maybe even all of our theories with Giuseppe here. Hey, I may even be able to clone my *main man!*" Jared exclaimed while starting their old VW bus.

While they drove, they discussed what they must do; preserve Giuseppe and the cells they've carefully dissected; the time they have to book with the lab in order to unravel the DNA. On this uncharted ground they needed to find the steps to cloning – that was going to be the hardest part of their experiment. The controversy around human cloning and in-vitro birth methods were hot topics around the medical community at the time, and they had many discussions with professors and fellow students on the implications of such technology.

"Sal, I've been thinking, we need to talk to Dennis about this."

"What's Dennis got to do with this?"

"CIA. If this gets out to the public; even a breath of what we are up to, this could be the end of a very good thing, *and* you know what I mean, we need protection. Besides, *they* may need what we have to offer, the CIA has some of the best labs around." He shot a glance in Sally's direction. "Hey, if you've got any other ideas, I'm willing to listen."

"Whatever," Sally grunted, "we haven't looked into anything else. Don't you think we should at least look at the alternatives?"

"Hon, besides the lab, we need the cover up, don't you see? The CIA will keep an iron lid on this. If this gets out into the public, we will be dead meat. I mean our careers are over. Nobody would hire us. Hell, we could even end up in jail. We'd be facing pretty stiff penalties for this sort of thing, you know."

"Are you running scared all of a sudden, Jared Houghton?" Sally asked sarcastically.

"No, I have been thinking a lot about this and the last thing I want to do is to risk the most amazing Swansong of our careers."

Jared's older brother, Dennis, had become a CIA agent. Since the Cold War was still brewing, he was busier than ever, tracking suspected terrorists, protecting top-secret missile installations and watching out for other potential international war related events. He had been away from home for two years but called frequently from places all over the world. Due to the secrecy, nobody knew where he was at any given time. He just showed up from time to time without warning. The only way to keep in touch was through letters to an address in Washington, D.C. Jared got along with Dennis but noticed his brother was changing, becoming more cynical, more militant and certainly less tolerant as his tenure with the CIA stretched out.

"What about Professors Jones and Smith? You promised that if you ever stumbled across a woolly mammoth, let alone an ancient human, they'd be the first to know? How are you going to keep such a secret?"

"We'll have to figure that out as we go along; I really think we should consider the CIA."

They discussed all the angles; the need for the agency's labs, the protection and secrecy the CIA could offer. The potential discoveries that could lead to history-making, earth-shattering results that would give someone the opportunity to bring positive change to society by destroying dreaded diseases and producing a healthier human were all very healthy and attractive prospects for anyone interested in persuing these goals with them.

They speculated on the response from the CIA and how they would have to sell them the idea.

"Jared, you're a born salesman, you'd have them eating out of your hand in no time."

"I'm not so sure of that, this isn't the latest spy device, you know. We are talking about a concept that needs to be explained and then proven, they won't pull out a check book and ask how much it'll cost. They will want a lot and we had better be ready to give."

"Do you have any idea where Dennis would be?"

"I think Mom has ways of getting a hold of him."

As they got to Jared's house, the phone rang. He picked it up, his mind still on their discovery of sperms in Giuseppe's jewels.

"Jared, heard you were in Europe, congratulations on your engagement, when's the big day?"

"Dennis!" Jared couldn't believe his ears. "Where are you?"

"L.A."

"When are you coming this way?"

"Couple of weeks. When are you getting married?"

"November twenty-eight." He paused – Jared was still stunned. This was lucky that his brother would call when he needed him. "Dennis, I need to talk to you about something real serious."

"Okay, I'll be your best man."

They both chuckled.

"No, I mean, CIA serious."

There was a long pause before Dennis spoke. "Are you in trouble?"

"No, no, I just don't want to talk about it over the phone, besides, I have something to show you."

"Why does the CIA have to be involved?"

"DENNIS!"

"Well why? I can't just pack up and leave. I have assignments, reports, I have someone I'm accountable to, you know…" He raised his voice. "I have to have a damn good reason to leave LA. *And* now you're asking for the agency's help." Quieting down a little he went on, "*But*, if it's that important, I'll see what I can do."

It was Jared's turn to show his excitement. "This is *that* important, believe me, this could be huge! *You* won't be disappointed. By the way, nobody but Sally and I know about this. Neither of our parents, nobody, so…, you're coming up on assignment, got it?"

"You've really got my curiosity, Jared, this better be worth it."

Chapter 8

Dennis arrived in Seattle on Sunday. Jared and Sally still had not told him about their find; Dennis was starting to get antsy. They finally had some private time without other family members and friends, as Jared and Sally drove Dennis to the school laboratory.

Dennis was exactly the opposite of his younger brother. He had dark hair and brown eyes offset by a square jaw and high cheekbones. He stood about five foot eleven and his stocky build made him look much older than the four years that separated the two. He was cold and calculating. He had chosen business and political science as his majors compared with the creative and anthropology-type courses Jared loved. Their parents always wanted Dennis to be a lawyer or doctor and Jared to be a marine.

Since Dennis's involvement with the CIA, he had grown colder, more calculating and hardened toward a corrupt world. As a youth, he loved to read about spy activity and knew every author of all the pulp fictions and had seen every spy movie dozens of times. His parents used to shut off his TV in the wee hours of the morning after he watched some B grade flick about drug trafficking or sleazy counter-intelligence activity with the Russians. His two year tenure with the CIA had led him from a file clerk to communication with front line veteran spies and a jaded look at cold war and failed missions to oust puppet governments. He was still very keen to take calculated risks, but with his fearlessness trait, he was becoming anxious for the thrill of adventure. At the age of twenty-four, he had very little interest in women and the only close friend he had grown up with, Jason Heward, had moved to Salt Lake City to sell advertising.

"This better be good Jar' ol' boy, this better be good. Here we are in the middle of a crisis with Idi Amin, Khaddafi and a bunch of banana republics that are about to explode and I'm on a joy-ride in a beat-up VW van, driving through Seattle, listening to Steve Miller and nobody's telling me what's going on. Damn, I'm good!" Dennis yelled as he ran his hands slowly and forcefully through his scalp from the front to the back of his hair and slammed back into the aging blanket-covered rear seats.

"Knock it off, Dennis. You've said that about a hundred times." Jared lowered the radio volume and paused, turning around briefly. He smiled at Dennis. "Thanks for doing this bro', you have no idea how incredibly important this is to us." Dennis was sitting well back with his arms folded and a tense look on his face, staring out the window.

All three remained quiet as Jared drove the van down the tree-lined, manicured-lawn streets on the way to the I-5. Behind them, a faded green, seventy-six GMC pick-up truck pulled onto the freeway a few cars behind, following them well back in the traffic.

"Okay, here it is, Dennis, let me ask you what would be the ultimate scientific experiment?" Jared inquired while he maneuvered his seventy-two blue and white VW van on to the I-5. Vehicles of all size and shape blew by them easily as they gathered momentum.

"C'mon, Jared, are you on to that cloning a wooly mammoth thing again?" Dennis chided his little brother.

"Do you think I'd make you leave your work, fly all the way from L.A. for a mere mammoth clone? Are you kidding? No way, man! Think about it, what could the CIA really use for spy material in their organization?"

Dennis forced a laugh. "Some good-looking women!"

"Women! You wouldn't know what to do with it if one of them fell into your arms and said, "Marry me!" Seriously, who could the CIA *really* use in their organization?"

"Well, I don't work for the human relations department or the R&D division," Dennis replied while reaching for a Marlboro in the breast pocket of his khaki shirt. He lit it up, deep in thought, drawing a big drag as he began to relax. Jared threw a glance at Sally.

Dennis looked out the side window and stared into the passing city skyline. "The agency can always use intelligent people who fit their mold – people who are accountable, who can think for themselves and are fearless to the point of no return. Someone with no regard for their own life and little regard for others, when push comes to shove, they will always defend their country, their boss and ideals. I'm not sure what order." He blew a big whiff of smoke toward the window, sucked another drag off his cigarette, and then focused on the rear view mirror to catch Jared's eye. "Are you telling me you have cloned a human?"

Jared locked his eyes on Dennis in the rearview mirror. "Not quite, but you're close – that's why I need the CIA's help. You told me one time; the CIA had top secret laboratories that conducted experiments on all kinds of things."

"They have been working on human cloning for years. What makes your theories and or experiment so special?" Dennis asked.

"Sal and I have stumbled across one of thee most amazing finds in archaeology, or should I say *anthropology* since the pyramids." Jared glanced at Sally again. "That's why we're taking you to show *you* our secret find."

Dennis's dark eyes flashed in the rearview mirror. He shifted to the edge of the seat and leaned his arms on the backs of the front seats getting closer to Jared and Sally. "Why the hell the CIA? Are there not government and private agencies who would be overjoyed to take on such an experiment?" His cigarette was dropping ashes all over the floor.

Jared replied, "Of course they would, but we have a huge problem. We have smuggled in our clone host from another country and we would be in deep shit if we went to the government or private companies to help us. It would be scientific suicide for us to even begin to broach the subject. Hell, I mentioned human cloning once in one of my biology classes and the prof. nearly threw me out. I can't imagine bringing up the origin of the host. We're talking about a very serious hot potato. The world isn't ready for anything like this."

"We're already in deep shit," Sally remarked quietly.

There was a brief silence as Dennis, deep in thought, took another drag off his smoke and looked down at the bright green carpet samples used for floor mats. He flicked some ashes into an empty Coke can he found rolling around under his feet.

"You are probably thinking why couldn't we use a red-blooded American and you are exactly right." Sally turned in her seat toward the middle. "Many theories have been postulated over the years about the origin of species; about how much stronger we are today as human beings. How we have supposedly evolved to having a stronger immune system to ward off diseases. How our intelligence has increased, my God, look how technology has exploded. We are supposedly living longer today and mankind is better off, et cetera, et cetera," she went on. "Dennis, you know Jared and I have done a lot of studying from unconventional sources. We have never been traditional in our thinking and we see an opposite picture. Sure, we may be better off than humanity was a couple of thousand or so years ago. But, we have never bought everything education has taught us. We *know* there are two sides to every story. In our studies, our findings have shown us that mankind actually lived longer, a hell of a lot longer than we do today. The Bible talks about people living to be hundreds of years old, they had a higher immunity to disease. Although they may not have enjoyed technology as we know it today, there is a very good chance our long lost forefathers were a whole lot more intelligent than we give them credit for – just look at how the pyramids were built."

Jared picked up where Sally left off. "You have heard the expression, "We only use ten percent of our brain"? We believe there is a lot of truth to that. We believe there was a paradigm shift of thinking when technology became our god. This all started back in the eighteen hundreds when the Wild West was being tamed and Europe was undergoing an industrial revolution. The theory of evolution was born and the search was on to prove origins of species, transitional species and things related to how did this all come about from a pure physical existence. Science was bent on trying to prove dates, times and events rather than explore the human condition. It eliminated, ever so subtly, pursuit of the existing, relative to the pre-existing, as we know it. What this has done has caused science to approach antiquity through a whole different set of rules and consequently, it has laid aside some elementary things."

"Herein lays some amazing truth," Sally interrupted. "There are all kinds of speculations how the dinosaurs disappeared, how the world has had cataclysmic events. We found an article from an obscure Russian biologist, Igor Kravistsky, who died in 1911. Now get this, while he was doing tests on the frozen wooly mammoths located in Siberia, long before they became famous, he found they had an incredible immune system, they actually were about five hundred years old when they met their demise, and get this, some had man-made harnesses attached to them!"

Sally caught her breath and continued, "Apparently, our friend Igor was so blown away by the find that he removed the harness so that he could do more research on it. In doing so, he completely altered our theories of evolution and everything else. Nobody believed him when he showed them the harness afterwards. He had opened up an incredible can of worms about the immune system and age factor, but completely screwed up by taking the harness off the mammoth. Apparently, he went insane and committed suicide, and that's why he has never become well known. His writings were discovered years later sealed in the wall of the asylum where he died, when they were tearing it down. Do you know what this means? This means that humans were alive and well during a supposedly no-human era, and weren't supposed to be on the scene for another few million years."

As he put out his cigarette in the Coke can and slid back in the seat, blowing smoke at the side window, Dennis scornfully retorted, "Where'd you find that Russian crap? Are you expecting anyone to believe that? I don't care if it was authenticated by Albert Einstein; you are talking about altering science as we have known it for the last thousand years. I have heard your position on all kinds of things over the years, but this takes the cake. Besides, what the hell does this have to do with cloning?"

Jared cleared his throat and stared into the rearview mirror at his brother. "Look, *you* may not buy that story, but this has everything to do with our experiment. Just suppose we could take a human from the past, clone him and find out if our little theories are correct or not. The worst case scenario is that we have an average human with exactly the same characteristics as we do today and that's all she...."

Sally was hurt by Dennis's retort. She turned completely around in her seat to face him. With a dramatic passion wavering her voice, and pointing with her right hand to each finger on her left hand, she began, "The *best* case scenario is a), we discover the cure for cancer, heart disease, multiple sclerosis, and every other major disease known to mankind, b), we would have a human who may be a way more intelligent, c), they may live for a hell of a long time," she yelled, "And d), they just may be all around better persons!"

Her glare into Dennis's eyes caused him to look down at the floor. She then swung around quickly and deliberately slammed her back into the seat.

The noise of the straining motor of the old van coupled with the impending road noise filled in the void when the conversation stopped. Jared looked over and winked his approval at Sally. Her flushed face and flashing eyes made up for the unbecoming, tense, knitted vertical lines between her eyes as she fought back the tears. She held back a sob that was locked in her throat. She rested her right arm and hand between her mouth and the edge of the door and gazed off into the distant skyline in silence.

Dennis took out another Marlboro and lit it up in a cloud of smoke. This time he cracked the side window to let the smoke out while the traffic noise increased inside the van.

Jared exited the van off the freeway and drove it into the vacated parking lot at the university. The green pick-up parked on the street well away from the parking lot. A few vehicles were a good sign; there was someone there to let them into the lab. They silently piled out of the van. Very little conversation had taken place since Sally's impassioned speech.

"We have to keep our conversation down, I don't want anyone to know what's going on here," Jared said authoritatively before entering the Science Block.

At the other end of the lab, there were a couple of students absorbed in their work on experiments of their own. Jared got into the frozen specimen area and took his key to the liquid nitrogen container out of his pocket. He grabbed a pair of long tongs and after unlocking the lid of the container, reached around with the tongs and very carefully lifted out the frozen genitals amongst the cold swirling fog of the evaporating liquid nitrogen.

He briefly showed the leathery, shriveled, ancient specimen to Dennis while quietly describing the story of their find. Carefully he slid them back into the nitrogen deep freezer and sealed the container again.

Almost in a whisper, he then explained, "We have found frozen sperms on our friend here. This is all we need to proceed. You see, a sperm cell is like a stem cell or the completely stripped version of all the information we need to tell us everything about the person. If we used cells from say the skin or hair, we would have to go through a huge process in order to strip off all the other info we don't need in order to get to the basic cell. Also, the neat thing about the sperm cell is that it doesn't need to be alive. What's really amazing about this, Dennis, is that the DNA for this guy is ever so slightly different from ours today. We have run it through the school's computers and microscopes. All the chromosomes and telomeres are there, but the telomeres tell us how we age, in a normal modern cell are, let's say, this long." Jared showed an inch spread between his thumb and index finger. "I might add that they get shorter as we age, in this guy's cells are like this long." He showed a distance of about six inches.

After that little exposé, they moved into the computer room off the main area of the lab. Jared took some disks out of his coat pocket and slipped them into one of the computer's drives. The monitor came to life after a few groaning noises. He then typed some commands and the monitor showed off a series of numbers and graphic symbols.

Sally, feeling slightly more enthusiastic now that Dennis seemed to listen with interest rather than mockery, got into it. She pointed to the monitor and quietly explained the DNA code layout, the importance of the stem cell and what would be necessary to complete the experiment.

Jared took over. "We thought we were measuring something else or doing it incorrectly, but we verified it over and over, and as far as we can tell this is true. Furthermore, there may be many more of the same kind of things we can't ascertain. So far, his DNA appears to be a way more complex than today's average Joe. What we need is a more sophisticated computer and lab equipment to complete the count of chromosomes and crunch the numbers. Then we can proceed with the process. What we do is somehow inject the sperm into the egg and fertilize it. Then we do the in-vitro and Sal will give birth to the descendant. By the way, this guy was virile; we have lots of frozen sperms to work with."

Dennis had grown quieter and pensive, his abrasive attitude had melted away in the presence of such a daring adventure, and his doubts had all but abated. He was starting to think of how many ways the CIA could benefit from this. There were a lot. Foremost was consistency, this could mean undeniable loyalty, no turncoats. They could custom-clone by department. Like a beehive, there would be the drones, the inside workers, the no-minds who had no interest with front line, dangerous missions, they would be much more efficient and loyal than the crowd that presently work in the many offices and departments. Then there would be the warriors – the people who love to live on the edge, they could care less about office procedures and bureaucracy, they could be technically adept to do everything from flying helicopters to implanting micro-chips into someone's body. They could use any kind of weapon and have the audacity to steal the steak off Idi Amin's plate while he's eating. Then there would be the clones of the masterminds – they could see the whole picture, like chess masters, able to forecast trouble zones and set up counter-measures before innocent lives were lost. They wouldn't get bogged down with menial management responsibilities that so many of the leaders presently do.

Then it hit Dennis like a brick – this could ultimately mean a huge promotion and a lot of recognition, even money. To him, this was right out of a movie. He started thinking of ways he could sell his boss on the idea.

"How does this *in-vitro* work?" Dennis asked almost dreamily, trying not to show a lot of emotion, just like any good agent would do.

"You *are* with us; I thought for a minute we had lost you," Jared scolded. "I said in-vitro is this: we take an unfertilized egg from Sally and fertilize it in a laboratory setting and then re-implant the fertilized egg back into her. If all goes well, in nine months we are parents."

By this time Dennis was trying to hold back his enthusiasm toward the idea. "What guarantees or risks do we have?"

Almost startled by the change in his brother's attitude, Jared looked over to Sally with raised eyebrows and then back to Dennis. "There are certainly no guarantees and the risks are no different from any other pregnancy."

"How much do you think this would cost?"

Again, Jared looked at Sally, only this time he was like a lost puppy. "We never thought about this in dollars and cents. We were thinking more of the time factor. But, you're right; I guess there has to be a dollar value attached to it."

"You gotta have some kind of dollar figure in order for anyone to buy your concept," Dennis said, shrugging. He shook his head side to side. "My little brother, off in the clouds somewhere. Besides the computer and lab time, what other expenses are there? You guys need to be rewarded somehow for your time and effort." He stopped and looked at both of them in turn. "Let me think about it."

"Does this mean you are willing to help us?" Jared asked, anxiously.

"I know nothing about what you are doing here, except, I think the CIA can benefit from it," Dennis replied uncommitted.

At the same moment, they heard voices and footsteps approach the room. Jared motioned to be quiet as he escaped from the program and ejected the disk out of the computer. The two students, one older man and a younger Chinese girl entered the computer room. They exchanged the usual greetings. After which, the new comers made their way around the lab.

"We're just leaving; it's all yours," Sally said, gesturing to the students. The couple thanked them and sat down in front of the computer.

The trio left the lab and soon piled up again in the VW. A slight drizzle had replaced the afternoon sun as they made their way back home along the glistening streets. The conversation was ignited by the possibilities. Dennis was conservatively excited, as any good agent should be and even tossed around some cost figures that may work.

"Can't be too damn expensive, but being too cheap is just as bad," Dennis growled as he lit up a smoke.

"Look, Dennis, we don't want a whole lot of money for this. Besides, we are not *selling* this to the CIA. This isn't some commodity or piece of machinery or something. We are simply asking for assistance to complete our experiment. It was you who brought up the dollar figure," Sally remarked. "But I think we could certainly use help in the area of our expenses as well as support when the child is born. Why don't we do a contract of some kind where the agency doles us a monthly check over a given period? If the experiment *is* a success, then we will have a specimen to conduct further experiments, with our assistance and under our care, 'cause after all, the child will still be ours. If the experiment is a failure and the child turns out to be a normal red-blooded American, then the dole is terminated and we are proud parents and we continue our research at our own expense or find a job in the medical field. Or whatever."

"Sounds all well and good to me, but I've got to convince my superiors. We're in the middle of Reganomics and huge budget needs for the agency, and I'm not sure they would be open to a daring risk venture," Dennis replied.

The wipers slowly, almost awkwardly smeared away the rain on the windshield as Jared looked over and gave Sally a love smile. She was sitting stiffly with her arms crossed over her chest, pensively looking out the windshield.

As clouds of smoke from Dennis' incessant smoking began to invade the whole of the van, both coughed and spluttered. "One day those god damn things will be banned," Jared shouted, annoyed. "They've killed enough people. Can't you crack open a window a little? We're dying up here."

Dennis reached over, opened the window and flicked the butt out. "Right! And smoking probably killed your man on the mountain, too." He snorted and rolled the window back up.

Jared looked at his brother in the rear view mirror. "So how do you want to work this?"

"I'm thinking about it." He paused. "Would you be willing to sign a contract?"

"The CIA makes up contracts?"

"Of course. Who do you think they are? Some kind of slimy underworld hit men or something. They make up legitimate binding business agreements all the time!"

Sally and Jared looked at each other with a "why not?" look.

"Sure. But that still doesn't answer my question," Jared continued, "how are you going to sell the agency on this?"

Dennis stretched his arms over the back seat. "Jared, are you insinuating I can't present this case to the powers-that-be at the office?" Dennis barked indignantly.

"No, I just want you to make sure you convey our intentions clearly and they have a clear understanding we are not creating a monster."

"I think I can do that quite well thank you. However, I'm sure a written proposal from you guys would make it a whole easier."

"No problem," Sally said excitedly this time. "We already have one – all we have to do is include the dollar amount."

The rest of the trip home was animated with the possibilities of the experiment mixed in with reminiscing and wedding plans. The tension had long abated and they were back to being family, laughing at old times and silly jokes.

Meanwhile, the green pick-up several cars back, changed lanes un-noticed, keeping a safe distance from the van as it exited the I-5 toward the residential area where the Houghtons lived.

Chapter 9

The family had a meal together and discussed the wedding. Dennis had to catch a flight back to L.A. that evening.

The parents wanted to come along as well. So, everyone got into the VW van and headed for the Seatac airport.

The family bid Dennis good-bye as he grabbed his overnight bag out of the back of the van and headed into the terminal.

He looked at his gate number on his ticket and decided to stop at a washroom before going through the newly installed metal detectors.

For some reason, he picked one of the smaller washrooms that only had a couple of urinals and stalls and stepped up to a urinal. Suddenly, the door burst open and a tall, rugged-looking man, dressed in a dark blue suit, entered the washroom. He quickly checked out the stalls, pulled out a .38 and stuck it into Dennis's ribs.

"Shake it real good and put it away, we're going for a walk," ordered the assailant as he picked up Dennis's bag while still holding the revolver in his back. "And don't turn around."

Dennis slowly did up his fly. "Can't I at least wash my hands?"

Without replying, the rugged man clasped his gigantic hand around Dennis's arm and forced him to the door, out into the airport foot traffic.

"Later," growled the gunman, "we're going for a walk."

Dennis knew it was an agent and swore to himself that he never checked for a tag while they were driving around – shit, he cursed, the "students" in the lab – never even thought. He shook his head in disgust at himself.

"OK, I know you're an agent, put the gun away – so that we both don't get busted, I'm not some mole or double agent. I only work in the office and I can explain the whole thing," Dennis pleaded with his captor. All he got in reply was another grunt.

49

They exited the terminal at a different entrance where he had originally got in and from there; Dennis was shoved into a black limousine.

The gunman got in behind him as Dennis found himself in the company of three agents.

"Dennis Houghton?" the middle-aged man dressed in an ill-fitting, grey suit asked gruffly.

"That's me." Dennis's heart was beating wildly. "Who are you?"

"You left L.A. yesterday on a leave of absence to visit your family. Previous to that, you had a phone call from your younger brother pleading to see you about the agency's potential involvement in something big. What the hell is going on, Houghton?"

"You wire tapped my phone? You sleazy bastards – I thought there was a little more trust than that! I deserve some personal time."

"What kind of experiment is your brother doing up at the university?"

"Well, let me explain." Dennis was flabbergasted by his own employer's unscrupulous means to keeping track of their own. "Firstly, I *did* come to talk over wedding plans with my brother. Secondly, he and his fiancée are students. I don't even know who you are. You haven't told *me* anything. You're holding me hostage and my plane leaves in ten minutes."

"Houghton, if you've got something the agency needs to know about, we're here to find out," the grey suit snarled.

"Anything I have to say will be to my superiors, besides, where the hell do you think I was going? Look, here's my ticket. I'm headed home and tomorrow I am going to talk to Chambers and go from there. Besides, I still don't know if you're CIA, moles or KGB."

The grey suit slowly reached into his breast pocket, nodded to the other two and they all pulled out IDs and held them in front of Dennis.

"Gees, that's better! Look, I appreciate your efforts, I don't have to tell you guys anything. I've got to catch that eight o'clock flight or I'll be in bigger trouble than I am now and so will you."

"Don't worry, Houghton, you'll have company on your flight – we are here to make goddamn sure you get on that plane, and if you do something silly, you will be attending your own funeral."

"I can't believe I'm taking this from fellow workers!" Dennis exclaimed, flustered.

"Get used to it; this is nothing. Now get outta here and catch your plane, you'll have company on board, and somebody waiting for you in L.A. Say "Hello" to Chambers from the *Norwest's*," the grey suit smirked as he nodded to one of the agents closest to the door.

Dennis slid out of the limousine, in defiance grabbed his bag off his *assailant* and dashed through the terminal to catch his plane.

As he walked down the aisles of the Boeing 737, he checked out the face of each seated passenger, looking for clues to a possible agent. He thought he saw one, a thirty some year old woman seated next to the aisle, dressed in a charcoal suit, piercing eyes, short, straight brown hair, plaquish skin, little make-up, flipping quickly, almost nervously through a Seattle daily newspaper. Their eyes met and they both sized one another up like two dogs sniffing each other's butt.

He slowly walked up to her row as he waited for the passengers in front of him to get their things away and into their seat, all the while checking her out. She did the same, and just before he passed her; she lit up with a big smile and said a muffled "Hi." Dennis, who was so intense on his mission, grunted a "Hi" back as he shuffled toward his seat about five rows back from hers.

He felt his face and neck heat up in embarrassment as he sat down.

He gathered his thoughts and mentally planned a meeting with Chambers. He clicked in his seat belt and took out the paper with Jared and Sally's proposal. He decided not to open it as he still felt paranoid about the fellow passengers. Sitting next to him on his right was a young Chinese, college-aged girl wearing glasses. *Strange*, he thought. *Wait a minute; she looks like the girl that came into the lab at the university. Can't be. Then again, could be.* To him, all Chinese looked alike. Besides, CIA using college kids?

His intelligence training had gone out the window. He tried to remember a spy movie with this many turn of events in such a short period of time, and all that came to him was Woody Allen's spoof, *What's up Tiger Lily*. Using a fast paced, tacky Japanese B movie, Woody had turned it into a comic "thriller" with English over dubs.

51

The story line was turned into agents who were trying to secure a secret egg roll recipe from the enemy.

Dennis couldn't believe he was in the middle of this. All he wanted to do was help out his little brother who had a fantastic idea. He slipped the proposal back into his pocket; put his head back in the seat only to wake up in LAX.

Chapter 10

The next day he was in Chambers' office.

"Have a nice trip back home, Houghton?" asked Chambers, a heavy set, middle-aged, balding father of three grown boys. He put on his glasses, picked up some reports that were on his desk and started to read. "Have a seat."

"I did, sir. Thanks for asking," Dennis replied nervously as the leather-winged chair squeaked in response to him seating himself into it.

Chambers looked up from the reports at Dennis, his eyes narrowing and penetrating.

"What *were* you doing in Seattle, Dennis?"

"I was visiting my family, discussing wedding plans with my youngest brother who's getting married in November. He is an aspiring biologist slash geneticist and him and his fiancée are working on something that I believe the agency should take a serious look at."

"How come you didn't tell *me* you were out scouting new business on behalf of the CIA?" Chambers barked. "We had three agents involved in your little escapade, which cost this department a lot of time and money. Next time you decide to take a vacation, you'd better make sure you take a real vacation or you'll be taking a permanent one."

"Yes, sir, I'm sorry, sir," Dennis replied meekly, looking down at the floor between his legs.

"Well, what have you got?" Chambers' voice was softening.

Dennis, who started to loosen up, told him the whole story starting with Jared and Sally's theories, then the discovery of the frozen specimen and how they had cracked the human DNA code for cloning and were now ready to produce a clone of their *Ice Man.*

"Hmm," Chambers grunted, "sounds a little far-fetched to me."

"Sir, it did to me as well until they took me to the university lab and showed me the private parts off their mountain man and the computer stuff they have come up with. I could hardly believe it was being done by my little brother."

Dennis went on to explain the value human cloning would be to the CIA, how they could actually have consistent staff. "Just like a beehive, the drone bees do all the work, they have no aspirations to go to another department or leave the hive. They simply do, say office work and all the paper work," Dennis continued. "Then there's the warrior bees, the ones who defend the hive, they are the ones who ward off predators; just like our field workers. They feed information to the queen; they are fearless and have no regard for their own lives. Then there's the…"

"I get the picture, Houghton," Chambers cut-in. "Why do they need us?"

Dennis then explained the dilemma Jared and Sally faced; the fact that they had in their possession a stolen artifact and that the computer and laboratory at the university were not up to par to complete the process. They needed a complete covert operation. He mentioned their proposal and how they would like to see the process managed.

Chambers was seemingly warming up to the idea. He got up and began to pace around the room in silence.

"Mind if I smoke?" Dennis asked as he watched Chambers walk around the room with his hands clasped behind his back.

"Yes, I *do* mind."

God, I hope I don't turn out this way. This guy needs a diet and some exercise, Dennis thought.

Chambers continued pacing for another minute or two in silence, his large frame and girth causing him to breathe with some difficulty.

"I'm curious," Dennis said, looking up at his boss, as he was pacing in front of him. "How did you know I was up to something when I went to Seattle?"

Chambers stopped behind his desk, leaned toward Dennis with both hands on the desk. Their eyes locked. "We are the CIA and you are going to learn how to be a good agent – no – a damn good agent, so I'll let *you* find out when you're ready."

Dennis squirmed in his seat, crossed his legs. Chambers sat down, put his hands behind his head and leaned back while his chair creaked in protest. Seconds ticked by into minutes.

"I'm going to think about this." Chambers finally broke the silence. "Did you say something about a proposal?"

Dennis reached into the breast pocket of his jacket, pulled out the rolled up piece of paper and slid it across the desk to Chambers.

"By the way, Norwest's says "hello"." Dennis remarked flippantly as he reclined in his chair.

Chambers jerked his head up, flung his upper body to the table and stared at Dennis. "Did he see this?"

"No, sir."

"Did you tell him what you were up to?"

"No, sir."

"Are you sure? What about the lab?"

"Positive, my brother had shut down the computer before they had a chance to see anything. By the way, that was very clever, having the two students coming into the lab while we were there. I never knew we had female, college-age Asian spies working for us."

"We don't," replied Chambers, snickering. "She is a tour guide. The other guy is one of ours." He looked down at the proposal and silently perused the piece of paper.

Dennis felt more wind come out of his sails and cussed to himself about his spy's obvious inabilities.

Once Chambers finished reading, he lifted his gaze to Dennis. "I'm going to have to run this up the flag pole and see if it will fly. As far-fetched as it sounds, I personally like the concept. However, I will have to convince Washington then get somebody to cough up the dough. As for you, I should send you back to the farm team for some re-training." Dennis bit his lip and looked down at the slightly soiled carpet under his feet. "But I think you have learned a lesson. This is the CIA, the most powerful intelligence network in the world. There is no room for slip-shod practices. We pride ourselves in being the best," Chambers preached concluding his little spiel.

"Yes, sir, I believe I have committed a grave error, sir, and I'll make sure it doesn't happen again," Dennis replied patriotically.

"It won't happen again, Houghton."

Dennis, feeling a little better about the encounter, left Chambers' office and went back to his own cubicle to work. Later, he went to a pay phone on his way home from work and relayed the meeting with Chambers to Jared. He instructed Jared to make sure they watch every move they made as there may be tags put on them.

He also wanted them not to talk on the phone about it as their phone lines might already be tapped.

Dennis informed Jared that the agency might contact him and Sally directly in order to set up a meeting, or they might want to use Dennis as the liaison.

Chapter 11

The next day the phone rang in Jared's home. It was 7:00 am. The CIA agent, disguised as a job recruiter, wanted to set up an appointment with him and Sally. They were to meet at one of the coffee shops on the main level at the Seatac Airport the following morning at 8:30. He also instructed them not to talk about it to anyone, only to say that it was a job interview for both of them in response to an ad in the paper.

Time dragged by like an eternity as they excitedly prepared their documents and files for the meeting.

The next day at the airport, two men met them and quickly escorted them through the terminal to a waiting helicopter. A little apprehensive about the whole cloak-and-dagger stuff, they were whisked off to the roof of a high-rise office building in the Seattle downtown core.

Within minutes they were searched and then escorted through an incredible labyrinth of stairs, secure doors, video surveillance equipment, security guards and finally into a small, windowless, plain office. In it, there was a desk, typewriter, a metal filing cabinet and three rolling chairs. Sally and Jared were asked to be seated. Their escorts melted away as quickly as butter on a hot skillet, locking the door behind them as they left.

Jared and Sally had been unable to speak with each other except through body language and they were still in shock from the whirlwind events.

"Wow! Wasn't that an incredible ride? Never been in a chopper before. I wonder why? We could have just driven here," the ever-practical Sally remarked in a hushed voice.

"I wonder if this room is tapped," Jared whispered.

"This is exciting!" Sally exclaimed, as her zest for adventure seemed unquenchable.

In a few minutes, the door opened and two men entered. The first was in his mid-fifties dressed in a blue suit with a leather briefcase, the other was of similar age, dressed in a white lab coat, wearing very thick glasses and sporting a rough, graying beard.

Sally and Jared jumped to their feet as they were introduced.

"Mr. and Mrs. Houghton?"

"Ah, just about…," Jared corrected demurely. "We are engaged to be married in November."

"My name is Douglas Riddenhall," the first man said, "forensic specialist with the Central Intelligence Agency. This is Andrew Lowenstein, head of scientific research and development."

They shook hands, exchanging pleasantries.

"Please have a seat." Riddenhall gestured to the couple.

Andrew remained standing.

"I understand you two have something we may be interested in," Riddenhall commented as he opened the briefcase and shuffled through a file folder.

"Well…," Jared began.

"Before we go any further," Riddenhall interrupted, "I would like you to take a look at this non-disclosure agreement. We have drawn this up as a precaution to both you and ourselves. Since what we are going to discuss is very sensitive, we are in no position to have unnecessary breaches of confidentiality. This is a life or death document, please read it over carefully and Mr. Lowenstein and I will return in a few minutes. Do you have a pen? If not, there is one on the desk."

Riddenhall and Lowenstein left, and, once again, Sally and Jared were by themselves.

They slowly read through the ten-page document and tried to understand the legal terms.

"*Hereto with, circumvention, misconstrued…,* man, what the heck do these words mean?" Jared blurted, shaking his head.

They pondered over the agreement for several minutes and only gathered that they maybe signing their lives over to the CIA as a scientific experiment.

Riddenhall and Lowenstein came back into the room with an extra chair for Lowenstein. They both sat down.

"Sir, we have some questions. Is it possible we can have a lawyer look at this?" asked Jared.

"We can have a copy sent to your lawyer; however, this is not a contract, only a non-disclosure agreement. That's all we need to do to proceed with this business. Please sign on the necessary lines. This is not a deal, simply a non-disclosure," Riddenhall reiterated as matter-of-factly, pointing to the signing lines.

Still unsure, Sally and Jared signed and dated the document and handed it back to Riddenhall.

"Thank you. Now, we can proceed. Mr. Lowenstein here would like to ask you some questions."

Lowenstein nodded and turned his attention to Jared. "Mr. Houghton, I understand you have a very interesting experiment you would like to perform?"

"Yes, sir."

"Please let me see what you have."

Sally pulled out a bulky, well-used file folder from a leather briefcase she had borrowed from her father.

Jared and Sally went on to describe the whole experiment, beginning with the ancient find to their theories and ultimately their need of microinjection equipment. The frozen sperm or stem cell had to be inserted into the egg. Then the in-vitro process could begin and Sally would carry the child to term.

They also went over their connection with Dennis and the reasons for which they thought the CIA could benefit from the experiment. Riddenhall took notes and listened intently to the couple's proposal while Lowenstein browsed through the files, also making some notes on a separate sheet.

"Very interesting observation on the length of telomeres," Lowenstein remarked. "If this is true, this guy could have lived a long time." He glanced over to Riddenhall a concerted look on his face.

Lowenstein's demeanor was rapidly changing from a professional skepticism to a deeply interested behavior, as he read through the file.

"Well, I think this is a very interesting project you two have come up with. I read your proposal and preliminary findings and I was, quite frankly, skeptical at what you had found out and what your plans were. As a scientist, I don't buy into a lot of things you speculate on, but some of the characteristics of your mountain man's DNA look to be amazing."

"As you can imagine," Jared interjected. "The lab at the university we did our work in is pretty basic and we still aren't sure of everything we have mapped. That's one of the reasons why we are here; we want to ascertain that we would get access to the equipment needed."

Lowenstein turned to Riddenhall with raised eyebrows. They both got up and walked toward the door.

"We'll be back in a few minutes," Riddenhall said as he closed the door behind them.

"I think Lowenstein likes it," Sally whispered.

"I don't know about Riddenhall. He is a bit of a stick in the mud," Jared said quietly, shaking his head.

Time dragged on as the two sat quietly in the stark fluorescent-lit room.

"I can hear my heart beating," Sally mumbled. "It's so quiet in here. I wonder what floor we are on."

"I don't know. But I still wonder why the helicopter ride?"

Five minutes passed. Jared was getting impatient. He got up in a jerk, which sent the chair flying against the opposite wall. He paced around the room like a trapped animal while looking for hidden microphones and cameras all the while trying not to be too obvious about it.

Eventually Lowenstein and Riddenhall burst through the door.

Riddenhall stood in the doorway declaring, "Mr. Lowenstein would like to take you on a tour through our facility. I would like to brief you on the next step from here."

The laboratory was something out of a science fiction movie. There were white coated scientists everywhere. The lighting was subdued around groups of computer monitors. The equipment was like nothing Sally and Jared had ever seen.

There were people walking around with head microphones connected to telephones located on their hips. Some were talking in broken English, still others in foreign languages.

They were escorted then to a separate room that required security and inside they met four scientists who had an incredible array of beakers, flasks and equipment spread out over the tables at their backs. Several computer monitors flickered as numbers flashed on and off the screens. Banks of equipment with red, yellow and white flashing lights lined the walls. The air smelled peculiar, like solder and electronic equipment mixed with exhaust from Bunsen burners.

Jared and Sally were spellbound by what they saw.

"Wow! Color monitors," Jared pointed out quietly to Sally.

"Here is where we do our biological experiments," Lowenstein broke through over the hum from the equipment. "And this is where we will complete yours. The rest of the lab is out of bounds to you and there will be no talking to anyone in that area. You will require an escort to and from the entrance. Washrooms and lunchroom are right around the corner.

"Because this is such an unusual experiment, and since this is a first for the CIA, you are the very first civilians ever to be allowed inside a facility like this," Lowenstein went on. "A breach of any kind of security will seriously jeopardize not only the experiment, but your own safety. Mr. Riddenhall will fill you in on the details. As well, you will have to have assistants working with you in order to operate the equipment."

Lowenstein escorted them back to the office area and back into where they had left Riddenhall. Riddenhall was finishing a call on his cell phone.

"Is that…, what do you call it…, a *cellular phone?*" Jared asked in amazement.

"Yes it is," Riddenhall replied matter-of-factly.

"A formal agreement is being prepared to lay out compensation and security issues. I want you two to know that you are the very first civilians ever to be allowed into this area and to do this type of project. I can't emphasize how gravely important it is for absolute silence about this project. If anyone outside of this building knows *anything* about what you are up to, the project will not only be cancelled immediately, but you may find yourselves, umm, relocated. Is this very clear? Do not discuss this with any members of your family, certainly not friends, and no one at the university. You will be working for a company called Pacific Laboratories. Your job titles will be lab technicians and the company specializes in the study of marine life. If anyone asks specifically what you do, you assist in various lab functions. I am sure you can make up any number of things that it entails. You will report to Mr. Lowenstein at all times. Your telephones will be monitored and someone has been assigned to follow you. Take that as a comfort as well as a caution."

"Can we request lab equipment if necessary?" Jared asked innocently.

61

"Yes," Riddenhall said, visibly annoyed by the interruption. "Let me continue. A legal contract will be couriered to your address, Mr. Houghton, in the next day or two. I expect it back on my desk within forty-eight hours. It is fine to have it checked out by a lawyer. Do not mention CIA or you will risk ever seeing the inside of this lab again. I cannot stress enough the absolute secrecy that is at stake. The only reason we are even considering this is because of your relationship with one of our employees."

"I think we get the message loud and clear, sir. One more question; why did we have to come here in a chopper?"

"You will find that out later," replied Riddenhall as he shot a sidelong glance at Lowenstein.

They were then escorted out of the lab area, this time through the front doors. They exited through several doors and security barriers before reaching the foyer. The foyer to the lab looked like that of any government agency. There were cubicles with office workers and desks and filing cabinets and computer monitors. The big ceiling-to-floor oak doors had simple locks on them and exited to a main floor, which included a bank of elevators.

They returned to Seatac in a black sedan, picked up their old van and headed home.

Jared was still astounded as he drove. "Did you see the equipment in there? Wow! I've never seen anything like that, not even in the movies. Now I know why they do such incredible things. Dennis will be blown away by this!"

"Can we tell him?" asked Sally. "Remember Riddenhall said *no one*, not even our families."

"Well, Dennis, will know, I mean, hell he got us this far."

"I don't think we should say anything to him unless he asks, and then we can make up a story – I don't know, we had better ask Riddenhall or, what's his name – Smart. What a name, I was going to ask him if we can call him "Get" for short. He even looks a little like the blundering agent from the TV show."

"Baby, we are going to see our dreams come true!"

The old van lurched along the I-5, a faded green pick-up followed them staying back in the traffic.

During the drive, they discussed their plans for the project.

Sally said, "I would like to keep our lives as normal as possible. Once we finish with the lab, we should be able to have a normal pregnancy. I don't want a bunch of agents scrutinizing and following every move I make. I would really like to give birth at the hospital where me and the rest of us kids were born. It would look real dumb if everyone saw me pregnant one minute, then I was whisked off and gave birth in a laboratory somewhere – talk about drawing attention to suspicion. We should really stress that point with these guys."

"Yeah," Jared agreed. "And I don't want my kid to be taken and raised by the CIA. Wouldn't that be awful? Can you imagine?"

"Jared, what if the kid is different? What if they insist on keeping it? We have to be prepared for the worst. This would be a case of an unplanned adoption, the state taking and raising your kid against your will."

"Yeah, but we are going to get that straight in the contract."

Sally laughed. "You're dreaming, this is the CIA we're dealing with." She quickly grabbed her mouth. "Oops, not supposed to say that word, damn, this may be harder than we think. We gotta remember; Pacific Laboratories and we are doing menial marine testing stuff. How are we going to keep this quiet, Jared?"

He turned to Sally with a very serious look on his face. "Sal, this is the most important secret we have ever had to keep. This is a dream we have waited for all our lives. This is more important than keeping Giuseppe under wraps. We have to play their game, we have to follow the rules – something we have struggled with all our lives but this is the most beautiful nemesis."

Their gazes into each other's eyes could have filled a library shelf of books on the art of communication.

Jared dropped Sally off at her home and headed toward his folks' place where he still lived. The green pick up followed well back and parked a few houses away from his home.

Both Sally and Jared announced their new job prospects to their respective parents and congratulations went around all day long.

The next day the courier arrived at Jared's place right on time and he immediately arranged with a local lawyer to have it read over. The lawyer Okayed the standard initial contract and Jared had it couriered back the following day. They told their parents not to tell a whole bunch of their friends about their jobs as it could be temporary and they themselves would like to break the news to their own friends.

The first few days on the job consisted of security checks, aptitude tests and cross-examination by CIA personnel. They were being treated as clerical employees working under Lowenstein and the lab crew. They were never allowed into any of the very high security areas and were escorted virtually everywhere.

"This is boring," lamented Jared on the way home after their first week. "I want to get on with this. I mean, I'm bored stiff."

"Yeah, me too. Hey, where's the agreement for the proposal we put together? I think we should get that signed and sealed before we go any further. We should get Riddenhall in there and find out what's going on."

"Yeah, let's get that done tomorrow, first thing. I want to get Giuseppe down here and start makin' some babies."

Sally glared at Jared. "Easy for you to say that, Studley. You don't have to have something rammed inside of you prodding around for an egg. Then carry an experiment around inside you for nine months."

"I'm sorry, sweetheart. Guess I'm just bored."

The next day they met with Riddenhall and Lowenstein and a much-modified agreement was ready to be signed.

"We changed some of the wording around to make the agreement clearer legally. Go ahead and take it to your attorney. There is no mention of the agency in it and I would suggest you get this back into my hands as soon as possible."

The agreement spelled out terms and conditions and agreed upon compensation. They took it to their attorney and had it back in the lab within a couple of days.

There were things that had to be adjusted but it eventually was agreed upon and Giuseppe was transported from the university lab.

Chapter 12

More than two weeks had passed by and it was now the middle of September.

In an old, industrial section of Seattle a long ways from the downtown core, Pharmaco, a floundering laboratory, specializing in the new world of DNA mapping, was having its telephones cut off for the second time because of lack of payment.

"Great, just what we need. I hope one of our investors doesn't try calling about now," Steve Giles, the forty-five-year old owner and manager of the lab, yelled as he slammed the receiver down on the cradle.

Giles was a heart attack waiting to happen. He stood five-foot-ten and tipped the scales at two-eighty-five. He smoked two packs of cigarettes a day coupled with numerous Jim Beams he hammered back for lunch and at home. His ruddy complexion and thinning red hair screamed out behind his bulging eyes and spider veins that marbled his cheeks and chin. Sweat stains constantly hovered around his armpits. He carried a handkerchief to keep his forehead and face dry. He breathed like an old heifer in heat when walking the shortest distances. His wife had left with their two kids three years ago to live in a trailer court on the other side of town; the mental abuse, resulting from the pressure of the business, had been too much for them.

The lab had been a pace setter in the race to get DNA mapping done quickly. Its claim to fame was several patents pending on the process of DNA mapping as well as some cellular mapping treatments that saved time and money. The problem was that his top biologists who worked there had been swooned away by big money to larger labs and many of the private investors were getting nervous because there had been nothing new in more than two years. The residuals from the rights to their patented processes were becoming less and less as other labs came up with their own short cuts and processes. They needed a major break through.

Giles was a great salesman and could keep a story going for a long time, but, time was running out and so was the investors' patience.

Now with his sweaty head in his hands he was combing his mind for answers.

"If there is a God, I need help," Giles blurted hoarsely aloud. At that moment, the mailman walked in the door and handed him the mail. He had to let the receptionist go so he took over the duties. He normally wouldn't get too excited about the stacks of bills; however, he thought there might be a check mixed in with it all. Sure enough, there was a check for an overdue receivable.

"Thanks, that was a quick answer," a surprised Giles said as he reverently looked up while holding the check in his hand.

Giles knew he could come up with a solution to increase the value of his company. At this point, nothing less than a miracle would do. The following day he restored the phones and had a long meeting with the three surviving employees to explain the crisis.

During the meeting in the front office, they were interrupted by a young woman.

"Excuse me; is the person in charge of hiring available?"

"We're not hiring," Giles answered roughly, annoyed by the interruption.

"Could I leave my resume?" the girl asked timidly.

"Well…, why not." Giles got up, and huffed and puffed over to her and took the envelope from her. "We'll be in touch," he grumbled.

"Thanks a lot," she meekly replied as she backed out the door.

"Where were we? Oh yeah…, Bob, do you think we can work on improving the speed of that computer in your department?"

"It's a beauty; we need more RAM and a way faster processor," Bob replied.

"I'm talking not costing us anything! Can we rob some RAM from another computer or something, damn it you're the nerd around here. We need to speed up the mapper; we still haven't got close to count yet. We're getting left behind. I can feel it." Giles mopped his face and the veins on his temples popped a little further out.

They discussed the things that had to be done and after a break, the workers went back into the lab area to the contract work they had committed to.

Giles made his way to his office; the resume from the young girl still in his hand. He ripped the envelope open and quickly leafed through the simple two-page resume of work experience and objective of the applicant. All the while he kept on thinking, *why am I doing this? I've got to make some calls and get some more business in here, there are three families in the back that I'm responsible for.*

OBJECTIVE: To work in a laboratory where DNA mapping
is being done. I have a deep interest in plant and animal
cloning, for the betterment of mankind.

Something about the girl and her education was very attractive to Giles. She was a recent university graduate and top of her class, plus she had worked on some unusual projects. Stuff he wished he could introduce in his lab.

"Cloning, now that's a field we should be pursuing," Giles thought aloud.

He flipped the resume into a *Hiring* file and went about his work.

Chapter 13
The Experiment

Sally had been taking fertility drugs in order to increase her egg count. She was now ready for the crucial timing of the release of the eggs.

Lowenstein was sitting on a stool beside the operating table. "About five years ago," he began, "the world heard about the birth of the very first test tube baby born to a thirty-year old Englishwoman. As you may remember, the Aussies repeated the process successfully several years later." He cracked a smile. "However, we had achieved the same feat back in the late sixties at one of our labs in New Jersey. The result was a fine young man who graduated from high school this year. It actually wasn't done in a test tube. As you know, normally, the fertilization is done in a glass dish. One of the eggs is then put into a nutrient bath and placed in an incubator for a few hours. Then it is exposed to a bunch of semen, which have been swimming around in a salt solution. Shortly thereafter, one of the little buggers penetrates the egg wall and life begins. Once the fertilized egg is replaced into the female, the pregnancy can begin." Lowenstein paused. "By the way, ranchers and farmers have been using a similar process for years, they call it artificial insemination. Not quite as sophisticated as this, but has turned into a big business."

Lowenstein went on as if he was teaching a biology class, but looked directly at Sally. "What's different here from a regular in-vitro is that we are going to inject the sperm from your mountain man directly into the egg. We had to design an extremely small needle, less than half the diameter of a human hair, the first one ever used anywhere. His sperm cell is what we classify as a stem cell. Even though it has been frozen for a long time, it has all the information needed in order to bring forth life and pass along his traits."

Jared, working the long tongs, carefully pulled a vile from the swirling liquid nitrogen. "In here is the sperm. I separated as much as I could find, there may be more in the testes. I didn't want to take

68

anymore than I needed to do the experiment." He placed some of the frozen sperm into a solution in order to thaw out.

The operation room was set up with a full complement of staff in order to perform the laparoscopy; a small incision made below the navel to provide a passage for a camera to be inserted along with surgery equipment into the ovaries.

"What we have to do is find an unfertilized egg from Sally and we can begin," Lowenstein went on. "We have this device, which can help us locate an egg."

"Well, shall we?" Lowenstein asked, looking at Sally.

"No problem, let's get it done," she replied nervously.

The nurses brought out a machine that looked like an ultra sound. The anesthetist did his business and Sally slipped into a gentle unconscious state, setting her eyes on Jared before closing them.

The lab was equipped with high-powered microscopes with probes and manipulating devices hooked up to them. These, in turn, were connected to sophisticated monitors displaying the contents of the Petri dishes, which the technicians would swap back and forth.

Lowenstein explained how it worked on the screen before them. He tweaked the knobs while running the probe over Sally's pelvic region. Jared was in awe as the images streamed across the screen. Lowenstein then pointed to the different areas and explained what they were seeing. Several minutes went by as he slowly moved the probe around. Silence was overcome by the whirring and grunting noises from the machine while Lowenstein looked for the egg. Half an hour went by and he finally found what he was looking for. He zoomed in on the image and pointed to Jared and observers what he saw.

"Now it's your turn," he said to Jared. "I need you to hold the probe while we extract our find."

Jared held the probe while Lowenstein made the small incision. The minuscule camera was inserted and images started to show up on the monitor.

"Wow, you guys do have awesome equipment!" Jared exclaimed. "I have never seen anything like this."

Lowenstein worked the camera around and maneuvered it until the target easily showed up on the screen.

"You won't see this equipment in a hospital for a long time. We are generally five to ten years ahead of civilian medical practices.

We usually perfect this sort of equipment long before private companies get their hands on it."

He looked at the screen again. "I can see that the fertility drugs have been successful, Sally has a few eggs we can choose from," he remarked, turning his head toward Jared and smiling.

He then returned his attention to the camera and inserted a tiny suction device to extract the eggs. As soon as he retrieved the instrument he handed it to one of the assistants. "I guess we have all we need for now," Lowenstein said as he pulled out all of the equipment.

Jared was still in awe at the apparatuses as he sat beside Sally. He slipped his hand down and took a hold of her hand, gripping it with excitement.

The eggs went into a solution and under a microscope that was connected to yet another overhead screen. Lowenstein swirled the mixture around until he found an egg all by itself. He quickly isolated and "froze" it into a static position with a glass slide.

An assistant brought over the dish with the sperms in it and he changed places with the first dish. He swirled the solution around, looking for a sperm cell. He came across a bunch of them floating along like little chunks of ice.

"Boy, these guys are cold." Lowenstein was slightly annoyed. "Would you mind getting this in the incubator," he told the nurse beside him. "Warm it up for about three minutes at ten degrees above room temperature.... That should do the trick." He smiled at the nurse as she took the solution from his hand. Lowenstein then returned his gaze to Jared. "You know, another good thing; thankfully men have a huge amount of sperm in them at any given time. We'd be in big trouble if we only had one to work with."

"That's better," he said when the nurse brought the vial to him. The sperms are floating with much greater flexibility. "Now let's try something that's never been done before."

An assistant manipulated the tiny syringe and with the help of the TV monitor he found a lone sperm and sucked it up into the tube of the syringe.

Another assistant switched the dishes, and the solution with the egg sandwiched in a glass case came into view on the monitor. Lowenstein took over and very carefully injected the content of the syringe into the egg and slowly implanted the sperm cell into it.

70

The scientist then let out a big sigh of relief and handed the controls back to the assistant.

"We normally would let these two dance for awhile to see if they can waltz in time. However, because we are dealing with a non-living sperm, we will apply some electricity to zap the process into life, so to speak. We need to see if it will take once the egg divides. Then, we need to get them back into Sally fairly quickly."

The first few attempts failed and finally after some frustrating moments, one of the eggs divided and the excitement began. The fertilized egg was then implanted back into Sally's ovary. After the medical assistant had closed the incision, Sally came out of her sedation a few minutes later. The whole lab had a different atmosphere from before she went under. Now, everyone congratulated her and she sensed a whole more positive mood in the place. She was asked not to move around for the rest of the day and to lie down as much as possible.

Jared was so excited he couldn't quite contain himself. "We're going to have a baby, baby doll!" he whispered in her ear. Sally, in a drugged daze, smiled wistfully without speaking.

The experiment worked. Sally had definitely become pregnant. She experienced mourning sickness and began to gain weight. Wedding plans were well under way and they were glad she hadn't started to show. She was having mood swings and her parents were a bit concerned. She put it off to the pending wedding and they went along with her.

Both she and Jared kept in touch with their university friends and they frequented the campus cafeteria regularly, visiting friends. Nobody had a clue what was happening. They had everyone convinced that their jobs were legitimate, lab technician type, mundane jobs dealing with the marine industry.

Jared and Sally were married in a modest wedding in November. After a short honeymoon down the Oregon coast, they rented a small apartment close to downtown and continued to work at the agency.

They kept their secret well and even Riddenhall and Lowenstein were impressed with their ability to keep the whole thing under wraps. Each day they went to work, they got more involved in the research at the lab and the agency was becoming more impressed with their abilities and contributions.

As the days turned into weeks, and then into months, Sally became agitated and had a hard time sleeping. The pregnancy appeared to be normal, but she was becoming elusive and moody.

She then went into a brief depression. At night, her thoughts went from a positive note to a negative one. *This child isn't ours. What if there is something really wrong with it? I feel like I have been raped. I don't need to prove anything about my theories, besides I will be too busy being a mother. Maybe I should have an abortion. What are my family and friends going to say when they find out I'm carrying a scientific experiment? The poor child will be a freak of nature..., no, of science – that's even worse. Is there supposed to be this much discomfort from a pregnancy? My friends never had this much discomfort.*

She needed to talk to someone. Her close friend, Jane, worked at a small lab in the downtown core and one day they decided to meet for lunch at a little restaurant. The eatery was packed and they ended up sitting next to a low divider. Next to the divider, Giles who happened to be in the neighborhood and stopped in for lunch was sitting by himself, reading a newspaper. Then a younger, well-dressed man came in and sat down at the table right behind Sally.

Sally and Jane went through their greetings and pleasantries, recalling old times, Sally and Jared's trip to Europe, the wedding, the honeymoon. Jane was a tall, buxom, large-framed girl which made her larger than life to anyone looking at her. She had a square jaw and steel grey, piercing eyes. She had always been a good listener and Sally seemed to gravitate toward her when it came to bouncing ideas or sharing some of her deepest thoughts, concepts and concerns.

"Jane...." Sally lowered her voice. "I'm pregnant."

"Pregnant?" yelped Jane. "I knew it! I knew you were going to tell me this, I just knew it!"

"Quiet..., will you." Sally looked around; people at tables close by, including Giles, glanced over, throwing Sally smiles of congratulations.

"Yep, pregnant." Sally looked down while she fingered her hair back. She was uncomfortable. She felt depressed and wanted to talk about it.

"Are you all right, Sally?" Jane inquired, seeing that her friend was quite fidgety.

"Yeah, well not really … just a little down. I don't know, this pregnancy thing can really throw you for a loop."

"Maybe you will feel better after you eat."

"Yeah, I sure hope so."

Sally drank some water, her hands trembling when she grabbed the glass from the table. Jane looked at her a tad concerned about this change in her friend. She put it down to her being pregnant.

As soon as the waiter left after taking their order, Sally opened the valve of her repressed anguish. "Jane, you remember me and Jared and our ideas on DNA and all that?"

"Of course," Jane laughed, trying to cheer Sally up. "How could anyone forget your grandiose ideas about changing the world of medicine with your return to Adam and Eve theories? I thought there were some brilliant postulations you two had about early man being smarter, healthier and all, but quite frankly, I thought you had both lost it."

Sally narrowed her eyes, leaned forward and whispered, "Jane, listen to me, those crazy ideas are happening. My baby, this isn't Jared's. This is science!" She pointed to her stomach.

Giles pretended he was not there. He looked the other way and flipped noisily through the newspaper. However, he shifted his large overweight frame to listen in even more.

As the server decided to choose this moment to bring the two women their salads, Jane, dumbfounded, mumbled, "Sally, you must be joking. What do you mean "science"?"

"I mean science, Jane…. You can't tell anyone, though," Sally groaned, passing her hands over her face. "I can't believe I'm doing this." She looked at her dish distractedly. She was no longer hungry. She pushed the plate aside.

On the other hand, Jane seemed ravenous. She gobbled down a few forkfuls before she said, "I won't tell anyone, Sally, trust me, I think this is awesome. Whatever you two are doing, I think it's great. When are you due?"

"Around the first part of June, we are going to have it at the Northwest Hospital; you know, it's a Medical Centre. That's where both Jared and I were born. Listen, you won't tell a soul, Jane, please…, will you?"

Jane continued eating with visible gusto and with a mouth full of food "I'd swear on a stack of bibles, cross my heart and hope to die.

June, that's less than four months from now, you're amazing that you don't show a whole bunch. Man if it were me, I'd be out to here and probably have gained fifty pounds by now."

Sally went on to tell her about the discovery of the Ice Man, the sperms, and the in-vitro. She managed to leave out the CIA part.

Jane's eyes widen, and she stopped eating. As she listened, she kept saying, "Wow! That's incredible – this sounds like a movie!" every time Sally described another part of the things she and Jared went through.

Meanwhile, and after he finished his coffee, Giles who was next to the divider got up and left.

Sally recovered her composure while she told the story. Having poured her heart out to her friend felt fantastic but she began to feel guilty to have blurted out everything.

"Did you see the look on that fat guy's face sitting next to you?" Jane giggled.

"No, do you think he was listening? My God, don't tell me he heard us talking…, Jane…, do you think?"

"Naw, it's too noisy. Besides, I was just so amused at the initial look on his face when I yelped about you being pregnant. After that, he was more interested in the newspaper. I swear; he wasn't interested in a couple of chicks talking about a pregnancy. C'mon, Sally, loosen up, you're awfully edgy. Besides, even if he heard what we're talking about do you think he would be the slightest way interested. You'd really have to know what we were talking about or be from the FBI or CIA or something." Jane shook her head in dismissal. "Don't worry about it."

"My God, Jane, I should have never told you." Clearly overwhelmed by what she had done, Sally began to cry, her body heaving in great sobs. "Jared will kill me if he finds out that I told you. I can't believe I told you. Jane, please, please, please don't tell anyone, I beg of you."

Jane got up and went to sit beside her friend. She reached over and grabbed Sally by the shoulders, "Sally, get a grip, I won't tell anyone. This is really important to you two, why would I say anything? Besides, nobody would believe me except some of your old profs and I won't be seeing them none too soon."

"You really mean that, Jane? You really can keep this an absolute secret?" Sally eventually looked up from reddened, mascara-streaked eyes.

"As I said a minute ago, I'll swear on a stack of bibles."

Chapter 14

Steve Giles, sweating and puffing profusely, threw his overweight body into his old car, sat at the wheel, and waited. The two girls, still in the eatery, continued to talk for another half-an-hour until Sally settled down. Jane had to return to work and they finally both left the restaurant.

Giles followed them, driving slowly as they walked down the street. Sally got into the VW van and Giles scribbled down the license plate number. He knew somebody who could get an address off license plates.

His heart was pounding. His mind was racing. He was sweating so hard, he had to wrap his handkerchief around his hand so he could wipe the sweat off quickly before it got into his eyes. He had never been so elated. He rushed back to the office and got on the phone to his last and only financing partner to tell him the story.

"Jim, you know this little gal, she is going to give birth to the most incredible human in modern day history! And we, as a company, need to be there. I don't know how at the moment, but I can tell you, I will figure this out."

"You'd better figure something out real fast or you are going to be giving birth to something besides a baby. I don't know if I can wait four more months for one of your hair-brain ideas to take place."

"Jim, it's less than that. Please, trust me. This time it's no joke, I will get pictures of her to prove it. Let me call you back."

Giles then dialed his friend at the licensing office. He got the call back that night. His friend gave him the address and not waiting a minute longer; Giles got into his car and went looking for the VW van. Sure enough, he found the van and decided to go to the next step. He followed the van to Sally and Jared's place and with a telephoto lens on his camera, he started taking pictures and documenting their movements. Little did he know there were other sets of eyes doing exactly the same thing.

Sally never told Jared about her wild mood swings and her spilling the story to Jane.

The next day, they got a call on the intercom from Riddenhall to meet in his office.

"We need to check Sally out and see how the fetus is developing. I'll have one of our resident doctors do a routine physical and make sure things are going well in the baby department. How have you been feeling, Sally? How are your friends and family handling it?"

"I've been feeling much better, Mr. Riddenhall, thanks. I had a bit of nausea and stuff at first, but, that's seems to have subsided and I am starting to feel normal."

"Sally, who was that friend you had lunch with yesterday?"

Sally's face turned white and her eyes grew big. "J-j-Jane Higgins, an old friend from university. My God, how did you know?"

"I assure you both that we monitor every move you make. Apparently, you were very emotional, what were you two discussing?"

Sally was dumbfounded. "Well, you should know, your guy was right there. Anyway, I…, I told her about my pregnancy."

"Go on."

"I was very emotional, I have been very emotional, haven't I, Jared?" Jared's steely stare told it all – disappointment, bewilderment.

"I'm so sorry, you guys, I don't know what came over me, but I had to talk to someone." The tears welled up in her eyes. "Jane is my best friend, I've known her for years, we have shared every secret with each other. I know enough about her to embarrass her in front of God. I assure you, she knows nothing about the CIA involvement in this. As far as she knows, it is an experiment between Jared and I. Ask your…"

"I thought we had an agreement." Riddenhall cut in abruptly. "The agreement states that if there is any kind of a breach, that it can be terminated without cause."

"Even though this is the first time I have heard about this, Mr. Riddenhall," Jared piped up, "This would be true if, the CIA has been mentioned, or, was somehow involved in the breaching. By the sound of it, Sally never brought the CIA into it and it was a very innocent mistake. I don't think we should jump to conclusions and assume the worst."

"We always assume the worst and work back from there. You've been around our operation long enough to see how things are done." Riddenhall paused and eyes furrowing with great seriousness, he added, "We are not going to terminate this agreement, we are however, going to make sure this little lesson will never have to be learned again. Is that perfectly clear? There will not be a second time. The next time you need someone to talk to, Sally, come and see me. Now go see Doctor James, he is waiting for you."

Sally got through the check up and went back to the lab to work with Jared. He was quiet and listless.

They left work and were driving home when he exploded. "What in hell do you think you were doing, Sally?"

Sally was very despondent. Between clenched teeth, she said, "I knew that guy was a spy, I just *knew* it. I don't know what came over me, I had to tell Jane. I felt so depressed, I don't know why. My God, Jared, I feel bad enough. I'm so sorry."

"You mean you knew there was a tag there?"

"Well, the place was packed and there was a big fat guy sitting like this far from us, reading a newspaper. He got really excited when I mentioned pregnancy. I don't know how he heard the rest of the story. It was so noisy in there."

"Do you think Jane will spill her guts?"

"Absolutely not!" Sally yelled.

"I can't believe you would do something like this."

"Don't start; I feel like the biggest terd ever already, I don't need you barking at me."

The short drive to their apartment was kept under now two pairs of watchful eyes, unaware of each other.

Chapter 15

Spring arrived in Seattle in its own soggy fashion. The Japanese cherry blossoms and rhododendrons bloom incessantly in the myriad of intense colors they are famous for, despite the rain and gloomy days, slivers of sunshine parting the clouds sporadically.

Giles's company, Pharmaco, struggled along. A small government grant here, more royalties there. His whole attitude had taken on a fresh, new positive outlook. He was talking to his kids and his employees were wondering what got over him, he was actually conversing with them civilly. The plan he had laid out for Jim Shanks, his one and only investor was brilliant. Shanks thought Giles was only going to get DNA off the baby right after it was born and do a human clone. Giles had the plot for the perfect crime. He had the hospital staked out; he had the records department, the birthing ward, all the procedures worked out down to the smallest detail. Nobody would ever suspect what happened or even how he was going to get the DNA specimen off the baby.

Cloning was a priority, he knew it was the wave of the future and he must position his company to be a leader in the field. He attended every work shop, researched as much material as possible and started gearing up the lab for the big switch. He rifled through the *Hiring* file looking for the young girl who had dropped off her resume a few months back. He called and left a message for her to give him a call back. His plan for the birth of the ultimate clone was about to take place in a few weeks and he needed to muster everything possible in order to facilitate the experiment.

Within a few days he contacted and hired the girl who originally applied for the job. His motivation was twofold. Once he had the DNA swab he could put her to work on the clone. Secondly, she could be an alibi in the event anything went wrong during his time at the hospital.

Chapter 16
The Birth

Sally's contractions grew more intense – they were already fifteen minutes apart.

"Honey it's time," she groaned as she shook Jared out of his sleep. It was 5:30 AM and she had been preparing for this moment for weeks. Jared pulled himself out of bed and threw on his clothes. Sally, groaning and wheezing, gingerly lifted her bloated body off the bed and put on the robe she had ready by the bed. Few words were exchanged.

With Sally's duffle bag in one hand and an arm around her, Jared carefully shuffled them toward the VW van. The cool June morning air bursting with the smells of freshly cut grass and spring flowers washed their faces with a newness and vigor.

Jared sped to the hospital and had Sally admitted through the Emergency Entrance. As soon as she was wheeled of to the maternity ward, he went to park his car and rushed to the desk where all the documents were to be filled out.

"It must be baby day today," quipped the clerk. "You are the third couple to come in this morning already."

As Jared arrived to the maternity ward, a nurse led him directly into Sally's private room. She was screaming "blue murder" by the time he sat down. He had never seen Sally, or anyone for that matter, in such a pain. She could hardly talk. As each contraction subsided, Sally rallied up enough strength to tell him how much she hated this and how much she wanted out of there. And then, she yelled loud enough to alert the nurse across the hall.

"All right, Mrs. Houghton, we're getting there," the nurse said, after she checked if Sally was dilated enough to be wheeled into the delivery room. "Just a few more minutes," she concluded, draping the blankets over Sally's feet again.

"What can I do?" Jared asked all nervous.

"Just hold her hand, Mr. Houghton, and try to have her breathe as they taught her at the Centre."

Jared had never attended any of the pre-natal sessions with Sally and he had absolutely no idea what the woman was talking about. All he could see was his wife in excruciating pain.

"Couldn't you give her something for the pain?" Jared asked in desperation.

"Too late, Mr. Houghton, but your wife is doing very well. We'll come and get you both in a few minutes," the nurse declared, marching out of the room.

The few minutes the nurse had been talking about seemed to have stretched into hours by the time the attendants came to wheel Sally's bed to the delivery room. Jared breathed a sigh of relief when they finally reached what looked more like an operating theatre than anything else. He wondered if they called it a "delivery room" because of the delivery of the father from anxiety or because of the mother delivering a baby. He would have said the former would have been more appropriate.

It still took several hours before Sally gave birth. The afternoon was well on its way, according to the clock in the room – it had taken 13 hours for their progeny to arrive in the world.

"It's a boy!" Jared had exclaimed to every other expectant father that had been waiting with him in the lounge. The doctor had just told him that mother and child were doing fine.

He rushed inside as the nursed placed the brand new bundle of life in the arms of Sally's exhausted body. The dark hair and bluish, yellow skin look like any new baby, and Jared was so excited he couldn't contain his joy.

"You have done well for a first timer, only a thirteen-and-a-half hour labor for a natural child birth, congratulations," said one of the nurses. Jared looked up at her – he couldn't disagree more. He would have thought three hours of such a torture as the one he had witnessed would have been way too much already.

The delivering obstetrician then asked if they wanted him to contact their family doctor and they agreed instantly, knowing that the CIA would be all over this immediately.

Meanwhile, Steve Giles had found his way into the maternity ward dressed as a doctor and was waiting for the baby to be delivered into the ward. His heavy, overweight body was drenched in sweat as he maneuvered his way around. He tried to be inconspicuous despite heavy, rapid breathing, and he purposely slowed his footsteps, trying not to appear hurried.

The new babies were brought into the nursery ward for observation, where all the proud parents could gaze through the one window at their own. There were a lot of newborns and they all looked alike, so the nurses had each crib clearly marked with the last name. The door to the ward was locked to keep over zealous parents from accessing the tiny infants, thus preventing infection or even abduction.

Giles, however, had managed somehow to make a copy of the key to the room and when no one was looking, he went inside and found another baby boy that looked similar to the Houghtons' boy. He switched their paper work on the cribs and even the tiny identifying ankle bands. He intended to get a mouth swab and possibly some blood for the DNA. This way, too, there would be no attention drawn to the baby. He would then return the babies to their rightful cribs. He left the room and quickly (as rapidly as his labored steps would allow) and found his way out of the hospital to retrieve his little medical kit from his car. Then all of a sudden it happened, just as he was opening his car door, pain like a freight train overran his sweat-soaked, obese chest and grabbed him like a monster, and threw him onto his car seat. He tried to yell for help but the incredible pain from a dying heart squeezed the breath completely out of him. Struggling for a last gasp of air, he slumped over onto the passenger seat like a sack of potatoes being tossed in slow motion, dead from a massive heart attack.

A few hours later someone found him in his car with the driver door ajar. Police and hospital staff were summoned to deal with the body. As soon as it was removed to the hospital morgue, they notified his wife and she came immediately to identify the corpse.

"Curious, Mrs. Giles," a police officer said, "why was your husband dressed as a doctor and why do you think he was here today?"

She stared blankly back at him. "I have no idea. I thought he was at work. He normally wears laboratory gear."

"What did he do?"

"He owns, rather, owned a medical laboratory."

"Oh, Okay, I guess that accounts for the bag of medical stuff we found in his car. I am so sorry about the loss of your husband, ma'am. I'm sure he was a good man. We'll complete this report and then turn him over to you. There doesn't look like any foul play. Again, sorry." The officer gently placed his hand on her arm and gazed steadfastly into her eyes.

"Thanks." Ruby Giles was emotionless, stunned by Steve's death. She had put up with such upheaval and roller coaster behavior from him, she didn't know how to feel, relieved or otherwise, but, deep down, she still loved him and remembered better days. She knew that smoking and poor diet would one day be his nemesis despite everyone telling him he needed to exercise, quit smoking and change his diet. She also knew she had to face a whole new world, dealing with closing or selling the company, insurance companies, estate issues, raising a family and making a new life.

With her head and shoulders down and purse almost dragging on the ground, she slowly shuffled her way to her car and drove off. Tears began to fill her eyes as she left the parking lot.

Chapter 17
The Adoption

"There he is, Diane. Look, he is so tiny. I never realized newborns were so small," Bob reflected, as they looked through the window into the nursery. The Lindstroms were at the hospital eagerly waiting to sign the paperwork and to pick up their new baby as it had been pre-arranged by the agency to pick him up the moment he was born. The birth mom was a young college student who had wanted to keep it a complete secret that she had been pregnant and that she had gone full term. She didn't want to have an abortion as she believed a life was worth living. Just because she did not want to compromise her family, her reputation or her studies was not enough reason for her to terminate the pregnancy. She believed there were wonderful parents willing to raise her child. She even opted to sign off completely from having any contact with the baby. She was also told that, under the circumstances, the adopting family would have to sign an affidavit promising not to try to find the mother. As far as she was concerned this chapter of her life was over.

Bob and Diane Lindstrom had tried for years but it turned out Bob had an extremely low sperm count, and Diane had had complications during puberty, preventing her from conceiving. Even with medical intervention, there was virtually no chance for them to have children.

The nurse walked over to a crib marked Lindstrom and brought their precious bundle to them. With hands out drawn, Diane clasped the little child, the whole time trembling with excitement and tears of joy welling to her eyes. The baby awoke momentarily from being moved around but went back to sleep almost instantly.

"Thank you, Joy," Diane said to the nurse in a low voice, as she read from her nametag. "You have handed me the greatest gift in our lives. We have waited for this moment for years; you have no idea how much this means to us. He is beautiful – a gift from God."

"Do you have a name for him yet?"

"Caleb – a name we found in the Bible. It means *my servant,* as in servant of God. If you know the story; Caleb, Joshua and ten others came back from scouting the Promised Land. Ten gave an evil report of giants and a bunch of negative stuff. But those two gave a positive report. And they ended up to be the only two – him and Joshua – to go into the Promised Land."

"That's nice . . . and a very strong name," Joy said. "I'm sure he will live up to his reputation."

"Yes, we think so, too, and it is not a common name."

The nurse made sure they had all the documents completed and told them what to expect over the next few weeks.

"Oh, we have been to classes," Bob said all excited. "I think we are prepared as we can be, and realize there is nothing like hands-on experience."

They stood there, looking at the infant, lost in a world of wonder. Thoughts rushed through each of their minds of the journey they had in front of them to raise a precious life, of their responsibilities, of an uncertain future – all the things that any responsible parent would think.

"Well, Caleb, let's take you and your mom to your new home," Bob said finally, taking his wife's free arm and leading her out of the maternity ward.

They left the hospital and headed toward their home on a beautiful June evening. They had adopted Sally and Giuseppe's child.

"Honey, there is something wrong here, this just doesn't seem like our kid, I dunno, I have a strange feeling about this," Sally lamented as she was breastfeeding the little boy the next day.

"Really, Sal? I don't think so.... Look, he has the same amount of hair, his eyes are the same color, he has the same little wrinkles or skin folds or whatever you call them..., see right under his chin. Same bracelet, same blanket, everything.... You're being paranoid, Hon," Jared concluded, smiling at his lovely wife and child. "Besides, how can babies get mixed up in nurseries? The doors are locked, there is always staff around, and there are records...."

"Yeah. I guess you're right." Yet Sally didn't sound at all convinced.

There was something uneasy, something not right and unsettling roaming around Sally's mind. She had a gut feeling.... What if there actually *had been* a mix up?

On the fifth day, Jared and Sally were ready to take their son home. The CIA doctor met them at the nursery.

"We want to run tests on your child within a week to make sure he is healthy. Which one is he?"

"He is over there in the crib marked Houghton," Jared replied, pointing to the crib.

"I am merely here to make sure we all follow procedure and I will expect to see you sometime next week in my office. Just come in during office hours – no need for an appointment."

He left the nursery and went to the record's department. He conferred with the record keeper to place a special government marker he provided on all the babies charts born that day. His reason for doing so was a test that the government was doing to potentially implement new security measures to track immigrants and aliens from illegally entering the country and putting a burden on the welfare system. Little did they know the real reason.

The Houghtons took their new son home without incident and made their way to their apartment without realizing the tragedy that had occurred.

"I hope they don't start all kinds of weird tests on our boy, Jason, here, until he is at least a year old so that we can raise him normally. I am so excited and looking forward to seeing what unfolds," said Sally as she brought her son close to her face.

"Yeah, I know it is an experiment, but I feel really bonded to the little guy already, like he is our own, don't you?" an emotional Jared softly mumbled out as he drove along the I-5 toward their home.

"Don't forget, he has been inside me for nine months, Hon, we have been very close."

Chapter 18

A few weeks later, after exhaustive tests had been performed on Jason, the CIA doctor concluded that Jason Houghton was a normal, healthy Caucasian boy and that the parents could continue to raise him without their interference. Their only commitment was to keep an oath of secrecy about their experience with the agency. They had to commit to annual tests on Jason so that he could be assessed for unusual behavior.

Meanwhile at the Lindstrom residence, they, too, were experiencing the growth of a normal baby. They felt very blessed and thankful for Caleb.

This, however, was about to change. Caleb, turning three years old, started having trouble sleeping and would wake up crying for no apparent reason in the middle of the night. This went on for sometime. The Linstroms consulted their doctor who said it was normal for youngsters to experience dreams and sometimes nightmares, which would wake them up. They tried leaving a light on in the room, they tried soft music and prayers and eventually it subsided. However, they knew he was awakened because he would giggle, coo and kick.

As the years passed, Jason Houghton grew into an average teenager – if there is such a thing. His sandy colored hair, blue eyes set in a rounded face and fair skin made him blend in with his peers. His DNA and life skills, behavior, and physique were the same as any other all-American child. He now had two younger sisters and one brother, who didn't resembled him in the least.

Sally and Jared kept the secret of his origin well hidden. They still thought Jason was Giuseppe's son and didn't press the point when asked why their eldest didn't show any of his father's traits. He usually responded by saying, "He's just like my great-grandfather. I guess he just skipped a few generations." Which statement was true enough in many ways.

Jared had become a professor at the University of Western Washington and Sally was a stay-at-home mom, tutoring students in the evenings. The CIA terminated their financial contract and temporarily closed the book on the human cloning experiment they so desperately wanted to develop with them. They were now faced with global terrorism and a whole new set of challenges that had changed their directives. They were still interested in cloning, but were looking into other ways of producing similar results.

Jared and Sally Houghton, although disappointed in the results not being what they expected, still had hopes in some day pioneering another form of human cloning.

Chapter 19
The Descendant

The Lindstroms, on the other hand, who had the real Ice Man's descendant in their care, were experiencing the raising of a supernatural child whose abilities, physique and skills were anything but normal.

Caleb bolted upright in bed awakened from *The Dream*. Looking at his clock – 4:24AM. He slumped back into his pillow and attempted to go back to sleep.

Going over the dream in his mind for the hundredth time, he saw slight differences from the last one, two nights ago. He fumbled for the light switch on the bedside lamp, flicked it on and wrote notes in his "dream" diary. He had even developed his own language in an ancient cuneiform way, something that seemed to come naturally to him. The components of the symbols each had a consistent meaning to them. For example, a brontosaurus had four distinct strokes while a pterodactyl had two distinct strokes with little paddles on the ends of the strokes. He could record large portions of the dreams, or visions, in a few symbols, even with actions. Little did he know he was revealing something far deeper than a dream.

This dream included huge tropical ferns, which could hardly hide the "lizards" – his nickname for the massive brontosaurs, T-Rex's, reptiles that were all becoming restless. He chuckled to himself as he recalled the first time he described the creatures to his girl friend, Darby. *She had to think I was some kind of nut case back then.* However, the look of disbelief on her face was changing into conviction as she was drawn into the fascinating world Caleb was unfolding through his "dreams." Her fondness for him had evidently grown as well, as she saw the struggles he went through while keeping these stories from his friends.

After all, who else would believe these crazy "dreams" anyway? How could he go about telling the public about live dinosaurs, huge vegetation, ancient mountain ranges and strange skies that he was so intimately involved with? Things that were so real, he could reach out and touch them. As he pondered all these things repeatedly, sleep finally overtook him.

The 6:30 alarm woke Caleb and he slowly dragged his six-foot-one, one hundred and eighty pound frame out of bed, while wiping the sleep out of his turquoise-green eyes. After a quick breakfast, he pulled on his gym gear since he had to be ready for an early morning basketball practice. Something he really looked forward to. He ran some gel through his unusually wavy, dark chestnut hair with both black and blonde streaks running through it. His olive colored complexion and high cheekbones set off the hair and eye coloring in such a way that he looked like someone out of the Greek mythology.

Diane was a lively redhead with flashing blue eyes, five-foot-five, and petite. She kept in shape with regular workouts. The constant search for Caleb's birth parents and a string of volunteering events she was involved in kept her on her toes and busier than ever.

"Don't forget your session with Dr. Stevens tonight…," Diane said as Caleb sat down at the kitchen table. "How did you sleep last night?"

"The big ferns and the lizards were acting a little weird…, I dunno, this Stevens…, nice guy, but, he thinks I'm having pizza dreams or something, Mom. I don't think he's much help, I've told him tons of things and he just smiles and writes stuff down. I mean, Dr. Peters was at least interested in what I had to say, but this guy is a dead beat. He's not helping at all." Caleb continued to eat.

"Should we continue taking you to him, then?"

"I don't know, I guess he's okay for the time being. My coach told me there's an NBA scout interested in checking me out." He looked up at the clock. "I gotta go, Mom. Justin must be waiting for me." Then looking down at his mother, he lifted her chin. "Don't worry, okay? Things will work out." Diane nodded.

Caleb then grabbed his things and ran toward the door, yelling from over his shoulder, "Love you, Mom!"

"Love you too, dear…. Call if you're going to be late!" Diane shouted as she heard the door close on her son.

Diane's gaze moved from the door to the curtains she had put up when Caleb was in grade six. It suddenly dawned on her that time was flying by faster than she was willing to admit. She started thinking about re-decorating their modest home.

The drain on time and expenses taking Caleb to clinical psychiatrists had taken a toll on both their emotions and finances. This latest doctor was getting nowhere with Caleb and she could sense the frustration mounting in her son.

The shrill ringing of the cordless phone jarred her out of her little dream world, and the unfamiliar voice at the other end asked her if she was Mrs. Lindstrom.

"Yes, who is this?"

"This is Mrs. James from the Clements Adoption Agency; you had been in touch with us a few months ago regarding your son, Caleb. Sorry this has taken so long but we have found some important documentation on your son. We would like for you to come in to our office and verify some of the information. When would be a good time for you?"

Excited, Diane looked at the calendar on the fridge and asked if Caleb should be there as well.

"Does he know he is adopted?" Mrs. James asked in reply.

"Oh yes, of course," Diane said as she quickly scanned the calendar. "Let's see, how about ... this Thursday? What are your hours? Can we say five-thirty? My husband will be home from work by then and Caleb should be around, as far as I know. I am very curious, what kind of information have you found?"

Mrs. James paused. "I am not in a position to discuss it with you over the phone; our policy is a face to face meeting with our clients. As you can appreciate, this can be very confidential information and we want to make sure of the utmost discretion with any of our clients." Mrs. James went on to confirm a time. "Thursday looks okay. We'll see you, Caleb and your husband, Robert, on Thursday at 5:30PM then. Do you have our address?"

Diane, a little disturbed and feeling funny about the call, slowly copied down the address and parking instructions, thanked Mrs. James and hung up. She slumped back in one of the kitchen chairs. She gazed for the longest time at the address she had scribbled on the family calendar.

She really wanted to get to the bottom of this mystery about her son. After all, he was more than just their only child, he was noticeably different and people around them asked tough questions. The psychiatrists, where she had sent Caleb, just kept coming up with "an incurable psychotic, treatable with drugs only." As a family, they didn't believe any of the results and felt there was something far deeper.

The endless hours of searching adoption agencies and attempting to find hospital records and the agony of not finding the birth parents, had weighed heavily on her mind until this phone call. For the first time, she felt a twinge of hope.

They had decided to adopt after the first five years of marriage. They had thought about adopting a girl as well, but Caleb had turned out to be enough of a handful.

Despite all of the trials, she and her husband, Bob, and Caleb got along very well together. Caleb rarely needed harsh discipline and despite his "quirks", he was very balanced in his nature. He rarely got angry and if he did, it was over in a moment. He had a deep respect for his parents and others. He never spoke badly against anyone and his teachers and friends thought highly of him.

At school, Caleb excelled in practically everything. He had an A+ average, and what ever he put his hand to, he had little difficulty achieving results. The school suggested he write an IQ test and he took an aptitude exam to find out what profession would best suit him. Caleb felt it wasn't necessary as he had made up his mind to pursue archaeology and sports. They insisted and he was rated at 180. As a child he had great running speed and co-ordination. Even when he had a paper route, he would finish delivering papers in record time.

As Caleb grew older, the dreams and visions became more vivid and detailed. Even though there were no other humans in the dreams, he was becoming increasingly aware of something else, something like *a spirit* that he could communicate with.

Bob, now in his late forties, was tall, thin, with wavy brown hair, graying at the temples. His steel blue eyes hidden behind stylish glasses, accented his handsome features, especially when he got into a serious discussion and he knitted his forehead while contemplating answers. Bob had been quite athletic in school and he liked to work out regularly and keep in shape. His career as an insurance broker had been very lucrative and he counted the years to retirement.

At the next basket ball practice something else happened that renewed the NBA scout's belief that he was watching a *star* in the making. The ball easily went in the hoop as Caleb laid up an unbelievable shot and rushed back into position. The frustration was starting to grow on the faces of his defense teammates as they tried to keep the ball far away from him.

In the bleachers, the NBA scout was amazed at the speed and agility and sixth-sense Caleb exhibited during the game. *Michael Jordan, look out,* he thought. *This kid is going places!*

The whistle blew and practice ended. As the boys gathered around the coach, the scout made his way down from the bleachers.

The coach pointed out some weaknesses the offense needed to correct and sent the team back out to work on them. Among the defense, with his head down, somebody murmured, "Lindstrom is invincible. He is too hard to stop."

Someone else then piped up, "Yeah, what are we supposed to do, maim him or something? I mean, this is only a mid-season practice!"

"Watch your language, Jones!" scolded the coach. "You are going to get this kind of game from Tacoma or Lynnwood. Hey, welcome to the real world, kid. Now get your butts out there and work on hoops and blocking. We have Tacoma on Wednesday and we *do not* want to lose to them for a third year in a row – so get to it!"

The scout walked over to the coach, stretched out his hand and introduced himself. "My name's Bill Maxwell, scout for the Sonics."

"I heard you were going to be here – what do you think?" the coach asked.

Maxwell was trying to keep back his enthusiasm, when he yawned, stretched his arms cracking his knuckles. "Yeah, you got some talent here; defense needs some work, though." He paused. "Hum ... what's number thirty-four's name?"

"Caleb Lindstrom – pretty amazing, huh?"

"How long has he been playing?"

"This is his first year."

"First year?" Maxwell could hardly control himself. "How old is he?"

"Sixteen – all six foot one and a half of him – a late starter. This boy is going places.... You should see him play hockey, football..., and even baseball – there's nothing he can't do well.... I wish I were about 20 years younger and in his boots."

"You're playing Tacoma on Wednesday? I would like to see him ... huh ... them play in some real competition. What time is the game?"

93

"7:00PM. We're going to kick their butts!"

Maxwell forced a smile and excused himself; all the while keeping an eye on this amazing young athlete as he walked away.

Later at Dr. Steven's office, while Diane flipped through magazines in the waiting room, Caleb recalled last night's dream as the psychiatrist took notes. The tape recorder was running while the young man described things in the only way he knew how. Steven's scribbled notes continuously. Caleb finished describing his dream and Stevens, who was a quiet individual, carefully read over what he had been writing.

He questioned Caleb on different portions of the dreams, and then asked him about his daily activities. He had been trying to formulate a pattern of behavior but could not seem to pin down anything conclusively. Once the session was over, he asked Caleb to get his mother – he wanted to have a word with her. Diane came in and sat down – anxiety written on her face.

Stevens leaned back in his chair. "Look, I know you two don't think we have achieved a lot in these sessions. I have to admit, the dreams coupled with Caleb's behavior appear to be very unusual; however, without prescribing drugs, I cannot go any further with Caleb. I can log this incredible tale of a pre-historic world for years and suggest all kinds of mental gymnastics to overcome this condition, but it won't do a thing unless Caleb's chemistry can be altered. This will sedate the mind and eradicate the over stimulation of these dreams." Stevens shook his head. "Sure, there are side effects but minor in comparison with the present experience."

Without leaving Diane time to comment, Stevens wrote out a prescription and handed it to her. "I want Caleb to take these pills, under your supervision, twice a day for two weeks, one before breakfast and one at bedtime, then once a day only at bedtime for one more week. I want to see him again after the third week." Again, without looking up, the psychiatrist wrote out an appointment card and handed it to Diane. "Please call my secretary, only if this clashes with your schedule. Otherwise, I'll be seeing you then." He switched his gaze to Caleb. "If you are having any symptoms other than a little groggy in the morning and excessive urination throughout the day, call me right away."

"What are in the pills?" Diane asked.

"They are a new mild form of sleeping pill with melatonin, something the labs have been experimenting with," Stevens replied. "They're supposed to be quite effective."

"What if we decide not to do this?" Diane knew her son was not going to take any medication.

Dr. Stevens puckered his lips pensively and took a deep breath. "Well, I can't help you any further. I'll have to pass your case on to another psychiatrist."

"OK, thanks for your help, Doctor," Diane said while she got to her feet and shook the psychiatrist's hand. "We'll think about it, won't we, Caleb?"

Caleb nodded in agreement and loosely shook the doctor's hand as he slowly rose to his feet, too.

The doctor showed them out without another word.

Diane and Caleb were quiet on the drive home. Caleb knew what his mother was thinking and he silently agreed with her that pills, or any sort of meds, would not prevent him from having these strange dreams.

Chapter 20
A scout

The phone rang and the young girl's voice asked for Caleb. "Caleb, it's for you. It's Darby," Diane said from the kitchen.

Caleb ran to his room and picked up the phone. "Thanks, Mom," he said as he heard his mother hang up.

Meanwhile, Diane filled Bob in on the events at the doctor's office and showed him the prescription.

"Bob, we can't do this," Diane declared, running her hand through her hair, her blue eyes flashing with defiance.

"Why not? What are a few pills going to do to Caleb?" Bob asked as he grabbed the remote control and muted the TV sound.

"You know, I'm afraid. Not afraid of stopping the dreams and other things, but this may change him, alter him into someone else, a different guy."

"You're acting paranoid. That's what the medical profession wants to happen, isn't it? He is different, too different for the world to accept. And isn't that what we wanted to do initially?"

"Bob!" Diane was not about to accept her husband's comments without a fight. "We originally wanted to find out if Caleb had some kind of birth defects, or something they could easily tell us – something he will grow out of, a conclusive prognosis. All we have gotten is, drugs, that'll straighten him out, not one of these turkeys have said, "Here it is, folks, it's a whatever condition." Not one! I'm so fed up with this whole damn thing!"

"Honey, you know, I think this adoption agency is going to shed a whole lot of light on this situation, you just wait and see."

"You'd better be right," Diane replied as Bob restored the TV sound.

Meanwhile, Caleb was talking to his girlfriend.
"What you're doing?"
"Studying."
"Studying? Let me guess, dinosaurs."

"That's right, dinosaurs. Hey, now you're reading *my* mind."

Darby sighed. "That's not hard. What kind of dinosaurs now?"

"OK, are you ready for this? T-Rex's and some of the carnivores.... You know, Jurassic Park and all the models of T-Rex's aren't quite right, they actually have a much smoother skin and they aren't nearly as aggressive as everyone thinks they are, plus, they eat mostly vegetation. The males have a much larger hump on their backs than females do and they actually have horns that grow out during mating season and drop off shortly after. Besides, they are mammals, and did you know they can swim...? This school information is wrong!"

Darby didn't answer right away. "Caleb, I know you've dreamed about them, but, that doesn't... I mean, you know, the authorities, they'll never believe you."

Caleb fell silent.

"I'm quitting Doctor Stevens. We just got back from seeing him, for the last time."

"Why?"

"He just wants to put me on drugs and Mom and Dad don't agree with that."

"I don't blame them."

"You know, it's like I was there, I've seen them, I can almost touch them, smell them.... The dreams are so real. How do you describe something like this? Why is it so difficult to get somebody to believe me?"

"You'll get through to somebody," Darby assured him passionately. "I believe you, your family believes you. You'll get through this."

"Mom got a call today from some adoption agency that she was in contact with quite awhile ago, and apparently they have some information on my – I guess you would call them – my birthing parents. We're seeing this woman Thursday night."

"Well, that's exciting, don't you think?"

Caleb laughed half-heartedly. "Hey, my parents could have been aliens or something." He looked dreamily around his room. The walls were covered with posters of Michael Jordan and dinosaurs. Models of pre-historic figures littered every shelf and desk, which was neatly placed in the corner of his room.

Darby giggled. "Well, at least you'll know where you came from."

They then talked about some school stuff and made small talk.

"I should go; the coach wants me to work on some shots early in the morning, so I'd better finish this homework. Thanks for listening, Darby."

"Yeah, okay...." Darby changed her tone. "We should go over to Alicia's party with the cheerleaders on Friday night. Everybody's going to be there and it would be good for you to take a break. We can celebrate kicking Tacoma's butt tomorrow night!"

"Well, we had better; it's been three years, you know. Sounds like a good idea. Let me think about it.... I'll talk to you later."

"See you tomorrow. Bye."

When Caleb hung up, he began to realize how much people were starting to count on him – the coach to win the game, Darby to celebrate with their friends and his friends to help them with their homework, which he did quite often.

Wednesday, at the game, Caleb's parents were there along with Darby's folks. He caught a ride to the arena with his friend, Justin, who played center.

The ball bounced off Seattle's hoop, a defense man grabbed the ball and fired it down the court toward a forward, he dribbled around the opposition and one of Tacoma's defenses knocked it loose, but, right into Caleb's hands. *Where did he come from?* Caleb passed it over to a charging forward and he easily made a perfect lay up. The score went up to 84 to 68 for Seattle.

On the Tacoma bench everybody was buzzing. The coach was hollering plays and the players were plotting how they could get number 34. He was embarrassing them almost single-handedly.

"He can read your mind!" the players kept insisting among themselves. The coach kept bellowing plays and, out of frustration, he started to call individuals over, and when the players mentioned about reading minds, he blew up and yelled at them.

Meanwhile, Maxwell, with a coffee in one hand, was freaking out – he had never seen anything like it. This kid got the ball off anybody and not only passed, he could run through traffic at an incredible speed. This was a live "Space Jam" happening before his eyes! "How does he do it?" he muttered under his breath.

98

The game ended with a score of 112 to 96 in favor of Seattle. The whole place went wild. It was the first time in three years Seattle had won over Tacoma.

Maxwell worked his way through the crowd and followed the team to the dressing room, looking for Caleb.

Caleb was already showering. There was the usual hubbub in the room from the winning team. Maxwell hung around outside the dressing room and took note of the young talent and the way they interplayed as a team off the court as they were leaving. There was nothing unusual about the rest of the team; solid relationships, disciplined play, positive coaching. But, what about number 34? *Got to talk to that boy!*

His discussions with the coach revealed a little bit about the way things were done, but, there was something else, something about that kid that was *extraordinary.*

Caleb emerged from the dressing room and his eyes locked on Maxwell's. He quickly looked away and went back inside. Maxwell felt a little funny from the encounter; it was almost spooky. The din of the kibitzing and the pranks dwindled while Maxwell downed the last gulp of his now very cold coffee and swung on his heels away from the dressing room. He crumpled the empty cup and quickly jettisoned it into the nearest garbage can, watching the boys file out of the locker room.

He was straining to look for Caleb in street clothes and couldn't spot him. *Where did he go?* He cussed to himself and headed back toward the dressing room. He stuck his head inside but still couldn't see him. He asked one of the boys where Caleb went. The boy looked around and shrugged. "I dunno – he was just here."

Maxwell thanked him and quickly headed out the door, muttering curses.

Meanwhile, Caleb emerged nonchalantly from a stall, grabbed his bag and sauntered toward the door. "Hey, some guy was looking for you, K," one of the forwards told him.

Caleb shrugged. "I know. Tell Justin to wait for me, will you?" The other boy nodded and made his way to the parking lot. Caleb then shoved his right hand in his jacket pocket and walked out the door, casually swinging his sports bag with his left, his muscular figure transporting him like a fleeting gazelle on a trip across the

Transvaal. His short, wavy, dark-brown hair glistened under the lights.

Maxwell was now out pacing in front of the stadium where appreciative fans were waiting for their heroes. He walked over to some giggly girls and excusing himself asked if they had seen Caleb leave.

They looked at each other tittering. One of them asked sarcastically, "Are you his dad?" The group broke into laughter.

Maxwell replied, "No!" He paused. "But seriously, have you seen him?"

The girl asked tauntingly, "If you're not his dad, are you his uncle?"

Big laughter.

Maxwell could feel his blood pressure rise as he glared back, biting his tongue.

Forcing a smile, he retorted forcefully, "Actually, I'm God! Look, has he come out or not?"

One of the girls, sensing his frustration, quickly piped up above the rest, "He hasn't come out!"

And Maxwell with a controlled "Thanks" folded his arms and meandered off into the darkness.

Just then the stadium door opened and the girls let out a scream as Caleb quickly slipped through the doorway, moving into the shadows, all the time looking toward Maxwell standing a ways off to Caleb's left.

How did he know I was here? Maxwell wondered.

In the meantime, the girls wanted autographs and tried to mob Caleb. He moved through them with ease, stopping and signing, leaving to his right.

Maxwell slipped around some cars in the dark and moved in toward the fans. He managed to get a glimpse of the fleeting star as he hot-footed it across the parking lot.

"This kid can move!" Maxwell puffed as he chased him. "Hey, Caleb! Hold on! I don't bite. I just want to talk to you!" Maxwell panted some more, looking around to see if anyone else was watching.

Suddenly Caleb stopped under a light, turned and effortlessly ran to meet Maxwell. The scout stopped head down. Gasping to get his breath, he took a moment to compose himself and put his hand out for an introduction. "I'm—"

"Bill Maxwell, scout for the Sonics," Caleb interrupted.

"How did you know my name? I guess your coach told you…," the surprised and much winded Maxwell wheezed out.

Completely relaxed and far from winded with his arms crossed over his chest, Caleb stared at him and calmly replied, "I have ways. Now, what do you want from me?"

Maxwell managed a frustrated smile between gasps. "Boy, *you are* popular! You sure know how to shoot hoops, where did you learn all that from? Besides, with your abilities I wanted to…" He stopped to catch his breath, which was coming out like wispy clouds under the dim light of the parking lot. "I wanted to talk to you about the possibilities of playing in the NBA."

Caleb quietly stared past him; then looked down at the ground, slowly bringing his gaze back up to the scout's eyes. An eternity seemed to pass. Maxwell's heart rate was slowly returning to normal and his breathing became easier. "Well?"

Caleb, riveting his penetrating eyes on him, finally answered with, "I'll think about it."

"*I'll think about it*!" Maxwell exclaimed. "Is that all you can say? Do you *know* what you're saying? Do you know what I am offering? I'm offering *you* a career, money…!"

"I believe I know what you're offering," Caleb interrupted quietly. "I said I'll think about it. I have to go, I have a ride waiting for me." He then turned and walked away.

Maxwell, stunned in disbelief, raked his fingers through his moist hair and rushed after Caleb. "Look, hey, this doesn't happen every day…." He was trying to catch up to Caleb's ever-quickening pace. Maxwell was getting annoyed; the cool air was refreshing to the face as his temperature was beginning to rise. "I don't know what makes you tick, boy, but I would really like to…" By this time, Maxwell was angry. He grabbed Caleb by the arm and stopped him. Through clenched teeth, Maxwell said, "Let me give you my card at least." He fished through his pockets, patting his breast, all the while keeping his gaze on Caleb's face. He then reached into his hip pocket and hauled his tattered wallet out, letting go of Caleb's arm. He flipped through receipts and money and, glancing back and forth between Caleb and his wallet, he dug out a business card and shoved it into Caleb's hand.

His heart was racing again against his mounting irritation. "My number is on there," Maxwell spluttered. "Please call any time. I would like you to meet someone who can, if nothing else, improve any weaknesses in your game."

Caleb took the card, looked at it briefly, shrugged again and turned toward Justin's vehicle. Maxwell looked after his quarry for a moment before he too, made his way to his car.

When Maxwell neared his old Ford, he lit up a cigarette, took a puff and threw it on the pavement in disgust. "I can't believe this," he said to himself as he rummaged through his pockets for his keys.

He was so upset that the keys on his key chain rattled like a wind chime while he fumbled around to insert the key in the car's ignition. He wanted to feel angry, violated, as though he had been sucker punched, but that didn't account for the nagging reality that this wasn't an ordinary encounter with a smart-ass high school kid trying to be coy. He felt as though he had been in the presence of something a lot bigger and a lot more intelligent.

Later, at home, Bob and Diane congratulated Caleb for his and his team's performance and commented on how good of a time they had with Darby and her folks.

Caleb crawled into bed and thoughts of his encounter with Maxwell flashed through his mind, mixed with highlights from the basketball game. He wondered if he had been too hard on Maxwell and almost felt a bit sorry for his actions toward Tacoma. He couldn't help it; he could hear the players' thoughts as clearly as if they were telling him what and where they were going to throw the ball.

His thoughts were quickly overridden by the face of Darby drifting into his mind. She was such a beauty; long, blonde hair..., and those tender, blue eyes that came to life and danced when she laughed. He knew she genuinely loved him a lot because he could read her thoughts. She was so different from all the rest of the girls he had met. All they thought about was getting him into bed or they were starry eyed by his sports abilities and just wanted to hang out with him.

He recalled the first time he and Darby had met. She was a cheerleader for the school football team and he was playing a wide receiver. The ball had been poorly thrown and he had to come a way back to get the pass near the sidelines where the cheerleaders had been located.

Caleb had been drilled from behind out of bounds just as he had caught the ball. He had ended up flying out of control, half-rolling and half-sliding through the cheerleaders who had scrambled to get out of his way. When he had finally stopped the "bull-dozing", he had been lying face up, staring into the face of this horrified, beautiful blonde. She had been knocked down, her legs pinned under the upper part of Caleb's body. She had been the only one he had hit and felt so bad about it that he had begun apologizing profusely since he had seen and sensed she had been in considerable pain. He *had known* she had sprained her ankle. It had been the first time he had sensed and identified "body energy" – the spirit of living things – and even had pin-pointed it. It had been his first experience with telepathy with humans, even though he had "communicated" with his dog and Aunt Cheryl's cat, and other creatures, including birds and farm animals. They really hadn't talked to him; he just *knew* what they were thinking, what they were going to do next and he could *communicate* with them.

He remembered sitting for what seemed like an eternity, quietly calming Darby down. He had looked her over and had "wowed" to himself at her beauty. Even in amongst her pain he had heard her thoughts. He recalled shaking his head and banging the side of his helmet as if he weren't sure he was hearing things. But, sure enough, he had heard her voice saying, "This is sure my lucky day; first I bang up my folks' car and now this! Hope it isn't bad … this guy is really cute, too, and here I am ow, ow, my ankle…. This really hurts…. Wonder how I can get his name…."

Caleb smiled to himself remembering how he had blurted out, "I'll give you my name. My name is Caleb." The look on both their faces had been one of total surprise but Darby's face had been priceless – even in her painful condition – because she had only thought it. She actually had given her head a shake.

He still shivered as he recalled how she had gazed into his eyes and had said, while mustering a smile, "I'm Darby," moaning, "We gotta stop meeting like this."

That's when Caleb knew he had to pursue this one.

Somebody had called a time out and the medical staff had come running over to attend. The medical staff had not been sure if she had broken her leg, foot or ankle and had probed and checked out everything for a break or what ever. Caleb had told them that it was a sprained ankle and they had looked at him as if he were crazy. "How do you know? Are you a doctor?" one of the young attendants had arrogantly asked.

Caleb had said, "No, I'm not a doctor, but I can tell you without a doubt it's a sprain. It's a bad sprain … right there." He had pointed to the exact spot. The attendants had looked at him with a smug "take a hike" look when he had sprung to his feet and had gone back to the game.

That was the last thing he thought about when sleep overtook him.

Chapter 21
A CIA connection

The next morning, the alarm clock jarred Caleb awake out of another encounter with his prehistoric world. He had been walking through an incredible valley, lush with giant ferns and enormous trees, plants and flowers with petals of red velvet and long slender silky fingers that seemed to pulsate with a rainbow of colors as the light caught them at different angles. Caleb swore he could recall a scent so enticing it was indescribable.

There was a family of spider-like insects about five inches high, with massive legs and antennae that scurried along the ground. He heard a symphony of sounds that emanated from the forest, sounds that could be best described as an orchestra of enormous proportions.

There were birds, some perched, some flying, but their colors…, unbelievable! He identified crows, doves, robins, and all kinds of familiar species mixed in with others he had never seen before.

That was when he noticed for the first time, mountains in the background, tall mountains, really tall – must have been summer because there was no snow on or near the tops – not even a glacier or any trees.

At breakfast he talked to his parents about the meeting with Maxwell. They both expressed their encouragement and were pleased with the opportunity.

"How do *you* feel about it?" Bob asked.

Caleb, buttering his toast, shrugged. "I dunno…. The scout, this Maxwell guy, he was a bit…" He stopped to think of a word that wouldn't sound too offensive in front of his parents. "He was a bit…, weird, I guess." He took a bite of toast.

"Weird? In what way?" Bob asked.

Through a mouthful, Caleb replied, "He really wanted to make sure I had his card. He wanted to get together with me real bad." He continued to chew, stared blankly into his orange juice.

His dad chuckled. "Hey, he's a salesman; he knows a good thing when he sees it! You must have really wowed him. Besides, that's his job. Hey, if he can bring extraordinary talent like you to the table" —he pointed to Caleb— "he could retire early!"

"You think that's all he wants?"

"Well, ultimately!" His dad laughed as he took a drink of coffee.

Caleb's gaze slowly descended toward his plate as he began to understand what was going on in the world of professional sports.

"You mean all those big stars – Michael Jordan, Shaq and all those guys – they had to go through the same kind of thing?" Caleb asked meekly.

His dad, sensitive to his son's innocence, quietly assured him that they did and went on to explain his own understanding of the process.

Caleb knew he had to talk to his coach about this whole thing.

Diane then interrupted this father-son talk, saying, "Both you guys listen, don't forget the appointment tonight with the adoption agency, we can go for dinner somewhere close to their office – after? Before? I just don't feel like cooking."

Caleb looked at his dad and then back to his mother.

"He wants to go to that steak and lobster joint he really likes – if it's the one that's close to their office," Caleb said.

His dad laughed. "Quit reading my mind! But you're right, haven't been there in awhile. One thing about you is that we can't get away with nothing when you're around!" He reached over and tugged Caleb's ear.

"Let's go after – and we can have dessert!" they both blurted out simultaneously while looking at Diane. Her red hair bounced around as she shook her head in a playful manner with a *disgusting* look on her face, her clear blue eyes clouded with mystery. "You guys and your sweet-tooth…!"

That evening, the conversation was quiet in anticipation as each one thought about the implications of the pending meeting. The thirty-minute drive to the adoption agency, located in a big, grey and glass building in the downtown Seattle corridor, was pleasant, with the April backdrop of Japanese cherry-trees shedding delicate pink blossoms in fleeting mounds, heaped by the curbs.

As it was just after hours, most of the buildings were vacated and stood in ominous, silent vigilance waiting for the next onslaught of activity in the morning. Many of the office lights were still on and yet others were being shut off, creating a twinkling effect.

After parking in a side street close to the entrance, they made their way to the huge open foyer. They checked in with security and followed the signs to the correct bank of elevators. As they walked through, they admired the somewhat ostentatious but cold foyer.

"This place gives me the creeps," Caleb mumbled as they located an open elevator door.

"Me too," Diane agreed.

"Me three," Bob added playfully. Caleb and Diane look at each other with a "groan" look.

The elevator reached the level with a subdued "ding" and a female voice announced the floor where the agency was located. The oak-paneled walls and sudden hush in the hallway increased the tension. The Lindstroms quickened their paces as they looked for the correct office number.

"Down here," Caleb whispered hoarsely, as he waved from the end of a long corridor.

There was a buzzer located on the outside of the office to the right of an impressive brace of oak doors. CLEMENTS ADOPTION AGENCY in shiny brass letters was meticulously etched into the wood.

Caleb pushed the button and in a few seconds, the door opened. A tall, willowy lady asked, smiling, "Lindstroms?"

"Yes," Diane answered quickly.

"Come in, please." The woman, dressed in a navy-blue, business suit, pointed to her office to the right.

They enter and she closed the door quietly behind them.

"Welcome to Clements Adoption Agency, I'm Mrs. Barbara James; I believe I spoke with you the other day. Please come into my office." She stuck her hand out and firmly shook Diane's hand. "You must be Robert?" She grabbed his extended hand in turn.

"Please call me Bob. Nice to meet you."

With a noticeable sparkle in her eyes and a lilt in her voice she turned to Caleb. "And you must be Caleb!" she exclaimed with a giggle.

"Yes," Caleb replied slowly, looking intently into her eyes and shaking her hand. Caleb was *scanning* her thoughts, listening for some clues on what was about to take place. He picked up that she thought he looked like a "pretty normal kid" and a bunch of other things he couldn't make out. He certainly didn't feel threatened.

The foyer to the agency was modestly decorated with plants and the usual prints of unknown artists on the wall. The reception area was sparsely furnished with a few chairs in a row facing a receptionist's desk. There appeared to be four or five offices lined along the windows with a spectacular view of the Space Needle and downtown Seattle. The shears on the windows created an unusual warm glow from the late afternoon sun.

They followed Mrs. James into her office. She stretched an arm to the three leather, winged-back chairs lined up in front of her desk and asked them to have a seat.

She spun efficiently around her mahogany desk and lowered herself comfortably into her black, executive chair that allowed her to swivel around in front of several huge filing cabinets.

They exchanged casual conversation, getting to know one another. Mrs. James was personable; she explained her role in the agency all the while gathering information about the Lindstrom family.

"Well, this has been a long, tedious search for Caleb's records," Mrs. James said, finally coming around the topic that brought them together that night.

"As you know, we've been at this since September last year. It might have been a faster process if we didn't have one of our top researchers go on maternity leave in the middle of your case, and on behalf of Clements, our apologies." She stopped, obviously looking for some understanding on the Lindstroms' part. They nodded sympathetically. "Let me first explain that we are quite different from most agencies since we specialize in unusual cases, mostly fed to us from the military, CIA, FBI, and other para-government jurisdictions."

"We also get involved when traditional agencies come to the end of their tether, as in your case." After a short pause, Mrs. James went on, "Since this is not public knowledge, we treat each case highly confidential – almost like the FBI would deal with criminal activity outside local law enforcements. This is done in order not to get the public alarmed. For example, if the governor of Washington was adopted, never knew who his natural parents were and it was found out either by him or someone else that his parents, either both or one of them was a serial killer, that could be devastating as you can well imagine, his political career would be over and he would be flipping burgers at McDonalds. We also do searches for people who have serious medical symptoms…" She paused, cleared her throat, and looked at Caleb. "As could be in this case, it may shed a light on how to treat individuals."

Caleb fidgeted and looked down and then up, rolling his eyes back and forth as if scanning the room.

Mrs. James paused again and looked at each surprised face looking at her. "What's this got to do with a young man named Caleb Lindstrom? Well, let's first review what prompted this search. I believe, as a family you were concerned with Caleb's recurring, excessive, and unusual dreams and aberrant behavior? Is this true?" Mr. and Mrs. Lindstrom nodded a slight affirmation. Caleb remained still.

"Caleb's behavior is fine, it is really the constant dreams and other phenomena he experiences that concerns us," Diane said.

"Phenomena?" asked Mrs. James. "What kind of phenomena?"

"This is something that he recently started to discover – he always has been very perceptive, but, it now appears he can…, well, read minds, something like mental telepathy or something."

Mrs. James raised her eyebrows and nodded affirmatively, while she took a few notes. "Very interesting, hmmm…." She made a clicking sound with her tongue. "This could be interesting…."

"What we found after exhausting the public records through electronic archives which is the normal procedure, was a 'tagged' file from the Seattle Memorial where Caleb was born. Being tagged or flagged, means there was one of a number of things that needed to be checked. We always start with the simplest things and go from there. Unfortunately, we kept drawing a blank. Your natural birth mother on the birth records did not match the main hospital registration records, which kept leading us into the dark.

"So, what we had to do was a physical search of the records from the hospital. Now, you can imagine how much work that is because every year birth and death records are moved to a records keeping department located somewhere else. To make a long story short, we finally located what we believe to be your file, Caleb. That's the good news. The only problem is that there is a flag on your birth records…." Mrs. James paused once again. "…from the CIA"—the Lindstroms gasped in surprise—"that might have even been tampered with."

Mrs. James quickly pressed on, "No need to get super alarmed, they haven't been contacted at the moment as we do not have conclusive evidence about your birth mother, but we have tracked down mothers who were in the ward giving birth at the time and they are willing to co-operate with us on some DNA tests. We would like to do the same with you as well, Caleb, so we can match DNA possibilities."

"Excuse me," Bob had to cut-in, "you keep saying the CIA; this is pretty serious. Why in creation would they be involved in adoption?"

"As I said, this is only because the records were "tagged" or "flagged" and because of the difficulty trying to pin down conclusively who Caleb's parents were. Besides, there might be something we just don't know about."

The quiet groan of the air conditioning became noticeable, as everyone grew silent, including Mrs. James.

"I'll do it, I'll do the tests," Caleb said calmly. "I think this is the only way to have me cleared from the rank of nut cases in the eyes of doctors and shrinks. When can we start?"

"Nobody thinks you're a nut case," Bob interjected sternly. "We've talked this over lots before and there is nothing much else we can do. Besides, originally, you were the one that wanted to find out about your birth parents. Then, you were the one that was having a real problem with the fact that no one else around you experienced things the way you did."

"I know, I'm…, I'm sorry, Dad, but I just like to find out. I guess I'm frustrated."

"Excuse me," Mrs. James jumped in, "thank you both for each of your remarks. Caleb, when can you do the DNA test? We all would like to put this case to rest. Meanwhile, we will still check out the CIA possibilities without ruffling too many feathers, or, should I say, open up any can of worms," she concluded. "Do you folks have medical coverage?"

"I have family coverage through work," Bob replied.

"What line of work are you in?"

"I'm an insurance broker," he chuckled.

"Well, that will certainly help," Mrs. James said, as she peered down at her *Reference Book*, looking through her contact management program. She wrote down some information on a piece of paper and handed it to Diane.

"This is the laboratory where Caleb will have to set up an appointment with; I will contact them beforehand with the details. Please give me at least one day. As soon as the lab has the results, they will be forwarded to me and I will set up another appointment with you all." She smiled at Caleb. "You must be feeling a little better that there is actually some progress being made."

Caleb shrugged, nodded and looked down at his lap.

Mrs. James got up and the Lindstroms slowly rose to their feet in response.

"I think this will help clear up a lot of questions and hopefully, not unearth a whole bunch more," Mrs. James said confidently as she pointed them out of her office. "I assure you, at this moment, you don't have to worry about the CIA."

They shook hands goodbye as the three dumbfounded visitors took their leave.

The Lindstroms remained silent while they made their way out of the office and back down to their car.

"Still want to eat somewhere?" Diane asked weakly from the front seat of the car while Bob drove out of the underground parking. "I can make something when we get home."

The silence she got from her two men gave her the answer. Bob pointed the car toward the way home. "I guess that means no."

A little ways down the road, Caleb broke the silence from the back seat of the car. "Boy, she sure seems efficient. You never know, I might have been one of those wild experiments the government is supposed to have done; you know aliens and all that."

"Yeah, like in the movie *Twins*, or something? Come on Caleb," Diane chided, "you heard her say, the CIA thing is a pretty far stretch. Besides, could you not pick up any "vibes" from her?"

"Nothing much at all. She spoke exactly what she thought and she was like lightning, the only thing I could pick up was: "I want to get home" and how much she liked your outfit, Mom."

They all laughed, helping to ease the tension.

Chapter 22

Diane made the appointment with the lab for the following Thursday after school and made a note on the refrigerator calendar for Caleb. She softly hummed a tune as she cleaned up around the table after breakfast. The telephone ringing startled her.

It was a lady from the church office calling to find out if they would be interested in attending a seminar on creation science. A bunch of the local churches were sponsoring a Dr. Schellenberg, an expert on the creation side of the origin of species.

Diane's spirit leapt as she asked, "When is he going to be here? Whereabouts?" She busily scribbled down the information on a piece of paper. "Count us in!" She hung up and went back to the now nearly filled calendar and wrote the date, time and place of the seminar on it with a black marker. She didn't want anyone to miss that date.

Even though she had taken Caleb to church as a child, she had seen his interest wane, as he became a teenager. She knew the peer pressure and his *condition* was keeping him from attending. He had so many questions that the church leadership and others couldn't answer, and his own spirituality overwhelmed most of the members.

This seminar will probably be dealing with stuff he certainly could relate to and hopefully, he would be interested. Heck, Bob could use a good dose of church, Diane mused. Even with his limited knowledge of the Bible, he had a hard time trying to explain things of God in his own way to Caleb. This might shed light on the dinosaurs and dreams he had had. She always thought there must be a connection to the spirit. She didn't feel he was possessed or anything like that, but she had been tempted to take him to a psychic on occasion, but she felt that just wasn't the right thing to do. Besides Bob wouldn't approve of it

Her mind continued to wander while she speculated, as she had done for years, that maybe his natural parents were involved in the occult. She sure hoped not. She shook her head as if saying "No Way!"

Although Caleb didn't buy the Theory of Evolution, he constantly researched the origins of species and along with his knowledge of prehistoric archaeology and geology he could have already been classed an expert. Although Caleb wasn't a regular church goer, he read the Bible all the time and was fascinated by the account of the big flood in the book of Genesis. He contended that it took far more faith to believe in modern theories than it did to believe in God, the Creator.

He had studied the many modern quests for Noah's ark and his desire to go to Europe and the Middle East grew constantly. Caleb's immense interest in science and biology made him crave knowledge. He spent a lot of time in libraries. He always found holes in the information that he came across, especially in the ancient historical theories of origins and geology. He had contacted dozens of experts on these topics and told them he had *first-hand* insight into whatever the topic was. The experts didn't take him seriously, and even when he started to prove his *findings,* they still claimed it was *lucky* or it was just *coincidental.* They usually got quite indignant when he blatantly disproved their theories.

No wonder he is frustrated, Diane thought. Still, both she and Bob had the nagging doubt he might have a mental or physical disorder that could cause him to be the way he was. She just wished there could be some conclusive evidence; maybe Clements Adoption was on to something, and she sure hoped so. The CIA *thing,* though, troubled her. "This just can't be part of the equation," she said aloud while shaking her head.

That night at dinner, Diane announced the Creation Science seminar. Both Bob and Caleb looked at each other.

"What's it all about?" Bob asked.

Realizing she knew little about the content of the seminar, Diane said, "Well, I don't know all the details, but Jan Smith from the Presbyterian Church called. She said that a bunch of the local churches are sponsoring this guy, Dr. Schellenberg, a specialist in creation science. I think it would be a really interesting topic, you know, dinosaurs, origins of species, and what not, from a biblical point of view. I told them we would be coming. Hope that's okay?"

Bob looked at Caleb with a 'Well?' kind of expression.

Caleb chewed on a carrot pensively while looking back and forth between his mom and dad. "Sounds interesting. Maybe I can help him with the seminar; some of those guys are so far off the mark."

Diane looked at Bob then to Caleb, and retorted, "I think it would be good for you scientific types to be challenged. After all, God made dinosaurs, too."

"Hope he's not just going to talk about dinosaurs," Caleb said. "I would like to hear what he has to say on other stuff like DNA. I wonder if he's got a book or something."

"I'll see if I can get a brochure from the church's office," replied Diane helpfully.

Bob then asked Caleb for a game of catch and as soon as dinner was over they helped clean up the dishes and put them in the dishwasher. While they were cleaning up, their discussion started out on the topic of origin of species and the Bible, and ended up on how well the Sonics had done in the past few games and how unlikely they would make the play-offs. Afterward, they went out to the driveway and threw the baseball until it was too dark to see the ball.

Thursday rolled around and Diane drove Caleb to the DNA clinic. An hour-and-a-half later they left for home. Caleb felt exhausted. However, for the first time, he sensed there was some progress made in his path of discovery.

The clinic informed the Lindstroms they would be contacted in about three weeks via the adoption agency for the results.

The phone was ringing as they entered the house. Bob answered it from the den and he yelled to Caleb, "It's for you, son."

Caleb picked up the phone closest to him.

"Hi, Caleb, this is Bill Maxwell, the scout from the Sonics, I met you at your last game."

Caleb paused and lowering his voice, he said, "Oh yeah, I remember, how did you get my number?"

Maxwell grunted. "We have ways…. Hope you don't mind the call. Are you able to speak for a few minutes?"

"Yeah, I'm okay for awhile," Caleb replied, adjusting the phone to his ear as if listening for Maxwell's thoughts.

"Have you thought any further about our conversation? The training coach I mentioned is still available," Maxwell continued on the other end of the phone. "How are your grades?"

Caleb suddenly seemed agitated. He kept forcing the receiver around his ear as if trying to hear better.

"Grade A+"

"A+?" exclaimed Maxwell, "that's pretty good! Have you thought about what you want to do for your post education?"

"I want to pursue archaeology, some scientific stuff and maybe sports."

"Those are good goals, especially the sports part. Any preference of school you wish to attend?"

"Haven't made up my mind – still looking."

"Well, with that kind of average and your abilities, you can pretty well name the school. Have you looked into Washington U?"

"Sort of. Thought it would be nice to try something out of state, don't really know yet," Caleb replied coolly.

"What about the hoops? Who would you like to play for?"

This guy is asking a lot of questions. "I don't know that either, I like the Pacers and Lakers. Look, I should be going now, I…"

Maxwell cut him off, "I know, Caleb, don't mean to ask you a zillion questions, I just wanted to get some direction as well as provoke some thoughts for you. You have a lot to offer a team and it would be a shame not to channel that ability properly. Do you think we can get together shortly? I have some other stuff I want to share with you."

"Oh, yeah, sure, that would be great, let me get back to you. I still have your card."

"How about next week?" Maxwell pressed, trying to pin down a time.

"That could be arranged, give me a call on Monday."

"Why don't *you* call me?" Maxwell suggested firmly, thinking, *this kid doesn't seem to get it.*

"Yeah, okay, Mr. Maxwell, I'll call you on Monday or Tuesday."

When he hung up, Maxwell felt better about this conversation and looked forward to getting a call – he knew he would call Caleb back if he didn't hear from him by Monday evening.

Caleb stood hanging on to the receiver for several seconds, contemplating how hard it was for him to *hear* Maxwell's thoughts over the phone. This is weird, he thought, he could *hear* the other person's thoughts much better when he was in his presence. He wasn't sure if he even could really *hear* them properly at all over the phone.

"Sorry to be nosey, but who was that?" Bob asked as he walked by.

"Maxwell – the Sonics' scout. You remember the guy I told you about. He wants to get together with me next week. I'm thinking, should I be looking for an agent, Dad?"

"Why don't I come with you next week? I would like to meet Mr. Maxwell myself. We can cover all that territory then. How would you feel about that? After all, these are pretty important decisions you have to make."

"Let me ask him that when I set up the appointment."

"Okay, let's eat. I think Mom has dinner ready."

After dinner, Caleb went to his room and got on the phone to Darby and related the events of the day to her. When he hung up, he did some homework, and got ready for bed.

Caleb quickly fell into a deep sleep that drove him to dreamland almost instantly. He was "transported" into a mountainous area, and from his viewpoint, he could see huge caves carved into the side of the range. He noticed the mountains weren't anything like the Rockies or any others he had seen. They were very steep and arid, void of vegetation, almost as if they were new. The valleys were lush and thriving with the big trees, ferns and vegetation, he had seen so often in other dreams. This time he was seeing them from above.

The caves were located several hundred feet up the mountain and the shape of the rock formations and outcroppings surrounding them were very symmetrical. The shiny rocks had a deep red hue, almost a ruby red color with translucence like he had never seen before.

In an instant, he was transported to a shelf located at the entrance of one of the caves. He looked back across the landscape and for the first time gazed across the horizon. The breathtaking view was inexpressible. What ever the direction in which his eyes traveled, he saw the dazzling colors glisten off the lush pre-historic world. The sky was filled with birds of every size, shape and color. The symphony of birds cooing and crowing, and animal calls was almost deafening. The fragrance that permeated the air was beyond description. He realized it was not the first time he noticed the smell of it all, but this time he could *feel* it peeling his nostrils.

Caleb's heart leapt with excitement and he felt incredible joy. He wept in awe at this overwhelming scene. Even in his dream, his first thought was, "I wish Darby could be here!"

He could see a river meander through the valley and tried to follow its course as it weaved its way into the horizon. The sky was very different from reality. The clouds were misty and hung low. Their coloring was like a painting, almost as if layered.

All of a sudden, as if his eyes were zoom lenses, he focused on a scene and then back and forth. He nearly lost his balance as he got used to this new discovery. He practiced on things closer, so there wasn't such a motion effect. He couldn't believe this was happening to him. He was thrilled with these latest developments. He *zoomed* across the horizon and picked out herds of elks with lions and tigers lurking in the shadows. There were even brontosaurs and a T-Rex working his way along the river. The T-Rex was of special interest because of the scar on the right side of its head. Caleb had seen the animal before. He thought that maybe his dreams were located in one area. *How big is this?* Then, as suddenly as the dream started, he woke up. His pillow was damp from the tears he had wept while viewing the scene from the cliff where he had been perched at the cave's entrance. "Why didn't I look in the cave?"

The room was dark except for the LEDs on the clock telling him it was only 2:37AM.

He cursed to himself about the time while thinking about the inconceivable experience he had just gone through.

He flicked on the light and grabbed a pen and his "dream diary". It was increasing in size and he knew that one day it would be worth the effort. Little did he know how valuable it was going to be.

He dozed off with the light on and woke again to the annoying beeping sound of the alarm clock. Sleepily he checked out his diary to make sure he captured the dream. He got up and readied himself for school. He then remembered the homework he hadn't finished last night and quickly got into the shower and back to the books.

The excitement of his dream permeated everything; he could hardly wait to tell Darby as well as his parents.

At breakfast, he recounted the dream to them as they sat quietly, and attentively listened to the incredible new experience their son had.

117

Diane looked at Bob as he said Caleb, "Man, you're getting pretty detailed in these dreams. What else beside dinner did you eat last night? That's pretty amazing. How are you feeling after the tests?"

"I feel fine; I'm ready to get to school. Can I shoot some hoops with Justin after school?"

"Sure, dinner is at six," Diane reminded him.

Bob and Caleb left and the house was empty again. After her shower, Diane did a bit of house cleaning, but her mind was on the DNA results. *What if Caleb is really different? What if there was something different about his birth parents? What if they used drugs and he has some weird disease or incurable problem? What about the CIA thing?* Her mind raced like an Indy car engine.

She had thought about this a thousand times, but she could see the beginning of an end. Diane had never been a real praying person, but, for the first time, she cried out to God aloud and almost shocked herself hearing her own voice praying. Her prayer was simple, "Please help us, God!"

Upstairs, she walked by Caleb's room and stopped. She slowly opened the door and looked in. She respected Caleb's privacy and rarely entered – only when necessary. The dimly lit room softly showed off the posters of Michael Jordan, Shaquille O'Neal and many other sports' heroes a teenager would follow. The dinosaur models and knick knacks, books and stuff a kid would collect littered the shelves and Caleb's desk. He was a pretty neat kid; clothes put away, bed made. She thought about his taste in clothing. He liked to wear stuff that was very different, woolen sweaters and rugged looking leather vests – quite different from others. His best friend, Justin, and Darby always tried to get him into something more with the times, but Caleb refused to bow to peer-pressure and was very often ridiculed for his dress. That too, never bothered him; it was as if he really marched to a different drummer.

She suddenly felt forlorn. A strange feeling invaded her mind, as if Caleb would be going away; it gave her an uneasy sensation. Diane had felt that way once before when she was growing up. Her mind took her back to when she was fifteen, and her younger brother went camping with some friends. She had gone in to his room for a pair of his socks. This same forlorn feeling startled her then, exactly the same way it did at the moment. Even though he had already left for the camping trip, she felt she would never see him again.

That weekend there was a freak snowstorm in the Snoqualmie Pass while on the way to the campsite. The van their family friend, Jack Crawly, drove, slid off the road and rolled down the embankment. Her brother was killed in the accident. Understandably, everyone was devastated. It took a long time for the families to get over the tragedy.

People she had shared the experience with called it a premonition; she didn't believe in that kind of thing and wrote it off to a coincidence.

It was the same feeling – a pang in her heart, forlornness, a feeling of great loss, deep sadness. She started to weep and cried out, "No Lord! No Lord. Not again!"

Through her tears she looked around the room, but she couldn't take the feeling anymore and walked out. As soon as she left, the forlorn feelings and sadness immediately left her. It left as suddenly as it had come upon her. This startled her even more. She went back into the room again and looked around – nothing. She wiped her tears with the back of her hand and walked back into the room and then out – still nothing.

This is weird. She felt tingling all over. She shrugged her shoulders, walked back to the kitchen and went about her day. The feelings never returned.

Diane had to get a hold of the brochure on the Creation Science seminar, so she phoned the sponsoring church and asked where she could pick one up. The closest place was the Baptist Church right around the corner. It was raining, but a good walk would clear her head. Maybe this seminar would spark some interest in Caleb's faith – maybe in the faith of the whole family.

The gentle west coast drizzle brushed her umbrella and a few drops landed on her face. It seemed to cleanse the recent sensation away and with each step she felt rejuvenated. Her round trip to the church and back home was short and sweet.

As soon as she settled on the living room sofa, she browsed through the colorful brochure. Its description was perfect for Caleb, the topics were exactly what he had talked about and it looked very interesting – even to the uneducated.

The family started heading for bed and as usual, they had the TV on for the eleven o'clock news as they went about cleaning up and getting ready for the next day's activities. Caleb came out of the bathroom with a toothbrush stuck in his mouth. "Mom, did you…?" He stopped in mid sentence as he saw an ancient corpse being exhumed from an icy grave on the TV screen. *"Today, archaeologists are describing the find of this perfectly preserved body discovered in the Austrian Alps as one of the oldest human remains ever discovered. At first it was believed to be a lost modern hiker, but upon closer examination it has been determined that this man is very old,"* the TV anchor said. By this time, Caleb had run into the living room and was glued to the screen. He stood there in awe, shaking like a leaf.

"Are you okay, Honey?" Diane asked.

Caleb didn't answer. He was transfixed by the images displayed on the screen.

The anchor went on, *"Archaeologists have discovered personal ancient artifacts and clothing near the body along with a bow and arrows and even food."* The camera showed a close-up of the body and panned from the head on down. A European correspondent with a heavy German accent reporting from the scene was next. *"This ancient man still has his skin and even his eyes are somewhat intact. However, a bit of a strange twist to this find is that the man's genitals are missing. You can see how well preserved he is, notice how flexible the body is as he is moved from this icy grave."* He went on to describe the region where he was discovered and other details. *"We'll have more on the Ice Man this coming Wednesday's science report at 7:30PM."*

The anchor came back saying, *"Fire ripped through a downtown Seattle warehouse this evening…."* Caleb was standing in the middle of the living room frozen like a statue. His eyes glazed over as if in a trance.

By this time, Bob and Diane were on their feet. "Caleb, are you OK?"

No answer. Bob took the toothbrush out, wiped the toothpaste that was oozing out of the corners of Caleb's mouth and grabbed his son's shoulders and gave him a shake. "Caleb, Caleb!"

Diane cried out, "What's wrong, Honey?"

Caleb's legs buckled like wet spaghetti just in time for Bob to grab his son and to hold him before he collapsed to the floor. He dragged him like a rag doll to the sofa and gently lowered him down. A minute passed and the parents were frantic as they stared into the glazed-over eyes of their son. They kept calling out to an unconscious body.

Diane ran to get the phone to dial 911. But, all of a sudden, Caleb came to. He blinked rapidly and swirled saliva around his dry mouth. He licked his lips, cleared his throat and looked up at his hysterical parents with almost an amused look.

"What...? Mom, Dad? What are you doing? Wow! Not sure, what happened.... The TV...." He jumped up off the sofa in time to see a commercial. "I was there ... I felt the cold ... I saw the rescuers ... I was there...," Caleb blurted.

"What are you talking about?" Bob asked, dumfounded at his son's reaction.

"The..., the news report, you know, the corpse, the man on the mountain, the man in the ice, the Ice Man. I was there!" Caleb insisted. He was adamant about what he had just experienced.

"Yes we saw that, it was about the discovery of an ancient corpse, but what...?"

"Mom, Dad," Caleb interrupted vehemently. "This is for real. I was there. I can't tell you how, but I was there. I could feel the cold, the scenery ... in my dreams, so familiar, over and over again, I have gone to this place in my dreams and the dream ends ... now I think I know why. I have got to find out who this man was and which country he was found in. I feel like I know him. I can't tell you how, I feel like there is a connection, a very close connection, something personal. I felt so sad to see how he was treated. I felt like it was me they were excavating.

"You see, I have never shared what I am about to tell you with anyone. It is too strange to repeat. Remember, I had mentioned about the animals getting restless and I could sense the presence of another being? Well, recently there was a change in the atmosphere; it started to rain a lot. The animals really freaked out and I actually saw other humans. Something I had never seen before. They were at a distance and running around as if something was about to happen. From what I know of the Bible and the great flood, I believe it was what took place in my dreams."

121

Chapter 23
The Seminar

Dr. Schellenberg, MDiv (Master of Divinity) from Yale University School of Divinity, New Haven, Connecticut was a typical graying, middle-aged guy with high cheek bones and long, boney fingers that seem to be connected at his wrist. He was of an average build with a spare tire around his middle, attesting of the good life he led. He pulled no punches when he talked. He had the highest credentials from a theological point of view, but he was passionate about the great struggle that existed between creationists and evolutionists, and had studied both sides of the argument extensively. He was obviously biased toward creationism. He often made it clear that the impact of teaching a one-sided theory to society was impractical and debilitating.

He opened with, "The teaching of the theory of evolution is, in fact, one of the top most diabolical attacks on the mere fabric of our society. Consider this; if you are convinced, by enough teachings, that you are nothing more than a form of elevated animal, or worse still, you have descended from the apes, then where does that leave any sense of societal responsibility? When you really stop and think about it, that would mean your pet monkey or even your dog, is not only your distant ancestor, but is, in fact, more highly developed, smarter and quite frankly, beyond you! Well? They have been around a lot longer, right?

"If it were the case, that we evolved from a former species, and looking at the animal kingdom, there can be a sort of respect for others, but what about human life, what about honoring others, what about respect for oneself? These things and hundreds of societal concerns are mysteriously left out of the theory of evolution. Notice it is called – "The *theory* of evolution". Why is it today, with all the brilliant minds that roam the earth, that this theory cannot be challenged in the echelons of Western education? Every other theory is openly discussed, challenged and openly put through a scientific process, but thinkers are not allowed to discuss this for fear of losing their jobs, their credibility, maybe even their lives because of the potential repercussions. Now tell me, what brought about these Draconian measures to deal with this? I would really like to know myself!

"Let me give you my opinion on this. I believe that this anti-Christ document is being ferociously protected in order to control our society, to bring division, to incite everything from bigotry to hate and to mock believers as being narrow-minded, uneducated fools who have blind faith and should shut up or be dealt with harshly. It also is a huge money mongering industry. If you can bring strife, you can throw money at it to control it, then it can be kept in check – maybe – but there needs to be more taxation to hire a bigger police force, military, homeland security, bigger penitentiaries, more judges, lawyers, and the list goes on. I am not a quote "conspiratist", but I do believe there is a devil and he has been given a way too much power, both by governments as well as the church.

"If you examine western societies today, I say western, because most Middle Eastern and eastern countries openly teach and believe in a creator. Sure the theory of evolution is talked and discussed, but in the context of any other theory.

"If society is a fabric, you will notice there are serious concerns that run with threads dyed the same color. These same colored threads are made up of the things we see on the news every day – drug and alcohol and other forms of addictions, violence, unrestrained anger, murders, suicides, hate, wars, split families, physiological and psychological diseases, etc. – these threads are woven into the fabric of society and weakened, certainly not strengthened it in every way."

He paused. "I should point out that although the theory of evolution is not the only cause of all mankind's ills, it certainly is one of the major pillars in the foundation of where the sin nature of man is built on, to show its ugly glory.

"Does anyone know what the charter of the Religion of Secular Humanism or as it is now called, the Council of Human Secularism says? This is number nine in their charter; let me read it for you:

Today the theory of evolution is again under heavy attack by religious fundamentalists. Although the theory of evolution cannot be said to have reached its final formulation, or to be an infallible principle of science, it is nonetheless supported impressively by the findings of many sciences. There may be some significant differences among scientists concerning the mechanics of evolution; yet the evolution of the species is supported so strongly by the weight of evidence that it is difficult to reject it. Accordingly, we deplore the efforts by fundamentalists (especially in the United States) to invade the science classrooms, requiring that creationist theory be taught to students and requiring that it be included in biology textbooks. This is a serious threat both to academic freedom and to the integrity of the educational process. We believe that creationists surely should have the freedom to express their viewpoint in society. Moreover, we do not deny the value of examining theories of creation in educational courses on religion and the history of ideas; but it is a sham to mask an article of religious faith as a scientific truth and to inflict that doctrine on the scientific curriculum. If successful, creationists may seriously undermine the credibility of science itself.

"Folks, this is the folly that has been written against God and you. These tenets are the foundations or building blocks for a godless society.

"Did you notice they admit right off the bat, that the theory of evolution has not reached its final formulation? That's like saying; this is not an exact science and certainly not the truth. However, we will believe anything that supports our mandate as long as it speculates or propagates some form of the evolutionary process. Or, putting it into a practical explanation, how would you feel if I told you that the house you are living in – no one is sure if there is a foundation, there appears to be one, but some contractors will drop by now and again and check it out. Sure enough, one by one they drop by and report back they haven't found one yet. Somebody thinks there is one because the house is still standing, so therefore there has to be one, but he is not absolutely sure. Another contractor comes by and looks and can't find it either and reports something different. And so on, each contractor speculates about his findings but no one will sign off to the truth. Time goes by and another contractor comes and looks, and suggests looking up the original builder, but you have been told repeatedly that the original builder no longer exists. So, what are you thinking? Either the contractors are giving you the run around, the original builder built shoddy houses, or you continue to hire more contractors? Or, duhhh, maybe you should find out more about the original builder? And they say the Bible contradicts itself? Let me read this again:

"Accordingly, we deplore the efforts by fundamentalists (especially in the United States) to invade the science classrooms, requiring that creationist theory be taught to students and requiring that it be included in biology textbooks. This is a serious threat both to academic freedom and to the integrity of the educational process."

"Wait a minute; there is a caveat...." *We believe that creationists surely should have the freedom to express their viewpoint in society. Moreover, we do not deny the value of examining theories of creation in educational courses on religion and the history of ideas; but it is a sham to mask an article of religious faith as a scientific truth and to inflict that doctrine on the scientific curriculum. If successful, creationists may seriously undermine the credibility of science itself.*

"Wait a minute, did I just miss something? Teaching Creation is a *"serious threat both to academic freedom and to the integrity of the educational process."* What? A serious threat? Come on, what kind of statement is that? That is libel. If Christianity said that teaching evolution is an assault to our intelligence, there would be a huge price to pay. In other words, we think it is Okay to talk about Creation, but don't ram it down our throats.... Like the theory of evolution has been rammed down our throats for decades. They speak with forked tongue. Note the potential fear of loss of their precious doctrine ... *"it is a sham to mask an article of religious faith as a scientific truth and to inflict that doctrine on the scientific curriculum. If successful, creationists may seriously undermine the credibility of science itself."*

"Any Creationist worth his or her salt is a pure scientist. Nothing is speculated to affirm someone's belief system. Let me repeat, *nothing* is speculated in order to get you or me to believe in some religious order or, there is some hidden agenda to get the skeptic to believe in Jesus. I don't know where these guys get their doctrine from. Well, I think I know. If you read their charter, it slams anything to do with religion, especially Judeo-Christian doctrines and makes an atheist a believer – in the Religion. Oops, I mean, Council of Secular Humanism.

"Although the theory of evolution cannot be said to have reached its final formulation, or to be an infallible principle of science, it is nonetheless supported impressively by the findings of many sciences. There may be some significant differences among scientists concerning the mechanics of evolution; yet the evolution of the species is supported so strongly by the weight of evidence that it is difficult to reject it.

"Show me the evidence! There is not a shred of evidence to back these statements. Carbon dating and other forms of time dating try to point out that the earth and the universe is millions of years old, therefore, life *had* to have been different back then, and that age is the key factor in the beginning of life. After all, if something is that old, there *had* to have been a chance of the right mixture of chemicals in order for life to begin. Okay, let's say the universe is a trillion years old, or whatever. Have you ever noticed what happens when you leave an apple on the counter for a few weeks? Or a piece of meat? Or any other living organism? Hanging around, waiting to evolve? Okay, even some dirt. It degrades from one form to another, lower form – nothing has ever been found, anything that has transitioned up to a higher life form, or evolved. If the truth were known, things are devolving, certainly not evolving, even according to the second law of thermodynamics.

"Yes, there certainly are creatures that have adapted, just like humans, if you live in the Arctic, you will have a different body, in certain ways, such as your skin or blood or other minor characteristics, than someone living in the tropics. But, that doesn't mean there is an evolutionary process going on; you and they are still humans."

Schellenberg, pointing his long, boney fingers at large flip-charts he had prepared, went on with his postulations and theories of pre-flood atmospheric conditions, potential for sudden appearances of different forms of life found in the many layers of earth. How water was broken up from the deep and potentially from outer space, how amazing the human body consists of many trillions of cells and the intricacy built into each cell and how each person is completely unique. How everything works together in a synergy, using examples of bees that could not exist without flowers and flowers could not exist without bees. How everything pointed to an intelligent designer, a creator, rather than a hap hazard, come by chance formulation.

"You know, the odds that the Big Bang theory has any credence, is about the same as an explosion in a printing factory would produce a dictionary. I could go on, but that is not what I am here for, I want to talk about how great our God is. He is concerned about everything. He loves us, including the atheist, the agnostic, the skeptic. He loves all of us and guess what? I believe we were created, I believe He planned our lives. I believe He not only knows our address, but wants to dwell with us. I also believe He wants the best for us, I believe He will never over step His laws of the Universe, but He wants to give people the keys to His power in order for them to rule with His son, Jesus, in perfect harmony. He is truly the expression of perfect love, and that He has always existed – the Alpha and Omega, the beginning and the end.

"I also believe, according to His word, that He has revealed Himself in His creation and it is our choice to look for Him. I believe the reason there is all the strife over Creation, theories of evolution, etc. is because God gave us a curious mind, an inquisitive spirit, the ability to think, to rationalize, to perceive, to create. After all, the Bible says we were created in his image, and I think you've gathered by now He is *very* creative. Moreover, if we accept that God has created us in his image, we must therefore accept that He would not have created a being *inferior* to Him. In Luke 17:20 we read: "The Kingdom of God is within you." I think that sums it up pretty well."

A large, biker-looking guy with tattooed arms crossed tightly across his chest took offense to Schellenberg's remarks. He was getting more agitated as the evening wore on and would mutter things under his breath.

"I would like to go on about the statements in the humanist's doctrine which are riddled with a continued onslaught to this country's heritage, belief system and weaken the family, lower the beauty of creation, including humanity, to conjecture and hap-hazardness. Another glaring problem with evolution is the division of the human race. Besides the many racial atrocities we are aware of, there are pictures of the Australian aborigines chained together like animals because they thought they were less than humans – the term 'race' implies that someone, usually by color, is superior to another. This was originally preached by evolutionists for years, and guys like Hitler used this as their doctrine or platform of hate and evil in order to mercilessly kill people – in the name of a superior race. How evil is that?

"Now...." He paused. "Enough of the evil, I would like to take you to a place where there is truth, where there is evidence, where there is an explanation – no, an exciting explanation – of the events that have brought creation, that have shaped society, and continues to unravel the mystery of the past.

Schellenberg went on and read Genesis and gave his views on what the atmosphere was like and how it changed after the fall of Adam. Then he started on the subject of the great flood and Caleb's ears perked up. It was as if his ability to read Schellenberg's mind was tuned in to a radio station. It was so powerful, he wasn't sure if he was listening with his natural ears or his "inner" ears. Schellenberg described it in a way that Caleb had never heard before. All of a sudden his dreams not only made perfect sense, but made him realize, he actually had witnessed the dawn of creation unfold before his eyes. Caleb was shaking like a leaf. He was in awe when Schellenberg described in great detail, dinosaurs, extinct plants and other forms of life wiped out by the flood that Caleb had seen in his dreams.

Schellenberg went on about the great flood and how the waters covered the Earth and how the mountain-tops were exposed briefly to outer space and how present weather patterns were formed. He pointed out the frozen river of fish that was discovered in northern Russia and how it would have had to freeze in minutes in order for them to be found within the ice the way they were. How the wooly mammoth elephants were found flash frozen with tropical vegetation in their stomachs and even their mouths, in Siberia. "...Some of the exposed flesh had been eaten by modern day wolves. One of them was standing on its hind legs! How does Darwinism and a supposedly protracted length of time account for this? How do fossilized clams and other sea life get to the tops of the Rocky Mountains?" He pointed out the human footprints inside the fossilized tracks of dinosaurs. How so much scientific evidence pointed toward an intelligent design. Schellenberg went to the book of Job where God spoke and asked questions related to creation and how those things continued to point to a deeper science, which is being uncovered today.

"Faith is like gravity, you can't see it but it sure affects your life. We all have faith. You have faith that when you breathe, there will always be air. When you eat, you will be given nourishment, when you press the brake pedal in your car, you will stop. Those are simple acts of faith, but, there is no difference in having faith in the infallible truth of the gospel, which I should remind you has been around a whole lot longer and has been tested, disputed, ridiculed, reveled, for over two thousand years. Mr. Darwin's theory has been around for one hundred years or so and is being touted as truth. One of the reasons for its adaptation so readily to society was due partly to the industrial revolution, which was bringing great discoveries of science to the world. In the eighteen hundreds, the world was beginning to shrink rapidly with the advent of steam and gas powered machines making travel easier. Scientists were traveling to places on Earth where civilizations had lived untouched for thousands of years. It was a time of wonder, of adventure, of speculation. Darwin happened to be one of those who had his theory published on a printing press that had only been around for a few years. So, the spread of his theory was faster, easier and to a far greater audience than if he had been around fifty years prior.

"At this time I'd like to open the meeting up to questions."

Immediately hands went up throughout the church and people were contesting his view on creation.

"Why is it all you religious bunch won't accept the blatant scientific findings pointing toward solid evidence of an old earth and the fact that there is overwhelming facts that things have evolved?" one attendee asked.

"I am not going to argue the age of the earth. There are parts of science that points toward an old earth. I will however, ask you the question about the quote "facts" of evolved species. Has there been ANY transitional species found?"

"Plenty," replied the attendee.

"Name or show evidence of just one."

"Well…, there is the sightless frog found in New Mexico."

"You're right; it was discovered in caverns filled with underground water ways, where it is pitch-black. You see, this is not a form of evolution, but rather a case of adaptation. There are lots of those types of creatures around. Take any of those creatures and place them into normal surroundings and they morph back into their original state – they "de-evolve" rather than evolve. Also, there are no creatures *or even plants* that are in the middle of transitioning, none, zero," Schellenberg retorted.

The agitated biker-looking guy got up, with a red face – obviously very offended by the deliberation – turned to the audience and declared in a loud voice, "I came here because my wife forced me to come. I have never been so belittled in my life. Not once have you given any credible data about timelines, about fossils in strata layers, about real science. How is it that you creationists only talk about a so-called creator and not about scientific data that points to the obvious? I don't believe in God or religion. I was a Christian, I know all about your salvation stories and the flood and all that nonsense, but after awhile I started to question this faith thing and started reading about other religions, and they all say they have the truth. You know what religion is, it's a way to control the masses, it came out of a pagan society that was happy to do its own thing but somebody wanted to control them. So they invented a god because, hey, out of their ignorance they couldn't explain anything any other way. You know, if you read about messiahs, there have been many of them appear throughout Asia and the Middle East. Heck, even here in North America. This Jesus, he ain't anything special. Shucks how do we know he even existed? The scriptures were written from hand me down stories. Come on, people, religion is fear mongering. Genesis is a fairy tale. Anyone who believes in that needs their head examined."

Schellenberg had heard it all before and knew how to handle the guy. "Whew, I guess we all came to the wrong meeting. Would you like to come up here and tell us about the origin of species?" The audience gave a nervous chuckle. "Or how about your opinion on the geological findings at the Afar Depression in Africa? Look, I know that whatever *I* say, *you* will find a reason to argue against it. Any self-professed atheist has to defend his reasons for their existence; after all, this is a free country founded by *believers* – oops, there's that disgusting word again – who came from a religious, oppressive society where you would have been hanged for saying what you just said. Now, if you like, I would like to meet with you personally after the meeting and we can have a discussion."

The guy laughed, grabbed his wife by the hand and dragged her out of the church, cussing and mumbling all the way down the aisle.

Questions came forth in rapid succession and Schellenberg answered with grace and humility, admitting he certainly didn't know all there was to know about creation.

Caleb leapt to his feet and asked, "What if someone has witnessed the world before the flood? Like maybe the Ice Man that was just discovered."

Schellenberg gave a little chuckle and said, "Yes, that is quite a discovery, apparently so well preserved, besides the discoloration of his skin from frost bite, it is like he was buried yesterday. Remarkable! But to say he witnessed a pre-flood world, well, that would certainly make it a whole lot easier for science, but the Bible says that all of mankind was drowned. However, further to that, I don't know anyone personally who witnessed the flood." The audience laughed.

"I will wrap this up with the word *faith*. The Bible describes faith in the book of Hebrews chapter eleven verse one in the new testament as *"the substance of things hoped for, the evidence of things not seen."* So faith is a substance and evidence of things not seen. Maybe hard to grasp, but well documented and certainly proven repeatedly. I believe it takes far more faith to believe in a theory than to believe in the simplicity of the gospel, which will point toward a loving God who created you and gave you a free will to love or hate; to do good or evil, live or die. He even has paradise waiting for those who want to spend eternity with Him, or to be forever separated."

Schellenberg finished with a call to repentance and a relationship with God the great Creator through Jesus Christ who went to the cross and died, and shed His blood and rose from the dead after three days for all of humanity's sin or separation from God by Adam's disobedience. He pointed out that without Christ an understanding of both Genesis and the New Testament's Gospel was virtually impossible. "So come today as you are I would like to pray – a prayer is simply a communication link with God – to receive Christ as your savior."

At the conclusion of the seminar, Caleb jumped out of his seat and ran toward Dr. Schellenberg. He could hardly contain himself, his heart was pounding and he was sweating. He stood in line to speak with the man.

Bob ran up to join him. "Do you mind if I joined you?"

"If you want." Caleb's voice was wavering. "I think I can handle it."

Bob could see Caleb had some new hope. Something was suddenly different. Besides the shaking and sweating and flushed face, there was intensity in his eyes like Bob had not seen before.

Caleb introduced himself to Dr Schellenberg and started to unravel his dreams. At first, Schellenberg showed little interest but when Caleb began to describe in great detail, the skin and fur, the eye color and sounds of long extinct creatures, Schellenberg started to pay close attention.

"Caleb, whoa, we need to talk to others here. I am staying in town for a couple of days and would like to meet privately with you. I think you are onto something. Can we do a lunch or dinner?"

"Of course, we can," Bob cut-in. "I'm Bob Lindstrom, Caleb's father, and we would love to get together. How about dinner tomorrow night at our place?"

"That would be fine," Schellenberg said, smiling.

Caleb was so excited; he had never met anyone with credentials who believed him, and even when reading Schellenberg's mind, he could tell he was sincere.

That night, he could hardly sleep. Time seemed to drag on like molasses in January.

Dr Schellenberg arrived for dinner armed with a video recorder and asked if he could record the meeting. He assured the family this would be for his personal use only.

Over dinner, they exchanged pleasantries.

"I have to tell you, I was a little taken aback by the comments of that big guy at the seminar the other night," Bob said.

Schellenberg nodded. "That happens frequently. As I said, it is impossible to reason with characters like that. Especially the ones who have maybe experienced salvation and some kind of church life. I'm beginning to think there are a lot more out there who are jaded by religion. I don't know where they went off the rails and what they are looking for; obviously they have bought a lie. They see all these different denominations and the petty bickering over doctrine and who's right and who's wrong scenarios and they start to question everything. It must make God pretty sick. That guy is what you call an "anti-thesist", or atheist with an anti-Christ spirit. He has been spending a lot of time researching why he *shouldn't* believe, rather than why he *should* believe and there is a ton of propaganda out there to support his cause. It is very sad. I feel very sorry for their situation and pray that they have a real God encounter that will flip their polarity back aright. There is a saying that you become the thing that you hate the most, maybe that will happen to our friend."

They went on and discussed the fact that Caleb was adopted. The fact that they hadn't located the birthing parents was interesting to Schellenberg. Caleb was bursting at the seams to tell his story and talk about his abilities and dreams.

As he described the intensity and reality of his dreams – the detail of the flora and fauna, the mountain ranges and everything he had seen. Schellenberg was becoming animated with every story. There was a bond forming quickly between the two. Caleb's description of something would lead into a question or remark from Schellenberg and an incredible story would then unfold.

The young man's description of a prehistoric world was not only fascinating, but it was accurate. He answered every question Schellenberg would pose, however impossible they seemed, or difficult they would be to answer.

"How are you able to describe the skin of a tyrannosaurus so accurately?"

"I have touched it, I have felt it with my hands, I have smelled it, just as a horse or a cow or any other animal has a peculiar smell, so do these creatures," Caleb replied.

"But how did you get so close? Weren't you afraid?"

"No, because I have authority over them, if they get aggressive toward me, I can speak to them and tell them to back off or go lie down."

"Really? That's hard to believe!" Schellenberg exclaimed.

"Well, you wanted to know; didn't Adam name all the creatures? He had to get up close and comfortable with all of them, right?" Caleb paused. "I can also sense some kind of strife or conflict."

"Have you got a Bible?"

Diane went to the living room and brought back her New International Version.

"I want to show you something in Genesis six...."

1 When human beings began to increase in number on the earth and daughters were born to them, 2 the sons of God saw that the daughters of humans were beautiful, and they married any of them they chose. 3 Then the LORD said, "My Spirit will not contend with humans forever, for they are mortal[J]; their days will be a hundred and twenty years."

4 The Nephilim were on the earth in those days—and also afterward—when the sons of God went to the daughters of humans and had children by them. They were the heroes of old, men of renown.

5 The LORD saw how great the wickedness of the human race had become on the earth, and that every inclination of the thoughts of the human heart was only evil all the time. 6 The LORD regretted that he had made human beings on the earth, and his heart was deeply troubled. 7 So the LORD said, "I will wipe from the face of the earth the human race I have created—and with them the animals, the birds and the creatures that move along the ground—for I regret that I have made them." 8 But Noah found favor in the eyes of the LORD.

9 This is the account of Noah and his family.

Noah was a righteous man, blameless among the people of his time, and he walked faithfully with God. 10 Noah had three sons: Shem, Ham and Japheth.

11 Now the earth was corrupt in God's sight and was full of violence. 12 God saw how corrupt the earth had become, for all the people on earth had corrupted their ways. 13 So God said to Noah, "I am going to put an end to all people, for the earth is filled with violence because of them. I am surely going to destroy both them and the earth.

"Let's look at the word Nephilim in verse four. In the King James it is written "sons of God." There has been a lot of discussion over this passage. Some have seen this as a group of ancient people, and it looks like a reference to men only, well known heroes, or as it is written, "...men of renown." Were these nice guys? Or were they thugs? It isn't clear, but it looks like outright anarchy ruled, because verse five shows that the earth's population was pretty wicked. I want you to examine something here. Follow me for a moment, there are some who believe the Nephilim were fallen angels... "Sons of God." When Satan was thrown out of Heaven, he brought a third of the angels to the earth with him. Could this passage be referring to those fallen angels? It says they were mating with the "daughters of men." This poses another dynamic, there appears to be a separation or differentiation between the two groups. We have "sons of God" on one hand and "daughters of men" on the other, one spiritual in nature and the other physical in nature and we see them mating and having offspring. Then we see the Lord referring to great wickedness throughout the earth. Could it be that this inbreeding produced a hybrid human? They were in a human body, but they had supernatural, spiritual powers. Were they, for lack of better words, *possessed*? Stay with me.... I don't mean like something out of one of those creepy movies; I mean they had amazing abilities because they were a hybrid. Because they were banned from ever getting back into Heaven, they were ready to wreak havoc here on earth. One way to do that was to mess up God's crowning creation: man. Man was made in the very image of God. Also, as far as I understand, angels cannot reproduce; since they are a one time eternal created being. This sexual mating thing with humans would have been a hey day for them. Obviously the Lord wasn't very happy with the outcome of these hybrids because they had extraordinary powers, which corrupted humans. Where am I going with this? Well, have you ever wondered where present metaphysical culture, where witchcraft and other forms of ancient mystical practices came from? Is it possible that its roots came from these hybrids? Even after the great flood, there may have been enough of a residue left to exist today. Caleb here may have somehow tapped into this." Schellenberg turned to the young man. "Caleb, have you ever played around with the occult?"

Caleb shook his head.

"Have you been around friends who have?"

Again, Caleb indicated a negative.

"What about you, Bob, Diane?"

Both answered, "No."

"Okay, I won't belabor the point, I was just making sure. Sometimes when people have had experiences with the occult, there can be some telltale signs, even if there is a history of it a way back in the family tree. Maybe there was some activity in birthparents' lives, who knows."

Schellenberg was spell bound by this teenager's incredible

experience and asked if he could make a documentary. Caleb looked at his folks, who only showed their enthusiastic approval, and he agreed. Schellenberg didn't want to give Caleb a firm date, but he promised to get back to him with a schedule as soon as he got home.

The man was amazed by Caleb's first hand experience. Every one of his dreams seemed to be linked in order to tell the story of creation.

"How do you read minds?" Schellenberg asked.

"I don't know, it is not a physical sound, but rather a perception of thought, you know like I can't hear everyone's thoughts at once, only the one I am focused on. For example, I can tell you that you are going to ask me a question, but I can't read Mom or Dad's at the same time, even though they are sitting right next to you, it is like a radio station that I can tune in and out. I can read animal's actions as well – I can't totally explain it, it is an ability."

"What do you make of these abilities?"

"Well, after hearing your presentation last night, I believe what this is all about is that God wants me to tell about the birth of creation from a first hand experience, and somehow, He wants me to share it with the world. You are the first person who actually believes me. I have not shared this with my friends, well…, outside of my girlfriend Darby, and she is sworn to an oath of secrecy not to tell anyone else. I have been to a few psychiatrists and they all think I am a nut case. They want to drug me up to keep me from being delusional or something like that. Lately, in the dreams, I actually sensed the presence of someone – another human or humans. The animals were very restless and there seemed to be a big event coming."

"That is true, Doctor," Diane interjected. "We did not know how to handle this and sought medical advice and they all said the same thing. You certainly are the first one who has brought out the story. It is the first time even we have heard of some of the encounters in such detail. We have heard him brush over his experiences in a roughed out manner, but not to such an extent. He has had this pretty much all his life. I can remember him telling us about his dreams when he was just able to talk. At first, I thought he had a vivid imagination, but as he grew older, he would wake us up in the night terrified of some of the encounters. That's when we started with the medical advice. Both Bob and myself are not great supporters of medication and when any of these psychiatrists started wanting to administer drugs, we would move him to the next one and so on. Now sixteen years later, here we are."

"Thanks, Mrs. Lindstrom, a truly amazing story." He returned his attention to Caleb. "So, what big event do you think is about to happen – in your dreams?" Schellenberg asked.

"I think it is the great flood," Caleb replied assertively.

Dr Schellenberg pondered for a moment. "Are you making this up to substantiate your story or are you really sensing this?"

All of a sudden, Caleb shrank back from his enthusiasm, as if the wind had been taken from his sails.

Schellenberg realized he had gone a bit too far. "No, no, I am not doubting your experience, Caleb, please believe me, it was just a reflex question to where this was going." The scientist reached out his hand toward Caleb. "I am not trying to punch holes in your experience, please understand, a lot is at stake here. If you are who you are, I personally believe you have some profound answers and perhaps guidance to the history of mankind. I am for you, not against you, I want you to go before the top archeologists and anthropologists as well as Biblical scholars in the world and tell your story."

Caleb looked up with encouragement once again and continued to recount his pre-flood experiences. "You know, before the flood, it never rained, there was a mist that went up from the earth, right? Well, I have seen that too, it was like an underground sprinkler system without the sprinklers, again hard to explain but it makes sense when you see it. There are rivers and lakes for the animals to drink from, but this mist, it waters everything."

Schellenberg kept the video camera rolling and continued to make notes. He asked more questions about specific things related to creation science. Then he abruptly ended the interview.

"You know, I think I want to have this professionally videoed for a documentary. How about we leave it off at this point and after I get home, I'll arrange a crew. I want to get this moving as quickly as possible. Even what I have here is amazing in itself, but I want to get it done properly. At least, I have enough evidence to show the world that this young man, through his abilities and experiences has an incredible story to tell."

Schellenberg then packed up his gear, said his goodbyes and left.

Darrell Swanson

Chapter 24
Evil lurks around the corner...

Dennis, Jared's brother, became a double agent. He was so jaded with the CIA and even Western society that his whole mission solely focused on how much money he could get from terrorist groups and dissenters in exchange for inside information on the CIA's operations. He cared little for any emotional attachment or responsibility to American ideals, because of what he had seen done in other societies where the people were forced into acceptance of democracy and Western ideals. He walked a fine line; often caught in literal crossfire as he pitted one group against another, while salting huge amounts of cash away in a Cayman Island bank account.

When he wasn't working, he was very much a loner. He drifted between sordid female relationships, hung out with anti-establishment types and smoked, and drank a fair amount. In his forties, he felt disconnected and empty.

His boss called him into the office one day. As Dennis sat down across from him, he wondered what this was all about. Without preamble, the CIA man plunged forward. "Do you remember the experiment we attempted to do with your brother and his wife back fifteen, sixteen years ago? How we had closed the books on it because it appeared your nephew was pretty much normal?"

Dennis crossed one ankle over one leg and reclined in the seat. "Yeah, Jason, he is pretty normal."

"Well, I just received something interesting from the Clements Adoption Agency in Seattle and they have been in touch with a strange kid who was born the same day, same hospital as Jason was. Our agent back then was pretty thorough in one respect; he had all the babies that were born that day flagged on their birth records, and this kid was the last one to be tracked down, or rather, show up." Dennis moved forward in the chair, quite interested now. He already saw another opportunity to make some money.

His boss went on. "Apparently, the agency claims he is very unique. The kid has some strange qualities." With his elbows on the table, the CIA man leaned forward all the while rubbing his chin with his left hand. "Wouldn't it be something if the babies got mixed up in the nursery?" Dennis nodded. "Possible, you know; it's a long shot, but I want you to do some detective work on this kid and find out if we need to open the books on this case." Dennis looked down at his lap. He knew what was coming next. "I want you to interview the kid and send me a report on what you find. If he has some strange characteristics, we will need to bring him in for questioning."

Dennis rose from the chair and was about to leave when his boss added, "And, for God's sake, don't spook the kid, don't let him know you are CIA. I trust you, Houghton, because you have been with us a long time and you have a pretty good record of getting blood out of a stone. Let us know if you need help; don't try and be a hero."

Before Dennis left, his boss gave him the particulars on Caleb and then accompanied him to the door, visibly satisfied.

In the hallway, Dennis thought this was a waste of time. Yet, money was the lure of the game. All he wanted to do was to locate the kid, make up some big story and sell him to the highest bidder within the stable of underworld connections he had amassed. He lit up a smoke, hopped in his car and headed for the airport.

On the way, he contacted Ji, the head of an underground bio terrorist group known as FTW, an acronym for *Free The World*. They wanted to eradicate polluters and stop global warming and global free trade by taking heads of major corporations hostage. Their goals was to drive fear into the hearts of all humanity with suicide bombings, beheadings and torture, to stop polluting and ruining the planet, and make an economy based on only sustainable agriculture and a less complex lifestyle with one religion. They had recently developed a "dirty" bomb with a potent virus that was so virulent that once released over any major city, most of the inhabitants would be dead within hours. It would be a mass pandemic with no known antidote or vaccine. The FTW was funded by Islamic extremists, Middle East money, Greenpeace and other sympathetic underground economies.

"So, Ji, are you aware that there is human cloning going on?"

"No, I have heard of sheep clones, no humans. Why?"

"Let me ask you a question; your suicide bombers, how long does it take for you to convince your followers to pull the trigger?"

"Not long, I have a waiting list."

"What if you had access to a super human who had special powers, who could outsmart everyone around him, which would allow easy access to the top guys in any corporation and basically, you could do what ever you want with them? You could program them before they were born and they would always be the same. Exact replicas of each other."

"Have you had too much to drink, Dennis? Are you kidding me?" Ji sneered.

"No, I'm not."

"How much?"

"This is a big one." Dennis took a drag off his smoke. "Five hundred."

"Dollars?"

"Five hundred million dollars."

"You're crazy!" Ji shouted and laughed. "I am not interested, Dennis. Way too much money and trouble. You Yankees always big dreamers."

"You *will* be interested," Dennis replied calmly, "because if you don't take the offer, I already have somebody willing and able and knowing that with this weapon, will make FTW and other groups like it, go away real fast."

Ji stalled on the phone but agreed to get back to Dennis after he thought about it.

Arriving in Seattle, Dennis got in touch with Jared on the phone.

"What brings you to town, Dennis," Jared asked, surprise etching his voice.

"On a domestic assignment, nothing pressing. Are you guys available for some time over the next few days?"

Jared was taken aback. "Yeah, sure, Dennis; you never make time to see us. Are you getting married or you coming out of the closet?"

Dennis laughed. "None of the above, no. I just haven't spent much time with you guys and thought it was about time. Your kids will soon be married or something and I'll be wondering where the time went."

In mild shock, Jared invited him over to dinner that evening. None of the rest of the family knew about the cloning experiment and Jared reminded Dennis that it was still a secret between the three of them.

"Uncle Dennis, Uncle Dennis," the younger kids yelled as they ran for him and hugged him when he came through the door.

Jared had arranged for their parents – the whole family – to be there to welcome Dennis and have dinner with him while they would talk about old times and reconnect.

"Jared says you are in town for some domestic assignment, what's this all about, Dennis?" his dad asked.

"Oh, I'm just driving around looking for trouble," Dennis shrugged, casting a sideway glance at Jared.

"Okay, we understand. It is so great to see you home; you are looking pretty good, gaining a bit of a spare tire, too. You know, it's your mom's side of the family that has a real problem with weight gain, especially around the middle," his father chuckled.

"Jason here is turning out to be quite the basketball player as well as a great arm for pitching. He is one of the stars on his high school basket ball team, you know."

Jason blushed as he looked down. His dark hair, flashing brown eyes and chiseled features made him a magnet for the girls in his class.

"That's cool." Dennis grinned. "The girls must be knocking at your door."

"Yeah, he has more than a few; I would say the pick of the litter," Sally piped in.

Throughout the evening, they exchanged stories and laughed over things they used to do. Slowly Dennis loosened up a bit and began to feel safe around his family. He had only seen them a few times in the sixteen years since the clone experiment and he realized how much he missed them and cared for them. Jared and Sally's kids were so adorable that they had won his heart.

Later, after the parents had left and the kids were in bed, Jared and Dennis retreated alone in Jared's home office.

The TV was on with the volume down low and the eleven o'clock news was about to come on. Jared liked to watch the sports highlights reels that came later in the broadcast.

"How are you guys doing?" Dennis asked. "Your kids are great. Jason, my God, he seems pretty talented and good looking, too."

"Yeah, well, nothing special, with all the tests the lab ran on him, he is just another all-American boy. Even his DNA is nothing special. Sal and I really had our hopes pinned on him being, for lack of better words, superhuman. I don't mean like Superman or something, but there would be a definite difference. It has been really hard on Sally. She still believes in her theories of a disease-free world and perfect DNA. One day I hope we can repeat the experiment, but for now we are raising our family."

Jared leaned in toward Dennis, making sure there was no one listening.

"I still have part of the Ice Man frozen in captivity," he whispered and stopped, switching his gaze to the TV.

The newscaster had a picture of an ancient corpse behind him. Jared grabbed the remote control and cranked up the volume.

"*...he is believed to be the world's oldest, best preserved human,*" the newscaster went on. "*His remains were discovered by hikers high up in the Austrian Alps....*"

"Do you think there was a mix up in the nursery at the hospital or something?" asked Dennis, completely lost in thought and avoiding Jared's whisper.

"Ssshhhh," Jared cut-in, annoyed.

The anchorman continued, "*...Archaeologists have discovered personal ancient artifacts and clothing near the body along with a bow and arrows and even food.*" The camera showed a close up of the body from the head to toe.

A European correspondent reporting from the scene commented next, "*A bit of a strange twist to this find is that the man's genitals are missing. You can see how well preserved he is, notice how flexible the body is as he is moved from this icy grave.*"

He went on to describe the Schnalstal Glacier where he was discovered.

Jared jumped up, ran out to the door of the den and yelled, "This is him! They've discovered our Ice Man!" Sally heard him. "Sal, they have found Giuseppe our mountain man!"

Sally scurried to the den. "Whaaat? That's incredible! Who found him? When?" She looked at the screen then back at her husband.

"I guess they just found him where we left him. We'll have to get a newspaper and more details. This is amazing!" Jared turned the TV volume down.

"How do you know this is the same guy?" Dennis asked.

Jared growled, "Listen, how many ancient corpses have been discovered in the Alps … with missing private parts?"

Dennis looked from his brother to his sister-in-law. "So, what does this mean?"

"Well, this means we are potentially in a race against time by other cloning guys!" Jared cussed to himself.

"What makes you think there are others wanting to clone? I think you are being more than a little paranoid, dear brother."

"Possibly, but we need to get to work and try this again. I have a feeling there still has to be something different about the Ice Man."

Chapter 25

Completely out of character and all of a sudden finding a conscience, Dennis looking down like a little kid caught with his hand in a cookie jar, admitted, "Jared, Sally, I have to confess. I am in town on assignment to interview who maybe your experiment … errr… your lost son."

"Whaaat?" Jared and Sally exploded in unison.

"Don't get too excited," Dennis exclaimed, "I haven't met with him yet. I have to find a way to interview him without him knowing what's going on. You guys maybe able to help me since I have been trying to figure out how to get together with him. One of your kids could be the catalyst."

"Whoa, before we go there, how the hell did this all happen?" Jared raised his eyebrows.

Dennis explained the hospital connection and the potential for a baby mix-up and why the CIA had re-opened the case when the adopting family brought their kid to the adoption agency to trace down the birthing parents, because of his incurable and unstable mental conditions.

Sally was so excited she could hardly contain herself. "So they are saying he's different?"

"That's what the agency – the adoption agency – is saying," Dennis replied.

Jared shook his head. "Okay, Dennis, what happens if he really is what the CIA is looking for?"

"Well, I can't speak on their behalf, but I can tell you what I know from other operations. With a clone, they would pre-program them to be like automatons, you know, some would be clerks, some would be single minded agents, unable to be tempted by other foreign interests, some would be heartless killers with zero conscience. Still others would be the best information gatherers and if caught could pass any lie detector on earth. Still others would be, what we call cannon fodder, throw them up on the front lines and let them be gunned down as if they were a dime a dozen."

145

Shocked and disgusted, Sally and Jared were agape. "You mean, that's what they had planned for our boy all along? How come you never told us this, Dennis?"

A remorseful, teary-eyed Dennis squeaked out, "I'm truly sorry," while staring at the floor, "I never thought of that back sixteen years ago. I wanted to make a mark; I wanted to let the agency know I was not only an asset, but a hero and a great agent. When they found out that your Jason was normal, they almost fired me. I was sent back to file clerk for quite awhile. I hated my job, I hated the CIA, and I started to hate our society. What the CIA does in other parts of the world in the name of protecting American ideals and big business, you wouldn't want to know." Dennis wiped the tears streaming down his face with his sleeve, all the while sniffling like a little baby. "I haven't cried in years. Don't know what's come over me. Ever since I saw you and your kids and Mom and Dad and how happy you guys are, it hit me how much I have missed. I wanted to be the rock, the cool guy with an elusive lifestyle."

There was an empty silence as Jared and Sally looked at each other and over to Dennis.

Their minds raced. The plans that had been shelved sixteen years previously could be resurrected once more.

Jared got out of his chair, went to sit beside his brother, and wrapped an arm around his shoulders. Dennis was slouched over, staring at the floor.

"Dennis, we'll help you with this kid," Jared said calmly while looking at Sally, nodding in approval.

"How can we be sure that he is not going to end up in one of those situations?" Sally asked.

"Oh, I can fake my way through this...." Dennis sat up with renewed confidence. "Mind if I smoke?"

"Yes, as a matter of fact we do," Sally said. "When are you going to kick that awful habit?"

"Do you know his name and where he lives?" Jared asked.

"Yes, his name is Caleb Lindstrom and he lives on the south side. We need to see how we could get Jason and Caleb together."

The whole evening, they worked out a plan whereby they would wire Jason with a "bug" and get him to go to the Lindstroms' door as a surveyor, canvassing for a local sports charity. Part of the survey was having a meet-and-greet with a famous basketball "star" the next night at a local hotel. This way they could get Caleb in front of Dennis alone. They agreed to descend upon the Lindstroms' place the next evening just before dinner.

The next day, as planned, Dennis, with Jared and Jason as passengers, drove his rental car to the Lindstroms' home and in his enthusiasm failed to notice he had been followed. It was an early Seattle spring day with heavy clouds blocking the setting sun. Darkness had already started to fall.

They parked a few blocks from the Lindstroms' residence and Dennis wired Jason with a microphone and transmitter. The teenager was equipped with a clipboard and some questions that Caleb needed to answer. The vehicle that had followed them was parked across the street, facing them.

Just as they arrived, Bob Lindstrom arrived home and parked his car in the garage.

"Perfect," said Dennis, "this way we can have the whole family involved. We may have to come back, but this way we will have some idea what and who we are dealing with."

After a couple of rehearsals, Jason was ready. He was a confident young man. He made his way to the door and rang the doorbell.

Bob answered the door and let Jason in.

Dennis and Jared could hear the conversation. Jason apologized for the late notice and asked if Caleb would be interested in the meet-and-greet the next night. Caleb hesitated at first and there was a pause interrupted by Jason's enthusiastic salesmanship.

At that very instant, two men got out of the van parked across the street and headed toward the front door.

"Wonder who those guys are," Dennis thought aloud.

"Could be guests," Jared replied.

Dennis cussed a streak. "I should have known it, dammit! We've been followed and set up. Let's hope for their sake this Caleb is the right guy."

"What's going on, Dennis?" Jared asked in alarm.

"We could be witnessing a kidnapping," Dennis snapped back.

"Kidnapping?" Jared yelled as he reached for the car door handle. "My kid is in there…. Do something, Dennis."

Without giving his brother an answer, Dennis coolly locked the doors.

Jared frantically tried to get the passenger one opened. "Damn you, Dennis, let me out of here…."

"Hang on, little brother; let me call the man…"

Jared stared while the CIA man picked up his mobile phone from the box between the front seats and dialed Ji, turning down the "bug" receiver.

"What the heck are you doing, Ji?" Dennis asked matter-of-factly as he surrendered to the situation and slumped back into the seat.

Sounds of laughter could be heard at the other end of the phone as Ji answered.

"I figure if you want big money this guy must be worth it, Mr. Dennis!"

"Well, *Mr.* Ji," Dennis replied, "nobody knows if this is the right one, you know."

"Come on, Dennis," Ji sneered, "you expect me to believe a Cracker Jack spy like you would be wrong?"

"I have been wrong before. If I were you, I would call your guys off until you know for certain this is the right guy." Dennis got out of the car and started walking toward the house with Ji still on the phone. "I'm on the way to your guys. Do you want me to start shooting?"

"I wouldn't do that if I were you. Look at the van where they came from," Ji replied.

Dennis wheeled around staring down at an M16 with a silencer, aiming at him from the van.

"Are you in the van?"

Ji laughed, "Are you kidding? Why would I risk reputation? I have good workers, they listen well, I tell them what I learn from you – you good teacher, Mr. Dennis."

"Cut the crap, Ji, call your men off before we all get embarrassed," Dennis snapped.

"You cut crap, damn Yankee," Ji retorted boldly. "I am in control now. I want boy. Allah is great!"

"You can't get away with this, Ji. There will be police all over this place in a minute." He clicked the OFF button on the phone.

It was too late; the gun toting kidnappers had forced their way into the house. There was a lot of commotion going on as they yelled out their demands.

At that moment, a car drove slowly toward Dennis through the quiet neighborhood. He used it as a cover to run quickly toward the Lindstroms' house.

Having heard all he could gather from the conversation between Dennis and this Ji guy – going completely off his head when he saw his brother crossing the street gun in hand – Jared literally flew out the rental car and ran toward the house. He didn't care one iota if he got shot in the process; his son was in that house and he needed to get to him before it was too late.

As they both reached the front door at the same time, the sniper got out of the van and yelled at them to freeze or he'd shoot. He tried hard not to draw attention to himself and slowly walked toward them with a nine mm pistol dangling at his side.

"Go ahead, go on in," the gunman said. Dennis and Jared had the frozen, deer-in-headlights look. "I said get in the house or die on the street."

Dennis thought about every angle to get out of this one. He had been in similar situations before. The most recent was in Columbia where he was working on a drug cartel take-down and he had sold off information of a major raid to a high ranking cartel official. The official's bodyguards didn't know that he was a double agent and he ended up being kidnapped, and spent several days in a secret hideout somewhere in the Columbian jungle. His only way out was to bribe one of the guards to speak to his boss to let him know of his plight. The cartel official had Dennis released immediately and apologized for the incident.

Dennis knew this was way more complex and had to play it by ear.

The three of them entered the house as they witnessed the Lindstrom family, along with Jason, being hand-cuffed with zap-straps and their mouths duct-taped by the two original captors.

All the while, the captors talked in what sounded like an Asian language.

"Are you okay, son?" asked Jared.

Jason nodded.

"Is this your son?" one of the kidnappers asked. "That's why you almost die."

Next thing Dennis and Jared were zap-strapped and duct-taped, too. Dennis's gun and phone were confiscated on the spot.

"Where are keys to car in garage?" asked the man facing Bob. "Tell me!" He grabbed and ripped the duct-tape off Bob's mouth.

Bob winced in pain from his five o'clock shadow being up-rooted. "What in blazes is going…? Over on the wall by the door. The ones with the leather holder."

The captor quickly re-taped Bob's mouth as he tried to speak behind the tape.

Another man left the house and the other grabbed the keys, opened the garage door and drove Bob's car out while his companion drove the van into the garage.

The lone captor waved his pistol toward the garage and ordered the Lindstroms, along with Jason, into the van, while the van driver kept a drawn pistol on Dennis and Jared. Once the four of them were loaded into the van, they pulled out of the garage.

Since Dennis and Jared had left the rental car so quickly, the keys were still in it. One of the captors drove it in the garage and the two brothers were forced into it at gun point.

One of the men then drove Bob's car back into the garage after the rental car was driven out. He then closed the garage door and let himself out through a side door.

One kidnapper drove the van with his accomplice, the Lindstroms with Caleb and Jason, and the third drove the rental car.

They went a few blocks then suddenly stopped. The gunmen then tied black scarves over their captives' eyes and continued on the journey.

Several hours later they stopped and exited their vehicles inside a large, dark warehouse.

The kidnappers removed the black scarves, shoved their live booty out of the vehicles and up a few steps into a windowless, paint-chipped, twelve-by-ten room with nothing but a sixty watt light bulb dangling from the ceiling and some old wooden chairs strewn around. It smelled like a wet blanket mixed with rotting vinyl and seemed to be part of the old warehouse or factory. There was another door immediately to the left that was locked.

The door slammed behind them and was locked. Another vehicle rumbled into the garage, the motor was shut off and doors slammed. Muffled dialogue could be heard in the room. The sound of a vehicle starting up and more doors slamming, and then they heard the car drive away.

Keys rattled in the lock of the door, the door opened and in walked three gun-toting men in balaclavas and military fatigues – obviously different from the first three. They motioned to the captives to back away from the door and to turn around to face it. Another smaller figure entered the room. He looked a midget besides the other men. He was wearing a Che Guevara hat, large dark glasses, and military fatigues with an open shirt and large, black, army boots that definitely seemed a size too big for him.

"Welcome to my abode, gringos," he said with a smirk on his face. "I would like to talk individually with you, but I can see you are all tongue tied," he cackled. "If we all co-operate, no one will get hurt. There is no room for error; we will kill you like dogs if you disobey." He paused. "What am I here for, you may be thinking. There is one person here who is very special to us, and the rest of you, well, are worth bargaining dollars. The more we have the more bargaining dollars we can get to complete a very ambitious experiment."

Dennis was furious, both at himself and at the situation. Never before had he allowed himself to get into a kidnapping situation. He had never met Ji face to face – they had only talked on the phone – but he was convinced this must be him. He also knew these were master killers and nothing would stop them from slitting throats or beheading any one of them in front of a camera for money or a cause.

"We will now introduce you to your home away from home." Ji gestured toward the second door. One of the gunmen unlocked and opened it while one of the other gunmen got around their hostages. Behind the six of them, he herded them into an area with several large rooms leading off in different directions. There were cots, laboratory equipment and food supplies strewn throughout the rooms amongst garbage, paper and dust. There was only one small, dirty window located high on one of the walls – it was barred.

They noticed the door being locked behind them and the gunmen frisked each one carefully, gathering keys, and other personal belongings before removing the duct-tapes and zap-straps. There were yelps of pain as the duct-tapes were removed. The gunmen kept their weapons pointed at the six hostages.

"No use yelling for help, you are far from civilization," Ji stated calmly. "Oh yes, there is toilet around corner." He pointed in the direction. Diane immediately scurried toward it with one of the gunmen following.

"What the hell have you got us all here for and who the hell are you," Bob blurted out, while he rubbed his tender face where the duct-tape had sealed his mouth.

"I don't have to answer that – but I want to know *you*," Ji said. He walked over to Caleb to grab his arm. "You come with me." Caleb recoiled like a leopard.

"Aren't we jumpy!" Ji exclaimed as he leapt toward him to re-grab him. Caleb moved like lightning around his attackers and knocked one of them down. Bob lunged toward the other one just as he stepped into him with a knee to his gut. Bob folded up groaning.

"Hey, no funny stuff!" Ji shouted as he pulled a pistol out of his belt. "We are not going to harm your son; we need him for a test."

Ji took hold of Caleb and arm-wrestled him out of the room with the young man twisting and turning around, looking back at his dad moaning on his hands and knees. Ji took him into another room while the rest were left with the two, now nervous, AK-47-toting guards.

Dennis and Jared picked Bob up and sat him down on a dirt-crusted chair.

"Don't try any heroics here," Dennis ordered, "these guys will slit your throat in a heartbeat."

"Where's Caleb? What happened to you, Honey?" Diane asked as she returned from the bathroom. "Who are you guys? Can someone tell me what's going on?"

"Your son is off in another room," Dennis said. He was standing by a groaning Bob who clutched his groin. He looked at the floor and then to Diane. "Your husband will be okay." He paused. "Please, before I go on, I repeat, our kidnappers mean business, do not try anything stupid. I'm afraid this is all my fault. I came to your place…, err…, *we* came to your home to talk with your son and some guys followed us." He looked up at the two armed-guards still with their balaclavas on and guns drawn.

"This is really my fault…," Jared countered.

"Let me speak," Dennis cut him off in mid-sentence. "What we have here is a case of mistaken identity. These guys think there is something special about your son that they want – for whatever reason. I would like to talk to the leader of this before this goes too far." He looked over to the gunmen and asked if he could talk to their leader. The gunmen didn't move. "Understand English?" There was a pause as the guards looked at each other. Dennis made motions with his hands and mouth. One of the gunmen left the room. In a few moments, he returned, and motioned to Dennis to follow him.

He was ushered into an office where Ji and Caleb were located. An open door led into another room full of all kinds of lab equipment and guys dressed in white lab gear. There were high-tech gas masks and strange looking devices. Ji got up and quickly closed the door.

"So, Mr. Dennis, we finally meet face to face." Ji reached out his boney hand.

Ji was a small Asian man with a stringy Fu-Manchu moustache and a large scar by his left eye, which made him look naturally evil. His Indonesian upbringing drove him to make money, and just like Dennis, he, too, was disgruntled with his native society as well as capitalism. He had learned very early that in order to get ahead in life he had to bully his way, stopping at nothing to get what he wanted. He was very charismatic, and attracted uneducated Muslim radicals out of the Jakarta slums. He knew how to get funding for his latest venture: FTW, a movement to eliminate exploitation of farmers in the Third world, by kidnapping heads of large agricultural conglomerates and demanding return of stolen land back to their original owners. He also supplied crews for international drug and arms smuggling. His reward was more funding from Middle East money and international drug cartels. He spared no punches with ghastly videos of slit throats and beheadings if demands weren't made immediately. He had garnered a large reward from international agencies for his arrest. He knew he had little time to do something big before the CIA would arrest him or eliminate him. His latest venture consisted of a form of bio-terrorism. His goal was to release a deadly air-born toxic cloud over an unsuspecting major American city and wipe out every living thing in it. The demand was to demobilize the US military from their various command posts around the world. He also wanted all American-owned companies to surrender to the governments of the countries where they were present. His policy was to shoot first and ask questions later.

His lab in Jakarta had already produced a form of the toxic, virulent bacteria, far stronger than Anthrax or other known "boutique" bacteria. Any prevailing wind could carry the bacterial cloud. Fuelled by its oxygen-eating propellant, once the bacteria had reached its target, it would lather inside the lungs' pleurae with an invisible cloak, and suffocation would be mercilessly imminent. Only certain types of gas masks combined with a special antidote would qualify as protection.

"So it is you, Ji," Dennis growled, not bothering to extend his hand. "What the hell do you think you are doing? These are innocent people; this young man has nothing to offer you!" He looked over at Caleb sitting calmly across the room.

"Oh, we will find out soon enough. If he has been cloned, he is exactly what we need." Ji smiled wickedly. "We have big plans for boy. We want to clone him for our trump card. We create super human race that will be unstoppable."

Dennis hadn't wanted Caleb to hear that. He glanced over at his *nephew*. The latter remained mute and visibly shocked.

It had hit Caleb like a brick as he slumped back into his dirty chair; he now knew he was a prize. The Ice Man he had just seen on TV, the dreams, his differences from everyone else – he had been cloned. He sat there, stunned by what he had been hearing. His own thoughts swirled like a high-speed blender. Darby, his family, his career, and his whole life were flashing before him. How was he going to get out of this, he wondered.

"So what are you going to do to the kid?" Dennis asked. "What if he *is* a clone?"

"All we need is simple blood test," Ji replied.

Ji summoned the guard to get a lab technician and in Indonesian, he instructed him to get a needle. The technician returned with a needle, tourniquet, and some vials and drew some blood from Caleb's arm.

Ji then instructed the guard in Indonesian to take them back with the rest.

As soon as the door was opened for them, Caleb ran to his mom and dad and hugged them. He blurted some comforting words and sat beside them once again.

Dennis then asked one of the guards for a drink of water and the guard did not respond. He asked again, neither one responded.

"So, I heard that your boss is a faggot. He's gay, right?" No response from the guards.

"I heard both you guys are gay and you love pigs?" No response.

"Heads up everyone, either these guys are bluffing or they don't understand English."

All of a sudden, both guards looked at their watches, got up and proceeded to leave the room, locking the door behind them.

"We were scared to speak, Dennis," Jared whispered.

"So what is going on?" Bob and Diane piped up in hush tones.

"This is my turn to speak," Jared said. "Introductions: this is my brother, Dennis, and son Jason and my name is Jared. And you are Bob and Diane Lindstrom and Caleb, I believe. Did you folks see the news on TV the other day of the find of the old man on the glacier?" They all nodded. "Seventeen years ago my wife to be at the time, Sally, and I – fresh out of college – decided to go to Europe for a final trip before settling into a job or more education. We ended up on a hiking trip and we actually discovered this ancient Ice Man, back then. We are both biologists and we wanted to study DNA and cloning. I presently teach biology at Western Washington and am actively involved in the human Genome project. My wife, Sally, was and still is convinced that our early ancestors had a superior DNA and held the key to eradicating disease. There are other potential benefits such as a longer life and maybe even higher intelligence."

Jared went on, "What we did when we discovered the old man, is remove his genitals and when we returned home, we found useable stem cells which we were able to create…, well, for lack of better words, a test tube baby. Through in-vitro, Sally became the mother of the first cloned human. I know it wasn't right, but at the time I was young and ambitious and it seemed to be the thing to do. She gave birth at the Seattle Memorial Hospital to a perfectly normal baby boy. Somehow, to this day, we don't know how, but there was a baby mix up and we ended up raising Jason here, who has been an amazing kid and we are not disappointed with him in the least. And by the looks of it, you have had the privilege of raising the world's first human clone, the descendant of a five-thousand-year-old man," Jared concluded, directing his last comments to Bob and Diane.

They were in obvious shock. Everything that had transpired in their lives, with the raising of Caleb and all his abilities and dreams, all of a sudden made sense in a way they hadn't imagined. They were relieved on the one hand, but in wonder on the other.

"What does this mean and why are we here?" Diane asked.

"My turn," Dennis piped up. "I work for the federal government on an international level and have contacts all over the world. One of my contacts happens to be Ji here. We go back a few years. I have helped him out with things and he has helped me out. Unfortunately, he is really mixed up with major underworld activities." Dennis tried hard not to make himself look bad. "And I had confided in him about the possibilities of having a human clone connection and he jumped all over it..., umm..., us, immediately. I'm not sure why he is so massively interested in Caleb; that is one thing nobody here knows."

"Well..., human cloning has many implications," Jared began to explain. "Clones can be programmed for good or evil. They can also be great living laboratory specimens, and in Caleb's case I suspect there may be a vast treasure house of things no one knows anything about yet."

Jared couldn't take his eyes off Caleb, he studied every part of his face and hands and structure. He could see a lot of Sally in his physical make up, the high cheekbones, the slender hands, the long neck, the shape of his nose. But his olive colored skin, penetrating turquoise eyes and dark hair were certainly characteristics from the Ice Man.

"I believe I know what is going on here," Caleb whispered. "They have built some kind of super bacteria bomb, something to wipe out a bunch of people. I can read minds and that is what I have picked up so far. I think the leader wants to clone me and create some kind of evil, super race. He took some blood from me to check my DNA. I could pick up from his thoughts that he needs a specialized lab to check that all out to develop his clones. He is not a nice man."

The room was hushed; not exactly an atmosphere for what should have been a fantastic family reunion.

"Can you block thoughts? Can you speak thoughts into someone else's mind?" Jared asked.

"I can't block thoughts, but I am learning to speak into someone else's thoughts, I have to be very careful 'cause it startles most people when they hear a voice in their head and not in their ears."

"Just like this…." Caleb switched to telepathy. "Nod your heads if you are hearing this." Dennis, Jared and Jason looked at each other in a sudden shock and nodded affirmatively as they heard it in their minds. Diane and Bob smiled.

"Isn't that some sort of psychic power?" Dennis asked.

"Psychics and others call it ESP. I don't believe what I have is some mystical power, but rather a natural gift, and now that I know who my ancient father is, I believe at one time, all of mankind communicated this way; there was no need for any one outward spoken language; they came after the Tower of Babel."

Chapter 26

Meanwhile, Sally was now quite concerned. It was well past midnight and she had no idea where the Lindstroms lived. She paced the floor with her mind racing. Should she call the police to see if there had been any accidents reported? Should she call or drive to the Lindstroms place? She opened the massive Seattle and area telephone book and was relieved to find only four Lindstroms listed and wrote down all their addresses and phone numbers to call in the morning.

"This is crazy," she said aloud, "I've got to get some sleep." She set her alarm for the usual 7:00AM call. With the cordless phone on Jared's pillow, Sally got ready for bed and tried to get some sleep. The night dragged on and her heart pounded louder at every beat. After what seemed like an eternity, she drifted off in an uneasy sleep from sheer exhaustion. The alarm brought her out of a horrible nightmare of Jared and Jason in some kidnapping situation.

Sally got her other three children breakfast and ready for school. She fabricated a story that their father and Jason decided to stay overnight at a friend's place. She looked and felt like she had been hit by a truck. Her stomach was in a knot and her heart was still pounding. She was washing the dishes when the phone rang. She literally jumped out of her skin. She wiped her hands on the towel and picked up the receiver – her hands shaking.

It was a friend and she asked to call her back the next day.

Sally knew her stalwart man very well and her gut told her he was in some kind of trouble.

She drove her children to school and came home to make calls to the Lindstroms out of the phone book. Two of the Lindstroms that answered were unrelated and another one went to an answering machine with a young female voice. The last one listed as an R. Lindstrom, she dialed, the answering machine picked up and the woman's cheerful voice said, "You have reached the residence of Bob, Diane and Caleb, we are unable to come to the phone, leave your message after the tone." Sally knew this was the right place and the tone came and went waiting for a message. She hung up in a bit of a trance, fearing the worst.

She dug out a map and drove to the Lindstroms' residence. She drove slowly into their secluded driveway and waited in the car for a while to see if anyone noticed her. Cautiously she opened the car door and lifted her statuesque frame out of the seat. All the while with her heart racing; she looked intently at her surroundings.

As she walked up to the door, the daily newspaper wrapped in plastic, was leaning up against the front door. She rang the door bell several times and there was no answer. She tried the fancy brass door latch and the door opened freely. She left the paper outside.

"Hello, hello, anyone home?" Sally asked nervously. Then hesitantly she walked in to the spacious foyer. Her ears were tuned for any noise, but the silence was deafening. Her shoe heels clattered across the wooden flooring and echoed throughout as she made her way into the bowels of the house. Walking toward the kitchen, she glanced at neatly framed pictures of the Lindstroms on the walls of the living room. She was drawn to a familiar looking clipboard on the kitchen table and remembered that one of the guys had given it to Jason to use in their plot to approach Caleb. As she picked it up she immediately recognized the handwriting. She also noticed there were three place settings ready for a meal and food was still on the stove.

She wasn't sure if she was in a trap or completely alone. As there were no other sounds, she felt a little more at peace. She jumped as the phone rang. Eventually the answering machine came on, "This is Doctor Schellenberg confirming tonight's video shoot and interview. The crew will be arriving about six thirty and…" Sally knew she had to pick up the phone. "Hi there, …um, sorry to interrupt your message but I don't think the Lindstroms will be home for your meeting."

"Who is this?" Schellenberg quickly asked gruffly.

"My name is Sally Houghton, you don't know me and I know I shouldn't be answering strangers' phones but I believe the Lindstroms have been kidnapped."

"Kidnapped?" Schellenberg exclaimed. "How preposterous! I spoke with Caleb yesterday."

"What time?" Sally asked. "I believe the kidnapping happened around dinner time. My husband and son, and brother-in-law came here to meet with Caleb just before dinner and it is still on the stove.

I never heard from them after they left home which is not like my husband. I was worried sick and decided to drive over here. I found the front door open, no one home and just before you called, I found a clipboard with my son's handwriting, lying on the kitchen table. You have to understand, I do not know the Lindstroms, but I am Caleb's birth mother."

"You are his birth mother?" Schellenberg was stunned. "I interviewed Caleb briefly a couple of days ago and what a remarkable young man. I have hired a professional crew and was going to videotape an extended interview with Caleb tonight and that is what prompted this confirmation call. I was thinking of contacting you, his birth parents to be part of the interview, Mrs. Houghton…"

"Call me Sally."

"Yes, well, Sally…, what do you know about Caleb?"

"Seeing as we *just* discovered that he lives here, I know little, but I understand he has special abilities," Sally replied.

"He is very unique, Mrs. Houghton. He has an incredible insight into a pre-flood world. He has supernatural abilities, like reading minds, like communicating with animals and other things we were about to find out in the interview."

"A pre-flood world – do you mean the flood in the Bible?" Sally asked.

"Yes," Schellenberg replied. "Dinosaurs, large foliage and lots of water. I could go on, but I think we need to find everyone. Do you have any idea where they might be?"

"Not a clue. My next call is to the police."

"Perhaps I can help. I am staying at the Ramada a few blocks from the Lindstroms. I can be there in a few minutes."

Just as they hung up, the phone rang and once again it went to the answering machine. A worried young girl's voice came over the speaker. "Hi, Caleb, it's me, wondering where you are. Jonathan came by to pick you up this morning and you weren't there. Don't forget we are supposed to meet Jessica and Randy at the library at three-forty-five. Oh yes, am I supposed to be there for the big interview tonight? Bye."

Sally couldn't resist and picked up the phone again. "Hi, heard your call come in and thought I should pick up. My name is Sally Houghton and I am at your boyfriend's house. I think something strange has happened to the family. Try not to panic." Sally paused. "I think I can use your help."

"What's going on?" a very shocked Darby asked. "Of course, I will help, are you the police?"

"No, you may not believe this, but I am Caleb's birth mother. Through a series of rather bizarre events, we have come in contact with him for the first time. I have not met him or his adoptive family yet. I believe they, along with my husband and son, have been kidnapped. I came here to look for them and found an empty house."

"This is weird," Darby said. "This is not like this family at all. Have you contacted the police? Look, I will leave school right now and come over."

"Please do not tell anyone about this, I maybe wrong and would not want to embarrass you or anyone else. Just so you know; the fellow who is doing the interview tonight is on his way over as well," Sally concluded somewhat abruptly and hung up the phone.

Sally felt strange being in somebody else's house and was worried she could be an accessory to the kidnapping.

A vehicle pulled into the driveway and she quickly clattered her way through the silent house, each step creating big echoes off the walls, to the front door.

When Sally opened the door, Schellenberg stood looking at her for a moment before saying, "Jeffery Schellenberg, call me Jeff." He held his hand out, puffing. "Excuse me, I'm a little winded…, I tried to get here as quickly as possible."

"Sally Houghton. Sorry for the cold hand." She grabbed his hand, her face taut from worry. "I hope we can get to the bottom of this, after we spoke, Caleb's girl friend called and I answered, again, which I felt funny doing in a stranger's home. Anyway, she is on the way over from school, I think she can be of assistance."

They stood in the foyer after Schellenberg closed the front door.

"What kind of doctor are you?" Sally asked.

"Theology," Schellenberg replied. "I specialize in creation science. I met Caleb and his family at a local church after one of my seminars. He lit up like a Christmas tree when I talked about the great flood and dinosaurs, and afterwards we talked and then it was me who lit up about his knowledge of the old world. I came over for dinner that night and that is when we decided to do a professional video interview. Why do you think they have been kidnapped?"

Darrell Swanson

"Well...." Sally paused. "I don't want to get into details, but I do know that because of a recent incident with my brother-in-law, who works for the C..., well..., government, I do know that he uncovered something unusual about Caleb through the adoption agency."

Another vehicle arrived in the driveway; it was Darby, who quickly stepped up to the front door. Schellenberg let her in and introductions were made as she ushered herself into the foyer.

"Have you called the police yet?" Darby asked eyes red from crying and puffing from her sprint up the long driveway.

"No," Sally replied. "Before we all get too hysterical, I thought we would do some detective work of our own to see if there is some evidence of a kidnapping. When was the last contact you had with Caleb?"

"Around 4:30 yesterday afternoon. Caleb was pretty excited about doing this interview. I had to cut the conversation short as I was helping mom with dinner." Darby wiped her eyes with a tissue that she had pulled out of her jacket pocket. "Then I tried calling later and there was no answer, I think it was around eight."

"In your estimation, would there be any reason for the whole family to be kidnapped?" Schellenberg asked.

"Oh Heavens no," Darby exclaimed. "This is a church going family. Caleb's father is an insurance agent, he sells all types, health, life, you know, like..., a salesman. His mom doesn't work. If anyone would be kidnapped, it would be Caleb." She started sobbing again. "He is very special, very unique; I hope nothing has happened to him."

Sally put her arms around her shoulders and brought her close to her. "Now, now, it will be okay, you obviously care for him very much, and together we will find him."

Schellenberg went through the house from top to bottom, making sure they weren't tied up in the basement, or in another room, looking for clues. He went into the garage through the door by the kitchen and found Bob's keys in the ignition. He never touched them, thinking about potential fingerprints.

"I think we should call the police," Schellenberg said, coming back in from the garage. "We may be sacrificing precious time trying to be detectives."

He called the police and shortly two cars arrived, a regular squad car and an unmarked one. Four officers came to the door. Two with

162

drawn guns burst there way through the front door, startling the three people inside, while two others remained outside.

Two officers took down statements from Sally, Jeff Schellenberg and Darby while the other two searched the premises.

Once all of the questions had been asked and all of the answers written down, one of the officers concluded, "The main thing with this is that the FBI will be responsible for the case from here on in. They have been contacted and are on the way over. We have to turn ya'll over to the Feds. Kidnapping is, well…, a federal offence and they are the only ones allowed to handle this. They're gonna ask you the same questions all over again and then some."

Three FBI officers arrived in an unmarked car and were debriefed by the police in another room away from Darby, Sally and Jeff Schellenberg. After several minutes, the head FBI agent, a tall, bald African-American, entered the kitchen.

"Greetings, my name is Darnell Conor. I am with the Federal Bureau of Investigation and me, along with my two partners here, are sorry to hear of this unpleasant event. Because of the nature and the potential size of this, we must first verify that this is not some hoax. We are treating this very seriously. The military has been alerted, and once we are through here with you, we will determine if and when the White House will get involved. If we feel this is some two-bit underground punk trying to act big, then we will keep it low-key and not instill fear and panic into the general population. However, if it is for real, then we have a large challenge on our hands. We hope we can help locate their whereabouts in a timely fashion and bring everyone home."

They went through introductions and immediately started their investigation from where the police had left off. His two colleagues followed him closely, taking notes or making phone calls.

Conor then ushered Schellenberg, Sally and Darby into the living room. They sat on the over stuffed furniture that was comfortably laid out for intimate conversations.

"Just so that we can rule out local foul play, who here was the last person to see the Lindstrom family?" Conor asked.

"I did," Darby replied. "I saw Caleb as he was leaving school."

"Were they planning any vacations or time away?"

"No, not to my knowledge. I am Caleb's girlfriend and like, he tells me what the family is up to. They take their vacations in the summer, and usually head north to Canada."

"They don't take vacations other times of the year?"

"Rarely, they may go skiing for a few days in the winter, but certainly not at this time of year."

Conor turned to Sally. "I see you are Caleb Lindstrom's birth mother, Sally Houghton. Besides the obvious, what other vested interest do you have in all this?"

Sally opened her mouth and closed it again. The abruptness of the question and its implied accusations rubbed her the wrong way. "My 'vested interests' as you call it, Agent Conor, are quite obvious, I should think! My husband and son and brother-in-law have been kidnapped with the Lindstroms." Sally paused annoyingly. "I thought you would have that written down already because I have told the police officers."

Meanwhile, Schellenberg was observing the exchange with interest. He had already noted the resemblance between Caleb and his mother, but now, her attitude and character traits became the obvious similarities between her and her son, which he had observed in Caleb.

"Oh, that is interesting. How did they get involved?" Conor asked, all the while looking down and writing notes on his pad.

Sally sighed and repeated the story to Conor.

Conor, a seasoned FBI agent, finished his interview and they all sat in an uncomfortable silence while he reviewed his notes. After several minutes, he scratched his baldhead and began, "I'm having some difficulty with this. The son, Caleb, he is adopted, he is different, and the apparent target of a kidnapping. Your brother-in-law, Dennis, works for some government agency of which nobody seems to know anything about; the Lindstroms are innocent parents and your husband and son got pulled into some kind of strange sting operation. Too many holes and unanswered questions. I'm going to start all over, I need more information."

Before he started, he excused himself and along with his agents, went into another room and he debriefed them with plans of action.

Conor scratched his head and folded his arms while pacing the floor. "I have no idea where to begin here. I don't think there is any foul play. This Dennis character has me intrigued. One of you guys do a search on a Dennis Houghton, he could be from one of ten thousand government departments; hell, he could even be one of us."

One of the younger agents in his thirties piped up, "What about the older guy? He seems a little too smug or something, I dunno, why is he hanging around?"

"He's a theologian, preacher, some kind of religious guy. I think he is sincere, it says here he was supposed to interview the kid tonight," Conor stated while reading off his notes. "Look, my gut tells me these guys are all innocent. Any news on the phone trace?"

"Looks like it may have come from a payphone and they are back checking the lines," the other agent concluded.

"Can you get prints off these guys, Smith?" Conor ordered as he continued to work on his report.

They did all things they needed to do to keep records correct and satisfy procedure.

After several hours, they decided to let Sally go and attend to her children. Jeff and Darby stayed and offered to make something to eat while they waited for answers. The minutes dragged into hours while Conor and the other agents kept in constant contact with their home office. As the day dragged on....

Chapter 27

Somewhere near an abandoned warehouse on the outskirts of Portland....

"Come back here, Buddy, you little stinker!" The two year old yellow lab bolted after something through a hole in the chain-linked fence and bounded through the litter of the sprawling industrial property. The run down buildings located a fair distance from the main road, seemed to loom up reluctantly out of the weed ridden, cracked and faded asphalt resulting from years of neglect.

The ten-year-old kid got off his bike and while pushing it, he tried to find an entrance large enough to breach the barbed wire re-enforced, eight-foot-high fence surrounding the property.

"Here, Bud, here, Bud," he called out as he surveyed the fence for openings. His dog was nowhere to be seen.

He quickly got back on his bike and pedaled hard toward the gate at the main entrance. It appeared locked, but when he pushed on it, it easily slid open. He pushed a little harder and squeezed himself and his bicycle through the opening. Back on his bike, he pedaled furiously in the direction his dog disappeared. As he approached the buildings, he slowed down and a little fear started to set in as he realized he was all alone amongst some abandoned buildings.

"Here Bud..., here Bud...! Where are you?" he called out again in a subdued, nervous voice that echoed back from the silent buildings. He pedaled ever so slowly, gyrating his head back and forth, looking for his dog and any other movement. He was now both angry at his dog and creeped out by the quiet, ominous surroundings.

Suddenly, from around the corner of a building, just in front of him, his dog barked and started to whine. He stood up on the pedals and pumped as hard as he could. He rounded the corner and there was Buddy in a large, covered loading bay area, pawing at a small door leading into what would have been formerly a receiving area.

Buddy's bark and whining echoed ominously in the darkened loading bay. The dog would stop barking, whining abruptly and cocking his head as if he heard something from behind the door. He then started barking furiously and became very animated, his blond tail wagging uncontrollably.

"Bud…? What is it? Come on let's go," the kid yelled from outside the bay. The dog wasn't about to go anywhere, he kept repeating his little act and looking back at his master as if to say, "*Hey, get over here, there is something goin' on behind that door.*"

The kid knew he had to get his dog, leash him and haul him out of there. Scared half to death, he rode toward the darkened, rusted stairs leading up to his dog. The dog was now even more agitated knowing he had his master's attention. Bobby grabbed the dog and quickly secured the leash to his collar. As he turned around to leave, a voice said, "*Help, we are inside.*" The kid froze. "Who said that?" His voice echoed back in the dark loading bay.

The voice said, "*If you can hear me, I am not speaking out loud, you are hearing me in your mind. There are six of us inside. We have been kidnapped. We need help.*"

This freaked Bobby out. He stumbled down the dark stairs and with his dog now leashed, he hopped on his bike and pedaled as hard as he could, with his dog straining to keep up back to the main gate. Quickly exiting the abandoned property and closing the gate, he *flew* home to the condominium development where he and his single mother, and two siblings lived, which was about a mile south.

Between hard gasps, he told his mother everything that happened.

"I swear, I never heard a voice with my ears!" he exclaimed. "Mom, it was freaky. I really think there is somebody in there. You should have seen Buddy, he was going crazy."

His mother, who was busy wiping down the kitchen counters, a recent divorcee, mother of three kids and looking for work amongst everything else in her life, had a lot more important things on her mind.

"Bobby, you have a way too big imagination," she casually replied, shaking her head, wringing out the cloth in the sink. "You're tellin' me you heard a voice in your mind…. First, I ask you to walk the dog, which you don't like to do, and *then* you end up with this cock-and-bull story. The last story you came up with, was almost believable, except one of the Smith kids saw you at the pool when you said you were walking Bud over in the park." She paused. "I can't trust your story, Bobby…. Look, I need you to help your sister carry some of her boxes in the basement up to her room."

"Mom, I swear, this is no story. I was too scared to go in there."

"OK…." She stopped cleaning the kitchen counters and focused her gaze on her son, hoping to call his bluff. "I think you need a man, someone with authority who will check this out for you. Umm…, I think I know the perfect guy – Dan the cop, over in unit seventeen, I'm sure he would be up to it."

Bobby never flinched while he stood like a wide-eyed statue staring at his mother. His mom made arrangements with the cop to take Bobby into the industrial park first thing in the morning. As it was a Saturday, Bobby was out of school and Dan happened to be off.

****

The vehicles pulled into the receiving bay area, up the ramp and inside the warehouse. Ji and his entourage unloaded supplies and made their way into the office and makeshift lab. They had driven the long distance and dropped their first video tape off at a Seattle TV station, showing the captives and outlining their demands. The two Indonesian guards told Ji about the barking dog incident and he became very angry and agitated, flailing his arms around, and reamed them both out for not killing the dog and the kid.

Everything else, it seemed, was going as planned for Ji and his crew.

****

As arranged, on Saturday morning, Dan picked Bobby up and they made their way to the abandoned industrial park. On the way, Bobby explained the whole ordeal. They drove up to the main entrance and Bobby got out of the car and ran to open the gate. It was locked. He was stunned. He looked back at Dan while he shrugged his shoulders in disbelief. Dan got out of the car and walked up to the gate. There was a massive chain and padlock on it.

"So this wasn't here yesterday?" Dan asked.

"I swear, I just pushed on the gate like this and it slid opened," a very perplexed Bobby replied as he attempted to shove the gate open.

"Where did Buddy get in?"

"Away over there."

They got back in the car and drove around the far side of the property to search for the breach in the fence where the dog had initially entered. Like soldiers, older stands of maples lined the property fence and some of the mature branches reached high over it. Their ever thickening trunks almost cut off the view from the road. After a few slow drive-bys, Bobby spotted the place where his dog bolted after some animal and slipped through the fence. It was a place where the roots of one of the maples had lifted the bottom of the fence and snapped off one of the upright posts, allowing small animals to enter easily.

They got out of the car and went over to the fence. "Boy, I don't know how Bud got through that," Bobby said as he examined the broken fence. "But he flew through it like if he was after a rabbit or something."

When they got back to his car, Dan was now convinced that Bobby wasn't lying. When he dropped Bobby off, he told his mother he would try to get into the industrial park when he was back to work on the following Monday.

***

The TV station immediately forwarded the tape to the police. The police in turn notified Conor and along with Darby and Jeff, they drove to the FBI office in downtown Seattle where they met Sally to watch the grainy homemade movie. Conor and his colleagues watched the video first and they all felt it was appropriate to let the three view it. Conor wanted to make sure there was no collusion between them, the hostages and the kidnappers. His staff was trained to watch the reactions of the three in their eyes as well as in their body language and speech to look for clues of any possible connection.

"I should warn you, there is extreme emotional graphic content in this video. This is also a highly secure and sensitive piece of footage that cannot be shared with anyone at this point. Any leak of this to the public can jeopardize the lives of the hostages. I repeat, you cannot, and should not breathe a word of this to anyone. Do you understand?" The three nodded and verbally agreed. "Please have a seat."

Conor gestured toward the chairs in front of the TV, which was located in the middle of the room. His men found their way to their positions and sat off to one side pretending to focus on the screen. They were there to watch the two women and Schellenberg's reactions – not the video. Conor rolled the tape.

"I can stop the tape at any time if it is too much for you," Conor said calmly. "Oh yes, I need someone to identify each person in the video by name."

Sally and Darby gasped and clamped their mouths in horror, their eyes grew to the size of small saucers and their faces became pallid when they saw Caleb and the two families on the screen. Even Schellenberg was shaken.

Behind the hostages were a makeshift banner with the FTW logo and two men in black balaclavas with foot long knives sticking vertically out of their folded arms, standing on either side of the families. At this point, Conor paused the tape and Sally and Darby gave him the names of the hostages.

Ji's voice came on, off camera. *"Hello America, we are Free The World, an organization dedicated to free the world of capitalist pigs. You average Yankees need to know that outside your country, little families are treated like animals, slaves to your Yankee dolla..."* Some blurry video clips cut in, showing Third-World farms being bulldozed by some smiling white guy while the family pleaded and cried as their livelihood was destroyed. Then short clips showed an endless series of atrocities, depicting agricultural and human exploitation such as overseas sweat factories. All the while Ji went on with explaining his motive behind the ransom and his demands.

"Furthermore, we need our first installment of twenty-five million within forty-eight hours. If not received in bank account, we will unleash most lethal weapon on big US city, there will be no living soul after forty-eight hours. I repeat; there will be lot of Yankee lives lost if our demands are not met immediately. Next, rest of money need deposit or we will start with beheading one of six lucky contestants sitting between my two soldiers, and then we wait for a few more hours and off goes another head. We expect full co-operation or there will be no more heads. Free The World mean business, if no co-operation, then a very big Yankee city will be nothing but a concrete jungle with no living souls and six heads will roll like soccer ball!"

After the viewing, Sally, Darby and Jeff sat quietly in shock. They stared at the floor, shook their heads in disbelief and with dazed looks, all that could be heard in anguish was "oh my God, oh my God." The three had many questions and for the next hour, they discussed the dynamics of the incident. Conor would not discuss the FBI's strategies or methods of releasing hostages in any detail. He wanted to make sure he knew what and who he was dealing with.

Conor had the tape dusted for fingerprints, and a video analyst replayed the tape over and over in regular and in slow motion, all the while looking for clues.

"He had the editing done on a pretty basic manual editor, something that could be bought at Radio Shack," the analyst commented. "If you look at the wall the banner is hung on, it looks rough, and it is definitely not some office or board room. There is some writing on the wall over there…, let me zoom in." He did, but the words were illegible. He noted the color and condition of the run-down furniture, the clothes they were wearing, their shoes, and every little detail – something that would suggest a clue.

"Well, boys, this is the real deal." Conor folded his arms over his chest while he paced the floor of the operations room. "We have heard about this group headquartered out of Indonesia, I believe. These guys are very serious terrorists and mean business. Their demands are unusual. They are asking for a down payment of twenty-five million deposited in a Swiss account in order to suspend the launch of some kind of *dirty* bomb. Which could be Anthrax, but *it* takes too long to be effective. Personally, I don't know of any other type of bio-chemical stuff. Has anyone heard of something else?" Conor paused, looking around the room. "Then they want to start beheading the hostages if the rest of the money isn't received. Interesting, they only show two guards in the flick, I think there are a lot more of them. This beheading thing is a typical Middle Eastern terrorist thing…. They must have some connection to each other if this group is out of Indonesia. Intelligence had warned us about some potential FTW *cells* in the US. We are going to need some…" He stopped. "Did any of you guys get any intel on the Dennis Houghton fellow?" He looked around the room again.

"The only thing we could find out is that this guy is CIA," one of the surveillance agents piped-up.

171

Conor didn't hesitate. "Someone get the CIA on the blower. We need some answers, NOW!"

As soon as he got an agent on the line, he laid out the case to him. The CIA already had a file on the FTW and immediately dispatched some Special Agents to the FBI office. They agreed to contact the White House and warn of the potential danger but not to let the media get a hold of it. The Seattle TV station was warned not to broadcast anything until it was advised otherwise.

The CIA contingent arrived and after viewing the tape someone recognized Dennis. "Hey that's Houghton." Conor smiled from behind the agent's shoulder. He was proud that one of his agents had found about Dennis before being told by the CIA. "What the hell is he doing there?" the CIA man went on. "He's one of us. I know his boss, Alex Chambers; he works out of L.A...."

Conor immediately got Chambers on the phone and explained the case.

"What would your agent be doing in the midst of a hostage taking?" Conor asked.

There was a sigh of frustration on the other end as Chambers explained Dennis's assignment and his relationship to Jared and Sally, and their family.

"I don't however know how the FTW got wind of this unless Houghton has let it slipped, or has played double agent and it back fired. He has worked with this agency for over twenty years and despite some minor blunders, he is one of our best agents. He has a pretty clean record. He had been working on international FTW surveillance for some time. They are heavy into human and drug trafficking around the world. You probably don't know much about them here in America because our intelligence has turned up little except a small cell connected to a mosque in L.A. I would like to think Dennis slipped up somewhere – he was identified and followed. FTW is a very serious organization," Chambers concluded.

"Thank you for the intel, Agent Chambers. We are working with your local agency and have notified the White House, and I will notify SWAT when ever we've got it set up for a hostage release. What else can you tell me?" They then discussed strategy, manpower and resources and agreed to be in twenty-four hour contact.

"How are we going to arrange twenty-five million dollars?" one of Conor's men asked.

"I will get to that, this will be a cat and mouse game," Conor replied. "We are going to pull every stop; the last thing we want to do is be embarrassed by some two bit, third world puke." Conor then marched back to his office and then, through the intercom, requested Sally to be brought in.

She entered his office. "Please have a seat," Conor told her without looking up from his desk. She did. He then reclined in his seat and finally riveted his gaze on her. "Why didn't you tell me about your involvement with the CIA? I don't appreciate half-truths, Mrs. Houghton," he flared, his brown eyes flashing with contempt. "You mentioned something about your brother-in-law being a government agent, but you deliberately omitted to say anything about *your own involvement* with the CIA. Do you realize in how much trouble we could have all been, if we hadn't put two and two together?" He paused. "You could even be indicted as an accessory to a hostage taking, or obstruction – both of which incur several years in a penitentiary."

Sally was still shaken with what she had seen on the video. She responded with simultaneous embarrassment and anger. "What was I supposed to do? I had a strict oath to protect the CIA's interests in the birth of my son." She paused as emotion suddenly overwhelmed her. "My family is in the hands of terrorists and you are accusing me of hiding someone's identity? Good God, man! Who cares if Dennis could…, could be the President's brother? I just want my family back!" Tears welled up for the first time in her ordeal as Sally snapped, "Do something! Just bloody well do something!" Her body convulsed as wave after wave of emotion poured out of her. Conor got up from behind his desk and quietly offered her some tissues.

"Forgive me, Mrs. Houghton, but, you see, the only way we'll get your family back is for you to come clean." Sally looked up at him, dismay filling her tearful eyes. "We are, and will do everything humanly possible to free your family," he went on. "But, *we need* your full cooperation and assistance wherever possible."

Once he saw that Sally had settled down a little, Conor ushered her back to the counseling room and walked back into the operations room.

Chapter 28

Back to Portland....

The hostages had been confined for three days and tensions were growing between them and their captors. Ji knew he held the trump cards in every hand that could be dealt. He was secure, he had the bio-bomb ready to go and he had the US intelligence scratching their heads ready to drop twenty-five million dollars into his account. He was a gambler. He had learned all the tricks by watching his grandfather clean up at the underground poker tables, hidden away from the authorities in his native Jakarta. He learned that you never give your opponent the slightest hint of your hand. You always played from a position of ultimate strength, even when the cards were rubbish. His face or eyes never moved a muscle between twos and threes or a royal flush, but, he could see his opponents' hands like there were mirrors on their eyes and knew exactly when to fold and when to call.

He knew the CIA would call his bluff, he knew they would buckle when a life was lost. He also knew they would hunt him down like a dog and spare little mercy. He had smuggled a litany of weapons into his camp but knew if the bio-bomb worked he wouldn't need to use them. He knew he held the ultimate royal flush and there were no other trump cards available. Except he didn't know about one that had never been played before.

One of the lab technicians released a live rat into the testing compound, a small room, within a larger room, completely enclosed with a sealable trap door and some pipes sealed into the wall, well below an observation window. Donning gas masks fitted with an asthmatic-type inhaling device filled with the antidote and a detection meter, Ji and several of the lab technicians armed with their deadly concoction held in, were ready to try the experiment.

"We are releasing a trace amount of the serum into this pipe and will blow it into the room, representing a gentle wind. The monitor here will let us know how it is working. It should remain working until it completely removes all the oxygen molecules from the air, because, Mr. Ji, it *loves* oxygen. Of course, in a large city it will weaken and eventually burn out but not before it will have eliminated all air-breathing creatures. This other pipe contains the antidote which we will release to monitor the activity, and this pipe is connected to this meter." The lab technician continued, "I will release the serum and watch our rat."

The rat scurried around the room, inquisitively looking for food and things that rats like to do. The quiet hum of the fan gently blew air into the room and within seconds, the rat went crazy as it tried to escape and within a minute after convulsing, trying to get air, it laid on the floor in a lifeless heap. The monitor indicated zero oxygen. They stood around the meter and watched it remain there for several minutes.

"We will now apply the antidote." They did.

The meter slowly climbed back up to normal. There was a big cheer as they ripped off their masks and high-fived each other, they knew it was a huge success. "Allah is great!" they shouted and danced around the room. "We can wipe out the infidels!" they cried out in Indonesian.

Ji now knew his men were both very afraid of him as well as more loyal than ever. He left for privacy to his makeshift office and called his Swiss bank to see if any money had shown up. Nothing. It was now more than forty-eight hours. He kept a TV on to see if the public knew about the plight of his hostages and his onerous plans. There was nothing. He knew the policing forces were either not taking him seriously or they were willing to wait out his demands to the last minute. There was a knock at his door and one of his guards brought Dennis in.

"Mr. Dennis, what do you want? Are you ready to die for your country?"

"Not exactly," Dennis replied, "but I might die for a cigarette right about now." He sat down and crossed one leg over one ankle – outwardly relaxed. "Look Ji, you're not going to get away with this much longer. Someone is going to find out about your little hideaway sooner than later. They haven't played your little video over the air waves yet have they? The TV station would never play something like that without first giving it to the authorities. You know that. Besides, no one knows if you are serious or not. For all they know you could be a hoax, a staged event from some whacko in order to get some cash. This happens daily in the USA. There are ridiculous demands, everything from swapping the president for some white supremacist to blowing up the white house in exchange for the homeless. There are whole departments funded by taxpayers dedicated to checking these demands out. The press is under advisement from the authorities to turn tapes and threats and letters, et cetera, to them first. If the authorities can authenticate its origin, then it will become an All Points Bulletin to all police and security departments and eventually the public will get a version of it. Speaking of cash, how much did you ask for? If it is a lot, they will need time to assemble it. I know you are drooling all over the young fella here to get cloned, but you've got a problem, you *need* his mother don't you, to give up her eggs and how the hell are you going to do that? You start knocking us off or trading us in for ransom and there is going to be a big confrontation, right, Ji?"

"Shut up, damn Yankee!" exclaimed Ji, clearly disturbed by the lack of response from the authorities. "I should kill you one by one in front of camera and see how police respond. *That* would get their attention. Do you realize we have successfully created weapon that could wipe out Los Angeles or New York in less than forty-eight hours?"

Dennis laughed. "Yep, that would solve everything, wouldn't it? You could always drop your big bomb and *then* they would believe you." At that, Ji got up from behind his desk and slapped Dennis across the face.

"Don't mock me, Yankee pig!" Ji yelled angrily, "Get out!" He ordered the guard to roughhouse him back to the hostage room.

Dennis was thrown head first into the room with the rest.

"Well, Mr. Ji has no sense of humor," Dennis grunted, picking himself up off the floor while checking his jaw out from the hit.

"What happened in there?" everyone asked simultaneously.

"He's having a bad day ... not getting his own way," Dennis went on as he took a seat, being careful not to comment too much. He was still not sure how much English the guards understood.

Caleb had been trying telepathy with the guards but it hadn't seemed to be working until he stumbled upon a simple mental gesture of distracting or "off-loading" communication, almost primitive animal sounds or a sixth sense. He internalized a "grunting" sound in different tonalities; an "urgent" sound made the guards look at each other with a perplexed look and even get up and walk around and talked in Indonesian while they looked for the source of the voice in the room. The rest of the hostages in the room "heard" it as well and they looked around in dismay. Caleb would follow with something to alleviate the urgency. He would repeat some of the "commands" and each advance of his power to communicate was becoming a weapon which he needed to relay, in telepathic confidence to the others.

Needless to say, the hostages' morale was very low. Each day dragged on into night. They slept in their cramped quarters, waiting and praying for release. A quiet gasoline generator was the single source of electricity sustaining Ji's operation. At night there was only light from small flashlights.

Ji knew his next move was the most drastic; he had to videotape the murder of one of the hostages or he had to swap hostages for Sally. After his discussion with Dennis, he counseled with his chief lab technician who confirmed the need for Sally to complete the identical cloning and the ultimate plan for a superior race of humans under his command. He also needed to smuggle her out of the country to Jakarta or get her into a well-equipped lab locally to retrieve her eggs. He would also have to place a call to the CIA in order to make the deal. He knew this would break all hell loose in the CIA and he would have to make sure his escape route and ship – an old freighter – was waiting in the Portland harbor as soon as the money arrived or in the event they started closing in on him.

On day four of their captivity, after breakfast, Ji had his three guards and four lab technicians – all armed with AK-47s – herded the hostages at gun point into another room and ordered them to sit in two rows facing the camcorder mounted on a tripod. Ji then recorded his second demand video. He silently panned and zoomed into a close up of each hostage. The men had grown substantial beards and their faces were starting to look gaunt from malnutrition. Diane still looked fresh. She kept her hair tied up but the guards made her wear a scarf. The same guards masked in balaclavas stood on either side of the six with arms folded and long knives pointed vertically.

"You're a creep, you bastard! We don't deserve this," Bob yelled at Ji as they were shoved through the door back in their cramped quarters after the videotaping.

After they settled down, Diane turned to the rest and calmly said, "You know, this is a battle between good and evil and from day one I have personally been praying for a break through, a release, safety, all the things to keep us alive and Jesus has been answering my prayers. But, I think we need to corporately pray – out loud, all together. I don't know whether you have a bone of faith in you in or not, 'cause at this point we are going to need all you can muster."

At that, they all bowed their heads and Diane simply prayed, *"Lord, we need your help to be released, we need forgiveness for our captors, we need strength to endure and your love to carry us. In Jesus name, amen."* There was an immediate sense of peace in the room. The captors even softened.

"We are *going* to *need* a miracle to get us out of here alive," Bob muttered.

***

Back to Conor's war room in Seattle….

"Good morning gentlemen, we have now put out an APB to all policing forces and have alerted local TV stations to keep their eye out for unusual delivery people and delivery activities. We have arranged for the money to be dropped into FTW's account and Interpol is working with the Swiss bank to co-operate. The only phone call we received was from a phone booth, not a mobile, at a gas station off the I-5 not far from Seatac." Conor went on, "we have intel in Jakarta and L.A. looking into FTW's recent activities in both places. Apparently, the mosque in L.A. has Indonesian affiliations and we are connecting the dots there as well."

He detailed his men and called Sally at home. He briefed her with the activities. Each hour seemed to drag into eternity. Even the early spring weather was wet and gloomy.

***

In Portland, Monday morning, Dan Oliver reported for duty as a traffic cop out of the local 106th precinct. His superior briefed him along with his colleagues about the daily run of activities.

"We have an APB about a possible hostage take-out in Seattle. Six people, four adults and two minors were taken from a home a few days ago by a terrorist group called FTW, short for Free The World."

Dan cut his superior off. "When did this happen?"

"It says here late last Wednesday."

"That's wild! On Saturday, I took a ten-year-old kid from my complex. He had been playing around that old abandoned warehouse property about a mile from my place. He said he was told by some kind of mental telepathy that there were six hostages inside. When we went back, the front gate was locked, but, apparently, it was open when the boy went in the day before. His mother thought the kid was makin' up a tall tale in order to get out of doing chores and wanted me to call his bluff. I guess he has pulled stunts like this before. *I* think the kid is on to something."

"Okay, come and see me after briefing. Let's just finish this...." The officer eyed Dan curiously. "FTW is not only armed and very dangerous, they may have a dirty bomb or some form of bio-weapon. Please use caution. If you know their whereabouts, do not attempt to approach or arrest them. All sightings or irregular activities should be reported to me immediately – do not attempt anything on your own. Wait for further orders or back-up. That's all."

As he was walking out, the chief waited for Dan to file out of the room. "Okay, I heard you in there. I think you better call on someone in CSI and go over together to the property. If your suspicions are making any sense to CSI, we'll advise the FBI." Dan nodded. "And don't do anything foolish like going into the warehouse by yourselves..., okay?"

"Yes, Chief."

"Okay, on your way then."

As soon as he got back to his desk, Dan made arrangements to meet Clint Shatford, his CSI buddy, at the abandoned warehouse. He explained the scenario to his friend as they surveyed the property from the locked front gate. The distance from the front gate to the first building was about one hundred yards and the building, where Bobby had had his experience, was fifth and last in line. Other out buildings were spaced randomly on the estate, looking very tired and worn out, with windows smashed out from vandals and doors kicked in with graffiti sprayed randomly. The main road leading to the front building was lined with a series of ominous skeletons of rusty looking steel I-beams on both sides, used at one time to suspend heavy equipment and part of former warehousing. Because the property was located off main roads and surrounded only by other commercial and industrial properties on three sides, the infrequent traffic was more noticeable.

Clint knelt down and examined the road.

"There has been traffic here recently.... See the tire tracks.... The weeds flatten out..., see, over there.... One thing about a place like this, it will give you evidence. Mind you, these tire tracks could be left from the owners... Let's see if we can find *them*." They walked to the gate. "Look at this padlock.... That's new; way too new for the age of this property."

The two of them went over all the possibilities and Dan drove Clint around the two sides of the sprawling warehouse estate, showing him where Bobby's dog had gone through the breach in the fence. They knew they had to find the owner or caretaker, obtain a warrant, in order to gain entry.

"Look, a way over there, isn't that a *"For Lease"* sign?" Dan pointed. "Looks like that sign was put up in the fifties. Man, I can't believe how anyone could allow a big property like this to just rot away."

They copied the phone number down and drove back to the precinct. The contact number had been changed to a Washington state number and went to an answering machine. Dan left the precinct number and an urgent message.

"I think we had better get a search warrant; city will have the owner's info on file anyways," Dan said and then as an afterthought, "I better report to the chief first, otherwise he's liable to have kittens by the day's end if I do this on my own."

Both men laughed at the thought on their way out of the precinct. Then Dan drove Clint back to his office.

***

Meanwhile, later in the day Ji had completed the editing of his second videotape and sent one of his men dressed in a courier outfit to Seattle to drop it off at a TV station – a different one from where the first tape was left. The TV station immediately contacted the FBI and one of Conor's men rushed to the station to interview the receptionist who received the tape. Ji's man had followed a local courier company and managed to do a switch when the driver left his packages unattended for a few minutes. The receptionist identified the driver as a regular, leaving a cold trail.

The video was an intense plea for the lives of the six hostages. The video also revealed how the captivity was taking a toll on the hostages as the camera panned across each stressed face. Ji's voice-over off-camera not only expressed anger, but frustration at the funds not being dropped into his Swiss account yet.

"FTW will no longer accept complacency from Yankee imperialists. We are now demanding both money and exchange of one life for five lives."

The camera panned to the Lindstroms and Jason. *"We have new demands. Our patience run very thin. We will not use lethal weapon once we have twenty-five million dollar in bank account. Next, we release this couple and young boy for next twenty-five million deposit in bank account. When we see good faith by Yankee imperialist, we release two more."* The camera then focused on Dennis and Jared. *"Last, we need mother of young boy to deliver six bearable bonds, four million dollar each. We also want amnesty for thirty days at which point we release both mother and child unharmed."*

Ji went on to describe a complex time line and location of the exchanges. He also left an African email address for confirmation of receipt. This was the first time Conor could reply and start the negotiations. He called Sally immediately into his office and showed her the video.

"What do you make of this change in FTW's position?" Conor asked.

Sally, who rewound the tape over and over to see her family, began weeping.

"I know exactly what they want," Sally said amidst her tears. "They need my eggs to complete the exact clone. They could use other women's eggs, but they need mine to make exact replicas of

Caleb. There would be no guessing, it would be a human assembly line."

"What do you mean?" Conor asked.

Sally composed herself, wiped her eyes and pushed back her naturally blond shoulder-length hair. "They will fertilize my eggs with sperm from Caleb and implant host females through in vitro. It doesn't matter who the host mother is. All they want is the results, a perfectly cloned Caleb that they can turn into a super human being that is capable of doing things you or I have never seen. It could re-write the book on evil. Believe me, this is what my husband and I never wanted to happen when we started this experiment over seventeen years ago. We knew we were playing with fire, but we didn't know it was a forest fire."

"This is incest!" Conor exclaimed.

"Well, yeah," replied Sally expressively, "not only incest, but potentially, an open door for some form of the human race that we have never seen."

"Why in God's name did you guys ever do this?"

"Look, it would take me quite a while to explain our reasons. You have to trust me that it was all done in the name of science. We meant it for good, never for evil. I will explain the details to you at some point, but at the moment, I want my family back…."

Conor leaned back in his chair and looked up to the ceiling in deep thought.

"What are you waiting for? I will do whatever it takes," Sally blurted.

Time ticked by ever so slowly. "I have to think this one through, Mrs. Houghton, please." He got up and showed her to the door, saying, "I'll call you when we've made a decision."

Sally looked up at him a trace of anger in her eyes. As far as she was concerned, she was the only one who should be making a decision in this case. She didn't say anything and walked out.

Conor then assembled his men in the war room. "Any intel on FTW in Indonesia?" was his first question.

One of the agents was ready with his report. "Oh yeah, these guys are legit. They were responsible for the beheading of three western sympathizers, four suicide bombings, which killed thirty-nine and destruction of western-held food co-operative offices throughout Indonesia, Malaysia and Pakistan over the last four and a half years. They also have connections to arms and drug smuggling in the same areas. They are funded mainly by Middle East money and have quite a loyal bunch of followers – mostly Muslim radicals."

Conor nodded in response. "With the release of the APB yesterday morning, and now a contact, I believe we will make head way. I have called the president's security advisor and we may go public sooner than later, otherwise we could be responsible for some innocent people's deaths. Also, I am sure there are a fair number of people like family, friends, neighbors, and so on, that want answers. I am amazed that we and the police have received such few concerned phone calls." He looked around at the men. "Okay, I'll just have to make a call," he said, getting his butt off the table where he had been perched for the last few minutes, "and I'll get back to you...."

Since Conor had put the wheels in motion already, and had decided that Sally should make the exchange – much against his better judgment – he called her.

"Mrs. Houghton, are you still willing to do anything to free your son?"

Conor's brusque question was met with an even terser answer from Sally, "Get on with it, Conor!"

Annoyed with this consenting rebuke, he returned to the war room and went on to discuss Sally's willingness to do the exchange and how they should handle the confrontation. They would need SWAT and possibly the Army to take out the captors. They also knew this could be a blood bath if things got out of hand.

"We need to find out where that email came from. How are we doing on the satellite recon? Anything unusual happening? What about the airlines and airports? Any strange activities?" Conor asked.

The agents read off their reports and all had come up blank other than the Asian report. The African intel server would not be able to be accessed by the CIA or any other agency due to the secrecy of its location.

Conor assigned duties to his men and women with the hope of getting a break in the case. He knew he was running out of time and being a seasoned professional, both disappointments and frustration were always lying at his feet. Busyness seemed to help, but advice from experienced managers and agents was far more productive. His first call was to Chambers in L.A. Even though Chambers was CIA, he had quite a lengthy experience as well as a personal dossier on Dennis and his family.

"So what was CIA's intention with a cloned human?" Conor asked casually.

"We were experimenting with the thought of a unified agency. Our plan was to, for lack of a better word, program agents and staff for specific duties. If we could start with a known entity, one that was constant, no surprises, hell, you know what it is like trying to staff an intelligence agency. You can't put an ad in the paper, *"Interested in a career of subversion, murder and espionage? Please apply to the CIA."* With clones, they could easily be programmed, even right in their DNA, to do what ever you want them, almost like automatons. We had high hopes on the Houghton kid or *descendant*, or whatever he is. After we had determined, what we thought to be the kid—the wrong kid—was normal, we scrapped the idea. Besides, I couldn't get any more funds to try and prove any more of the Houghtons' theories and the risk of security leaks was getting too great."

"That is pretty heady stuff," concluded Conor. "A good lesson for us all to learn I guess."

"So how is the FBI going to handle this? Why don't you send me an email, I'd be curious to see your plans," Chambers suggested.

The two talked at great length about past hostage taking incidents and how they had been handled. They both agreed a negotiator was needed. Simultaneously they concluded Jeremy Raftus, a seasoned vet from the L.A. office of the FBI, was perfect. His qualifications and extensive experience had allowed him to swing deals with the most hardened criminals in the bleakest of situations. After a few more pleasantries, Conor and Chambers hung up and Conor was immediately on the phone to Raftus.

He filled him in on the details and arranged for him to catch the next plane to Seattle. Conor knew he had to prepare a media release and turned to his computer and started typing....

It hit the fan.... The six o'clock news came on TV and every radio station, and like a scene out of a Hollywood movie, the announcers spun out the known details of the drama and tension of the hostage-taking incident along with edited clips of the two videos.

Conor had released the news without a mention of the bio-bomb, as he knew it would potentially create mass hysteria.

Ji received a message from Jeremy Raftus notifying him that the first twenty-five million had been deposited in his Swiss account along with Jeremy's mobile phone number and a request for a phone call. Ji smiled wickedly, scratching the menacing-looking scar around his left eye as he watched the news break on his TV. He would check his Swiss account early the next morning for confirmation of the transfer. Ji knew not to call Raftus as they could trace his location, so he opted for email to outline the drop off of the Lindstroms. His reply to Raftus was short; once the next twenty-five million was received, Ji would then release the Lindstroms at a pre-determined location within twenty-four hours.

Raftus, knowing this was the oldest swindle on the planet, quickly replied, *"in order for us to comply with your demands, we need assurance that the hostages are still alive, unharmed and will be left in a safe place. A telephone call would be a faster way to get your money, feel free to call me anytime of the day or night."*

Raftus knew that emails were unemotional, and impossible to negotiate properly, and that is why kidnappers hid behind the impersonal print media. A war of words on a computer screen was no match for a voice on the other end of a line. Psychologically, a phone call was where he worked his magic by listening for the slightest intonations; he knew when they were lying, if they were injured, if they were armed. He even knew if they were alone, if they had been sleeping or shopping. He would record a conversation and play it repeatedly in order to gain insight. Time was always of the essence; lives were on the line.

Within hours of Raftus's email, Ji replied, *"In order to show honorable intention, right now you will find woman, husband and child showed in video, unharmed, close by exit 501 off I-5. We will release Mr. Dennis and Mr. Jared when other twenty-five million is deposit in Swiss bank account. Then we want mother of young boy to bring bonds."*

As it was already dark, Raftus forwarded the message to Conor and he contacted the local police force. Within a few moments, the police located the Lindstroms in a field just off the edge of an exit ramp. They were still blindfolded and their hands zap-strapped. They were cold, hungry but otherwise unharmed. Conor immediately had an agent pick them up for their debriefing.

"Welcome back to civilization Mr. and Mrs. Lindstrom and you too, Jason. Is there any need of a doctor or medical assistance?"

The three simultaneously shook their heads "no."

"Please meet Jeremy Raftus, chief negotiator of your release. We are going to get you comfortable as soon as possible, but we are first going to need your help to release the others. Mr. Raftus will be recording this."

In order to put pieces of the puzzle together, Conor had the three separated. They each told their own version of the events leading up to the kidnapping as well as their own personal stories of being in captivity. He had to made sure this was not a collusion scheme. He also gathered more accurate intel during a one-on-one interview. One of the questions focused on the demands made by the kidnappers. They were still unclear as to the motive behind the last part of the ransom demands. Why did the FTW want Sally to go to them? The bio-bomb threat was no mystery – they had seen this before, but asking a mother to join her son, that was another matter altogether. Conor re-assembled them back in his office and played the videos. He asked them to verify the details of the surroundings – anything that would help the SWAT team or the military regarding the size of the place, door and windows' locations and ventilation openings.

"What about the making of the videos?" Raftus asked.

"All we did was to get herded into a room inside the warehouse to face this guy, Ji – a short little Asian guy with a stringy Fu Manchu moustache and a big ugly scar around his left eye. I am not sure, he may even have a glass eye – ran a camcorder he had perched on a tripod, for a few minutes each time and said nothing. I guess he put the voice over after," Bob Lindstrom explained.

"How many of them are there?" Raftus asked.

"I can't really say, it appears to fluctuate, anywhere from four to twelve maybe. We always had at least two armed guards. But they have a fairly well equipped laboratory with a bunch of technicians – we've only had brief glimpses of them – we have no idea how many are in there."

"How long was the car ride?" Conor enquired.

"Several hours," Bob replied looking at his wife quizzically. "I have no clue which direction I came from; I heard heavy traffic, light traffic, no traffic; they could have driven us around in circles for all I know."

Raftus knew Dennis and Jared were probably okay, but he had to ask, "What about Dennis and Jared Houghton? Are they OK? Any torture, violent behavior?"

"They roughed me and Dennis up a couple of times – nothing serious, though. We knew they were capable of killing us easily. We expected to die anytime."

"I think if I stayed there any longer I would have wanted to die," Diane put in, tears streaming down her cheeks. "The conditions were horrible, really…. I mean everything was dirty and smelled awful."

"Did they feed you?" Conor was curious.

"Sure, if you can call the slop they fed up "food", then yes we got some food." Bob grimaced at the recollection.

"We only got rice and something like chicken," Jason added. "And then they gave us some green water…, Mom said it was tea." He shuddered. "It tasted like nothing I'd want to drink again. That was gross!"

"That's one way to lose a bunch of weight," Diane smirked while wiping tears off her face.

"What about the rest, how are they coping?" asked Raftus, "what do you feel the relationship is like between Dennis and this Ji fellow?"

"Not great." Bob replied. "One day Dennis went in to talk to him and the next thing you know, he was thrown head first back into our room. He was OK, just a little rattled. Our son, Caleb however, is onto something. He is able to read minds and he can actually communicate through a form of ESP. I believe he can assist in getting the rest out. We actually witnessed a little experiment where he had the guards wondering what was going on. Pretty amazing! We are very proud of him and we now know why he would be in big demand for all this cloning business. By the way, I want to thank you, Mr. Raftus, for getting us out of there. You don't realize how precious life is until you've been taken against your will and held prisoner."

Conor and Raftus went over details with the family for quite awhile, making notes and emailing other agents.

After the debriefing, the Lindstroms were escorted to a safe house to be kept under twenty-four hour guard until all was safe, if and when the incident was over.

Chapter 29

Civilians of the Pacific Northwest were in the grip of fear. Neighbors and relatives of the Lindstroms and the Houghtons banded together with phone calls and meetings. Church groups gathered for prayer meetings. Dark skinned and Middle Eastern people were stared at and treated with suspicion. The news media had a hey-day. National and international TV crews flooded the Seattle area. Policing agencies along with airports, and public transportation were also on high alert and SWAT teams and the military moved in.

Ji knew he had to move quickly as he watched the news. He emailed Raftus demanding that the next twenty-five million be deposited immediately and that Dennis and Jared would be released the instant the money was deposited in his account. If it wasn't, he wrote, he was ready to behead them both.

Raftus wanted to stall for time but he knew he was under pressure from Conor to avoid blood shed. They relented to the demand and made arrangements to deposit the next twenty-five million as soon as possible. Conor also arranged for the bearer bonds at the same time.

Highway patrol on I-5 was notified that there could be a human drop along the Seattle to Portland corridor. Raftus received an email from Ji within three hours after he received confirmation from his bank where to pick up Dennis and Jared on the I-5.

Once again, they were blindfolded, zap-strapped and left at a remote exit, much like the Lindstroms and Jason. There were no witnesses.

Dennis and Jared were immediately separated and Dennis was brought into Conor's office.

"Sit down," Conor demanded firmly. "What the hell is going on, Houghton? Do you realize you have put five lives besides your own, into extreme danger and cost taxpayers millions? Your boss is on his way along with the local CIA agent to debrief you. You are going to have a lot to answer to, my friend. In the meantime, what is the latest on the boy?"

"The boy is safe; he is what they wanted in the first place. Look, I can explain everything…"

"There had better be *one* good explanation," Conor cut-in mid sentence, visibly angered. "Quite frankly, if you were one of my agents, I would see to it that you got the needle. Because you are CIA, I have to leave how you got everyone into this, up to your supervisor. Personally, I would like to horsewhip you, but that is up to your boss. *Now*, I need to know as much about this place as you can tell me."

Dennis described as much as he could while Raftus recorded and asked questions. When he was done, he was removed from the office and Jared was brought in to tell his side of the story. Jared spelled out the kidnapping story along with his experience in the warehouse.

After he was finished, Conor explained the demand Ji had for Sally. Jared went ballistic.

"That's incest!" he shouted. "What a piece of crap. That guy is plain evil; talk about a power tripper. You should see the way he treats his men…. He is ruthless…, the little bastard. I don't want my wife being exposed to this idiot! I'd like to kill him. I totally reject the idea!"

"I understand, Mr. Houghton," Conor calmly replied, "It's not every day you have your wife's reproduction equipment exposed to a foreign terrorist outfit. However, if you don't, you take a chance that you will never see your son again, alive or dead. If your wife does her thing, we stand a much better chance of locating and potentially eliminating FTW as well as retrieving both of them because we have more time to work with."

"One thing you should keep in mind," Raftus interjected, "if he is any kind of a Muslim, he wouldn't dare touch another man's wife. I would highly doubt if he would have anything to do with the actual medical part of the operation."

"Really?" Jared shouted. "You expect me to believe that? After how I saw this guy act…? Look, I have an idea. I still have frozen sperm off the Ice Man, do you think he would accept that in lieu of my wife?"

"No harm in trying," Raftus piped up quizzically. "Usually these guys get something in their mind and trying another angle is futile, but still worth a shot. So, run over the details for me."

Jared explained how it would work and what medical gear would be necessary to complete the procedure.

Raftus put together the plan and emailed it to Ji. As he thought, the reply was negative.

The next morning, at the warehouse, Caleb's ESP power was starting to become more refined. He had the guards running around looking for phantom people and animals. He was even beginning to understand their thoughts, even though they were in Indonesian. It was not only helping to pass the time, it made for great entertainment.

In his office, Ji rubbed his hands in a wicked glee as he saw his plans coming to fruition and the money was in his account. He knew the next step would be the most brazen and dangerous; getting Sally into his hands and performing the eggs' extraction. He had his lab technicians go shopping for the necessary medical equipment and was now outfitted to do the operation. He had packed everything into his ship and had left his lab technicians aboard. He would use Dennis's rental car and stolen van to pick up Sally. One would be a decoy. Everything had to happen in seconds. In the event of an emergency, he had found an abandoned underground industrial railway system underneath the property that led close to where his freighter was docked. It had been used to bring materials and supplies to the massive plant that once operated on the site.

Ji started to compose an email to Raftus about the time and place for the pick up of Sally and bearer bonds. An unusual noise in the loading dock area of the warehouse caught his attention and he went to the only door they had used in the covered area, to investigate. He cautiously, slowly opened the creaking door, and peered around in the semi darkness. Nothing. Then he thought he heard a guard call him, so he quickly closed it and locked it.

"What do you want?" asked Ji to a guard standing outside Caleb's room.

"Nothing! I didn't say anything," the guard replied in Indonesian.

"What was that noise out there?"

"What noise, I never heard anything?"

191

"Didn't you hear it? It sounded like some kind of animal sound," Ji replied annoyingly.

They went back and forth and Ji was getting angry as the guard kept pleading innocence.

Caleb now knew he could pinpoint the power of his ESP to individuals, something he couldn't do before. He knew he was on to something big and started to plan his escape.

Outside the gates of the warehouse property, Dan and Clint picked the lock and opened the gate to let themselves in. Clint pointed to the multitude of fresh vehicle tracks as they drove up and parked by the first building.

"This is some huge property," Dan mused as they passed by the rusty skeletons of I-beams and dilapidated buildings that once employed hundreds, maybe thousands of workers. They stopped at each of the first four buildings, peered in through broken windows and cautiously went inside to upper office levels with drawn guns, scaring pigeons and sparrows, which had long taken over. The stench from the piles of bird droppings and wet, rotting furniture and other garbage left by the homeless was overwhelming.

Dan's shoulder radio came to life and it was from his boss.

"Where are you?"

"We are at the warehouse site. We have investigated four of the five main buildings – so far nothing. We are about to go into the last one. Lots of evidence of the homeless using this as one of their hotels."

"Well, check out the last building and head back as quick as possible, there have been some recent developments you should know about."

"Ten-four. Shouldn't be long."

They had left their car on the north side of the first building and had walked on the west side of the warehouses, leaving the vehicle out of line of sight. They had put their revolvers back in their holsters and walked confidently past the side of the fifth and last building, and headed toward the loading area where Bobby's dog had acted strangely. It was well shaded and their eyes took a second to adjust to the darkness as they rounded the corner, only to be met with a blaze of machine-gun fire. Both Dan and Clint, fatally hit, instantly slumped to the ground in lifeless heaps as the echoes of the gunfire pinged off the metal and concrete enclosure in a deadly cacophony. The whistle of frightened pigeons winging their escape was the only sound left in the cruel darkness. Blood quickly oozed out of the bodies onto the parched grey dust. Ji and one of the guards gathered up the bodies and dragged them up the stairs and inside the main warehouse floor where the vehicles were parked. While squatting beside them, they stripped them of their weapons and found their badges and wallets. They looked at each other in stunned amazement as they pointed to the badges and yammered away in Indonesian.

Ji knew it was time to move fast. He had sent his email for Sally's pick up time and place at a busy intersection in Portland where he had planned for the decoy vehicle to be used. He also knew his place could be surrounded by police in minutes.

There were only Ji, two guards and Caleb left in the warehouse. Caleb had heard the gunfire and knew there were casualties. He had also heard the thoughts of each of the guards and how cruel their thoughts were justified by their convictions of the killing of the two innocent men. He was appalled and scared, but as he prayed, a peace and sudden power overtook him. He heard a voice he had only heard before in his dreams. The voice told him that he was to go and speak to the dead men and tell them to *rise up*. Caleb banged the side of his head – he couldn't bring himself to believe what he had just heard. The voice then told him that there would be a bout of confusion among his captors when they were getting into the vehicles and he would have time to tell the dead men to *rise up*.

"Let's go kid!" Ji zap-strapped his hands together roughly.

"Why did you kill those men?" Caleb asked.

"Police, come to get us," Ji snapped back. "We need to go, now." He shoved Caleb through the door toward the vehicles. Caleb stopped in shock and looked in horror when he saw the two dead men lying in small pools of blood on the dirty, cold concrete floor. He stood in a trance. All of a sudden, his three captors left him by himself and went back into the office area, arguing and shouting at each other in Indonesian.

Caleb stood like a statue with his hands bound, in a trance, staring at the lifeless bodies, eternity seemed to pass, and the words came back to him like a distant radio station being tuned in, "*Tell the dead men to rise up.*" And it began to echo around the inside of his head like a hula-hoop. *Who is saying this? I can't raise the dead. Who is this?* Like the tenderness of a father, the voice in him said, *"I am the Holy Spirit and you have been chosen to speak words of life to those two men. I will raise them back to life. Do not be afraid."*

For a moment, Caleb thought he was in a dream or a movie, yet there was such a presence of peace; almost like a reality warp. "I'm too afraid. What if they come back to life just as Ji comes back…?" While saying this, Caleb's whole being was suddenly filled with indestructible resolve. He screamed *silently,* "I have to do this!"

His eyes riveted on the two men, he said, "Rise up … rise up … rise up!" Each *'rise up'* got louder and his voice reverberated off the empty warehouse walls. One of the bodies twitched, and then the other. Caleb ran over to them. "Rise up! Rise up!" he yelled as he got down on his knees by them. He could hear groaning and gurgling sounds and their limbs started to move ever so slowly, he could see their chests starting to move as well.

"My God! They *are* coming back to life! But they are in danger of dying all over again. Please don't let my captors see this miracle, please!" Caleb prayed out loud excitedly.

Caleb then heard his captor's voices and doors opening behind him and he quickly got up and went back to where he had been standing. They slid the main doors, which opened to the ramp and Caleb was shoved into Dennis's rental car with one of the guards. Ji got in the van with a guard who was driving and he backed up to turn around inside the warehouse, narrowly missing running over the two men who were coming back to life. The rental car driven by the guard with Caleb, squealed around behind Ji and down the ramp and the last thing Caleb saw was the two men slowly raising themselves up on their elbows.

His captors never saw a thing. A big smile broke out on Caleb's face and he yelled out "Praise the Lord!" which startled the driver so much he nearly drove into the gate while leaving the property.

"Portland!" Conor yelled. "How the hell did they get to Portland? I thought they were near Seattle! Maybe they have been there all along. We gotta move. They are expecting to pick up Sally in just over three hours. Get this address APB'd out right now, I want the surroundings locked down with snipers in key places. Get Portland on the line, NOW!"

The head of the Portland FBI, Gerry Jones, was on the line. "There is not much we can do in that area without being very conspicuous and having a shoot out. That's a very busy intersection.... Lots of pedestrian and vehicle traffic and there are all high rise offices around there with no window or roof top access. These guys are either smarter than you think or really lucky in picking that intersection. We could set up a fake work zone with armaments, but if he turns the other way, we are SOL. If we set up a police diversion, he will turn around and we could lose him fast. If I were you, and as much as you want to nab the bastard in flight, I would do the drop and I'm sure we can catch up to him with road blocks and other means... You *do* have her GPS'd."

Conor went on to discuss the logistics and time line and hung up the phone. Sally and Jared were already on the way to his office. Once they arrived, he outfitted her with a tiny GPS tracking device, sewn to the inside of her bra. It was one of the very first of its kind. She could be tracked virtually anywhere in the world. They left his office with a convoy of armed agents heading down I-5 in unmarked cars.

About two hours later, in his car, the phone rang; it was Gerry Jones, the Portland FBI chief in hyper-excited mode.

"You are not going to believe this, two of our local finest city police officers were just in an ambush at an abandoned warehouse. They were shot and killed, but somehow they are now alive and are telling their stories. I'm not sure if there is a link. They have the place surrounded and are investigating it further.... Rather bizarre, but it all started with some kid who was rescuing his dog, or something, a few days ago and he heard a voice in his head about kidnappers inside when he was in the same area where the officers were shot. The officers had gone to investigate and, wham; they were eating lead on the *outside* of the warehouse. The next thing you know they are laying *inside* the warehouse deader than door nails. Then they had some kind of out of body experience or something and then they woke up in a pool of their own blood coming back to life, but yet they are now fine, no bullet holes, only, apparently, little scars."

"Quit telling me fairy tales, Jones, we don't have any time to waste on stuff like that," Conor caustically quipped. "There is too much at stake. Are your men in position?"

"Yes, they are in position. I know, until I hear the story from the horse's mouth and see the scars on these two guys, I'm just as skeptical as you, maybe those guys were out on some huge bender the night before … needed some story to cover their asses, this is a first for me for sure." Jones laughed. They finished their phone call, the car went silent, except for tire noise and the ear-phone radio traffic crackling back and forth, as agents reported their positions.

"How are you two doing, especially you, Sally?" Conor asked quietly as they approached the intersection for her departure.

"If I see the little bastard, I swear, I'll take your gun and shoot him," Jared seethed, hugging his wife, both soaked in tears.

"You have the bonds, you have your suitcase, and you are looking for a white Ford sedan. Be ready to lie down on the floor in the car immediately you are in and pull your son down with you. There could be exchange of gunfire – I hope not – but you never know with terrorists." Conor was worried sick. His cool confidence was rattled to the core as he had the car stopped for her departure. There was no place to stop long as the heavy traffic piled up and horns started honking. Sally kissed Jared her last good-bye, stepped out onto the sidewalk and walked around the corner where the get away car was to arrive.

Ji had insisted she wore a long black, ankle-length raincoat and black scarf around her head for both religious and identification reasons. She pulled her suitcase down the sidewalk as people stared at this tall slender woman dressed in black. She was too nervous to pay any attention to the stares, and slowly walked around the corner for the pick up. Right on time, the white Ford stopped in a no-stopping zone and traffic started piling up in the intersection immediately. The rear passenger door opened and a quiet voice in her head said, "It's okay, Mom, it's me."

The passenger in the front seat yelled in broken English, "*Get in, get in!*"

She threw her suitcase on the backseat, barely got in and the car squealed off like a jackrabbit as she attempted to shut the door while they flew down the street. All of a sudden the driver made a hard right into a narrow alley and down into an underground parking lot. They spiraled down and around into the lot and screeched to a stop by an old yellow van with "Jake's Plumbing and Heating" graphics boldly printed all over it. In seconds they were out of the car and into the back of the van. The van was equipped with large, locked metal toolboxes that were separated from the cab with a security wall. Ji, who snatched the envelope with the bonds out of Sally's hands and ripped it open like a kid on Christmas Day, stuffed Sally and Caleb inside each metal box.

"You make my day! You make my day!" He smiled wickedly, his left eye almost popping out of its socket and onto the scar while he examined the bonds for authenticity. He forced them down inside the toolboxes and latched them in.

He barked instructions in Indonesian to the driver, and they slowly drove out of the opposite side of the parking lot to the sound of sirens led by a stream of unmarked FBI cars racing towards the abandoned warehouse.

They pulled out onto the street and slowly made their way towards the anchored freighter. Being careful to observe speed limits and traffic as much as possible, the Indonesian driver made his way toward the dock. However, about twenty minutes into their journey, he drove through a red light in front of a police car.

A rookie Portland traffic cop pulled him over.

Stopping by the curb, the driver looked down and noticed that he had forgotten to wear his seatbelt. He swore under his breath, while the officer made his way to the van and noted the license plate on his ticket pad.

Ji was sweating bullets as the cop walked up the window.

"Driver's license and registration please," the cop demanded.

The driver coolly pulled out his forged driver's license and handed it to the police officer, and then he frantically searched for the vehicle registration papers in the glove box and above the sun visor.

"Do you work for this company?" the officer asked without looking, as he started to write out a ticket.

"Yes, I am a parts driver. Registration must be at head office," the driver blurted. "Sorry, officer, I was in a bit of a rush."

Ji, hidden in the back behind the separating wall, had his AK-47 aimed at the officer from the inside of the van.

"You just went through a red light and I see you are not wearing your seatbelt. Two hundred dollar fine for running the red light and seventy-five for the seat belt infraction; it is mandatory to wear seatbelts in Oregon. They save lives. The next one it saves, maybe your own. Instructions for payment are on the bottom. Have a nice day!" the officer said, handing the ticket and driver's license back to the Indonesian fellow.

The driver slipped the seat belt on and unhurriedly drove away.

In an inexcusable moment of memory lapse, the cop failed to call in and check to see if the van was stolen, which he found out later that day, while he was doing his paperwork.

They arrived at the freighter and unloaded Sally and Caleb. Blindfolded and zap-strapped, Ji and the driver helped them to walk up the gangway onto the first deck of the ship.

They were shoved, unbound and locked into an interior room of the freighter lit by a greasy forty-watt light bulb. For the first time mother and son officially met. Time stood still in the dimly lit, grubby room. In breathless silence they caressed each other with their eyes. It was an intense moment of maternal love for Sally to a long lost son and for Caleb, the reconnection to an inexplicable bond that was part of a journey that began thousands of years ago.

"Mom, I can read minds," Caleb blurted out as tears started to fill his eyes.

"I don't care," Sally softly replied as she reached out and pulled her son into an embrace that lasted for an eternity. They wept, and Sally caressed her son's head as tears streamed down her face and onto his curly dark hair.

"Welcome home, son, welcome home."

"Dad, errr ... your husband had told me you were beautiful, and now I know why. Are you OK? Did you get hurt in the van?" Caleb asked as he pulled back from the embrace.

"No, I am fine. What about you?"

"I am fine, too..., Mom. You don't mind me calling you mom?"

"No, not at all!" Sally blurted through sniffles, "It is a privilege to be your mother."

"Have you met Darby, my girl friend? I miss her a lot."

"Yes, briefly, she seems like a very nice young girl. She was very concerned about you and asked me to pass on her love. Sounds like you two are close." Sally paused as she wiped her nose and composed herself. "Do you know why I am here?"

"Yes, it is to do more cloning." Caleb's mood changed. "...for evil purposes. I have read their minds and I know their intentions. This Ji guy is evil. He killed two cops just as we were leaving, but

the most amazing thing happened. I saw the dead bodies and a voice
... I believe it was God. He told me to speak to them to "rise up",
which I did. Then just as we were leaving, I saw them come back to
life, right before my eyes!"

"Are you sure they were actually dead?"

"Well, they were not moving or breathing and they were in a
pool of blood. After I spoke to them they started to breathe, and the
last moment I saw them as we left the warehouse, they both were
raising themselves up on their elbows."

"That's amazing!" Sally exclaimed. "Is that part of the powers
you possess?"

"This is something brand new; it seems as if the older I get, the
more things like this seem to develop. It started with the dreams and
then the dream participation, then the sensory dreams then the
telepathy, and now this. I don't know what's next."

"Have you ever been sick?"

"No, I have never even had a cold."

"Didn't your parents ... huh..., foster parents, wonder about
that?"

"They wondered about a lot of things including that. That's why
they sent me to all kinds of counseling. They knew I was different
but didn't have any idea where to begin to get help. This all came to
a head after we got in touch with the adoption agency."

"So turning to them was sort of a last resort?"

"Yes, apparently there was some kind of flag on my file put there
by the CIA. Did you know about the experience I had when I saw the
news on TV about the Ice Man discovery?" Caleb asked.

"Jared and your folks told me a little but there was no time for
details. Please, tell me."

"When I saw the pictures on TV – I can't maybe explain it in
words – it was like a trigger ... like a bolt of electricity and it was as
if it was me that was being pulled from the ice. I felt so close to that
person ... corpse ... like I had always known him. Somehow, I was
there ... like I was hovering over the scene. I couldn't quite feel
anything but I could, for the lack of a better word, see almost a
mirror of myself. Like a close-up of my whole body. Something like
an out of body experience, I guess. That's the best I can describe it. I
must have gone into a trance. My folks freaked out. They thought I
was having some kind of weird medical condition."

Caleb continued, "I eventually came back from the mountain … it was the most awesome experience I have ever had. Mom, I have to go back there, I know there will be answers to some of the many questions I have. I just know it will finally make the dreams complete … put the pieces of a massive puzzle together."

"When you were in captivity, did you share these experiences with Dennis and Jared and Jason?"

"A little bit … mainly in whispers at night … we didn't know if the guards understood English. I even tried telepathy, but again, I wasn't sure if I was communicating with them as well. I did some experiments with the guards and animal sounds telepathy… It was actually quite funny. I think we can get off this ship the same way."

"We are being tracked by satellite right now, too," Sally interjected quietly, "I am wired."

Caleb nodded. "Jared told me about your original discovery of the Ice Man and the smuggling and the CIA business. Dennis…, Uncle Dennis is funny. He always wanted to have a cigarette and he would hassle the guards to go somewhere for a smoke. He almost had us out of there at one point. When he ran out of cigarettes, he got real grumpy. He would swear at the guards and throw things around. It was quite entertaining." Caleb paused. "Jared told me he always wanted to clone a human but that you were more interested in the medical side. I would like to hear your side of the story."

Sally told him her theories of ancient man having better DNA. About how long man used to live according to the Bible. At this point, she introduced her own story and pointed out that she wasn't religious but had always been fascinated by ancient literature and anthropology. "You know, the more you look at existing reptiles, if you were to enlarge them, they look awfully like the fossils of some of the monsters that walked the earth thousands of years ago."

"I know that," Caleb cut in, "there are several that way, I have seen so-called extinct fossils in live action. I have touched and smelled them. You're right, a lot are simply larger versions of the baby ones we see running around today. The great flood wiped out their grand daddies and many other species."

"How do you know that?" Sally asked puzzle, her scientific mind kicking in.

Caleb's face slowly changed to an intensely serious look as he knitted his brow and locked his gaze into her eyes. "Because I was there … the Ice Man … he was running up the mountain to avoid the catastrophe and mayhem of a world coming apart at the seams. He witnessed stuff that no movie could recreate. He…, I, saw saber-toothed tigers and whales, and T-Rexes annihilated by mountains fall and valleys explode with water and new mountains being formed. He…, I, saw the sky so black you could not see your finger in front of your eyes in the middle of the day. We felt the earth rattle and roll, and heave, and heard it roar and groan like a giant having a baby, and huge boulders whizzed pass at incredible speed, mowing down whole forests like they were match sticks. Guess it was because continents collided and were being moved around like pieces in a giant jigsaw puzzle all over the world." He paused. "I could tell you a library's worth of eye witnessed scenes…. Now, I know all of the Ice Man's life and stuff he witnessed that was stored in his genes and it somehow needs to be played out through me."

Sally's mouth had fallen wide open; her eyes were as big as saucers as her son spelled out his story. She knew he couldn't possibly have made this up, or was he some dreamer. She knew she was standing before a phenomenon.

Their privacy was shattered as keys rattled in the door. Ji made his way into the room with an armed guard immediately behind him and with his wicked smile, he said, "So nice to see mother and son in same place. In meantime, we separate you. Boy stay here, mother stay in other room."

He then forced Sally out of the room and down some stairs into a corridor and along an outer deck toward her room. She had been outside long enough for the GPS to transmit their co-ordinates. The ship had barely left the harbor.

"How could her GPS just disappear?" Conor asked. He was staring at an empty screen in the Portland FBI office, "I thought this was the greatest tracking device ever…. Wait a minute there it is … damn … it just disappeared. Is this thing working or is it intermittent?"

"I heard you have to have a fairly open access to the sky or it isn't reliable," Raftus replied. "It doesn't work that well inside buildings. You have to be near a window. It needs to be tracked off a satellite."

"That's Mickey Mouse!" Jared yelled angrily, raking his hands through his hair. He got up and began pacing the length of the room. "That's my wife and son out there in the great unknown and I trusted you guys with the latest technology…! That's just f… great. I knew I should have never let Sally go into the lair of this whacko. I may never see her again. My God, I can't believe I did this." He sat down again in a hopeless, helpless heap with his head between his hands and wept openly in bitter agony. "My God! My God! Help me! Help me! Help Sal, help us," Jared cried out desperately, between convulsive sobs.

Conor nodded to Raftus to help a very distraught Jared into an empty office. Raftus got up and walked across the floor, gently touched one of Jared's muscular shoulders and quietly asked him to join him in another room. At first, Jared was unresponsive. Then, mechanically, he stood up shakily, shoulders slouched and head bent. With a hand on his back, Raftus guided Jared into a more comfortable room and got him to sit down in an ancient leather armchair that Roosevelt would have used in the days of old.

Chapter 30

A few minutes later, Clint and Dan staggered through the 106th Street precinct's door.

"Chief…, we were toast, we got ambushed, and the last thing I remember was rounding the corner of that building and then, hot, searing pain entering my body in several places…. Unreal! See, look at the scars!" Clint pulled up his shirt and showed off the rounded purple marks sprinkled randomly over his large torso left from the gun shot wounds. "And look…, we got the bullets…!" He opened his hand. In the palm of it were four mangled bullets.

Their chief stared for a moment and then picked up one of the slugs out of Clint's hand. "Get these to forensics – maybe it'll give us a lead where these guys got their guns from." He looked up at Dan. He wanted to hear his side of this outlandish tale.

Dan looked as disheveled as his companion did, but couldn't stop nodding until he had to but in, "I just remember a long tunnel and a bright light at the end … I knew it was heaven … I knew I was no longer in my body. I had heard about stories like this but thought they were fairy tales or something. Then I heard a loud voice yelling, "Rise up! Rise up!" and I thought, what does that mean? Then, I was back in my body and excruciating pain searing throughout it, slowly it subsided as I rolled over on to my elbow … it was like coming out of a dream … or…, nightmare. When I was able, I propped myself up, and felt cold, wet, and looked to see that I was lying in a pool of blood…. Little did I know it was my own. Then I saw the bullet holes in my clothing and thought, "wow, I've been shot all to hell, am I dead or alive?" Then I saw Clint coming to, and tried yelling at him but my voice was too weak. Ever so slowly, we both were able to sit up and this feeling … indescribable, like a wave of shocks and cool liquid coursing throughout my body as it was being repaired. It seemed to take an eternity, but I believe it was only a few minutes, but this presence of love and well-being surrounded us kept welling up in both of us. We knew it was God. I've never been a religious person, but this was God … and He like…, gave us a second chance.

I know it has changed my life forever. I have never experienced a peace like this before," Dan added quietly.

Clint burst in again, "When we both were revived, there was no one around, the warehouse was empty. We staggered to our feet with our clothes dripping blood. We yelled for help but only scared off the pigeons roosting in the rafters. As we came to our senses, we remembered what we were doing and collected our thoughts. As we slowly, I mean very slowly, worked our way outside, we remembered our vehicle was around the corner of one of the buildings. We started to feel pretty normal, even though we had so many wounds. Every moment we got stronger and we were both in shock and disbelief that we were still alive. Then we found our car and drove here."

"Amazing, absolutely amazing!" their boss exclaimed. "Please do not share this with anyone."

Dan and Clint looked at each other and then back at their superior. "Too late, we've already told our families."

"Well, make sure they don't go blabbing it around, at least not until we break this case. Now go home, change and take the rest of the day off and make an appointment to be x-rayed, there may still be lead in your body.... One question, did you find any evidence of someone being in the complex? We are going to send over CSI to find out what went on there."

"Homeless maybe, we were just glad to get outta there," Clint replied. "That would be a great idea to get a team over there, something very strange took place."

Both men left the precinct as their colleagues stared at their blood soaked, bullet riddled clothing. "So what happened to those guys?" the other officers asked their chief, still astounded.

"Ummm..., close encounters with a machine gun..., I think I will explain later," he answered tentatively. He quickly assembled the CSI teams and dispatched them to the scene. Police and investigators swarmed the property within hours. Reports came back congruent with Dan and Clint's testimonies, along with discoveries of remnants of a lab, fresh garbage and the dirt scarred by spraying bullets, pools of drying blood and recent vehicle tracks inside the warehouse.

Chapter 31

Conor was briefed on the findings.

Another blip on the GPS receiver and then gone. "Damn," he muttered to himself, "technology sucks."

A couple of days into the sailing trip, Caleb knew his powers were ever increasing. Despite being slightly seasick, he worked out in his little room and kept himself limber and agile with instinctive kinetic exercises. He could do countless chin-ups, push-ups, and crunches. He meditated on the God in his dreams, began concentrating his mental and physical power on objects of steel in the room, and was able to twist parts of the metal bed-frame with his bare hands as if they were putty. He was careful not to reveal his strength to his captors, as they would put him through some kind of test to use against him. He was more interested in saving his mother out of this horrible situation.

One day as a guard was bringing him breakfast; he completely baffled him with an overwhelming flood of his thoughts and paralyzed him unconscious. He then quickly escaped and started searching the ship for his mother. He went down a flight of stairs and one of the hallways, listened for her thoughts in his mind, and eventually found her locked in a room just one floor below his.

"Mom, are you alright?" Caleb asked while talking through the top vents in the door, and then opening it carefully.

"Caleb! How did you escape?" a very startled Sally replied. "I had to get over throwing-up for two days from seasickness. Other than that, I'm fine. I'm OK."

As he slid inside the room, Caleb asked sternly, "Have they done anything to you?"

"No, nothing, thank God, nothing but feed me bad food. You better watch yourself, how did you get out?"

"I'll tell you later. Mom, I have been increasing in power and abilities daily, I am going to demand to see Ji and work on his mind to turn this ship around. Have they been letting you out on the deck at all? I remember something from science class that this new GPS system works only when there is an open sky. It can't work inside this steel boat." He looked into her eyes. "You got to demand that you get some fresh air and exercise out on the deck. They can then track you. I could bust this lock very easily but I don't want to give away any secrets." He hugged his mother in a burst of affection. "Love you Mom…. I better get back to my room," he added, releasing her and taking the few steps that separated him from the door – without looking back. His love for his mother stirred something in him that he had never felt. It was strange – something invasive….

Like a cat, Caleb vanished down the hall, up the stairs and back to his room to find the guard still unconscious on the floor outside his room. With some jolting thoughts from Caleb, the guard came to in a few seconds and Caleb demanded, in his thoughts to see Ji.

The guard jumped up, wide-eyed and excited, grabbed his AK-47 and thrust it into Caleb's ribs. "Get in room! Get in room!" He forced the young man through the doorway and onto his cot. He then turned around, grumbling. He went out, locked the metal door quickly and stumped away.

Caleb smiled to himself, and said a little *thank-you* prayer. He knew it was just a matter of time; they would be away from this evil.

He sat down on the edge of the dirty bunk bed with his head in his hands and elbows on his knees. His thoughts went to Darby. With all these newfound powers, he wondered if he could project himself to her. He pictured himself in her bedroom with her where they had spent many hours together talking and petting. He imagined her wearing the sexy outfit she wore when they first went out. He had too much respect and integrity to have sex with her but he missed her closeness, her gentleness and understanding and the soul connection they had.

He spoke out loud because he knew nobody could hear him above the noise of the ship's engines. "Dar, I love you. I really miss you. I'm sitting on a disgustingly dirty bunk bed on a disgustingly ancient boat somewhere out in the ocean. I have met for the first time with Sally, my birth mom, who is locked up in another room. She is such a beautiful lady both inside and outside, and you probably already know the rest. We are off to create some clones in a far away country. When I really think of it, it is pretty disgusting because it is like incest. I think I would rather die than to go through with it. As a matter of fact I may really fight to my death in order to prevent it from happening. Do you think that would be evil? I may even have to kill someone to protect my mom from this. I really miss my main mom and dad. They have been so good to me. I am so sorry that I have put you through all this... Who would have known that this could have happened so quickly? You know, the most amazing thing is that just the other night in one of my dreams there was all the commotion about something big going to happen. Then I saw that ancient Ice Man and we connected. I knew that was me up on that mountain. I know now totally why I had all those dreams and visions while growing up. What an amazing discovery! What an amazing thing that Sally and Jared did. I hope I can help science. I hope it will benefit mankind in so many ways. You know, Dar, I now can bend steel with my hands...when I concentrate real hard with my thoughts and focus on something metal. I can bend or break it..., it's another new power. I don't want to show it off though because these creeps may want me to use it for evil. I should tell you about raising a couple of guys from the dead. I'm sure you have already heard about that. I will wait to tell you face to your beautiful face. That was awesome – a total miracle." He paused his thoughts and stared quietly in the dimly lit room and listened with his finely tuned senses to see if there was a connection to Darby's mind and a possible response. "Are you there, Darling?" He listened intensely. Nothing. He lay back in the bunk with his hands behind his head. His little talk seemed to satisfy something within him.

This was a conversation he repeated a few times while in captivity. He also prayed aloud several times throughout the day and his faith increased daily.

Conor's men, CSI and the 106th precinct men gathered to exchange their findings at the Portland FBI offices.

"Thank you for your efforts, men. We have concluded that the enemy has slipped away by boat and is somewhere in the Pacific, probably on the way to Indonesia. We have intelligence in the South Pacific on stand by. We still have the GPS tracking system that appears to be working intermittently and hopefully we will be able to track the ship at some point.

"This has been one of the most unusual cases of blunders, narrow

207

escapes, lucky breaks for the enemy and miracles for others, I have ever seen. And this case is still very much active and certainly far from over," Conor reflected. "We will give a public newscast to ease people's fears and continue with a skeleton staff on the case until we retrieve Caleb Lindstrom and Sally Houghton back safe and sound. Thanks once again for all your efforts. If you have any questions or further input, please report to your superiors."

Back in Seattle, the CIA put Dennis under house arrest. He was under twenty-four hour surveillance while he stayed at Jared's place and babysat Jared and Sally's kids. He had never been happier. For the first time in his life, he experienced the joy of children and he actually stopped smoking. He took the fiasco with Caleb and Sally very seriously, and agonized over the gravity of the situation, but the years of CIA training had managed to callous a part of him not to own to the circumstances and dangerous predicaments he would have to face.

For his part, Jared was having a hard time trying to forgive his brother for his unscrupulous actions.

"Uncle, uncle, look at the boat we made!" Jared and Sally's youngest boys shouted in unison, bringing in their cardboard ship they had made in the basement to Dennis. "Does this look like the boat mommy is on? We hope she is coming home soon. Daddy said she wasn't going to be working too long on the boat and we wanted to remember her with this."

Dennis' countenance broke down. He was caught off-guard by the innocence of the kids.

"Yeah, oh yeah, that's just like it." He tried to muster some enthusiasm. "She…, your mom will be alright, I mean, she should be home soon. Nice looking boat, you guys. Hey, let's play hide 'n seek. Are you ready?" They quickly dropped their cardboard boat, squealed with delight and ran off to hide.

As the days dragged on, the ordeal played havoc with both Jared and Jason. Jared was on sabbatical from the university and Jason was on an indefinite leave of absence from school. They both attended counseling classes regularly. Despite the newscast that there was nothing to be concerned about on US soil, the press hounded them continually and many set up RVs on their street, waiting to catch a glimpse or get an interview. The media went wild with speculation about the fate of Sally and Caleb. Plain clothes FBI agents kept the paparazzi at bay and ushered the family around when they needed to go anywhere. They used sleeping pills and were on a special diet to ward off any further effects of depression. In a very short time, Jared had taken on an altered personality, started to drink heavily, was far more serious, and laughed little.

They met frequently with the Lindstroms and Darby, who were suffering deeply as well. Bob and Diane were determined to keep up their prayers and stubbornly cried out to God for the release of Sally and Caleb. They all managed to encourage each other that everything would be Okay; that Sally and Caleb were safe and would soon return. They, too, were at the mercy of the paparazzi and had plain clothes FBI staked out around them. Both families had their phones tapped and recorders littered tables and desks in their respective houses. No one could have ever imagined such an ordeal. They were prisoners in their own homes.

Back on the ship, Sally insisted on taking a walk on the deck to stretch and catch some fresh air. After breakfast, her guard relented after much sign language and explanation to Ji.

It had been the first time Sally saw the sun and the swollen sea. She squinted and her eyes began to water while they adjusted to the brilliant morning sun, which sparkled off the heaving water. The intense sea breeze, laden with the scent of the salt water, almost stung Sally's nose that had become accustomed to the acrid smell of diesel mixed with odors that emanated from the freighter's inner workings. She steadied herself, while inhaling huge lungs full of the fresh air then slowly started walking along one of the narrow decks. It was like getting her batteries recharged. She was amazed how atrophied her leg muscles had become after only a few days.

She had had plenty of time to think what this whole thing was about.

Her mind wandered back to the original discovery of the Ice Man.

I was so innocent. Jared and I were so in love. We were absolute idealists, everything was black and white. If we figured one thing out, then the results would always be the same for the next discovery. A smile crept upon her face as she thought about it. *We held the world in the palm of our hands; we knew that we would make a mark. I was convinced I would find the cure for cancer, MS and heart disease. It was all in the genetic make up. I still believe it is. I knew Jason wasn't the right baby. I just knew it. Why didn't Jared stand by me? It makes me so mad when he is so bull-headed. All we had to do was force the hospital to do a DNA test or something. I mean Caleb certainly ended up in good hands, but what a fiasco. How simple things would have been if we didn't have to go through all this. And that Dennis ... I could kill him ... hope he gets his reward for this. I hope his life is a living hell for putting us through this! We may never get out this alive with these creeps. My God, Jared ... I can't believe he caved to the CIA. I can't believe I offered to do this either. What am I saying...? This is for Caleb's sake. Come on, Sally get a grip. You're strong. Mom always said I had the constitution of a pit bull. Well, I'm sure to hell going to need it to kick in now. I wonder what my eulogy will be like? Will my friends and colleagues remember me as someone who kept nasty CIA secrets? Who stole ancient artifacts? I wonder if this GPS thingy is working? This ship is such a clunker. That Caleb is something else... Wow! What an amazing kid! I would like to dive into that water and swim to some deserted island right about now.*

The guard watched at a distance as she picked up her pace, walking back and forth, swinging her arms vigorously to up her cardio.

Bleep..., bleep..., bleep, the GPS receiver and screen sprung to life in Conor's empty Seattle office. One of Conor's assistants heard the incessant bleeping as he walked by the office, found the door unlocked and headed to the screen that sat on Conor's desk. He immediately got on the phone to Conor and told him what was going on.

"Can you read any coordinates?" Conor asked. "Write down anything that makes sense to you on the read out, I'm just around the corner." He hurried into his office in time to hear the continuing series of bleeps and to see coordinate lines traced across a map on the screen. The look on his assistant's face said it all. "Did you get anything?"

His assistant had scribbled down what he could discern, handed it to Conor as he slumped into his chair all the while dialing Raftus' number with his left hand.

"Looks like we have finally tracked them down; they are about seven hundred and fifty miles on their way to Indonesia," Raftus agreed. He had the only other monitor.

"Well, this Ji character is good to his word so far; he wanted to take them there for his lab and I guess that's where they are headed," Conor replied. "We need to deploy a rescue team and get permission from the Indonesian Navy Command to strike within their two hundred mile limit."

He proceeded to alert recon all along the South Pacific corridor and to deploy Navy Seals and other military forces ready for action. The ship's co-ordinates were relayed to an aircraft carrier in the vicinity and a recon plane was deployed for a visual. Coupled with satellite images and shots of the freighter from the high-flying recon plane, Ji had no idea that he was a marked man.

As the freighter steamed toward Sumatra, Navy Seals were deployed to a vessel posing as a customs inspection ship. Captained by one of the locals, they headed toward Ji to get "permission to come aboard".

Ji was suspicious of everything and everyone. Once the inspector had made radio contact, Ji had Sally and Caleb moved to the head, closest to the engine room. On their way to their smelly prison, both Sally and Caleb silently prayed. Caleb used his telepathy. The guard kept stumbling and eventually fell to the grimy floor, unconscious, outside the toilet.

Sally was stunned in disbelief. "What happened to him? Did you do that? Is he dead?" Her voice shrieked above the throb of the engines coming from beyond the next wall. She was in shock.

"He's not dead; I'll tell you later, Mom. Let's put this guy into the toilet because this is where we were going. Something is up. Give me a hand, quick…, he may have help coming."

They dragged the unconscious body into the smelly head. Caleb picked up the AK-47 the guard had dropped and looked it over. He had never fired a gun before, but he knew he might have to learn fast. He needed to disable the weapon permanently or to get rid of it – one or the other. Caleb did not intend to shoot anyone but he had an overwhelming responsibility to protect his mother. However, a nagging thought kept coming to him to disable and dispose of it as quickly as possible.

Darrell Swanson

"We need to hide…. I have an idea," Caleb said as they ducked into a room full of supplies. The old freighter was small and Ji had partially converted the hull to accommodate his lab technicians and equipment. A hotel with storage would have best described it. There were several makeshift rooms, some with doors and others with curtains. The captain's bridge was located aft of the vessel. The engine room was below it and extending toward the ballast room.

The loudspeaker system crackled to life as Ji barked out orders in Indonesian. Meanwhile, Caleb studied the AK-47 carefully and decided to jam the firing mechanism.

Outside the supply room, they heard footsteps running back and forth as the twelve-man crew prepared for the landing of the custom's officers. The engine's throb came to a halt and within a few moments, Caleb and Sally heard more footsteps along with voices from above their heads, as the inspection went underway.

The door burst open, and Ji came face to face with Sally and Caleb. The astonished look on Ji's face was priceless; his left eye nearly popped out of its socket as the ugly scar twitched in anger. In a flash, Ji grabbed the AK-47 from Caleb and started yelling just as machine gun-fire erupted from the deck above. The twelve Navy Seals, who were hidden on the customs ship, had watched Ji's men assemble with AK-47s on one of the outer decks as the customs officers disappeared into the hull. They came out of hiding, guns ablaze, taking down Ji's men. Bullets ricocheted everywhere and dead and wounded bodies dropped into the water.

The Seals secured the outer deck enough to start boarding as Ji forced his captives deeper into the hull. Caleb kept trying to confuse Ji's thoughts but because of the heightened excitement, it appeared to be less effective. Ji knew his only survival tactic was to use his captives as a human shield and as he grabbed Caleb to point the AK-47 at his head, like lightning, Caleb snatched the gun out of his hand and threw Ji to the floor. Caleb stared into Ji's eyes while he pinned him down and concentrated on his thoughts and Ji lost consciousness. The custom's officials and Sally dropped their arms in amazement as Caleb silently raised himself off the floor and discarded the AK-47.

"We won't be needing this," Caleb said calmly.

At that moment two of the Seals with guns drawn burst into the hold.

212

"Hands up!" one yelled.

"It's OK!" Sally shouted. "We have the captain disabled."

"Doesn't matter, get 'em up!" Once again, the group threw up their hands and the Seals frisked them for weapons.

"Is he dead?" one of the Seals asked as he pointed to Ji on the floor.

"No, unconscious," Sally replied. "My son disabled him."

"Is he hurt, need medical attention?"

"Only thing hurt is his feelings," Sally retorted with a smile. "There is another one in the toilet by the engine room."

The Seal ordered one of his sidemen to look for Ji's man as he handcuffed Ji.

"What's your names?" the Seal asked from the kneeling position beside Ji.

"Caleb Lindstrom."

"Sally Houghton."

"We have come to rescue you two, there has been a lot of people worried about your safety. Anyone harmed you?"

"No, but we were sure wondering what was going to happen to us," Sally replied.

The Seal radioed his command post that they had secured the freighter and the subjects were under detention. Just as he signed off, the other Seal came back from the engine room area empty handed, "Nobody down there, sir."

The Seal looked at Sally and Caleb in turn. "Where did you leave him?"

"In the toilet," Sally and Caleb chimed together.

"I put him unconscious," Caleb piped up, "and we dragged him there, he must have come to, and escaped."

The main Seal got on his shoulder radio and alerted his men to look for him.

"Well, let's get you off this wreck and back home. We will take care of your kidnappers."

They made their way to the upper deck and as they were transferring to the customs vessel, a cry for help came off the water from the starboard side of the freighter. A black head bobbed up and down in the waves, and arms flailed for help. Instead of stepping on to safety, Caleb stepped off the side of the boat and, much to the shock of the rest; he walked on top of the water toward the drowning man.

"Caleb, what are you doing?" Sally yelled as she and the others froze in awe.

Quietly Caleb made his way bobbing up and down on top of the swells. As he approached the flailing man, he looked up dazed and confused. Caleb communicated through telepathy to him to lift up his hands. At first, the man couldn't believe his eyes and shook his head in incredulity, trying to wipe the burning salt water out of his eyes. He tried to swim away in terror as though not wanting any help. Eventually, already in a weakened condition, lifted up both his hands and Caleb grabbed a hold of him and pulled him up out of the watery grave as if he was being extracted from quick sand. The drowning man wrapped his arms around Caleb's neck. He then walked him back to the boat where the Seals grabbed him. Everyone was in quiet shock as Caleb climbed aboard.

"How did you do that?" the officer in charge asked.

"Are there any others in the water?" Caleb asked by way of an answer.

"Dunno...." The officer turned to his men. "Anyone knows if there are more in the water to be rescued?"

The amazed Seals shook their heads and stared at the teenager in wonder.

"Are you related to Jesus?" one asked, "I've never seen this before. How did you do that?"

The customs boat bobbed up and down quietly in the massive expanse of the sea and all on board felt humbled as a sense of the presence of the Almighty overwhelmed them.

"This is the man we dragged into the toilet by the engine room; he must have escaped and jumped overboard. Go ahead and tell them, Caleb, what you can do," Sally prodded him confidently.

"I can't explain this," her son began. "I can only tell you that I was only obeying a voice in me to do it. If Jesus did it, then why can't anyone else? I'm just a teenager; I have seen and experienced many things as I'm sure many of you have. I have discovered that there is the voice of God in us that we need to listen for. I have never walked on water before, but I knew I could today because the voice told me. It was done to not only save this man's life, but yours also."

"But, this is my son and he is different," Sally said. "I'm his mother and I'll tell you...."

"It's OK, Mom," Caleb interjected almost inaudibly, "I will tell them later.... How is Ji? Is he still unconscious?"

"You mean the captain, the little guy?" one of the Seals replied. "He's conscious alright. We have him handcuffed and secured in the hull. Feisty little bugger; he has done nothing but cuss and spit at us."

Meanwhile, the medic officer revived the drowning man. Even in his weakened state, he murmured away in Indonesian and kept trying to point to Caleb and to the sky.

Communication was connected to the FBI office in Seattle and an elated and relieved Conor came on the phone first to the Seal commander, congratulating him and for the necessary debriefing and then to Sally and Caleb.

"We are grateful you two are safe and sound. We will patch you through to your families shortly, but first, we need to get as much information about FTW's operation as you can provide."

Conor's plan was to get to the center of their activities and eliminate it. Sally and Caleb recounted their experiences, but when it came to the mental overpowering of the enemy and walking on water, Conor wrote it down as part of the activities. He was beginning to be less skeptical about Caleb's abilities.

"I want to be clear on a couple of things, Caleb. You said you used some form of telepathy to over power the enemy. Is this something we should know about? Something that others can learn? The same with walking on water? Are these teachable skills?"

After a pause, Caleb replied, "I'm not sure, but I do know that it is not something that I can turn on and off; it's something built in, part of my make up, something like that."

"We can talk more about this when you are back here." He paused. "I will patch you through to your families now," Conor concluded as he switched the lines to the awaiting conference call.

 Understandably, the families were elated in hearing Sally and Caleb's voices. They talked, and talked and talked some more until it was time to hang up.

Once mother and son landed on Indonesian soil, the authorities escorted them to a hotel in Jakarta where they awaited repatriation with impatience.

Meanwhile, the CIA transferred Ji to a detention center near Washington D.C., where he, and what was left of his team, underwent lengthy interrogation for suspected acts of terrorism. They were bound for trial soon after that. The bio-bomb found onboard the ship was stumbled upon by the Jakarta militia and was almost accidentally released except for the confession of one of the lab workers who had a change of heart.

As for Caleb and Sally, after their debriefing, they managed not to share his supernatural powers with the media under any circumstances, under the advice and supervision of the CIA.

Chapter 32

The emotional reunion of Sally, Caleb and their respective families was awesome. The press hounded and the paparazzi followed them everywhere, talk show hosts clamored for interviews. It would be awhile before their lives returned to normal. However, during it all, the families managed to keep Caleb's powers away from the public eye. Caleb and Darby drew closer than ever in their relationship, but the secret drive to return to the Ice Man's frozen domicile drove Caleb more restless. The vivid dreams continued to haunt him and seemed to become more foreboding. His prehistoric dream world was coming apart at the seams. Floodwaters were forcing Caleb and the animals to scale the face of a giant mountain that crumbled and groaned, and shook like a leaf in the wind.

The CIA re-opened the file on Caleb and kept him for several days in the company of a battery of scientists, biologists, and psychologists. They studied his DNA with the hope of capitalizing on his powers.

During his time with them, they tried persuading him to doing miracles and he could do nothing. He was able to read their minds and he knew they wanted to synthesize his actions and clone him.

In a separate office, Conor and the local CIA manager, Clive Jenkins, had made arrangements to interview him, Sally and Jared at great length.

One day a knock came at the door and in walked two men.

Conor and Jenkins jumped to their feet. "Sally, Jared and Caleb, I would like you to meet Dan Oliver and Clint Shatford." They all rose to their feet and shook hands. Clive Jenkins retreated to the far wall, crossed his arms over his chest and prepared himself to listen to what promised to be an interesting conversation.

"Dan and Clint are the two men Caleb raised from the dead at the warehouse in Portland," Conor said, addressing Caleb, Jared and Sally.

Dan and Clint came over to Caleb and hugged him with great appreciation.

Dan said, "We are honored and privileged to meet you, Caleb. You saved me and Clint here's life." He then told the story of the neighbor kid who had lost his dog in the abandoned warehouse property, how his mother didn't believe him, and how she had wanted to teach him a lesson by getting the police involved. Apparently the kid was always lying or fabricating some cock and bull story.

"I remember that day very clearly," Caleb began. "It was on a Friday afternoon and some of our captors had left us locked in a room with a couple of guards. A bunch of them had left the compound. Everyone had fallen asleep except me. I heard this dog barking off in the distance outside and I could hear it was getting closer. I had been practicing some telepathy, so I thought I would have fun with the dog. A couple of years ago I had communicated with one of my aunt's cat and had got it to respond without saying a word aloud, so I thought I would try it again. The dog would stop barking, so I started talking to it … in my head, and I could hear it whining somewhere close by. Then I heard a kid's voice yelling for it. I thought this could be a great way of communicating to someone about being kidnapped. So, I spoke to him something in my mind, *there are six of us inside the building, we are kidnapped and we need help.* It must have freaked the kid out because I heard him say something and then there was silence. I was glad he left because one of the guards was about to go and do something to him. They would have thought nothing of killing him. They got in big trouble from Ji, their leader, for not killing him and the dog, when he got back. This made them trigger happy and on red alert or something, because a few days later when you guys showed up, they had someone posted to monitor the same area and kill anyone who showed up." Caleb then turned to the two officers. "So, what was it like?"

Dan shook his head and gave Caleb a timid, disbelieving smile before he went on with the story of the neighbor kid, how the gate was locked, how he felt the kid was telling the truth, and then decided to get Clint involved because of his experience.

"When we had searched the rest of the buildings of the compound, we were kind of relaxed, thinking that the last one would be pretty much the same, no big surprises. Boy, were we surprised when we rounded the corner and all of a sudden we were hit with gunfire. We never had a prayer. Hot lead entering your body is a sensation I will never forget. Right Clint?"

Clint nodded enthusiastically, adding, "It's like someone sticking white hot pokers from a blast furnace into you and your first reaction is to try and pull them out but your arms won't do what they're told. All your body wants to do is fall down, your legs can't move, you are instantly paralyzed. I guess you are in a complete state of shock from the bullets tearing through your body. Then those creeps came and dragged us like sacks of potatoes up the stairs and dropped us on the warehouse floor. They thought we were dead, but we could still hear everything. We couldn't feel anything and we could see, but couldn't move our eyes or blink. Our minds were still on how to escape. Then, the strangest thing happened. Gradually you feel like you are going to sleep but next thing you know, you are out of your body looking down at it and think, what is going on? I was calling out to my wife, my kids, that they should come and see this. Then I remember a tunnel with the white light at the end and someone calling my name like as if they were either in the light or were the light. But this other voice sort of over powered that voice by saying *Rise up, Rise up.* I then found myself back in my body as the *Rise up* voice got louder. It seemed to be coming from the horizon and I had to lift my body up on my elbow to hear where it was coming from. Then the pain started, it was like nothing I could explain. I have eight bullet holes in me and Dan has nine. Each bullet, for lack of better words, was extracted like it entered, like a hot poker, only in reverse and very slowly. I thought I was going to die all over. The pain was unbelievable. Then this liquid … best described as liquid healing, started flowing through me like a trickle at first, then a small stream, then a river and I regained full consciousness. Both Dan and I came back to life pretty much at the same time. All we could say was *what the hell was that?* When we had enough strength, we got up and saw our blood all over the cement and shook our heads in amazement. We kept rubbing ourselves all over to see if we were missing anything and if we were still bleeding. We knew this was a miracle. We left the compound, called our families and went to the precinct all bloodied and clothes with these bullet holes – totally bizarre. We brought back some of the slugs and the Chief told us to give them to forensics for analysis. He then told us to get X-rays and see if there was any other damage. There was nothing, what we have left are the scars." Both Dan and Clint open their shirts and they pointed out the purple marks left on their bodies. "All we can say is that it was an encounter with God. I wasn't a believer before, but sure am now. Thanks a million for saving our lives!"

"Yes, Caleb; thanks for saving me, too," Dan said, lowering his gaze timidly.

"Hey, you guys, you're welcome," Caleb replied. "Thank God, I didn't do anything, a voice told me to tell you to rise up. That's all I did. I was handcuffed, waiting for them to come out from the lab area. Even the fact that they left me alone for a few moments was a miracle. When I saw you both twitch and come back to life I thought I was in a dream…. It just didn't seem real. It seemed time stood still. I was petrified, I have never seen anybody killed and come back to life, only in horror movies. I was even afraid that as you were coming back to life, Ji and his crew would see it and try killing you all over again. I was glad we were leaving the compound."

Conor was agape. "You mean to say, that you didn't pray or, you know, start some religious ritual prior to them coming back to life?"

"No, that's all I did."

"Remarkable! You just heard this voice telling you to tell them to *Rise up?*"

"You see, Mr. Conor," Sally interjected, "he has codes in his DNA that our ancient relatives had. This young man has never been sick. Besides all the other supernatural things and abilities he possesses, he has never even had a tooth cavity. Somewhere along the line, those codes became extinct."

Totally ignoring Clive Jenkins' presence, Conor mused, "I can see why the CIA wants him."

Jenkins threw him a disapproving glance under Jared's piercing gaze. Both men looked at each other for an instant as if they were soldiers preparing to do battle.

Conor shrugged almost imperceptibly and then went on to make sure that Dan and Clint, Sally and Jared and Caleb never exposed this story to the public. "You have to understand, ladies and gentlemen, that the repercussions would be mayhem to police forces and other agencies around the world. It is imperative that none of your family members and friends know about this. I understand if you have told your spouses and kids, but they MUST NOT, I repeat, MUST NOT, tell ANYONE. Do you all understand?" Conor waited for nods of approval.

"What happens if we already have?" Dan asked meekly.

"How many have you told?"

"My wife and kids. And I think my neighbor and a really close friend."

"About the same amount for me, too," Clint said. "Our boss told us the same thing and I kind of down played it that we were just slightly wounded, I never showed any scars or anything to anyone but my wife – she'd have known anyway…"

Conor paused in an uneasy silence as he rubbed his face with both his slender hands and looked at Jenkins.

"Has the press been after you?"

Both Dan and Clint looked at each other and replied a resounding "No!"

"Well, that could be a good sign, just keep it silent. I am turning everything over to Mr. Jenkins of the CIA here, and will no longer be directly involved with any of you. Because this was an international incident, this is their jurisdiction from now on. Mr. Jenkins has been well briefed on this case and will continue as your liaison. I'm sure he will have much more to do to carry out their mandate." Conor glanced at his watch and got up to leave. "It has been an amazing experience working with you, but it is now my turn to leave you. Mr. Jenkins will be a great asset to you all."

Jenkins, remaining silent, only nodded toward the group.

Conor then made his rounds, shaking each person's hand and exchanging pleasantries and good-byes. He hated to leave; deep down he knew what the CIA were after and knew they would be ruthless in achieving their goals. Against FBI policy, he had grown very close to the hostages and almost felt personally responsible for their well being, but knew that was a red flag. He, too, had a family who had been battered for his many hours of time away from them. Now, he had to shift his thoughts and energy on making it up to them. There were also other cases beckoning his services and expertise.

Clive Jenkins was in his late forties. At first encounter he looked mild mannered. Yet, his steel blue eyes, and his short, wavy sandy colored hair, graying at the temples, could not hide his astuteness and perspicacity. His almost diminutive frame and steel smile that exposed perfectly white teeth and clean-cut appearance, was in perfect contrast to his extensive CIA experience. He always wanted to be a spy, and after high school in Chicago, worked as a private dick, following unfaithful spouses and looking for runaways and fugitives. His masterful work caught the eye of the Chicago office and they eventually took him on in junior roles until he proved himself locally and then on to the international scene. Very soon his management skills started to show and he was assigned more duties and agents. He had been assigned to the Seattle office within the past five years and ran a tight ship. With this incident, he knew he would have to interface with Alex Chambers out of Los Angeles and was not looking forward to it.

Chapter 33

Chambers, Dennis's old boss, made his way from Los Angeles to meet Caleb. He arranged a one on one meeting at the Seattle CIA lab.

"Caleb Lindstrom, I'm Ed Chambers," the man announced, entering the room. The now aged, very overweight CIA boss limped, supporting his massive body with a cane in the one hand and reaching out with the other.

"Finally, I get to meet one elusive young man." He forced a smile while he studied Caleb up and down as if he were some exotic animal. He kept holding the young man's hand. At one point, he even lifted it up to his narrowed eyes, and studied it closely.

Releasing Caleb's hand, Chambers went to sit on one of the lab's chair – the sturdiest one in the place. "You have caused quite a stir in our organization." He tried his best to look dignified with his right hand on top of the ornately carved cane, like some southern gentleman. But the ill-fitting, grey suit and large belly protruding over the top of his belt, and his legs swung open, made him look more like some cartoon character.

"Looks like our scientists have discovered your genetics could re-write some of our evolutionary theories. According to the reports, among other things, your DNA makes ordinary human's DNA look almost inferior. After our meeting, I want you to meet Dr. Riddenhall, head of our biology department." His eyes sparkled with devilishness. "As you know, we have been very interested in you before you were born. Your mother and surrogate father and I had a deal drawn up that we had … first right of refusal to examine you and work with you if there was something different with you to…, ah, shall we say, re-create your character. I still don't know how you got away from us in the hospital." Chambers shook his head ruefully. "I guess it's better late than never. And here we are."

Caleb could read his thoughts and knew what he was up to. "And you want to clone me," he said calmly.

A startled Chambers threw him a surprised look. "Well yes, I mean, kind of, I mean, we are interested in improving humanity here and you appear to have some qualities that no one else I know of has. Don't you think that would be a good thing to spread around?"

After a long uncomfortable pause, the teenager sighed and fixed his gaze at Chambers. "Sir, what I am about to tell you, either you or the CIA may not understand or appreciate. You see, when I was growing up, I had dreams that no one understood. My parents took me from one doctor to another to find out if there was something wrong with me because the dreams were not normal dreams. When other strange things started to happen to me as I got older, they took me to the adoption agency, and there is where we found out there was some involvement with the CIA at my birth. I then started thinking that I must be different if a powerful organization like the CIA was involved. I would ask myself, what would the CIA do with a dreamer and with some of the other abilities I possess? All I came up with was, something to control their enemies, something to rule the world, and you know what? Now that I look at it, nothing's different than what we just went through with Ji and his crew."

"Now just wait a minute, young man!" Chambers interrupted angrily. "Are you comparing the CIA to some two bit terrorist outfit? We are *the* most powerful intelligence organization in the world. We *are* interested in the integrity of the human social condition around the globe. It may *seem* like we are interested in imposing American policies only, it may *seem* like we set up governments or bring them down for our own interests, but I can assure you that where we have been successful in our activities; the people of those nations are way better off. We don't go into a situation and call the shots; we work with the existing governing bodies in order to bring about resolutions as peacefully as possible. These activities need an amazing force of talented people to bring peace to countries torn by war. Some civil wars have been going on for decades. Millions of people have lost their lives. If we had better agents, better facilitators, workers with the powers that you possess, it would not only make our jobs easier, it would save lives! Are you *not* interested in that?"

Another long, uncomfortable pause engulfed the two men into reflection.

"I would be a fool to say that I'm not interested in the betterment of mankind," Caleb replied, all the while scanning Chambers thoughts. "I will help you and the CIA in every way possible, under one condition, that I first return to the mountain where my father, the Ice Man, was found."

Chambers was taken aback by the request. "Why in God's name do you want to go there?" His rubbery face wrinkled into a quizzical grimace. "I understand he has been moved somewhere else, some museum in Italy or something! Besides, I can't just put you on a plane to Europe and hope you will return. Where are you going with this? What are your reasons?"

"I have my reasons. I also think I can show archaeologists some really neat stuff. Things I have dreamed about. Things nobody ever thought existed there."

Chambers' demeanor switched into one of wobbling laughter. Even with all of his knowledge of the boy and his abilities, at that moment he was having a hard time believing that Caleb was super human. He all of a sudden seemed to rub him the wrong way.

"Wait a minute; you want *me* to assemble a bunch of high priced scientists, plus security and who knows what else, to chase down some kid's dreams? That would go over like a lead balloon at headquarters."

Caleb knew from Chambers thoughts he was negotiating a deal to keep from sending him overseas. He also could read that the man was curious about the dreams.

"So, you want to know about my dreams."

Chambers was knocked for six again. "Well..., yeah, you know..., curious. Hey, it's not every day I talk to someone as unique as you."

"Do we have a deal then? I would like to be assured that I indeed will be going to Europe *before* sharing my dreams with you or anyone."

Chambers paused. The smile drained from his face. "You know, I think I should call in Riddenhall and his crew. They could help me determine an answer whether I should send you or not."

The CIA man raised his large frame off the chair and shuffled to a phone on a nearby desk. He picked up the handset and fumbled for an intercom button. He punched some digits and eventually got a hold of Dr. Riddenhall.

"Riddenhall, can you bring some of your cronies in here and settle something for me? ...Yes I want some of your evolution sharpshooters that have examined the lad here.... Right away, please." Chambers threw the receiver into the cradle, grabbed his cane and perched himself on the edge of the desk while he waited for the entourage to appear.

A few minutes later, Dr. Riddenhall strolled in swiftly with his white lab coat flapping around his body. His graying, unkempt hair and thick glasses made him look less dignified than his age would have warranted. His two younger cohorts were typical-looking lab rats with white coats, clipboards and an air of uneasy confidence. They strolled in as two little dogs following their master.

Chamber said, "The lad here says he has some things he wants to share with us and I thought you guys should hear about it since I am no scientist. He says he wants to go to Europe, to the mountain of the gravesite of the Ice Man, because he *may* have information about the terrain. Stuff he saw in a dream or dreams…. You know, I have read the reports on the lad and can't deny he has something going for him, but I can't be spending a bunch of taxpayer's money on a whim. So, I need you to convince me one way or the other what we should do."

The entourage pulled up some lab stools around Caleb and prepared to take notes.

Riddenhall settled his gaze on Caleb but addressed his two underlings. "As you know, gentlemen, Caleb can read our thoughts, so we need to focus on the business in hand. Let's try keeping things, shall we say, organized, in our minds." He returned his attention to the boy. "We know something about your dreams, Caleb. What brought on this sudden desire to go to the mountain?"

"As I have mentioned to Mr. Chambers, before I share any details, I wanted assurance that I can visit the mountain site of my father, whether it's paid for by the CIA or by me. I don't feel I should be a prisoner to you or anyone else."

"We understand, Caleb. But what is your purpose for returning to the site?"

"I have personal reasons, but I also have information I have seen in my dreams from that mountain that I know archaeologists would love to know about."

"Can you share a little of that with us? Something, even a small thing, can help us determine a positive decision on getting you there." Riddenhall visibly tried to be as persuasive as he possibly could.

Caleb paused, cycling between each of the men with his eyes, and his thought *antenna*.

He was unable to get a clear handle on any of their thoughts.

"Well, here is a small thing, I have never been to this mountain in person, nor seen anything else than pictures that were broadcasted on TV, but I can tell you I know of three caves somewhere close by. You can confirm this with my mother, Sally, and Jared. I have seen them both in dreams and in spirit. I can also tell you what is in those caves…, but not until I am assured I can go. I also know of several other things about that mountain that I will have to take you there to show you."

"What makes you so sure about these things?" Riddenhall asked. "That mountain is at least five thousand years older than when you were there in spirit or whatever you call it. Lots of things have happened during that time."

Caleb shrugged, a sigh escaping his mouth. He got up to leave. "Oh well, I guess I can't help you with any more cloning."

"Hey, that's not the deal, kid!" Chambers slid off the desk and stretched out his cane in front of Caleb. "You are under contract…," he bellowed. "No, you are actually under the care of the CIA, there is nowhere saying that you are free to go anywhere."

"Wait a minute, Mr. Chambers," Riddenhall interjected quietly while he rose from his stool. "I think Caleb may have a good point. If we take him there and he finds nothing, then his dreams are not really valid. Cloning him may have some advantages, but maybe not to the agencies' liking, that could be a contract breaker. On the other hand, if these dreams are what he says they are, then we need to warm up the cloning machine real fast."

"I thought you stupid lab gurus confirmed he was an excellent specimen for cloning, now you are back-pedaling, you're…, you're saying he's incomplete or something."

"Hear me out," Riddenhall said, trying to maintain an even tone of voice. "What we have here in Caleb is one of the most amazing human specimens alive. Not only is his DNA off the scale, he has demonstrated super human powers and much more. We could clone him as he is and no doubt his offspring would be the same. However, what the CIA needs to see is a demonstration of his mental and supernatural skills. We have pushed him in the lab and elsewhere, to demonstrate some of the things he did when he was a hostage and he was either unwilling or unable to reproduce them. His dreams are as much a part of his make up as any other of the abilities he has been able to demonstrate. We need to witness this. My vote is that we *must* get him on that mountain. This experience could be the thread to tie it all together."

The loud tick-tock echoing from one of the clocks on the wall and a low hum from the fluorescent lights were all that could be heard as silence brooded over the meeting. Several seconds went by before Chambers cleared his throat.

"I guess you're right, Riddenhall." Chambers smiled awkwardly. "Caleb, let's get you to your mountain."

Caleb's face lit up with joy for the first time in weeks. He jumped off the stool, took the few steps that separated him from Chambers with renewed energy and shook the obese man's hand vigorously. "Thank you, sir. You will not be disappointed." He turned to Dr. Riddenhall. "Thank you very much for understanding and listening. None of you will be disappointed, I promise you. None of you will be disappointed," he repeated eagerly. "Now can I go home to be with my families?"

"I don't see why that should be a problem. Who do you want be with first?" Chambers asked.

"My mom and dad Lindstrom."

Arrangements were made for Caleb to spend two weeks with his friends and families and then he and a number of people would go to Europe for the visit to the Otztal Alps on the Austrian and Italian borders, where the Ice Man was found. In the meantime, he was told he would be tagged and had to be very careful where he went. He was now very valuable merchandise for the CIA and they were not going to lose him again. Even if something happened to him, they could clone him, but they needed to see his powers in action in order to program his offspring.

School was off limits for Caleb. Given that he had missed a month of classes and it was almost the end of the school year, they decided for him to go back in September. He was allowed to see Darby, but as for his other friends, he was chaperoned at a distance, that only he would notice. Everyone was glad to see him. The media told them that he was just part of a hostage incident and no information was ever released about his supernatural feats. Caleb and Darby were under strict orders not to bring it up or discuss it with anyone if there were stories flying around about the incidents.

"So, K, what was it like?" Darby asked. "I heard you creamed some guy with a couple of hay makers and kicked him in the jewels."

"Na, that's just some story," Caleb laughed. It was good to laugh; he could just be a sixteen-year-old again. He had no pressure to fight to keep alive. He couldn't get enough of Darby. He went and shot some hoops and played catch with his dad. It felt so good. He felt alive like never before. He slept through the night and there were no dreams. He woke up refreshed. He was so invigorated.

"So, what was it like? Come on, K, we need to hear the whole story, we saw the news and it sounded really creepy and scary. Weren't you scared? Who were those guys?"

"These guys were passionate in what they believed, they were driven to take unbelievable risks and we just happened to be their targets. Yeah, we were scared. They could have beheaded us, but thank God, we live in a country that protects us and our freedoms, and stood behind us all the way. I learned a lot from the experience."

His friends were in awe.

"Wow, that's heavy, man. What you said, I mean, I would have crapped my drawers if I were there."

"Yeah, me too…."

One after another, his friends acknowledged his strength of character. He was a 'hero' to them, yet they only had a glimpse of what Caleb really was – an ancient man in the body of a teenager.

Chapter 34

Jared, Sally and the Lindstroms had grown very close through the ordeal and Caleb wanted both families to come with him, and, of course, Darby was a must. He was home, living with the Lindstroms but wanted to spend time with Sally and Jared and he would sometime stay weekends with them. They marveled at his abilities and developed a private study log of as much as they could, and studied his DNA.

Dennis Houghton had been forced to retire from the CIA and had gone on to work for a local private investigation firm. Jared had regained a semblance of his old self, but was now more determined than ever to study his long lost son. His association with the Genome project was now a priority as the scientific community had made large gains in the mapping of the human DNA. Both Jared and Sally were ignited about seeing their dreams and theories come-to-pass. They wanted to make a mark on humanity with their published findings.

Jason, their natural son, was having a hard time with all the fuss over Caleb. He had been *dethroned* as number one son within his family and was growing resentful of lack of attention. He became more aloof as he shrank away into a world where he could garner attention from the seedy side of his peer group. His girlfriend came from a broken home and clung to him for guidance and passion. They decided to hang around with drug dealers and gangs, where they felt empowered, and because it was cool. Sally and Jared were very concerned, but seemed to be powerless to resolve anything. The more they voiced their concerns and opinions to the Lindstroms, the more it seemed to drive Jason away.

For their parts, Bob and Diane became strong advocates of third world causes. Through their church, they researched and supported mission organizations that were making differences in people's lives around the world. They became flaming evangelists and carefully shared the gospel and their testimonies everywhere they could. They so wanted to talk about Caleb's abilities, but knew the CIA followed them everywhere, besides it was strictly prohibited.

One warm summer evening, the Lindstroms invited Jeff Schellenberg and Darby for dinner, and announced their plans for the trip to the mountain in Italy. During their time together, they recalled the many events that had transpired over the previous weeks. When the families were away in the hostage incident, Schellenberg had spent many hours with Darby and learned a lot about Caleb. He, too, had become a huge fan of the young man and spent days studying scripture and archaeological journals trying to connect the abilities and dreams, which he had shared with them. He wanted to make a documentary of Caleb's life for the rest of the world to see.

"We are planning to leave for Italy in less than two weeks," Diane said, bubbling with expectation. "In our group will be Jared and Sally, Dr. Riddenhall and several members of their lab, and some leading anthropologists, and I imagine, some secret service personnel."

"I want to join you!" Schellenberg yelled enthusiastically. "This would be a dream come true for me. I will pay my own way, don't worry…, I won't be a burden."

"We'd have to get that cleared," Bob said cautiously. "This is quite an undertaking for the CIA to be agreeing to this trip in the first place. I'm not sure where they will draw the line. We have to get passports and prepare for someone to look after our places. The Houghtons have to arrange baby-sitters and all that as well."

"I understand," Schellenberg agreed, his eagerness somewhat deflated. "But I *need* to be there. Can I meet with their scientists now? I would like to share some things with them."

"I can check with Mr. Jenkins at the CIA, but certainly no guarantee on what their answer will be."

"What were you wanting to share with them?" Caleb asked.

"I want to ask them this; what if the Ice Man was fleeing up the mountain ahead of the great biblical flood? I can't say it's a fact, but everything seems to be adding up to that. In your dreams, Caleb, you saw prehistoric creatures, T-Rex's, Brontosaurs, and so on. You *saw* the mountain where they found the Ice Man. You went into that trance when you saw him being extricated from the ice. You know incredible details of the landscape and, you, somehow, remember or, shall I say experienced, the catastrophes of a natural world heaving with massive change. What else could it be? I don't believe the Ice

Man was out there on a Sunday picnic.

"Furthermore, I have been delving into a lot of study and I would want to discuss the potential relationship to the *ancient mysteries* and so on, direct connections to the spirit realm. They need to know what they have. You are not just an interesting lab study; you actually could be fulfilling some kind of biblical prophecy. Listen; are you aware of the stories in the Bible about Enoch and Elijah? Scripture tells us that Enoch walked with God and "was not", in other words he was translated right into the presence of God … from this form into another – a sort of resurrected state. Elijah, we are told, was taken up into God's presence in a whirlwind, another form of resurrection. Then there was Jesus who also was resurrected from the dead. These all happened post flood. Before the flood, there was no mention of this kind of resurrection activities. There were people who lived long lives and then along came Noah and his family and they were the last to have extended lives."

Caleb smiled eagerly. "Oh, I've believed this all along, Doctor. I believe or, should I say, *I know*, there was some kind of massive cataclysm taking place, something that I will show traces of once we are on that mountain."

"Tell him about some of the plants," Darby said.

Caleb turned to her. "Well, in my dreams, I saw flowers the size of dinner plates and they were deep and long, like huge trumpets, that pulsated in the sun. They were an iridescent red with yellow stripes…, like a tiger skin. These humming birds – if that is what we would call them today – they were about the size of a robin or even larger and their beaks were about a foot long. They would fly right inside the flower and part of the petals would wrap itself, like a blanket, around the bird, and suspend it inside while the bird did its thing. After a minute or so, the bird would fly out in reverse, a different color, coated in pollen, then fly to the next one, and so on. Some of the ferns I have seen were twenty feet high and each leaf was about six feet across – like what they have in Australia. The smell in the air was…" Caleb seemed to hesitate as if trying to recall the aroma surrounding him at that moment. "…well, indescribable. I have never smelled anything like it. I have ridden on the back of a T-Rex. They actually have this amazingly soft fur. I know where there are some buried on this mountain. There are also some saber-toothed tigers, elephants, bears, and a bunch of other animals…, buried. I want to show the science guys a whole bunch more things like this. I have even seen metallic rocks ... like gold or something."

His audience was spell-bound at the dinner table, their imaginations running to the fairy-tales of their youth, or the TV shows they had watched indifferently at some time or other, or even going to the museums..., but there was nothing that could compare even remotely to what Caleb was trying to describe. Eventually, Bob, Diane and Darby smiled toward Jeff Schellenberg confidently, knowing Caleb was reaching into the depths of creation that no living person had ever experienced.

"Amazing...," said Schellenberg with a sigh heavy of anticipation and awe. "Just amazing. What an amazing creation. You know, the more I study this incredible young man, and how great our creator is, the more questions seem to crop up. What you are saying, Caleb, and what will be found on this mountain may very well re-write science books as we know them today. It will certainly create quite a kafuffle within the Darwin camp. Have these scientists talked to you about evolution?"

"Not really, all they were trying to get me to do was read minds and do some miracles like walk on water, turn water into wine, stuff like that. I told them that I can't do it at will. They even had me try to heal somebody who had the flu. I've never done that before, so I just touched them and nothing happened. They asked me a lot of questions; they got real excited about my DNA. They did a pile of blood tests and told me even my blood wasn't normal. I had extra stuff in it that they couldn't identify."

Schellenberg asked, "How do you feel about a documentary of your trip?"

"I think that would be fine, but not sure what the CIA would think of that. I can bet they will be doing the same. They had a lot of video cameras on me when I was in their lab."

"I think we need to get some clearance first before we do anything else," Bob insisted.

Schellenberg nodded. "When you were away in the hostage incident, I shared some of my views with that FBI guy..., Conor? He seemed quite interested in what I had to say. I would like to talk to these scientists anyways. So, can one of you arrange a meeting for me at their headquarters?"

"Mr. Conor is no longer in the picture," Bob replied. "The case has been handed over to the CIA and a Clive Jenkins is now your man. I will run it by him. What should I tell them you want to discuss?"

"Let me see..., how about something like, a creationist's point of view on the origin of species? Or, how about, where does the CIA fit into the mark of the beast timeline?" Everyone laughed.

"I think I can get something across to them," Bob answered confidently.

"So, what will your plans be after you leave the mountain, Caleb?" Schellenberg asked.

It was as if he had been cold-cocked. Caleb froze for a moment, as a seated statue and his normally flashing turquoise eyes clouded into a haunting gaze that caught everyone by surprise.

He eventually shook his head and shoulders and shrugged it off nonchalantly. "I..., I'm not sure. I will come back here; this is my home, I want to finish school and maybe even play some pro-basketball. I don't know. I want to study archaeology, maybe even biology."

The rest looked at each other with "a deer in headlights" look.

"Did I ask a deeply personal question, Caleb?" Schellenberg had the most serious look on his face. "...because that was quite a reaction you had...."

"No-no, no, not really," Caleb replied, a spark of laughter in his eyes. "I guess I was off in a dream world. I have been thinking so much about the trip that I sometimes forget where I am." His green eyes flashed with vigor once again as his glance went around the table and looked at each one steadfastly.

"I'm so glad I am able to go to Europe with you all." Darby's cheery voice buoyed the air. "I'm so proud of Caleb. I, too, really believe there will be some amazing discoveries."

Schellenberg took a swig of coffee, got up from the table quite unexpectedly and started to pace. With his hands behind his back, his slightly pudgy, medium build stature was straight as a poker as he strode around the table. His allure was as dramatic as that of a president about to deliver a speech of a lifetime.

"I have been wanting to say something for a long time and have had difficulties trying to formulate a coherent, believable address about this amazing young man. What we have witnessed and are witnessing is the closest thing to a modern Jesus. I have studied his life extensively in scripture and there are so many parallels, yet there appears to be so many other things that don't jive. First, there are no documented occurrences of him being a dreamer, which is fine. Second, Jesus' call was a human sacrifice for humankind's sinful nature that we all inherited in the Garden through Adam's disobedience – one thing Caleb does not have to repeat. Thirdly, his resurrection to Father God left him at his right hand and his return will be quite profound to the whole world at once. Caleb's entry via cloning is not exactly what was to be expected." He continued to pace.

"I don't think we are looking at the Messiah. Sorry, Caleb, but I do think we are looking at what a man was like before the flood. I think what has happened here is that God wants to show us what the human family was to be like from day one. We are to be in such communion with him that we are not just a bunch of living cells slapped together to procreate for the sake of procreation and simply to exist, living out every desire we dream up, but we are to be the very expression of love, the very nature of God, and to exhibit his characteristics. I know, I am preaching to the choir, but I want you all to know that when Adam fell, he dethroned the "spirit" man and enthroned the "intellect" of man into the very psyche of every human and that man has been ruling ever since. Our wonderful ability to reason is at the same time the downfall away from God and the very door way to which leads to faith that leads to salvation, which is supposed to mature us into sons of God. So, I am saying this because Caleb here defies our view of humanity in a way that science will never be able to explain. The most hardened evolutionist, the most hardened agnostic, the most hardened atheist will have to admit, no, I mean confess, that there was a very flamboyant creator at work here. It was impossible for Caleb to have evolved when his fleshly father, who is much older, and should actually be a lesser human, not a superior one, which we are seeing, defies almost every theory of the origin of species out there. What I propose to do is show this documentary around the world, churches, national and international TV, people need to see what real hope looks like. This could be one of the greatest events since Jesus."

He stopped behind Caleb and laid his hands on his shoulders. "To think, he is only a teenager, what amazing things are in store for this young man. I think it is our responsibility to support him, pray

235

for him, protect him and see what will happen."

Bob looked up at the doctor before he said, "There are so many arguments and so much compelling evidence in support of evolution, how can a creationist ever stand a chance in persuading the scientific world that there has to be a master design?"

Doctor Schellenberg smiled. "In reality, it is actually the other way around, but because we live in a world that asks the age old question, *"prove there is a God,"* which I liken that kind of subliminal ignorance to this scenario; a leaf asking where a tree comes from. You see, the scientific world has a real hard time with the spirit world. Because science cannot physically see it, it tries to explain it away. It will call it the psyche, it will call it emotions, et cetera. It won't come right out and call it the spiritual dimension, that is because it doesn't understand it. If it doesn't understand it, therefore it is not responsible to prove it or talk about it is it? On one hand, pure science will admit there is a perfect design behind everything; however, if there is a design, then, there has to be a designer, right? Unfortunately, there seems to be a comeback for every scenario that a creationist will bring to the table. It is, I would say, now, more of a legal battle for the minds of humanity. Science lawyers pitted against creationist lawyers, trying to win a fruitless battle; bringing strife, confusion and even fear" Schellenberg walked around to his chair, and grabbed a hold on its wooden uprights like a preacher at his pulpit.

"I would like to say that the book of Genesis is not a purely scientific document. Sure, one can find lots of scientific things to talk about, but let's first understand some things. The Bible is not an ordinary book. It states that every word is inspired by God. If that is the case then who is God? Isn't He a Spirit? Therefore, every word deals in the spirit realm. True, there are geographical and historical references, but that is only to point to something a human's finite, natural mind can relate to, but the book is a spiritual document. The closest it comes to a scientific document is in the second oldest book, the book of Job where God speaks and asks some very scientific questions. The bible is meant to speak to the spirit man; it is a love story aimed at the real you, your spirit, which he knew before the foundations of the world, according to scripture. When we pass on, our natural body returns to dust, but our spirit man lives on forever. Adam and Eve were, for the lack of a better explanation, fully aware of the spirit realm living in an earthen bound body. They intimately knew their creator and daily fellowshipped with Him. However, through disobedience, they willfully lost their intimate relationship – you know the story – and just like that, their own spirit man was suddenly playing second fiddle to their flesh man. Through sin, their spirit man all of a sudden had a long distance relationship with the very one that created them and the paradise that they lived in was no longer available. I could go on, but the point I want to make is that I believe that the book of Genesis is the beginning of the blueprint of a timeline of God's plan for mankind. If you understand that "one day is as a thousand years and a thousand years as one day," according to second Peter three, then could it be that each day of creation is relative to events that have already happened and are happening? More importantly, does not each day of creation in Genesis, point toward the story of salvation? If day one was without form and void, isn't that the way you were before you received Christ in you? Then God moved upon the waters – are you not made up of a lot of water? And then He said, let there be light, and if Christ is the light of the world, then didn't He shine His light into your very dark soul? Then day two, there was a separation between the heavenly, Christ in you separated from the earthy, the Adamic nature. Day three, let the earth be fruitful, the stability and fruitfulness of the spirit filled life. Day four, a spirit led life. Day five, the fowl that may fly above the earth, the sweet savor of a life of worship that causes open heavens. Day six, let us make man in our image or likeness, this is sharing his dominion. Day seven, God ended His work and He rested, in us, the Sabbath of perfection or rest, complete reliance and trust in the Creator. If you were to take this a step further, and multiply each day by a thousand, then, that will bring us to the close of the sixth day which we are living in – about six thousand years, going into the seventh thousand years. I could go on – didn't mean to preach, but I wanted to tie this in with the importance of Caleb's earthly appearance, how his father was there when the great flood wiped out a very debauched family of fallen humans and how God saved eight, which again is very significant, in order to replenish the earth. I believe before the flood, if we think the world is sick today, it doesn't hold a candle to what was going on back then. No wonder Caleb's father was trying to escape. Probably not only from the peril of the flood waters, but from a society that was pretty wicked."

"Wait a minute, man," Bob interrupted, "whoa; you are getting pretty deep here. I'm not a theologian, and I think I can speak for everyone at the table. I'm not sure if Caleb had those kinds of things imparted to him. I think we need to focus on the present task of getting him to that mountain and revealing what he knows."

"Dad, there are a lot of things I haven't told you or mom about because I didn't want to freak you out. Some of my dreams were pretty … shocking."

Schellenberg quickly asked, "Why don't you share some of these things with us, Caleb?" as he went back to his chair to sit down.

"Excuse me, why don't we all move into the living room and get a little more comfortable," Diane suggested. "Anyone for more coffee?"

The party quickly exited the dining room and found more comfortable seating in the living room with Darby and Caleb holding hands in a love seat by the front window.

Schellenberg took his note pad out of his briefcase.

Caleb began soberly, "Don't know where to begin. Before we were kidnapped, in my dreams, I was starting to see human activity. Some of the things that went on were more of a nightmare. They were awful. People having sex with animals, people burning their children, some kind of angels or strange creatures having sex with humans, self mutilation, like cutting themselves…. They would go into some kind of trance when they did this. I even saw cannibalism, it was creepy. I tried to stop them but I was invisible to them. During the kidnapping, when we were in the warehouse, I had more of these dreams. Sometimes I would have them even during the day which made it hard for me to know if I was awake or asleep. That's when I started experimenting more and more with telepathy. I was trying to understand how to communicate with them to get them to stop hurting each other. Instead, I communicated with everyone else who was around me."

Looks of surprise filled the faces of the party.

"You never mentioned anything like this before," Diane blurted, "we knew about telepathy, or, at least your ability to read minds, but not about all the rest!"

"I know, Mom, before I found out what was going on with the cloning and all, I just thought they were nightmares and didn't really tie it together. Besides, I didn't think you wanted to know the gory details."

Schellenberg said, "You wouldn't have known about the connection to this, unless you knew where to look. In Genesis chapter six, there are accounts of such activities. Besides, that is why the great flood happened in the first place. God was disgusted with what He saw happening here on Earth and He wanted to destroy it and start all over with a fresh canvas, so to speak. What is truly amazing however is that the Ice Man actually saw how debauched society was before the flood, and it was somehow indelibly captured into his genes. It must have been very, very traumatic for him."

"That sounds gross," Darby grunted in disgust.

Bob straightened against the back of the chair. "Because of what we heard tonight, can we make sure that this does not leave the room? What the CIA doesn't know won't hurt them, besides, who knows what they would do if they found out. It could be used for more harm than good. So, please, everyone, let us keep this between ourselves. Is that understood?" Bob looked each one directly, expectant of an affirmative nod. "I think we should get plans together for this trip. We are leaving in less than two weeks." He clearly intended to change the subject. "Anyone know what kind of clothing and hiking gear we need to pack?"

"Just a second," Schellenberg butted in, "something that has perplexed me all along is how did the Ice Man get from, let's say modern Iraq to the Austrian Alps? Was he that nomadic? Or, did the floodwaters carry him on some kind of flotsam? Caleb, do you recall any kind of transportation experience?"

"I don't recall anything like that. You see, some of the things that happened in my dreams are not necessarily in order like in a history book. The dreams became more real and intense as I got older. I have notes on almost all the dreams.... I can check them out."

"I would *really* like to see those," Schellenberg said enthusiastically.

Caleb went to his room and returned with three school exercise books, one quite thin and the other two that contained many pages. He sat beside Schellenberg and carefully opened one of the covers to reveal hand scribbled notes that spanned more than half of his lifetime. He leafed through the many pages, slowing down when he thought he was in the general area of where he may have had a dream about being transported to the Alps.

239

"You are going too fast, may I see what you have?" Schellenberg casually reached over to take the book from Caleb's hands.

"I would prefer not to show you anything at this time," Caleb replied, while quickly closing the book. "Nobody outside of Darby and my parents have seen my notes, not even the CIA. As a matter of fact, they don't even know I have these." He looked at Schellenberg fixedly. "Please don't feel hurt, Dr. Schellenberg."

"Oh my gosh, I'm not hurt at all. You own one of the most important documents in history. I can imagine how I would feel about somebody poking around these, if they were mine. However, if you recall anything like this, I would be interested in knowing."

Darby and the Lindstroms smiled at each other confidently knowing that even if Dr. Schellenberg had looked at the notes, he would never be able to decipher most of them since Caleb had written them in a form of ancient cuneiform which he had learned earlier on in his dreams. His first notes were printed in childish pictures with English subtitles when he was very young but as he grew older, somewhere in his dreams, the cuneiform symbols seemed to come to him as an expression of what he saw and it was a fast and easy way to record the fleeting scenes.

They went on with the rest of the evening discussing the trip timeline and details, prayed together and Darby and Dr. Schellenberg left under the watchful eye of the CIA, parked conspicuously across the street.

Schellenberg called from his hotel room to remind Bob to ask Clive Jenkins for his permission to accompany them to the mountain. Little did he realize that not only the Lindstroms' phone was tapped, but that the CIA had bugged their house. The agent in the car outside the house had heard their whole conversation.

Chapter 35

The next morning, Clive Jenkins listened to the tape from his agent. He would stop and start and rewind it while taking notes.

"Good job, Easton. Now we need to get our hands on the kid's notes. I will call them into my office to help them plan their trip; you and Smith get the notes, take pictures of them and bring them here. Make sure you use the cablevision truck to divert attention away from nosey neighbors. It should be in the underground parking. I will call your mobile when all is clear."

The Lindstroms were having breakfast. Diane was hovering between the stove and the table. "You know, Caleb, I think you should show your notes to Jared and Sally. I was thinking that last night. You have an English translation of them on the computer. Why don't you run a copy off for them?"

"Yeah, that's a good idea. After last night, I was thinking they may be interested, even though it's my own language and it maybe a little embarrassing." Caleb chuckled. "At least, I have the English... Yeah, that is a good idea. Do you think Dr. Schellenberg should have a copy as well? I was a little hard on him last night."

"I think so," Bob agreed. "Got an early call from Clive Jenkins, he wants us to come in this morning to discuss the trip. I said we could be there by ten. Why don't you bring the notes along and we can stop at the copier place by their office, on the way back?"

An hour later, Jenkins got a call from Easton. "Sir, no need for us to get into the house to get the notes, the kid is bringing them with him at your meeting."

"Good," Jenkins said. "Stay in position – they should be home in a couple of hours." He hung up and waited for the Lindstroms to arrive.

"Thanks for coming in. Please have a seat." Jenkins motioned to the Lindstroms to the three chairs in front of his desk. He rounded the desk and sat down in the black leather, executive high-back chair that dwarfed his diminutive frame. "You will be pleased to know we have made all the necessary arrangements with the Austrian and Italian governments to scour their mountain tops pretty much unimpeded. They will have a couple of their government people with us to observe our actions and keep us honest, if you know what I mean." He chuckled coldly. "There will also be some backhoes and other excavation type machinery on stand by. We even have blasting permits and a blasting crew from a mine not far away, ready to assist if necessary.

"We have secured your passports and international documentation that permits us to carry on the way we need to. Although it is summer, I recommend you outfit yourselves well with winter clothing and rain gear. You will be up as high as three thousand meters, or ten thousand feet on a glacier. You will need ice gear as well, I'm sure one of the local outdoor stores can recommend what to take."

Bob decided it was time to introduce the idea of Schellenberg accompanying them. "Mr. Jenkins, I have been meaning to ask you if a very close friend of Caleb and friend of the family, a Dr. Schellenberg can meet up with us there?"

"What kind of doctor is he?" Jenkins knew the answer to the question already. The CIA had run a background check on the man even before the kidnapping, and he knew how much of a meddling preacher the man would be. He had no intention of letting this busy-body anywhere near the Italian Alps or Caleb during their trip.

"Theology."

Jenkins nodded. "Due to the extremely sensitive nature of our trek, let alone the potential for dangerous conditions, I am afraid I will have to say no," he replied matter-of-factly.

Caleb picked up Jenkins thoughts and heard he was thinking that he didn't want some religious nut hanging around and getting in the way.

"Caleb, do you have any sort of plan of what you want our scientists to see first?"

"Ummm..., the caves, I would like to see the caves first. I..., we saw a couple of saber-toothed tigers, a brontosaurus and pterodactyl and some other animals get crammed in one of them there below me, by the rapidly rising water. Then, I guess some of the debris jammed in behind them. I…, we could hardly see because it was raining so hard and there was so much going on around. It was like the world was in a massive ride at the carnival."

"Weren't you afraid?" Jenkins asked.

"Beyond fear, a way beyond fear, you can't imagine what was going on around me."

"After the caves, what would be your second thing to do?"

"There's a river … not far away … I remember it had some shiny metal stuff, gold colored, just lying around near the banks. It was brilliant, almost too bright to look at when the sun hit them just right. I always kick myself for not going closer and picking up some of those beautiful stones. Nearby is a valley where a herd of wooly mammoths lived. I remember there were hundreds of them. Then I would like to see another valley where the T-Rex's and some other raptors lived, all not far apart."

"What do you think you will find there?"

Caleb's aqua green eyes sparkled and his face lit up with a huge smile. "I can't wait to show you."

Jenkins smiled back politely. "I'm confident that *if* we find any of these things, we will be satisfied in taking this project to the next step. Now let us discuss more trip details."

"Excuse me, Mr. Jenkins,"—Bob leaned rapidly across the massive oak desk toward him—"do you doubt my son's credibility and abilities?"

"Doubting is rather a harsh supposition, Mr. Lindstrom," Jenkins fired back. "I am merely a cautionary accessory to the escapades of your … talented son. I, along with the rest of the CIA, am betting heavily on positive results over there. We are all hoping for the best. So…, sit back, relax."

Bob settled back in his chair.

"I had my team prepare a slide show of pictures from the region where we will be exploring, including the Schnalstal Glacier where the Ice Man was discovered. I would like for you to identify some of the landscape if you are able, Caleb."

Jenkins got out of his chair after turning on the computer that was on his desk, dimming the lights and lowering a screen and a projector mounted in the ceiling, from the bank of controls located on the wall behind him.

"Cool," Caleb said as he smiled and looked at his dad who

nodded in agreement.

The first image slowly came into focus on the motorized screen located off to the Lindstrom family's left, labeled with global positioning co-ordinates and elevation, plus directions relative to the Ice Man's grave. Caleb stared quietly at the grainy image of barren rock, ice and snow. Seconds turned into minutes as he struggled to identify landmarks so clearly visible in his dreams and memory.

"Let me see another," Caleb asked calmly.

The next image was similar but had been taken off axis to the first one. Again, no identification marks. Jenkins flipped to the next one and then another. After ten or so slides, Caleb got Jenkins to stop.

"This, I recognize something a way off in the background." Caleb got out of his chair, walked to the screen and pointed to a partially snow covered ledge with dark shadows in the background. "I've been there … there are some caves … I think…. They are so far away."

Jenkins made some notes and flipped through more slides. Caleb identified a couple of more areas while standing beside the large screen.

Jenkins completed the slide show, turned the lights back on and logged off from his computer.

"I realize it is very difficult to identify something you are specifically looking for from pictures you are not familiar with, Caleb. I have to say, though, that you did very well considering. Thank you, please have a seat."

Jenkins leaned forward, putting his elbows on his desk with his hands folded in front of him. "Caleb, are you sure you have given the CIA all the information about yourself? You wouldn't happen to have a diary or notes of the dreams stashed away somewhere?"

Caleb, caught completely off guard, flashed a questioning look at his folks. They stared back weakly.

"I…, huh… yeah … as a matter of fact I do. It is written in my own language and rather personal. I actually have it with me… Oh, I left it in the car. I was going to make a copy of it…, in case it got lost. I can get it."

"I'll get it for you, son," Bob piped up. "Besides, I have the keys."

Photocopies were made of his notes and a set shared with

Jenkins.

"You were right when you said they were personal, do you have a translation for this?" Jenkins was perusing the cuneiform symbols. "Why did you use this language to record your dreams?"

"It just came to me … I dunno … it was fast and easy and to me, one symbol tells a whole bunch of stuff. Let me show you." Caleb pointed to one symbol and read out what each dash and graphic segment meant to him.

Jenkins look of controlled surprise was obvious; he now knew this was no ordinary teenager. "We would like to see the translation at some point. Maybe when we are on the plane on our flight to Europe."

They completed their meeting with details of the trip timeline and the Lindstroms headed home. Jenkins had recorded their meeting. He rewound the tape and made notes for his boss, an Agent Easton, and his assistant to let them know the Lindstroms were on the way home.

The CIA had invested a lot of time and money into this trip and they were hoping to capitalize on Caleb's final proof of authenticity by identifying the things he had seen in his dreams and visions. They also wanted to see the connection between time-travel in respect with DNA recording. If their scientists could see relevance in Caleb's unique DNA and what he discovered, they would be the sole owners of not only the most unique DNA, but the ability to encode clones to have super memories and "upload" them with duties they would do with impeccable accuracy.

It would be the most daring experiment the CIA ever embarked on; the proof would be in the proverbial pudding.

The next day, Caleb and Darby got together with Jared, Sally and their family – except Jason. Caleb was a hero to their kids and they would shoot hoops in front of their garage.

Sally and Jared lived in a comfortable home not far from the university district.

Jared had invited Uncle Dennis over to say "hello" and join them for dinner.

Dennis, the consummate bachelor, lived off funds tucked away in the Cayman Islands. He had recently purchased a nice yacht on which he lived, docked not far from Portage Bay where he had easy access to I-5 and Jared's place. After his expulsion from the CIA, he had become a real family man. He loved Jared and Sally's kids. He spoiled the two younger ones, and even reached out to the struggling Jason who was caught up in the drug scene and seedy characters. He had decided to quit smoking, and already the softer side to the man was emerging. Nevertheless, he still liked the thrill of the international espionage scene and stayed in touch with some of the more notorious characters.

"I've been meaning to give you a copy of this all along." Caleb shrugged, as he handed over the cuneiform notes to Jared. "These are my dreams recorded as far back as when I first started having them. Sorry, they are in black and white, the original has color, you need all the colors to understand them better."

Jared was stunned. "Why didn't you show us these before?"

"I dunno, never thought they would be that important. I remember everything that is in there anyways. Dr. Schellenberg was the one who brought it up, then, somehow the CIA found out that I had them. I gave both Dr. Schellenberg and the CIA a copy. I still have the original at home."

"The CIA has these as well?" Jared repeated loudly. "Why did you give them a copy?"

"Like I said, Mr. Jenkins asked me if I had any notes on the dreams. I wasn't going to lie. Besides, they won't be able to understand them without these." Caleb smiled as he handed Jared another pile of paper with the English translation.

"Sal, come here, take a look at this," Jared called out, making his way to the dining room table and sitting down. He ran his fingers through his graying red hair which he had coifed to look the cool professor that he was.

Sally sat down beside him. "What's this?"

"Caleb's notes of all his dreams in his own language I guess. This is interesting." He flipped through the pages of the photocopies, trying to make sense of the symbols. "Caleb, can you give us an explanation?"

Caleb sat between them and began deciphering the intricate cuneiform symbols for them.

"How in creation did you ever come up with this?"

"It came to me. I can remember when it happened. I was about eight years old, playing with these large butterflies and dragon flies in amongst some amazing flowers, and the light…, or something, glanced off the wings of a dragon fly that had landed on a rock and I saw this diagram form as crystal clear as if it was right here in the room. Then I turned my attention back to this amazing colored butterfly and another pattern or diagram formed … in my mind, I guess. This kept happening and when I eventually woke up, I copied down what I saw." Caleb turned to the pages at the beginning of the notebook and pointed out the symbols. Each line and dash and shape had complete stories.

"I tried writing … or actually printing … I was too young to actually write my dreams down, and it took too long and large amounts of paper. For example"—Caleb turned to some of his first dreams where he had written them out—"you can see how crude and boring the descriptions are compared to this." He turned to a complete cuneiform symbol and explained it.

"These seven symbols tell a complete dream. Here is the deciphered English version." He showed them how many pages it took to describe the same dream.

Jared grew quiet as he stared at the symbols. There was something resonating in him that looked familiar to him.

"Are you sure you never saw these symbols before?"

"Positive. Why?"

"I don't know, this looks like ancient cuneiform writings … what ancient civilizations used to record their history with as well as communicate, but there is something different. You said the original is in color? Like what? Can I see the original sometime?"

Caleb flipped to a symbol and described what colors should be where.

"Wait a minute…. Sal, can you get the kids crayons? I want *to see* what Caleb is talking about."

Sally returned with a colorful plastic container and Caleb went to work and started to color in the symbols.

"So, the color is really needed to tell the complete story?" Jared asked.

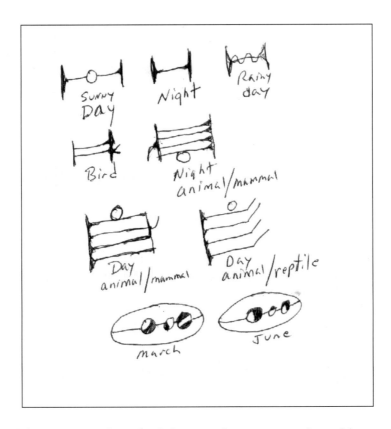

"Of course. Look, I don't know why everyone is making such a big fuss over these notes. I have the deciphered notes in English; wouldn't it be easier just to use them? I'm kind of embarrassed showing these crude symbols around to everyone." Caleb chuckled lightly.

"I can understand that, son, but, because you are so unique, everything you do is important. You never know, the way you sneeze may turn into some sort of signal." Jared nudged Caleb in the ribs with his elbow all the while laughing.

Everyone lightened up for a moment.

"But, I have to say, there is just something in these symbols that has me thinking," Jared said, stroking his clean-shaven face.

"Caleb…, Caleb, come and shoot some hoops with us!" Jared and Sally's youngest yelled from the front door. Caleb glanced around for approval.

"Go ahead, dinner isn't quite ready," Sally said as she gestured him toward the door and returned her attention to Darby, making her way back to the kitchen. "How's he doing with all this? Maybe I should ask how *you are* doing. Come on over here and help me with the Caesar's salad."

Darby drew up to Sally's side in deep thought while breaking off chunks of fresh washed romaine into a large bowl.

"It's bittersweet. I care for Caleb very much. He means everything to me. We have been through a lot together. I would just like to have some normal time with him." She sighed. "I'll be so glad when all this CIA business is over, but I'm concerned there are more twists and turns into an uncertain future for him. To be honest, as adventurous as he is, he has had enough and he's told me that he'd like to end the CIA business somehow."

Sally nodded. "I know how he feels. When I was pregnant with him, I had an emotional breakdown and almost blew the whole relationship with the CIA when I spewed my guts out to a girl friend over lunch at a restaurant. They had a tag sitting next to us and he heard the whole thing. I thought both them and Jared were going to kill me. After that I was ready for an abortion. I was soooo depressed. God only knows how close I came to terminating Caleb, which, by the way, I have never told anyone…, so please keep this a secret between you and me."

"No problem, Sally," Darby replied with reassurance. "Sure glad you didn't…. I think, in general, abortion is such a cop out. There are so many families desperate to adopt, and all these so called rights, satisfied by an instant fix with the elimination of a beautiful life at the altar of convenience. I have talked a couple of my girl friends out of abortion and into adoption. They were so afraid of carrying their baby to full term. You know…, the embarrassment, the supposed ruining of their figure and all the ramifications and the pressure from pro-abortionists and the negative garbage, they are lead to believe that there is no other choice. Afterwards, they have thanked me over and over again for not letting them abort. I mean, look what would have happened if you had aborted Caleb? Probably one of the most important humans alive today in the whole world and nobody would have ever known him. What about all the thousands of other voices that have been silenced in the name of convenience and rights of women? You know, what about the rights of the unborn?"

"That's enough, Darby!" Sally looked flustered – she had heard enough. "Sorry. I still shudder at the idea that I actually considered doing it." She finally smiled. "How's that salad doing?"

"Fine, nearly done."

They continued making dinner until they called everyone to the dining room table and sat down. They supped over lively conversations about sports, and the big trip.

After dinner, Dennis took Caleb aside and into the living room where they sat on a couple of comfortable chairs next to each other.

"Caleb, I have never told you this, but I have to get this off my chest. When the CIA asked me to track you down through the adoption agency, I was in a different headspace, different world, whatever you want to call it. You were just another piece of flesh to me, another number, another dollar in my bank account, even though I knew there was a family connection. But, that didn't matter. I guess you could say; I was just heartless. During the kidnapping, something changed – big time. I realized how far I had slipped away from reality and when I saw the love your parents had for you as well as Sally and Jared's passion, I really had to re-think my life. And that was not all. When I saw *your* love for your family and even for those terrorist bastards; which I still can't get over, I felt like a cheap violin beside a Stradivarius." He paused and gazed at his nephew. "So, first of all will you forgive me for putting your life in danger? And second, I want to help you out with your education. When you return from Europe, I want to give you some finances toward your schooling or whatever you need."

Caleb locked his turquoise eyes onto Dennis's. Looking into his eyes was like gazing into eternity. Dennis was transfixed as Caleb spoke directly into his mind, first inaudibly, with the sense of forgiveness that washed over and through Dennis like the cleanest shower he had ever had. He melted like a snowflake on a warm day. Then audibly, "Uncle Dennis, you are totally forgiven. Thank you for your kind offer. I am honored that you have chosen to support me in my education. Don't know exactly which place I will end up when I'm through high school. It all depends on what happens with this trip."

Dennis sat in his chair as weightless as a feather, yet he couldn't move. It was an emotional experience he would never forget.

The evening wound down, Darby and Dennis went their separate ways and Caleb stayed over night.

Over the next few days, they shopped at mountain outfitter stores and all who were going to Europe, purchased gear for their alpine experience.

Jenkins assembled his entourage of archaeologists, paleontologists, geologists, other scientists, and DNA specialists, including Doctors Riddenhall and Lowenstein who had worked with Jared and Sally at the very beginning. He sent them ahead to get established and acclimatized.

The little village of Maso Corto, Italy, next to the glacier was overwhelmed by the amount of rooms needed for everyone. The Schnalstal Glacier provided year round skiing; consequently there were diehard skiers from around Europe still hitting the slopes at this time of the summer.

Caleb's dreams had not happened for some time and for the first time, he started to second-guess himself. He began to think that maybe there wasn't going to be anything there when he arrived.

He called Darby.

"I've been meaning to run something by you. What do you think would happen if I can't prove any of my dreams once we get there?"

"Don't be silly K, that's not going to happen. Everything you have in you points to the stuff you are going to reveal up there. Don't tell me you're worried? You've never been worried a day in your life!"

"Yeah, I guess you're right…. It's just that I haven't had any special dreams since we came back from the ship."

"Have you dreamt of me?" Darby laughed.

"I always dream of you Dar…. Also, Mom and Dad aren't going now and the CIA wants to leave you behind as well."

"Whaaaat?"

"Apparently there aren't enough rooms in the town we are staying at, which is closest to the glacier. They say there maybe one single bed available in a room that you would have to share with a female scientist."

"Isn't that a rule of the CIA? I thought it was part of the deal. Your mom and dad are your guardians – they *have* to go."

"Yeah, I know, but Sally and Jared will be there, which are like

251

my parents … and Sally is my real mother. *I need her to be there.*"
Caleb had realized the importance of his mother's presence on this
trip long before anyone else had. He knew and felt that she had been
the key that unlocked him from his eternal prison. He was not about
to let go of the feeling of not only immense respect, but of deep love
he had harbored for her since they met. "…*and* I really want you to
be there with me," he added impetuously.

"I really want to be there, too."

Chapter 36

The day finally arrived for their departure. The CIA had found a shared room for a very delighted Darby and much to their chagrin; Bob and Diane had to stay behind. With the watchful eye of CIA under cover agents, Caleb, Sally, Jared and Darby and Jenkins, boarded a regular, economy flight to Europe.

Caleb was as impatient as ever. Waiting for a connection in one airport after another, drove him nearly crazy. He kept quiet but Darby could sense he was edgy, dismissing her in favor of solitude more than once. She didn't pressure him; she just let go. As for Sally, she wanted to get closer to her son. She couldn't resist his calls – he was speaking to her mind as if he were still a child – they were calls of despair and happiness. Caleb was at the end of a road of discovery of himself and he wanted to hang on to his mother's hand for dear life – the same as a kid at the fair – afraid to climb on the ride and yet anxious beyond words to have the thrill of his young life. Jared, for his part, was observing the people's va-et-vient; he felt as if he were in an ant colony – everyone going somewhere and maneuvering through the crowds as if the world around them didn't exist. Jenkins, on the other hand, was thinking of Schellenberg and his last conversation with him.

"You're not going, and that's final, Doctor," he had said to Schellenberg's visible dismay. "I can't risk having you preaching and blabbing what you'd see up there to everybody...."

"But, Mr. Jenkins," Schellenberg had said, "the world has the right to know...."

"No, Doctor, they do not – not yet anyway, and certainly not informed by you, they won't!"

Suddenly, and shaken out of his recollection, he heard the flight attendant asking everyone to fasten their seat belts – they were landing in Bolzano.

They took a bus ride through the lush green valleys of the Dolomite Range and at night fall, checked into a tiny lodge in Maso

Corto, high up in the Alps on the Austrian and Italian border.

Caleb was restless. He had spent time, on the last leg of the journey, with Jenkins reviewing some of the dream cuneiforms and explaining the details of the symbols in relationship to the activities in the dream. He had been unable to sleep on the trip as it was not only his first overseas trip, but his anticipation somehow outweighed the responsibility he felt to perform his duties. Once he was checked into his room, he collapsed on the bed in sheer exhaustion. He prayed for help and drifted off into an uneasy sleep.

The next morning, the team gathered for breakfast in a tiny, private room that smelled of newly varnished wooden tables and chairs. The ones who had been there for a few days were getting accustomed to the time difference, others, including Jenkins, who had just arrived, were suffering from the usual jet lag symptoms. The ski lodge was built in the quaint, rustic alpine style, popular throughout Europe. The elevated, weathered wooden structures with steep pitched roofs and carved gingerbread appointments brought to mind, a-typical impressions of the Alps, something right of a Hansel and Gretel storybook.

"Buongiorno, benvenuto al nostro albergo," the waitress cheerfully greeted the group while they were engaged in a lively conversation about the trip and the magnificent mountain scenery some had already explored. She took their orders and trotted away.

Jenkins greeted the group and introduced Sally and Jared to the team. He had roughed out a schedule based upon the meeting in his office with Caleb, Sally and Jared.

"Welcome to the official discovery home of Otzi, the Ice Man. After breakfast, I want a debriefing of what you have discovered so far and a lay of the land. Today will probably be an easier day for us who have just arrived, but tomorrow, I want to go full swing into our operation."

Jared wanted to re-connect with Riddenhall and Lowenstein to find out what was happening in their world of biology. The CIA was always a step ahead of the rest of the scientific world and because of Jared's involvement with the Genome project, he was constantly researching. Sally still had her dream of finding cures for deadly diseases and along with the rest, was elated to be here. Yet, the anticipation she felt for her son going on his discovery overshadowed most of her thoughts.

Breakfast was served and the hungry crew chowed down while exchanging laughter and stories.

"Bring back memories?" Jared whispered into Sally's ear as he pointed with his fork to the vista outside the window.

"Oh yeah, this was such a tiny village when we were here. Look at it now! They never had all year round skiing back then. There wasn't much here except that hostel and the pub. This is where it all began. We weren't even looking for our future, but somehow our future found us here. I thought you were a goner when you fell on the glacier.... Then your nose and the dry ice and the smuggled jewels.... What were we going to call it?"

"Giuseppe."

They both laughed as they sipped the hot coffee and continued reminiscing.

Caleb and Darby came in late and sat by themselves at another table. Jared and Sally got up and went to sit beside them. Caleb's red eyes and drawn look concerned Sally.

"Are you OK, Honey? Looks like you've been crying." Sally stroked his wavy, black hair.

"I'm OK, Mom," Caleb replied weakly, trying not to show his fear all the while staring blankly into space.

"You don't look OK. What's the matter, are you feeling alright?"

"He said he didn't sleep very well," Darby put-in, pushing back her blond hair. "I think he is very concerned. You know there is a lot resting on his shoulders." She gently rubbed his back.

"He was acting a little strange on the plane as well," Sally said, looking alternately into Jared and Darby's eyes.

"You'd better try and eat something, K," Darby urged quietly while she continued rubbing his back.

"I'm not hungry," Caleb answered weakly. He was still sitting motionless.

Jenkins had noticed Caleb and Darby coming in and the Houghtons going to sit at their table. He cleared his throat, turning towards the two couples. "Ladies and gentlemen, I want to introduce to you the reason we're all here on this mountain top and embarking on this amazing experience. Sitting over there with the Houghtons, his original birth parents, is Caleb – please, welcome Caleb Lindstrom and his friend, Darby Cook."

"Come on, get up son," Sally whispered into his ear.

A few seconds went by before Caleb rose slowly. His head and demeanor hung low. They were in marked contrast to Darby's. She had a bright smile adorning her gentle face and her blond hair bounced off her shoulders.

"Caleb is not feeling well…. You know…, jet lag." Darby spoke loudly and smiled confidently at the team. "He'll be alright after he eats and rests."

The men and women of the CIA team gave a short round of applause and returned to their chatting.

"Caleb, what's going on?" Jared asked quietly through clenched teeth.

"I dunno. I feel powerless. I feel like a fake. I don't know if I can do this, Dad."

"Caleb, please force yourself to eat something. We need to talk, back in your room after breakfast."

Darby had ordered some granola, yogurt and toasts, and a hard-boiled egg for Caleb, which she proceeded to prepare on a plate. She placed it before him. With his head still in one hand, he picked up the toast and slowly started eating while staring blankly at the floor.

"C'mon, Caleb, we'll be here all day at this rate," Jared chided impatiently.

"Stop it, Jared," Sally said, elbowing him in the ribs. "Give the guy a break."

Jared sat back in the freshly varnished chair, stretched his lanky frame out and crossed his arms over his chest with a disgusted "Humph."

Jenkins came over and stood by their table with some papers in one hand. "Hey, descendant-of-Ice-Man, how ya doing?"

Caleb looked up with a weak smile, "OK, Mr. Jenkins, just a little tired…. Feeling a little woozy…. I'll be alright."

"I'm sure you will. I've drawn up the agenda that we talked briefly about. Here's a copy for you and your folks to look at. I'll let you rest today, but I would like to get an early start tomorrow morning. Will that work for you and your folks?" Jenkins cast a look of confidence around the table. "We'll meet for breakfast here at seven AM?"

Everyone nodded in agreement.

He then went over general house-keeping things, rules and

regulations in respect to the use of the telephone, meals, curfews and body guards with them.

"Just so you know, Caleb, you are under surveillance twenty-four seven."

"Could I speak with Dr. Riddenhall? If that's possible," Jared asked.

"Should be no problem."

Jared left his chair and followed Jenkins back to the table where Riddenhall and Lowenstein were sitting, sipping on their coffees. Jenkins left Jared there and went to sit at one of the other tables.

Riddenhall got to his feet. After a brief greeting and a refresher of their previous history working in the lab with Sally and the in-vitro and all, Jared wanted to delve into a genetics discussion with him. As they exchanged general information about the Genome project, Riddenhall seemed to want to go deeper in the conversation, but held back as if he was about to reveal classified information. The latter then nodded a couple of times and returned his attention to the people sitting at his table. "I want to introduce you to Drew Adams and Nancy Andrews, paleontologists who came along with a couple of archaeologists and their assistants, and at that table over there, more DNA specialists, a geologist and biologists and assistants, are here to witness your son's revelations."

They all nodded in turn while Riddenhall invited Jared to sit beside him.

"Man, Clive Jenkins has assembled an impressive group here to record the adventure of my son," Jared said enthusiastically. "I'm impressed. I hope Caleb will be able to shed some light on everyone's field of interest."

"We are expecting big things," Drew Adams said with an effeminate laugh. "This area of the world is not known for any of the activity we are supposed to believe he is leading us to – not even in the slightest. There have *never* been any remains ever found in this region."

"And what do you mean by that?" Jared asked coldly.

"Well, firstly, T-Rex's, brontosaurus and saber-toothed tigers lived in different periods, and there were certainly NO homo sapiens, not even humanoids around for millions of years after their demise! Impossible! I dare say we will find nothing more than some fossilized ferns and frozen mosquitoes at this altitude," Adams lisped as Nancy Andrews smirked with approval.

"You'll eat those words," Jared replied with confident anger.

"I damn well hope so," Adams flashed back with a jerk.

"Darby is bunking in with me," Nancy said after a moment of uneasy silence, changing the topic. "I am looking forward to getting to know her.... She seems like a fine young girl. What is her relationship to you all?"

"She's Caleb's girlfriend. They've known each other for several years. She's been the only one Caleb confided in over the years with the dreams and his unique abilities. She has been a rock to him, and we're glad she is here to support him. That's my wife, Sally, over there, she is a biologist as well..., and Caleb's birth mother."

"So, tell us, how did this all get started?" Nancy asked.

The conversation went on as Jared told the tale of him and Sally finding Otzi, the Ice Man, long before his public discovery and the cloning, and events leading up to the present.

Sally waved to Jared from their table, to come over. Jared excused himself, walked over and sat down with Sally, Caleb and Darby.

"Can we go to Caleb's room and share a moment together?" Sally asked. "I think Caleb wants to catch some sleep but before he nods off he wants to talk with us in private."

"Sure, I'll let Jenkins know what we're doing." He looked briefly in Riddenhall's direction. "You know, that conversation I've just had with the guys..., well..., it was going nowhere...."

Sally raised an eyebrow. "How's that?"

"Well, it seems these scientists are not convinced they'll hear or see anything new."

"You mean they don't believe Caleb's story?"

Jared nodded. "They believe all of this is a waste of their time."

"We'll see about that!" Sally declared decisively, marching out of the room.

In Caleb's room, he propped himself up with pillows on the carved wooden headboard of his bed, crossing his arms across his chest. Darby sat close to him at the end of the bed and Sally and Jared found places to sit.

"What's going on, Caleb?" Jared asked his eyes riveted on the young man. "You have been acting really strange."

After a brief silence, Caleb looked up. His usual bright, flashing turquoise eyes were dark and cloudy. He looked like a scared sixteen-year-old kid, not the viral, larger than life specimen he always portrayed.

"I'm scared, Dad. I'm really scared.... There is something about this place that's freaking me out... I've never felt this way. I have lost the ability to dream.... I feel so weak.... I even feel shaky inside."

Sally got up and put her hand on his forehead. "Well, you don't have a fever. When did this happen? I noticed on the plane you were a little off."

"I'm not sick, I know that. As soon as I got on the plane, I started feeling a little funny.... I thought maybe it was because I hadn't flown on a long flight. The closer we got to here, the more intense it has come on."

"What does it feel like?" Jared asked.

"Seeing as I have never been sick, I can't tell you what it is, only what others have described.... I guess it would be like the flu? But it is not that.... It's like there is a bolt of lightning or something forming inside me. I know that sounds weird, but that is the best I can describe it."

Jared patted his son on the arm. "Are you ready for tomorrow's activities?"

"After some sleep, I guess.... I sure hope I don't disappoint anyone. In one way, I'm looking forward to show them stuff, but on the other hand, I almost feel like they don't exist.... They were just ... dreams."

Darby had to ask, "How could you have been so sure of yourself in the States and not so sure of yourself here?"

"I don't know, maybe it is just stage fright."

Sally shook her head. "Let's hope so, after all that you been through, of which none was rehearsed or staged and I saw you with Superman's strength, I saw you move like a wildcat ... walk on water."

Jared scratched is head; his long fingers danced on his scalp. "Tomorrow, they want to start with the caves. We remember those caves.... We found them shortly after I did a face plant crossing the glacier and just before we discovered Otzi. That was the most amazing thing. It will be interesting to see what those caves are like, the one was full of ice and the other was blocked with a bunch of huge rocks. The main one just sort of ended…. That's what I can remember."

Sally turned to Jared. "Honey, let's go so Caleb can get some rest…." Then to Darby, "Do you want to come with us for a walk? We would like to show you some of our old stomping grounds."

"That would be great, Mrs. Houghton, if you don't mind the company?"

"Not at all. Let's meet you at the front desk in twenty minutes."

"Okay, I'll be there."

They went back to their rooms and got dressed in layers for the ever changing alpine weather.

The sun in the cloudless sky was warming things up and a mist rose off the dew weighed down vegetation. The Alps were absolutely stunning. The higher peaks, which could be seen from their location, were still heavily laden with snow and ice. The others that were obviously lower had been snow free for sometime.

The aspen poplar and ash trees were lush, their lighter colored leaves reverberating in contrast to the stands of evergreens. The Houghtons met Darby and started on their little hike up a trail that opened onto a magnificent view of another valley. As they labored in the high altitude, they paced themselves slowly. Sally and Jared told Darby about their original trip.

"I don't remember this being so hard to do," Sally remarked when she stopped to rest, her chest heaving.

"Honey, you were a lot younger and in better shape back then. You could have run up this mountain then," a puffing Jared replied in delight.

For a few hours they explored their surroundings under the watchful eye of a binocular wielding agent who reported in to Jenkins from his walkie-talkie.

"Keep your eye on them and make sure they don't do any funny stuff," Jenkins ordered his man.

They returned in time for lunch and found Caleb sound asleep. As they passed the front desk, the clerk said, "Mi scusi, Signor Houghton, Ho un messaggio."

Jared stopped and picked up the piece of paper. "Jared or Sally or Caleb, call me a.s.a.p. at 39- 0471-555275, urgent."

"Excuse me, can you tell what place this number is located?"

Jared asked the clerk.

The latter looked at the message. "Penso Bozen... huh... Bolzano."

"Grazie."

For some reason, Jared decided to call from a pay phone outside the chalet. He had some liras in his pocket and after a few attempts, managed to get the phone to work. The rapid double ring tone brought him back to their first trip to Italy and reminded him of the monumental efforts it took to find dry ice and rebook their flights.

"Hello," a familiar voice answered.

"Jeff Schellenberg?" a surprised Jared asked. "What in hell are you doing here? I mean, what are you doing in Bolzano?"

"I couldn't stand being left behind ... and guess who else couldn't stand being left behind?"

"Who?"

"Bob and Diane."

"You are here, in Italy, with the Lindstroms? No way, you must have caught the next flight out after us."

"Kind of.... How's Captain Caleb?"

"Stressed ... or homesick or something.... He's sleeping now, though, which is not so good because it is only after noon, then he'll want to stay up all night..., you know, jet lag and all."

"What's the security like? If we dressed up a little, do you think we can get to see you guys?"

"Don't know about that; let me do a little research. I think there are actually quite a few agents around here and they don't walk around with name tags, you know.... How long are you at this number?"

"We are staying at a friend of mine. He is at work during the day, so I am answering the phone. He happened to have a couple of spare rooms for us here in Bolzano..., what are the chances of that? Thank God!"

"That's nice. Let me have a chat with Sally and Darby... I don't want Caleb or his folks to freak out over seeing each other. I'll call you back later today, after a little reconnaissance."

After a briefing with Sally and Darby, they decided to have the Lindstroms and Schellenberg come for an undercover visit and possibly find rooms. They would have to arrive at different times and dress as tourists or something which would make them unrecognizable.

Jared made arrangements with Schellenberg and the Lindstroms to meet with them after Caleb's first field trip.

Chapter 37

The next morning, at breakfast, Jenkins briefed everyone on the day's activities. He picked a skeleton crew, including Jared and Sally, and a camera crew, to accompany him and Caleb on their first assault of the mountain, leaving the rest of his team behind to keep watch on the village and any 'odd' arrivals.

Laden with ski poles, ice picks, ropes, shovels and other mountain climbing and safety gear, the brightly clothed, sun-glassed group found their way to the recently installed ski lift. After the extended scaling up the mountain and under Jared's guidance, they made their way onto the massive glacier. The caves were located clear across the glacier and somewhere along the face of one of the mountains. Although the glacier was groomed for skiing, it was treacherous to maneuver across on foot.

"This is the glacier I did my face plant on back then," Jared told Jenkins above the crunching of summer snow and ice underneath their feet. "If I remember correctly, over there"—he pointed to a location above the moraine—"where the rocky looking cliff sticks out, should be close to the caves."

It was a perfect day for the hike, not a cloud in the sky, the wind was light and it was quite warm despite the massive expanse of moving ice and snow beneath them.

After an hour or so of hiking with ski poles on a downward angle across the glacier, they reached its edge only to find a rapid stream separating them from the barren landscape that would eventually lead them to the caves. The team navigated the stream in knee deep, freshly thawed, frigid water and onto the moraine. Fortunately, they all wore waterproof mountaineer outfits which prevented them to be soaking wet after their crossing of the glacial stream. They sat down for a few minutes before starting once again toward the cave area.

"I remember the caves weren't so easy to find," Jared said to Jenkins, while he scanned the mountains with his binoculars. "Originally, we found them by accident when we were on the other side of the valley. Let's try working our way up this way. I think they maybe around the corner over there."

The team members were breathing heavily and walking slowly as they made there way up the incline. They went down a small valley and onto a patch of ice and snow. Caleb, who had been feeling weak, faltered to his knees.

"This is where we found him…. The Ice Man! That must be the marker." Jared pointed and yelled hoarsely through his heavy breathing.

Sure enough, a few meters away, there was a metal marker driven and fastened into the icy, rock strewn ground designating the spot where Otzi was officially found.

Meanwhile, Caleb was on his knees, head hanging limply forward with his mother holding him up as best she could. "Caleb! Caleb…, say something…. Caleb…, SAY SOMETHING!" She grabbed his wrist while she held him on a patch of snow.

Jared put two fingers on his carotid artery, checking for a pulse. Through his sunglasses, his eyes could be seen rolled back in his head. He was inert in his mother's arms. His complexion was turning pale and his breathing was shallow. "Let's start some CPR," Jared said as they smoothed out a place on the rocky landscape to lay Caleb down.

"No…, let's wait," Sally said calmly, while praying secretly. "Give it a little time. He just maybe suffering from altitude sickness."

Seconds turned into moments and minutes ticked by….

Just as Jared was about to start CPR, Caleb's eyes flickered and he started to blink. "Where am I?" He sounded groggy as he came out of his semi-comatose state.

"You are on the Schnalstal Glacier…, in Austria., Italy…, Europe," growled Jenkins annoyingly.

"Hey, wait a minute, Jenkins, this is my son you're trashing," Jared snapped back.

"He's been acting weird ever since we got here."

"Well, what if he isn't feeling well?"

"I don't care, we are on a mission and there is no place for this kind of behavior."

Jared shrugged and returned his attention to his son. "What happened, Caleb?"

"I dunno…. It felt like a bolt of lightning hit me, there was this hot flash that went through me and…, and I saw a very bright light…. Didn't any of you see that?" The rest of the party shook their heads. "Then, it was as if all the dreams I have ever had, fast forwarded before my eyes plus a bunch of things I've never seen before … like future events or something."

"This is bizarre," Jared said. "Right over there"—he pointed ahead of him— "is the marker where the Ice Man was discovered."

Caleb got up slowly and made his way to the marker, which was only a few yards away. He removed his sunglasses. Slowly and silently, he read the inscription about the Ice Man and returned to the watchful group. He scanned the surrounding mountains as if he was trying to use his eyes as binoculars, the same as he did in his dreams. He seemed frustrated with the results, so he grabbed the binoculars around his neck and slowly panned the all-encompassing vista, going back and forth looking for familiar markers. He stopped and focused for a moment on the ledge in front of the location of the caves – where Jared had found them all those years ago.

"I think that's where they are, the caves…, hard to tell from here."

"Let's make our way," Jenkins ordered.

"Are you feeling OK, son?" Sally asked. "Do you need to rest some more?"

"I'm fine now, Mom…. I haven't felt this good in a long time." Caleb flashed her a big smile. He was filled with renewed vigor; his turquoise eyes gleamed with confidence. His olive skin color was back to normal. He had a lilt in his walk. He even ran ahead to lead the party. He had to keep stopping in order for the rest of the team to catch up.

"Boy, something big happened to him back there," a panting Sally commented to Jared. "It's like he had some kind of divine download or something."

"No kidding. That was something. I've never seen anything like that before," one of the men, who had overheard Sally, said. Others agreed with raspy comments between breaths.

After a couple of hours of very slow vertical hiking, a winded Jenkins shouted to the newly energized Caleb to stop for a breather and join the rest of them for some refreshments.

The day was still picture perfect, a cloudless sky, a gentle alpine breeze which smelled "washed" clean from the ozonation of the sun. The panting team slowly found rocks to sit on, broke out snacks and drinks from their backpacks and silently drank and ate.

Caleb constantly scanned the rocky face with binoculars as he familiarized himself more and more with the terrain. He could hardly wait to scale the last gap to the ledge where the caves were.

After the break, Jenkins gave the orders to move on, and the party slowly trundled upward to their destination. Their progress was impeded by the steep gravel encrusted surface and treacherous incline. Caleb had arrived long before the rest, and once on the ledge, he sat down and scanned the magnificent panorama while his chest heaved with exhaustion and excitement.

It was beginning to look familiar. His dream and cellular memory resonated with the landscape. He saw how it had changed so dramatically. He could identify certain things, but remembered how the whole place heaved and buckled, like someone shaking a blanket. As he turned to view the caves, it was déjà-vu. In one of the dreams he was on this ledge and knew there were caves behind him but failed to turn around. He had seen flood waters rapidly approaching him and watched drowned and half-dead brontosaurs, T-Rex's, and other animals, too numerous to mention, coming at him and then crammed into the caves, debris and rocks stuffed in behind them like someone plugging holes in a leaking ship. He had grabbed some branches and floated away avoiding a drowning world in sheer upheaval.

Now, as he entered the largest cave, at the entrance, in the natural light, he read the graffiti carved in the rock left behind by modern spelunkers. With his flashlight he made his way into the darkness. The floor was quite smooth and easy to maneuver despite chunks of ice scattered throughout.

"Caleb, where are you?" Jared's loud voice reverberated in the darkness and brought him back to the present.

"I'm here." Caleb's voice sounded funny as it echoed back.

"Hey, wait for us." Jared's voice croaked between breaths.

The cave stopped abruptly about twenty feet in. "It stops right here anyways." Caleb sounded disappointed.

He *knew* it had to go on farther; he saw all those critters crammed in there. He looked for bones and any evidence of their demise. He swirled his flashlight around the back of the cave, looking for clues to something that would lead him beyond the back wall.

"Find anything?" Jared asked as he made his way to his son's side.

"Not yet. I know they are here. Have to find a way to get behind that wall of rock and ice."

As the entourage entered the cave, their flashlights helped to light up the interior. Caleb and Jared started moving rocks and chunks of ice by hand.

"We're going to need some kind of excavating equipment to take us much farther," Jenkins muttered.

"Let's all pitch in and try moving some of the rock debris," Jared suggested.

For a couple of hours, the search party removed a sizable amount of the giant wad blocking the way. As they worked, the rubble and ice became easier to remove and it grew into a large pile inside the cave. Jenkins kept his eye on the time and ordered the team members to take breaks individually at regular intervals.

They worked for hours until Jenkins ordered a halt to the operation as flashlights had failed and the sun was setting outside. Everyone's gloves had been all but worn out and they were exhausted from the thin air, hard work and lack of results.

He took Caleb and Jared aside as the crew filed out of the cave. Caleb had already read his mind. "I don't think there are any dinosaurs here." His voice was cold and matter-of-fact.

Jared looked at Caleb, whose face was calm and confident. "I'm sorry that we haven't found anything yet…. I assure you there is a treasure of creatures trapped in there."

"Well, why the hell is there nothing anywhere else around here to support your theory?"

"The same reason there was a five thousand year old human stuck in the ice just down the hill," Jared answered sarcastically.

"I can't answer that." Caleb sounded annoyed. "I just know the world was in complete chaos. I saw it. Mountains heaved up from below like … when you push a blanket with your hand, water roared through these valleys like monster rivers. The whole world was like a drunken man staggering down the street. It rained…, no, it flooded from above. The sky could barely be seen. I had no idea what was up and what was down…. Everything was drowning. I did everything to keep from drowning and from being smashed against the rocks or hit by floating debris. The last thing I remember was being here and seeing these caves and I'm positive this is the one. The other two are not large enough."

"Has anyone asked, how did you…, huh…, the Ice Man get here in the first place?"

"I recall, in one of my dreams that I was flying … on the back of a pterodactyl. I believe that is how…. I remember it being a long dream and knowing there was something strange going on."

"You mean we could find a pterodactyl here?" Jenkins asked mockingly.

"I believe so."

"Well, that won't happen today, let's make our way home before it gets dark."

The team made their way down the mountain, across the glacier and onto the ski lift. They were back to their lodge as the last bit of light faded behind the Alps and gave way to the Milky Way that was witnessing history in the making.

Chapter 38

Jenkins' tired, aching body got up slowly at breakfast the next morning to announce the day's activities.

"We have had no success so far in finding a thing; however, we are committed to this ... treasure hunt and will be employing some excavating equipment that is on stand by, to dig farther into the cave. I would also like to thank those who helped yesterday. You certainly earned your pay." He went on with the details of the day's agenda, which meant a repeat of the first day, except they had to wait to get the excavation equipment airlifted in, positioned and assigned fresh "troops" to the job.

Caleb, Jared, Sally and Darby were relieved Jenkins was still on with the program and the delay gave Jared time to call Schellenberg.

"I think it would be best to wait until you hear from me tomorrow, there is lots to do and we got home late and exhausted. Let's connect then," Jared told Schellenberg.

They hung up and Jared joined the rest of the team in their room.

"Are you surprised you didn't find anything, Caleb?" Darby asked.

"No, I am surprised at how easy it was to remove the rocks and debris. I actually thought we would need dynamite to get back there. The excavator will make it much easier, although, it will have to be small enough to get inside the cave."

"That's the first time you mentioned about the pterodactyl. That's quite the story."

"I was about ten when I had that dream. It didn't make a lot of sense until now. When we arrived on this mountain, it dawned on me. How did the Ice Man get up here? Sure the waters could have carried him, but he would have long drowned from the violent conditions. I think the only way he could have reached this height was on the back of a pterodactyl..., or in a helicopter," Caleb snickered.

"I think that's very cool," a wide-eyed Darby cooed.

The next day, the mini-excavator and operator were airlifted via helicopter onto the ledge outside the cave, arriving at about the same time as the team. The machine was barely small enough to squeeze through the opening, and, once inside, the operator had first to remove the debris to the outside of the cave, which the group had removed by hand the previous day.

As the excavator did its work, Caleb, Sally and Jared visited the other two smaller caves located nearby.

"Do you recognize anything special about these, son?" Jared asked.

In the larger of the two caves, Caleb was silently digging away at some trapped ice on the floor and systematically scraping away layers of loose gravel and dirt that covered ancient rocks.

"Not sure yet…. There *could* be something, but, it doesn't look familiar or remind me of anything like the first cave. We could try removing some of the debris with picks and shovels and I'll look for clues."

It was so small that only Jared and Caleb could work in the crowded space at the same time. They each had dust masks on. On their knees, they shoveled away layers of snow, gravel and ice as clouds of dust bellowed out of the opening.

"Jenkins signaled to me that the excavator has emptied the debris and is now digging," Sally's voice echoed slightly as she gave way to coughing from the dust.

"We'll be right there in a minute," Jared replied. "We can come back to this, Caleb, we'd better go."

The two, panting from the thin air and manual labor, emerged from the cave to shouts of excitement from outside the big cave.

"We've found something!" Jenkins yelled, flailing his arms to hurry. "We've found something!"

The panting trio ran as quickly as possible to the mouth of the cave. The excavator had stopped and everyone in the team – even the operator – ooohed and awed at something that poked out between the rocks. There, as the dust created a misty like cloud in the spotlights, in almost perfect condition, was the massive paw of a large cat.

"A saber-toothed tiger," Caleb's voice echoed calmly. He walked up and started removing more rocks from around the animal.

Sally tearfully hugged Jared as he looked at a quietly elated Jenkins with an '*I told you so look*'. The rest joined Caleb as the head archaeologist took over and gave orders how to remove the debris from around the big cat properly so as to not disturb it unnecessarily.

The thin air and arduous labor took a back seat to the sheer adrenalin of the find as the group worked furiously to uncover the remains of the ancient animal.

Jenkins left the cave and got on his walkie-talkie back to base, to relay the news to the CIA.

He made arrangements for the helicopter to return to the site with a gurney to have the remains taken to a pre-arranged refrigeration plant in Bolzano.

He stepped back inside the cave and ordered everyone to halt their digging.

"As I must remind each and everyone of you here today that you are under a written, sworn oath of secrecy that this find will remain in the possession of the CIA. This find or any of the activities surrounding it are not to be divulged by any member of this team to anyone not acquainted with the operation – and that means the general public. Severe consequences will befall anyone of you as a result in any leak to the public. God help the one or ones who are found guilty. Just so you understand: the only court you will face is the CIA and, no, you won't have access to a lawyer. This is actually written in section D, paragraph fourteen, of your agreement. Is that clear?"

The cold reality of the CIA and the frigid temperature inside the cave all of a sudden became equal. The group slowly went back to work and their enthusiasm returned as the big cat's well-preserved body came into view.

"I can hardly wait to tell Drew and Nancy," one of the paleontologists excitedly exclaimed to her assistant, "they will be really disappointed that they weren't here for the discovery!"

Jenkins had gone back outside and was barking orders over the walkie-talkie. Meanwhile, his cameraman was inside filming the historic find.

Within a few hours, the frozen tiger was completely uncovered. It was a perfect, complete specimen. Despite broken bones, to date, there had never been a find of this magnitude, and in such a perfect condition. The group stood back in complete awe as they surveyed this huge cat with the two, giant saber teeth over biting its lower jaw.

271

Measurements were made and they prodded and poked and examined everything they could get at while notes were made and the cameraman recorded dictation.

"We are so proud of you, Caleb. You have no idea how relieved we are. Darby will be beside herself," Sally said while the little family gave a group hug.

"I wish Mom and Dad Lindstrom were here to witness this."

"So do we," Jared said, trying to sound disappointed.

The helicopter arrived with another passenger weighed down with a large backpack. He removed the oversized gurney strapped to the helicopter and with the help of the team placed it underneath the remains, and carefully inched it along. Then a large thermal blanket was placed over top and sealed with ropes to completely cover the animal. They attached it to the excavator and the operator hauled it out of the ancient grave. After securing the precious cargo to the helicopter, the exhausted, exhilarated crew, along with the excavator operator, watched it lift off into the late afternoon sky.

Everyone was elated. They went back into the cave congratulating Caleb and thanking Jenkins for the opportunity to work on such a historic project.

"I assume we will be able to work further on examining the tiger?" one of the archaeologists asked Jenkins.

"I can't see why not. However, according to our hero Caleb here, there is much more to find and we will need time and your skills to uncover the rest. At the moment, however, we need to get back to camp as we are rapidly losing light."

Jenkins then went back into the cave, shut the lights off and gave instructions to the newly arrived guest.

As the team left the site without him, Jared asked, "Is he staying?"

"Yes, he's my security guard," Jenkins replied.

The tired, euphoric group returned to the village, off the last ski lift and made their way to their respective rooms as, once again, the last shafts of sunlight disappeared.

The Houghtons and Caleb went straight to Darby's room to announce the good news. She came to the door with a drawn face and she whisked them inside quickly.

"What's wrong, Dar?" Caleb asked in consternation as they hugged, his tired mind unable to get a reading.

"There's something funny going on. I was in the room this afternoon with Nancy – you remember; she's one of the paleontologists – and we had decided to go for a walk since it was so nice outside. I was gone for maybe an hour and when I returned, she was gone, including all her things, like she never existed. I went to the front desk and they said she had checked out. She never mentioned anything like that to me earlier. I asked if Drew was still here and apparently he had checked out as well. I don't know all the names of the people who are on the trip, so I didn't know who to ask for. You guys, I'm scared…. I'm so glad you're back, though." She hugged a baffled Caleb with a death grip.

"That is kind of creepy," Sally said with her tired, dusty face in a knitted frown.

"So, how was your day?" Darby let go and stood back with renewed energy.

The Houghtons smiled, looked at each other quietly and glanced over to Caleb.

"I know you were sworn to secrecy during the kidnapping, but now for the safety of us all and everything, you have to swear on a stack of bibles that you cannot and will not repeat what we are about to tell you, to anyone. This is the CIA we're dealing with," Jared said firmly. "And they will not hesitate to kill any of us just to make sure there are no security leaks, okay?"

Darby's young, crystal blue eyes widened in serious anticipation. "Of course, I believe my life is on the line as much as everyone else's."

"We found a saber-toothed tiger," Caleb announced quietly.

Darby shrieked with delight and hugged him all the more. "Really, a saber-toothed tiger? How big? What is it like?"

"He…, besides crushed bones, is in near perfect condition. The temperature and conditions of the cave have kept him almost like he died yesterday. His body is about eight feet long and he has the two big tusks, or sabers. His head is about this big around and he has paws the size of dinner plates with four- or five-inch claws. His fur and coloring is slightly different from modern tigers."

"Any different than your dreams?"

"No, pretty much exactly the same."

"Wow! That's amazing! Can I come with you and see him tomorrow?"

"He's already gone. A helicopter came and got him within minutes of us freeing him from his grave."

"I heard a helicopter off in the distance when I was out walking; that must have been his ride. Where would they take him?" Darby asked.

"Good question. This is the CIA; they have a lot of tricks up their sleeves," Jared said.

There was a loud knock at her door. Darby and Sally gasped. Jared, Sally and Caleb quickly and quietly ran into the bathroom and closed the door.

"Who is it?" Darby asked confidently as she walked to the door.

"Room servisio," a man's voice answered on the other side of the door.

"I didn't order any room service."

"Yes you did, Darby," a familiar sounding voice replied quietly.

Darby opened the door carefully, leaving the safety latch in place.

"Darby, it's me, Jeff Schellenberg," the voice in the darkened hallway whispered.

Darby flipped off the safety latch to let Jeff come in as he pushed a huge trolley covered in white linen in front of him. He closed the door quickly behind him and stripped off the linen. Huddled awkwardly on the trolley were Bob and Diane Lindstrom. Jeff already had his hand positioned over Darby's mouth and she gave off a muffled scream of delight just as he clamped it down.

"Shhhhh… Let's speak really quietly here, we snuck in to the lodge and borrowed some staff outfits…. We're probably in big trouble," Schellenberg whispered nervously. "Where is the rest of the clan?"

The bathroom door opened and out walked the Houghtons and Caleb. In a quiet huddle, they hugged as silently as their emotions would allow amid tears and whispers of love.

"I thought you were to wait for my call before you came here?" Jared asked in a whisper.

"We couldn't wait. We were as curious as the proverbial cat. We wanted to see you all so bad," Bob mumbled.

"Are you booked in here?"

"No, we got a ride from my friend Emillio, from Bolzano. We dressed ourselves with these crazy hiking outfits and these mustaches and wigs not to be easily identified. We saw there were security checks happening quite a way off, so we got out of the car and started walking away from the village, pointing at the beautiful scenery, like we had never seen a mountain before. When we felt we were far enough and hopefully, they ignored us, we circled back behind the lodge and found the uniforms and voila, here we are."

"How are you planning on getting out of here?" Jared asked.

"We aren't leaving," Diane flashed back staunchly. "We were kidnapped *against* our will once, now we want to be kidnapped *by* our will."

Everyone laughed quietly.

Chapter 39

After much hushed discussion, they decided to split up the group to avoid the watchful eyes of the CIA. Bob would stay with the Houghtons, Diane with Darby and Jeff with Caleb.

They worked out where they would sleep, how to get them food and when and where they would meet after each day; satisfied to be willing *prisoners.*

The next morning an enthusiastic group met for breakfast. However, only the ones who witnessed the find attended, plus Dr. Riddenhall and Lowenstein.

"Good morning everyone," Jenkins began as he rose to his feet. "As you can tell we are a much smaller group today. For security reasons, I have dismissed some of your newly-found associates from our team. They are no longer needed and you will not be able to contact them. Does everyone understand? Drs. Riddenhall and Lowenstein are staying on to assist us in our, shall we say, treasure hunt." He smiled wickedly. "Some of you asked about examining the carcass further. We have it stored in refrigeration at the moment in an offsite location. When we are done here, you are all more than welcome to do further examinations. We are back to the site today and I hope you are not too sore from yesterday's activities. Thanks for your efforts."

Caleb tried to read Jenkins' mind. There was something unsettling in his thoughts. Was Jenkins up to no good? He needed to get a better read, and the only way was to get closer.

The Houghtons and Caleb ordered extra breakfast for their guests and stuffed it into their backpacks when no one was looking.

After breakfast, the group met at the designated time at the ski lift and Caleb purposefully sat beside Jenkins to read his mind. Jenkins was ever cognizant of Caleb's abilities and made sure his mind was on his family back home or something innocuous.

Once again the helicopter flew in with the excavator operator, picked up the security guard and left. This time he also dropped off a small gasoline generator to power the floodlights.

After a short time spent in digging, the remains of more animals were revealed. All frozen in distorted positions and piled on top of each other, mixed in with the gravel and rocks and bits of wood, but in perfect condition. The yips, oohs and aahs and expletives from the group, echoed off the dust-filled walls of the cave as they rushed in to examine the vast treasure. There were big and small animals. There were reptiles and mammals, some were recognizable and common today and others were exotic, long extinct. This unusual cache of creatures created more questions than answers.

As the camera rolled, Jenkins grabbed a still camera and shot several rolls of film while the workers logged the numerous carcasses.

"We have discovered the mother lode of prehistoric creatures, this is like reaching into your great, great grandpa's pants pocket and finding several hundred million dollars," the head archaeologist commented while shaking his head incredulously. "No one has ever seen anything like this. This is not only historic in every sense, but absolutely mind-blowing. There are creatures here that have never been seen before and still others that we thought were long extinct let alone existing together in the same timeline. This will certainly challenge a lot of our thinking. What I can't get over is the fact that in the fossil layers around the world, many of these creatures should be much deeper and certainly found somewhere else, which leads me to ask, how come there are no fossils or any other evidence pointing in this direction? Amazing! Absolutely amazing! The whole world has got to see this."

The helicopter made trip after trip in order to accommodate the sheer number of carcasses. The exhausted crew finished up the day and went back to their rooms in amazed shock at what they had experienced. Their conversations were highlighted by radical changes to history, radical changes to the theory of evolution and other scientific protocols.

"You know, Babe, when we first came to this mountain what was one of our goals?" Jared asked Sally.

"We had lots of goals; I recall one was to get married." Sally's tired face smiled.

"Remember, I wanted to clone a human, which was just so far outta here. We talked about getting a hold of a piece of the wooly mammoth as a dream. Little did we know that *this* would happen.

One discovery led to another, which led to another and so on. The other night, I had a dream. In the dream those cuneiform images of Caleb became animated. As they moved around, they seemed to form familiar patterns. I can't shake it, they play in my mind like one of those tunes that you start humming and it won't go away."

Sally stopped and turned to face her husband. "You remember I always wanted to see if a prehistoric DNA was stronger, less polluted and so on, so that we could somehow emulate it into a method of strengthening modern man's immune system, in order to ward off everything from cancer, MS, heart disease, et cetera? Do you know, J, I believe we have everything here with the animals, with Caleb, in order to do that."

"I agree. Let's go eat and after, let's get together at Darby's, I think everyone else is there. We must remember to bring something back for Bob and Diane."

At dinner, the exhausted group was having a very hard time keeping the secret quiet. Even Riddenhall and Lowenstein were animated. They knew the consequences.

After dinner, Jared and Sally smuggled food for the captives in Darby's room and they all rejoiced in the news of the latest findings. They made sure they weren't followed and kept their tone of voices as inaudible as possible.

"When you were growing up, how could you keep all this secret?" Schellenberg asked.

"I just thought it was kinda normal," Caleb shrugged, looking at the floor. "Besides, because I was adopted, I thought there was something medically wrong with me, especially after I shared the dreams and full-on visions that would sometime happen during the day, with Mom and Dad. They didn't know what to do and asked that I kept them a secret from my friends so that I wasn't teased or picked on at school."

"What are you showing them next, Caleb?" Darby asked.

"There's a small valley down to the right of the ledge where the caves are and I remember seeing some bright shiny stones or something. Because it was a brief moment before all the earth broke up, I'm not sure if there would be anything like it left."

"Are you going to dig any further in the other two caves?"

"Absolutely," Jared piped up. "We are so close, we may as well check to see if there are more animals in them as well."

"Can I say something here?" Schellenberg said quietly as he leaned forward pensively. "I know I keep bringing up religious stuff, but I can't contain myself any longer. When Caleb is through with this mission for the CIA, can I kidnap him for a while and take him around with me when I do my creation presentations?"

"At the moment, I can't see any reason why not," Diane answered. "What do you think, Caleb?"

"I would really like to do that. You were the first person who connected my dreams to something concrete."

"I think we are getting ahead of ourselves," Jared said. "There is a long way to go before the CIA will be through with you. You are only at the beginning of a cycle of experiments and behavioral studies that could take quite awhile. Let's visit this again in a couple of weeks."

"I understand," a disappointed Schellenberg commented. "But, I still want to be the first to show him off to the church."

The little group sat in awe when the Houghtons and Caleb described all the creatures that had been unearthed in the cave.

It was a special reunion. Besides the supernatural, here was a family that had been knit together by science, adventure, danger, love, and history. They quietly sat in the little hotel room sharing such precious and powerful memories; little did they realize how precious this time was. Everyone left except Caleb; he sat beside Darby on the bed. They gazed into each other's eyes, arms around each other's neck as their souls connected in the silence. Caleb spoke his deepest thoughts of love into Darby's mind and she wept with happiness, knowing that he truly loved her.

"I love you so much, K," she whispered as they kissed in a deep lover's embrace.

"Um, sorry," Diane said awkwardly, as she walked in from down the hall.

The two lovers quickly untangled themselves and Caleb embarrassingly got to his feet.

"Uh, I was just leaving, Mom. See you at breakfast, Dar." And he quickly left for his room.

Diane smiled as she went about getting ready for bed. "You two really love each other, don't you?"

Darby nodded while still in a phantom embrace.

That night Diane was haunted by a dream that brought her back to Caleb's room a few months ago when she felt like something awful was going to happen to him. When she woke up, she smiled thinking that now, she understood that Caleb was going to leave home and get married to Darby. To her, it was a wonderful sign of maturity in their relationship.

Chapter 40

The early wakeup-call jarred Sally's tired, aching body out of a deep sleep. Jared was still glued to the bed and Bob was peacefully snoring, curled up on the love seat.

She stretched herself out like a cat, wiped the sleep from her eyes and parted the curtains to a fog covered view from her window. To get going seemed to be more difficult every morning and once again at the private breakfast, Jenkins and the group were quietly animated as they discussed their incredible find.

"Good morning," Jenkins began. "Thanks again for your profound efforts in securing the greatest archaeological find in the past ten thousand years. Nobody, except Caleb Houghton, seems to know how on earth they got there, but I'm sure we will find the reason. Today, we are splitting the group up. I want those who are more geologically interested in this trip to come with Caleb, Jared Houghton, and I; we will look for more…, different treasure. The rest will continue the work in the cave. As you can see, the weather has changed and the clouds have moved in. Apparently there is a cold front moving in and from what I understand, it can be unpredictable. Please, let's dress appropriately."

Up to now, the weather had been impeccable. Cloudless, sun drenched skies, very little wind and comfortable temperatures, despite the elevation. The glacier was melting rapidly and every day the stream they crossed had increased into an angry, frigid creek that carried gravel and minerals to the headwaters of a small river far below.

The group made its way to the caves and as planned, they split up into the two pre-planned crews. They had become somewhat accustomed to the altitude and moved much faster than when they first arrived. Caleb had gone on ahead to familiarize himself with the surroundings and get a bearing on the deposits he had seen in his dreams. The fog was becoming denser and the wind was picking up, blowing it into ghost-like wisps. The temperature was falling rapidly and any precipitation that formed quickly went from rain to snow.

281

Visibility diminished rapidly as the wind's velocity steadily climbed.

Jenkins, Jared and the geologist were a considerable distance behind Caleb who had descended into the valley off to the right of the cave's ledge. "I think we should call this off until the weather co-operates," Jenkins said to Jared and his assistant.

"Hey, Caleb, wait up for us," Jared yelled. It was almost fruitless calling into the swirling wind and snow. The crew rapidly descended into the valley, slipping and sliding on the mantle of gravel. The fog and snow were presenting a major visibility problem.

"Caleb…! Hey, Caleb!" Jared shouted. His voice was lost in the wind.

Jared knew mountain conditions. He had seen it first hand, hiking in the Cascades, how it could turn so quickly and deadly. He had had friends who were caught overnight in a blinding snowstorm just going on a simple day's hike.

Jared whistled and yelled as he went well ahead of Jenkins and the geologist. Visibility was down to only a few yards.

"Jared, hold on, I think we should be tied together," Jenkins yelled. "Jared, can you hear me?" he shouted again through the storm.

"What?" Jared yelled back.

Jenkins and the geologist caught up with him. "I think we should be roped together if we are going on any farther, otherwise we all could get lost."

"I'll stake a rope near the path toward the cave's ledge and let's use that as a marker."

"Good idea," replied a breathless Jared. "Now I am going to look for my son."

Thoughts flashed through Jared's mind that Caleb probably wasn't that savvy in these conditions, and being a typical teenager, he would be more concerned about the treasure hunt than his safety.

He yelled and whistled as he descended into the valley. He looked for footprints, anything in the accumulating snow. The wind was relentless. It didn't come from one direction; it swirled like something in a blender. Jared dug mittens out of his backpack and put on yellow goggles to cut down on the glare. It seemed to help and he could see his footing much better.

"Where could he be?" Jared muttered aloud while he panted heavily. He yelled and whistled again and stopped long enough to strain for a reply. Nothing. *My God, this is serious*, he thought, *I can't leave him out here, where in hell did he go?*

He was sweating profusely and that was not a good thing in those conditions. It can be almost certain death if ones clothes are too wet on the inside.

He stopped and gathered his thoughts. His rope was at its end. His chest heaved for oxygen. The blinding, driven snow in the fog made it impossible to go any farther. He yelled and whistled some more, the wind answered back with a mournful howl off the landscape. He stood, silently and angrily prayed. He felt helpless in the whiteout and knew he had to turn back. Slowly, he picked up the rope and coiled it as he made his way back to the ledge. He would stop and yell until he was hoarse. He whistled until he ran out of breath and stopped and listened for a response. Nothing. Eventually he reached the ledge and climbed awkwardly onto it.

"Any luck?" Jenkins asked as the three stood bracing themselves from a renewed onslaught of wind-blown snow.

Jared shook his head, wiped the snow off his goggles and shook the hood of his coat to clear it as well. "I don't get it; he wasn't that far ahead of us."

"We have to get back to the cave and see how *we* are going to get out of here," Jenkins replied.

"No way, Jenkins, this is my son. I don't care about the rest.... They'll be fine. I gotta find him," Jared yelled hysterically as he turned around to head into the whiteout.

Jenkins ran ahead and grabbed Jared squarely by the shoulders. "Look, you can't go back out there, man! We don't want to be looking for two of you when this weather lets up."

The larger Jared threw Jenkins aside as if he were a rag doll and rapidly retraced his steps. Jenkins picked himself up and yelled at his assistant to help. The two men ran after Jared and tackled him in the wet snow. The adrenaline-charged Jared punched and kicked them off after they rolled around in the snow, and ran toward his previous trail. The two men picked themselves up and ploughed after him; this time Jenkins brought a rope with him. Fortunately, Jared's hoarse yelling for Caleb was the only way they knew where he was. Again they tackled him and this time they tied both his hands and feet.

"Jared..., get a hold of yourself," Jenkins yelled between heavy gasps, "it's a way too dangerous for anyone to go out there."

"Let me go, you bastard! That's my son! He's gonna freeze to death out there. Why won't you help me look for him?"

It's no use. You were right behind him you couldn't see or hear him then. What makes you think we will be able to do any better now?

"C'mon, Jenkins, what if he's hurt? Knocked out from a fall or something…? Let me go…! I'd rather die trying to find him, knowing I did all I could to rescue him than lie here wasting precious time."

Jared was now soaked with sweat and starting to shiver as the cold crept into his being.

Jenkins knew common sense was out the window. So he stopped for a moment, gathered his thoughts and looked at his assistant and then to Jared.

"Okay Jared, we'll let you go…, under one condition, that we first get a longer rope. I am not letting you wonder off out there by yourself not tethered, but we have to go back to the cave to get it. Either we leave you here tied up on the ground or you come with us peacefully. It's not that far. This is for everyone's good…. I want to find Caleb just as much as you do."

Jared's shivering was turning convulsive and he nodded a shaky OK.

They undid the rope around his legs but kept his arms tied and helped him up off the snowy ground. Quietly they worked their way back to the cave.

Back at the cave, the crew had stopped working and was anxiously waiting for these guys to return.

"Where's Caleb?" Sally asked her face fast receding into grim dismay when she only saw three men enter the cave.

"We don't know, Hon. He had gone ahead of us and the weather hit us like a banshee out of hell. We have no idea. He wasn't that far, damn it…. He wasn't that far…. I went down into that valley on the other side and I yelled and whistled all the way down." Jared slumped to the ground in visible despair, shivering uncontrollably. "I want to go back out there…, we need a longer rope."

"Why are you tied?"

"He was desperate…. It was a way too dangerous and he was jeopardizing his own life," Jenkins replied quietly.

Sally squatted beside him. "Surely he would have heard something. He just vanished. Knowing him, though, he'll probably show up like nothing happened."

The group was understandably shocked and concerned at the news.

"Now, the challenge is for us, do we head back or stay?" Jenkins asked.

"I vote we get outta here as fast as we can. Who knows how long this could go on for?" one of the group members said.

"No, we stay here, at least we are in some kind of shelter and Caleb just may show up," Sally yelled adamantly.

"But we have no food and little water," someone lamented.

"I don't think this will last long," Jared muttered with a shaky voice, his arms folded around his knees and looking out the cave opening.

"Honey, you can't go out there, please don't risk it. Mr. Jenkins is right, no use trying to be a hero. Caleb will be alright. Okay? We need to warm you up somehow and dry out some of those clothes."

The snow had piled up about four to six inches already at the mouth of the cave and wasn't letting up. The cold wind whipped in blasts of frigid air into the cave now laden with snow. The group had grown quiet as they made brisk movements to keep themselves warm. The treasure of creatures all of a sudden had taken second place. Minutes turned into hours and slowly the light turned into darkness. Jenkins had been on the walkie-talkie outside the cave at brief intervals and was getting weather reports relayed to him. It wasn't good; it was a freak summer storm and the area, for miles around, was socked-in with fog and rain at lower levels and snow at higher elevations.

The ski lift had been shut down since there was no night skiing authorized at this time of year. Even if they had made it to the lift it wouldn't have helped them. Furthermore, it was far too dangerous for a helicopter lift. They were stuck.

"I apologize for leading you all into these conditions. I was assured by the local weather report that the fog was supposed to lift in the early afternoon…. This was totally a surprise," Jenkins said with authority, his voice reverberating above the howling blizzard outside.

People murmured in the background, their voices echoing off

the walls like an annoying buzzing sound.

Jared had removed his wet upper under-clothing and hung it to dry inside the cave. With only his down filled outer parka on next to his skin, he emptied a couple of backpacks and strapped them to his front and back. They helped cut down on the direct chill in the cave and the parka was acting as underwear. He ate some sweetened granola bars and quickly he started to warm up.

"In order to survive, we need to huddle together, far back in the cave," Jared said in the pending darkness. "I saw some of you earlier shaking from the cold; let's gather together. Our corporate body heat will keep us from freezing."

At first there was a little hesitancy to snuggle with a stranger, but as they pressed in, arms around each other in a tight circle while sitting on the ground, they all laughed and giggled at how comfortable it was. There were the usual remarks of being this close, but it was a relief and soon the group grew quiet as the storm raged outside. Both Sally and Jared's thoughts and prayers were on Caleb, and they could hardly wait for the morning and a break in the storm to find him. Some fell asleep and those who were awake made sure they were kept in close contact not to get hypothermia.

The night wore on, yet, and none too soon, the wind died down and the morning light filtered into the opening of the cave. Jared, who had not slept a wink, pulled himself slowly from the group and made his way to the opening. The snow had piled up in a bank about two feet deep at the cave's opening with a fair amount inside it. He stepped outside and in the very early light, he saw first hand, a winter wonderland. The fog had lifted but the sky was still overcast. There was an eerie calm as little wisps of wind chased handfuls of snow across the ground. The majestic peaks were completely white along with everything else. It was stunning to the eye – a Kodak moment in every direction.

Where's my son, he thought, as he scanned the stunning landscape. *I just can't believe he disappeared. Did the CIA stage a disappearance? Did he get scared and run? Did he have an accident? Is he stuck under a rock and froze to death because I didn't go far enough yesterday?"*

"Why are you up?" Sally's quiet voice and arm around his waist startled him back to the bleak, albeit draped in white, reality.

"Same reason you're up."

"I can't believe he is out there somewhere…, by himself…"

"Sal, the chances of anyone surviving in these conditions are…"

"Don't say that, Jared…, please…. He is Okay, let me believe that."

"I'm sorry, sweetheart…, we'll find him."

The morning light increased and the group began to wake up. Many were exceptionally cold and stiff as Jenkins got them up. He had made arrangements for the helicopter to bring a gas heater, some breakfast, hot coffee and a search and rescue dog and handler to the cave's ledge.

The throb of the helicopter was a welcome sound and the group yelled with hope as it neared the cave. Within the hour, they had heat, food and a whole different attitude. The dog and handler followed Jared to the spot where Caleb should have last been. As the sun rose, it became evident that the deep snow and snowdrifts could easily cover a body. They combed the area, zigzagging into the valley, looking for any clues. Nothing. They circled around and around. Nothing. It was as if Caleb had vanished.

Exhausted and frustrated, Jared and the dog and handler made their way back to the cave.

"We're going to have to wait until the snow melts…. We couldn't find anything out there."

"We need to get back to the lodge and tell Darby," Sally said. "Will the lift be running?"

"Yes, this would be perfect skiing conditions…. I'm sure we'll find quite a crowd," Jenkins replied.

The tired group trundled their way through the deep snow back to the ski lift and ultimately to their respective rooms for a much deserved rest. They had agreed to meet back for breakfast in the usual spot the next morning.

Sally and Jared assembled everyone in Darby's room and told them the news.

It was as if someone had slashed their tires. The usual buoyancy of Darby, the Lindstroms and Schellenberg, hit the floor like a lead balloon. They went into shock.

"You're…, you're pulling our leg," Bob said. "Is this some sick joke? C'mon, you're not serious."

"I wish it were a sick joke. I wish we were kidding around," Jared said, shaking his head in despair.

"What happened?" Schellenberg asked.

Jared described the scene.

Darby sat motionless as tears filled her eyes. She rocked back and forth in distress. She cried out, "No…, no…, it can't be!"

Sally stepped quickly over and sat beside her. She hugged her and gave her a tissue. Bob and Diane held each other in a compassionate grip as they began to weep.

Schellenberg sat down with his head between his hands and wept silently. The whole room went quiet except for the sounds of convulsive groans, weeping and sniffing.

"Is it possible he could be found alive?" Diane asked.

"Anything is possible," Jared answered. "Anything is possible."

Sally and Jared went slowly back to their room still cold and exhausted, and crawled into bed. Sleep soon took over. They slept right through until the next morning.

"I have arranged for another search team with dogs to comb the area as soon as the snow melts," Jenkins announced. "In the meantime, I still wish to complete the evacuation of all the remains in the cave. By the way, how is everyone feeling?

Heads nodded and Okays rambled about the group.

Jenkins had put the mineral expedition on hold until the snow melted. They ate their breakfast in silence and the sullen group made their way back to the cave to resume the dig.

The dog team searched all day and found nothing. Caleb had literally vanished without a trace. The weather had slowly returned to summer conditions and as fast as the storm had hit, as fast as any trace of it had disappeared. It was typical of mountain conditions and a lesson to those who experienced it to "always be prepared," when visiting the alpine.

Jared and Sally, the Lindstroms, Darby and Schellenberg inevitably mourned the loss of Caleb.

Diane replayed the incident from weeks ago how she was standing outside his room when he was at school; how she felt strange that he was going to leave. After seeing firsthand how close and in love, Darby and he were, she took it to be marriage. Now, she understood; it really was a premonition of him dying.

That night, as Darby was in a broken, fitful sleep, Caleb appeared in her dreams. He assured her he was okay, he was in

Heaven and he told her he was returning, how much he loved and missed her and to pass the news on to everyone. Jared wrestled in his sleep as well with the cuneiforms in his dreams, which somehow got mixed up with his DNA study and all of a sudden there was this connection, a flash of genius; could the cuneiforms be leading indicators in a double helix? When he woke up, he dug out Caleb's notes and perused them. Nothing made sense right away, but as he flipped through the pages, it started to sink in. He had to completely rethink the approach of viewing the symbols; these were no ordinary cuneiforms these were a code to something far deeper than some childish pig Latin.

The next morning at breakfast, Darby told the Houghtons about her dream. There was a little positive response upon hearing the news. After all it was only a dream, but it was an assurance, a form of hope, something to take away the sadness. Jared relayed his dream and the cuneiforms to her.

"You know, everything Caleb did and was had some impact on something. He has left a legacy far greater than who he was. For such young man, still a kid really, he led us to these dinosaurs which are in perfect condition. We now have his DNA to study, to prove that ancient man had superior genes. He showed us supernatural things that could only be God-gifted. He showed us unconditional love."

"Funny you should mention that, Jared," Sally began. "You know, after the terrorists were imprisoned, he kept trying to find out where they were incarcerated. He actually wanted to go and meet with them and forgive them. The CIA wouldn't tell him where they were."

"That doesn't surprise me in the least," Darby sighed. "I never knew anyone who cared for others and put everyone else first like he did. All his classmates were jealous of him because he dressed differently and paid no attention to peer pressure. He sure could play basketball, too. You know, I really believe he will return."

EPILOGUE

The CIA got what they wanted. They now had every part of the puzzle to clone super agents and dedicated staff. They literally could create "designer" staff that could man whole departments and offices in complete submission to their ideals. They wouldn't even need to hire outside, unstable staff that could be swayed to become double agents or turncoats to their system. Caleb not only proved his credibility, he led them to the greatest cache of ancient creatures ever discovered, in perfect condition. Caleb's cuneiforms turned out to be indicators of a whole new science. Instead of electronics being based on a binary system of ones and zeroes, or switches turning on and off, the cuneiforms pointed to a multi-level of intervals that functioned as an intermediate grayscale of action that meant there were now up to six distinct actions rotating simultaneously, like wheels within a wheel, spinning in multiple directions. This type of circuitry would revolutionize computers, memory and processing speed to supersede the human brain's processing by tenfold. The potential impact on technology was unimaginable. If Caleb's last outing had been successful, he would have led them to a vein of precious metals that would have stunned the world. He would have led them to the valley of woolly mammoths as well.

The two families, Schellenberg and Darby returned to Seattle and held a memorial service for Caleb. The church was packed to over-flowing. CIA staff, including Jenkins, Riddenhall, Lowenstein and Conor from the FBI, was in attendance. Even the press was there. The eulogy was given by Bob Lindstrom. The CIA insisted on them to keep the dinosaur discoveries confidential and to down play Caleb's scientific and supernatural contributions.

"Today as we celebrate the life of my son, I want you all to remember him for what he meant to you. Besides being a way too young to have left us, he will live on in our hearts as someone that seems ageless. His remarkable life, his amazing abilities, his curious love of dinosaurs, his passion for people should hopefully never be forgotten.

"When my wife Diane and I were in the hospital taking him home for the first time as his newly adoptive parents, I remember holding this little bitty body stretched out in the palm of my hand and forearm and wondering what kind of greatness he could bring to the world. You know the greatest thing that he brought to the world for us ... was love. He not only showed copious amounts of it, but he brought it out in us." Bob started to choke. "He made us aware that it didn't matter if he changed the world. It didn't matter if he was a genius or a superman or something special, but what mattered was unconditional love. What mattered to him was to make sure *you* were cared for first. I recall one incident where he saved a drowning man who hated him. He thought nothing of practicing random acts of kindness all the time. Many of you played sports with him. Was he ever violent? Did he ever pick a fight or, even raise his voice? He was an extraordinary young man. Over his sixteen years, my wife Diane commented several times about his uniqueness, how he never marched to the drum of convention. He always dressed differently, thought differently. He was very spiritual. He firmly believed in the God of creation through Jesus Christ and was filled with the spirit; he didn't need to say anything about his faith, it just was.

"He had rather a strange reaction the first time he saw Otzi the Ice Man on TV, you may recall Otzi was recently discovered on the Italian Alps. He became quite infatuated with Otzi and insisted on visiting the site, seeing his body and doing a study of him. You know the rest of the story; this is where he went missing during our visit.

"He believed Otzi holds the clues to modern man's health issues by having a more refined, or, less polluted DNA make up. He may very well be right and along with other things he discovered there, we all hope science can decipher something along those lines from this, so we will know that his death wasn't in vain. Let us all remember here today, young and old, to live our lives like Caleb, like there is no tomorrow ... and to love one another. One last thing I would like to do in remembrance of Caleb is to announce the Caleb Lindstrom memorial foundation. This is a foundation for underprivileged children to assist in their education as well as tutor them in life skills. You can find information at the back of the church."

The memorial was very different. Many young people from Caleb's school got up and honored him for the impact he had had on their lives. Coaches and teachers did the same. There was a time of mourning for many but for Darby she seemed to have a solid hope and kept the promise from Caleb.

Sally and Jared returned to their way of life and continued to raise their family. Shortly after their return, Jared began working with the CIA team. They had connected the cuneiforms to Caleb's DNA as well as the new, multi-dimensional electronics.

Darby went back to finish high school. She refused to date and clung to the dream and promise of Caleb's return. She prayed everyday to see him. One day she picked up the phone and called Sally.

"I've been thinking, a long time ago I heard that Jared still had some sperm left from Otzi. If Caleb doesn't return by the end of June, I would like to give birth to another Caleb."

"Whhhhaaatt?"

"You heard me; I think it would be exciting! You would still have to be involved as it was your egg that was used originally. I mean, I could go it alone too, but it wouldn't be the same."

"I'm going to have to think about that one," Sally replied, "Jared and I had talked about it awhile back and I'm getting too old. It *would* be nice to have another Caleb around, though; especially for you. How would you handle it? You couldn't get married to your own son."

"I wasn't really thinking that, I was just thinking that it would be an amazing experience."

Jeff Schellenberg continued with renewed vigor to teach on creation and what he had learned from Caleb.

John 14:12 Verily, verily, I say unto you, He that believeth in me, the works that I do shall he do also; and greater works than these shall he do; because I go unto my Father.

To be continued....

As Caleb promised, he is to return in Darrell Swanson's next book.

Darrell Swanson

Available in eBook and audio book and paperback at:
http://offthebookshelf.com/authors/1787-darrell-swanson
or
Contact:
swan1249@gmail.com
www.darrellswanson.com